Praise for F *Band Fags!*

"For those of us who came of age in the '80s, reading Frank Anthony Polito's novel is like being teleported back to high school. Filled with pop culture references that will have you saying, 'I remember that!,' this is a love letter to a time when happiness was a pair of Calvin Klein jeans, and every heartbreak could be fixed by listening to your Bonnie Tyler or REO Speedwagon albums. Most important, though, it is a portrait of a friendship between two boys struggling to find themselves without losing each other."

—Michael Thomas Ford, author of *Last Summer*

"Sweet and funny."

—Publishers Weekly

"With the Motor City running on empty in Reagan's America, Frank Anthony Polito's characters dance their mystery dance of teenage longing as if Motown never left for California. Sexy, funny, and wiser than it wants to be, *Band Fags!* pulses with a ragged beauty and bounces to its beat. I give it a 98.6."

—Thorn Kief Hillsbery, author of *What We Do Is Secret*

"This heartfelt valentine to coming of age in the '80s shows that the right jeans, a decent production of *Grease* and discovering a true friend do offer some consolation."

—The Advocate

"More than just a novel, *Band Fags!* is a virtual time machine that transports you smack dab into the cheesy heart of the '80s. It's like a queer *Wonder Years* as it follows Brad and Jack's memorable journey through high school hell. Screamingly funny, surprisingly charming and, ultimately, truly moving, it's a fresh take on the importance of friendship during the worst/best years of your life."

—Brian Sloan, *A Really Nice Prom Mess* and *Tale of Two Summers*

"Polito's refreshingly personable characters leap from the page with a flavorful magnetism that will leave you craving for a sequel, or better yet, a TV or film adaptation."

—Dayton City Paper

"The dialogue sparkles throughout the book. And his characters and situations are all quite authentic."

—Between the Lines

"Polito has perfectly channeled the voice of a closeted teen."

—Bay Windows

Please turn the page for more outstanding praise for *Band Fags!*

"A consistently hilarious story of the best-friendship we all seem to have had, set in a time we can never seem to forget—the totally awesome '80s—*Band Fags!* never misses a beat in its affectionate, moment-by-moment chronicling of the complicated journey we take from cradle to closet to what lies beyond."

—Matthew Rettenmund, author of *Boy Culture*

"Sexy and funny and filled with charm and sensitivity. The dialogue is perfect, the characters are loveable and the story cannot be beat for a light read that will make you forget the heat of summer and remind you of the warmth of first love."

—*Eureka Pride*

"Explores the difficulties of growing up gay in the 1980s, all told with a sense of humor and affection for its characters. *Band Fags!* shines with its clever dialogue and witty comments."

—*AfterElton*

"Polito does a good job of recreating the insecurities and rivalries that characterize relationships between high school students."

—*Bay Area Reporter*

"*Band Fags!* is like the gay teen flick John Hughes never got around to making. Let's face it, there's a Band Fag in all of us and Frank Anthony Polito has his on speed dial. This book is a sweet, funny, deeply felt valentine to the wonder/horror of coming of age in the 1980s. You might just pee your parachute pants."

—Dennis Hensley, author of *Misadventures in the (213)*

"If the words *Dallas, Dynasty* and *The Go-Go's* resonate with you, get this book."

—*In Los Angeles*

"These Band Fags march to their own quirky beat in a timeless tale delightfully syncopated against an '80s soundtrack. This surprisingly tender story of best friends locked in a tug-of-war of self-discovering is booby-trapped with Polito's pitch-perfect wisecracks and hilarious observations."

—Steven Sorrentino, author of *Luncheonette*

"A fun and quick read."

—*Out Smart*

And more outstanding praise for *Band Fags!*

"This former 1980s band fag declares *Band Fags!* totally wicked awesome. With pitch perfect dialog, and high stepping charm, Polito hilariously shows how not all hearts beat to the rhythm of the same drum major."
—Josh Kilmer-Purcell, author of *I Am Not Myself These Days*

"Hilarious . . . snappy dialogue drives the story, much more so than in most novels."
—*Echelon Magazine*

"Frank Anthony Polito's *Band Fags!* plays like an '80s after school special; it feels like dropping right back into the oh-so-important questions of who sits where in the lunchroom, who 'likes' who, and which friends might be 'fags.' Polito absolutely captures the voice of a not-ready-to-be-gay-teenager in the '80s, and spins characters who face real problems, ridiculous concerns, and the meaning of friendship over the years."
—Alex MacLennan, *The Zookeeper*

"*Band Fags!* is one of those rare books you may want to read not once, but like, totally a bijillion times."
—*H/X Magazine*

"Hugely enjoyable."
—*Dallas Voice*

"Polito makes you think, breaks your heart with the pain of having to 'hide' who you are and tosses in a whole lot of fun while showing 'us' how it is for gay teens."
—*Armchair Reviews*

"Enjoyable."
—*Edge (Boston)*

Books by Frank Anthony Polito

BAND FAGS!

DRAMA QUEERS!

Published by Kensington Publishing Corporation

DRAMA QUEERS!

Frank Anthony Polito

KENSINGTON BOOKS
http://www.kensingtonbooks.com

KENSINGTON BOOKS are published by

Kensington Publishing Corp.
119 West 40th Street
New York, NY 10018

All Kensington titles, imprints, and distributed lines are available at special quantity discounts for bulk purchases for sales promotion, premiums, fund-raising, educational, or institutional use.

Special book excerpts or customized printings can also be created to fit specific needs. For details, write or phone the office of the Kensington Special Sales Manager: Kensington Publishing Corp., 119 West 40th Street, New York, NY 10018. Attn. Special Sales Department. Phone: 1-800-221-2647.

ISBN-13: 978-0-7582-3164-2
ISBN-10: 0-7582-3164-4

First Kensington Trade Paperback Printing: June 2009
10 9 8 7 6 5 4 3 2 1

Printed in the United States of America

To Craig Bentley,
my favorite Drama Queer

Acknowledgments

Once again I must thank my editor, John Scognamiglio, for insisting I *not* become a One Hit Wonder and allowing me to expand upon this story. As always, to everyone at Kensington—from the Bull Pen to the Mail Room—for making me feel welcome and like part of the crew.

To my family back in Michigan, I love you all.

Thank you to Steven, Nanci, and Donna at Barnes & Noble for hosting my first book signing ever, and to Rich for taping it. To Keith and Martin at Common Language in Ann Arbor, and to Phil, Paul, and the members of the Great Lakes Pride Band who entertained us. Gary at Five15 in Royal Oak, Suede and the staff at Pronto!, and all the Hillbilly High alumni and other Detroit-area friends who turned up on June 12, 2008. To Jeffrey and Ryan, my personal PR posse, and Bonnie, my slave—I mean, *webmistress.* Also Chip and Ron of Spin Cycle for throwing my "1984" book launch bash . . . Jon-Erik Hexum, we will never forget you!

Others I must include: Kenneth in the (212), Matthew and Lee at Meefers, Marle at WBAI, Larry, Keith, Cynthia, Diana, James, and Kara at Sirius OutQ, the fabulous Sweetie, aka Daniel, for sharing Detroit Drag secrets, Leo at Live Out Loud, Amy and all the HPHS GSA members, and James at B & N, Royal Oak.

The writing of this book would not have been possible without the generous input of the following friends: Don at Between the Lines, my fellow ex-Detroiters, Mark of Fraser, and Mary Beth of good old Hazeltucky, and my brother, Shawn, director of Thespian Troupe #4443.

Last, but certainly not least, I thank my Best Friend since 7th grade, Grat Dalton, for loaning me his life and allowing me to embellish it.

This one truly is *fiction*—at least 98%.

Contents

—1987—

—1988—

—1987—

September–December

True Colors

"Oh I realize
It's hard to take courage . . ."

—Cyndi Lauper

"To thine ownself be true."

Wanna know what bugs the shit outta me?

When somebody tells me something they think I don't already know.

Case in point . . .

This morning during Miss Horchik's 3rd hour World Shit—I mean, *Lit*—we're studying the English Renaissance, even though we already covered it last year with Mrs. Malloy during English Lit. I guess maybe we're having a refresher course or something.

Anyways!

So Miss Horchik is reading to us aloud from *Hamlet.* You know, by William Shakespeare. Act 1, scene 3.

"'Neither a borrower nor a lender be / For loan oft loses both itself and friend / And borrowing dulls the edge of husbandry' . . ."

Da-dah da-dah.

She gets to the part when Polonius turns to Laertes, and tells him, "'This above all: to thine ownself be true.'"

Well, I don't know why, but Miss Horchik looks right at me when she says this. Pageboy haircut perfectly parted down the middle, hand to heart, beady eyes opened extra wide.

I'm thinking, *What's* that *supposed to mean?*

"To thine ownself be true."

I mean, I know what it means: be yourself, don't give a fuck what anybody else thinks, do what you wanna do. This is exactly the way I *always* live my life. I don't need some middle-aged, former-nun-turned-high-school-teacher giving me advice, you know what I mean?

"What the hell was that?"

Like horses outta the starting gate at the Hazel Park Raceway, the entire Hazel Park High student body bursts into the halls the second the bell rings.

"What the hell was what?"

Textbooks resting against his hip, Max Wilson stares straight ahead as we fight our way thru the throng of hungry Vikings on their way in search of sustenance.

"Why did Virgin Velma single me out when she said what she said?"

Max looks down at me with blue close-set eyes, totally oblivious. "What did she say?"

He acts like we weren't sitting in the same classroom mere moments ago. Maybe because Pam Klimaszewski and her tits just passed by and he's had a thing for her (and them) since we were Sophomores two years ago . . . God, we're getting old!

"She doesn't like you," I tell Max, hating to be a jerk, but it's true.

"Who?"

He whips his gelled head around just in time to avoid walking into the open Auto Shop door.

"Forget it."

When it comes to girls, Max Wilson loses all ability to pay attention. If he doesn't get laid this year on Spring Break, I don't know what's gonna happen.

"Bonjour, Bradley!"

We turn the corner down the middle hall en route to my locker when my French III Independent Study advisor, Mrs. Carey, appears from her classroom wearing this circa 1968 chocolate-colored turtleneck with a wool knee-length skirt over matching tights and boots. Not sure why since it's the middle of September. To me, she looks like a big brown blob. Maybe it's because Mrs. Carey happens to be black.

"Bonjour, Madame!" I recite *en français.*

Mrs. Carey nods and smiles. *"Comment ça va?"*

She reminds me of that guy from the 7-Up commercials. Only female. And without the accent. You know, the one who played Punjab in the movie version of *Annie.*

"Ça va bien . . . Et vous?"

I roll my eyes at Max. He doesn't know what the hell we're saying. For all he cares, we could be talking about taking a poop.

"Bien, bien," Mrs. Carey replies, thus completing the only conversation she truly comprehends. I guess her major back in college was Latin, but now that it's officially dead, French it is!

As much as I'd love to stay and chitchat, I'm jonesing big time. I haven't had a cigarette since this morning after Marching Band—yes, I'm a Band Fag. I only been partaking in the nicotine habit for about four years, but the thought of going without a smoke for more than a few hours makes me totally psycho . . . Imagine what I'll be like when I'm thirty.

I bid Mrs. Carey *"Au revoir."* Soon as she heads off to the

Teacher's Lounge, I bust open my locker, shoving my World Lit book to the back, in search of my secret stash.

Not that she's not nice, but from everything I witnessed during my two-going-on-three years at HPHS, sometimes Mrs. Carey can be a Total Ditz. I mean, how many teachers will write you a hall pass so you can skip their own class? And during French II last year, Mrs. Carey accidentally gave my friend Stacy Gillespie her *Scènes et Séjours* teacher's edition (with all the answers), and she never even noticed! I often wonder what it must be like being the only African-American in a school full of Caucasians just waiting to take advantage of you.

"Yo, Dayton . . . Can I bum one of them?"

Max watches as I jiggle my second-to-last Marlboro Light from its crumpled cellophane pack. Thank God I found my butts buried beneath my Advanced Grammar/Term Paper text, which I already had with Mrs. Mayer this morning during 2nd hour.

"Get your own!" I scowl.

At 85¢ per pack (plus tax) I can't afford to be giving my cigarettes away, can I?

"I'll be your Best Friend."

Max follows fast upon my footsteps towards the double doors at the far end of the hall.

"You already are my Best Friend," I remind him, even though he's already aware of this.

In fact, Max Wilson was the first person ever to talk to me when my family moved to Ferndale . . .

"You like *Star Wars*?"

I remember Max getting totally geeked when he saw me parade my Luke Skywalker action figure up and down my desk during playtime in Miss Norbert's 4th grade class back at Webster.

"Sure," I lied. The movie came out years before, but I still hadn't seen it. In fact, I had no real desire to. I just happened to think Luke Skywalker was cute from all the commercials, but I didn't tell Max that. Instead, I said, "I seen it like five times."

"I only seen it three," he replied, sounding disappointed that I had one up on him. "What's your favorite part?"

"I don't know," I said, not wanting to ruin my chance at making my first new friend. "What's yours?"

Max answered without hesitation. "When Luke Skywalker and Han Solo and Princess Leia are all trapped in the trash compactor and they're about to get smashed to smithereens!"

"That part's pretty good, I guess."

I tried my best feigning enthusiasm, even though I didn't know what the hell Max was talking about.

He lifted the lid to his desk. There amongst his purple Level 4 reading book, *Hooked on Phonics* worksheets, and *Ranger Rick* magazine, Max held hostage a collection of characters I only seen in the *Star Wars* section of the Sears Wish Book.

"I got an X-wing *and* a Y-wing fighter at home," he bragged, "but my stupid mom won't let me bring 'em to school."

"That's okay . . . I got *both* of them," I totally lied again.

Luckily, Max never found me out for the fibber that I am. Eight years later, we're still Best Friends.

"Today!"

Making a break for the parking lot, I tuck the slightly-bent-but-still-smokeable cig behind my ear, à la my new favorite actor, James Dean in *Rebel Without a Cause.* Oh, my God . . . He's sooo good!

The second we hit the pavement, I bust out my purple Bic and fire it up. I know we're not supposed to smoke on school property, but with only forty-five minutes for lunch, it doesn't give me much time to jump in Max's car, get outta the parking lot, head over to the BK in BF Warren, scarf down a couple bacon double cheeseburgers, *and* indulge myself in my dirty habit.

"Roll 'em down."

There's nothing worse than sitting on boiling hot vinyl, you know what I mean?

Crawling into the passenger seat, I immediately crank the window down. I hate Indian Summer. After spending the last three months in nothing but shorts and sandals, it always sucks being back in school all bundled up in jeans and shoes and a shirt.

"Dude!" Max groans the second I kick off my topsiders. "Your feet *stank*."

He turns on the stereo, as if cranking The Cure is gonna mask my stench.

Catching a glimpse of my freckled face in the sideview mirror, I drape my arm ever so dramatically out the open window, hitting my cigarette hard. I love the way the paper crackles as it burns. The orange-red glow reminds me of campfire coals on a cool summer's night.

I realize smoking is totally bad for me, but I gotta know how to do it, as an actor—yes, I'm also a Drama Queer. I mean, what if I get a part in a movie and my character calls for it?

"Step on it," I order, soon as Max puts the LeMans in reverse.

"I'm stepping, I'm stepping," he replies, sounding a tad annoyed.

We file in line behind all the other late '70s and early '80s model cars making their exit. Suddenly, I shout, "Honk!"

In front of us, I notice the blue Chevy Citation belonging to HPHS's own Viking Marching Band drum major, Ava Reese. In the passenger seat sits Ava's Best Friend and fellow clarinet player, Carrie Johnson. Both brunettes turn around and give a wave before Ava makes the right turn onto Felker.

"Where they going?" Max wonders, taking us in the opposite direction.

"Probably to Carrie's house to watch *Days of our Lives.*" She's a big fan, and tapes it every day on her VCR . . . Must be nice!

Me and Max have both known Ava since elementary school, but Carrie I didn't meet till 7th grade Varsity Band at Webb Junior High. In fact, she was my first French kiss. Too bad big mouth Max went and told my mom about it on the way home from the Fun Night. I got grounded for a week.

"What class you got 4th hour?" Max asks, after I remind him we don't have to hurry back.

"Chorale."

"What is that," he snorts, "some kinda *horse* thing?"

I roll my eyes. Max knows perfectly well that Chorale is the top choir at Hillbilly High in Hazeltucky, taught by Mr. Harold "Call me Hal" Fish.

Not that he's not a nice guy, but sometimes I think Mr. Fish—I mean, *Hal*—thinks he's one of us students and not our teacher. Sure, it's cool he lets us get away with stuff like being late for class and smoking when we're out at a gig, but it's like, *Dude . . . You're thirty!* Not to mention the fact that he's sorta heavy and he sweats a lot.

I mean, it wouldn't be so bad except he carries this rag around that he uses to mop himself off once the works start flowing. And since it's seventy-five degrees on the first day of fall, I can just imagine the mess Hal's gonna be by the time I finally show up to his class.

Oh, my God . . . Don't look now!

Burger King is packed with a bunch of obnoxious, postpubescent, hormones-raging high schoolers, but at least the air-conditioning works. Only I'm more in need of a cold shower when a maroon and gray Vikings Varsity football jacket catches my eye.

"What's up, Bradley?"

As me and Max snake around the mile-long line, who do I see coming towards us?

None other than #23: Rob Berger.

"Nothing much." I feel my face go flush the second his brown eyes meet my blues. "What's up with you?"

"You know . . . Getting some grub."

Rob flashes a sheepish smile. When I see the space between his two front teeth, it's just about all I can do *not* to wet myself right then and there.

"'s up, Berger?" asks Max with a nod, as if seeing Rob out in public is totally no biggie.

I'm sorry, but you should see this guy . . . For starters, he's got on these totally tight jeans, pegged at the bottom, with gray slip-on shoes, and no socks—love it! He's also SWB (Short With a Bod), which I also love. Like 5'8", 190 pounds, and built like a brick shithouse, with dark brown hair, cut over the ear, and buzzed in back. Did I mention his beautiful brown eyes?

Oh! And he's got the sexiest little mustache. Plus a totally hairy chest and a totally big dick.

Wanna know how I know this?

Every day after Swimming back in 7th grade, Rob used to walk around butt naked in the locker room. You can bet I took my sweet old time getting dressed while I secretly checked him out toweling himself off. I'm pretty sure Rob Berger was the first guy in our class to grow pubes.

"Hey, Asshole!"

Suddenly, I realize Max is barking at me.

"Huh?"

This is about all the response I can muster up.

"What do you want?"

I'm thinking, *Rob Berger's totally hot bod.* Until I discover I'm at the front of the line where the nondescript middle-aged woman behind the cash register patiently awaits my order.

"Two bacon double cheeseburgers, small fry, and a medium Pepsi," I tell her, polite as punch. Followed by, "Please." And then I'm right back to my staring.

"I'll see you in Drama," Rob promises, catching my eye. "Don't be late."

Again, I'm gonna wet myself!

I watch his every move while he picks up his double Whopper with cheese, large fry, and large pop at the opposite end of the counter. As he slips away joining his jock friends at a booth in the corner, I take in one final glimpse of Rob Berger's totally hot ass . . . 5th hour can *not* come soon enough, you know what I mean?

By the time 1:00 PM rolls around I've endured about as much of "Call me Hal" and his sweat dripping as I possibly can. The second the bell rings, thru the Choir room door I fly, like a bat outta hell.

"Brad!"

I'm about to enter the auditorium across the hall when I hear a voice call out my name. I turn to find fellow Drama Queer, Liza Larson, dressed in her uniform—black spandex pants, and black leather jacket complete with fringe. Her bottle-blond hair is perfectly feathered, and her signature penciled-on spider sits dangling from the web its spun in the corner of Liza's left eye.

"What's up?" I ask, slightly outta breath.

Liza gives me a look. "You gotta pee or something?"

"No."

I can't help but wonder why she's questioning me like this. Until I realize I'm hopping back and forth on one foot like I gotta find the nearest boys' room. Really, I just wanna get into the auditorium ASAP and save a seat for somebody . . . Guess who?

"Wanna head out to Skid Row real quick?"

In addition to being one of my Senior classmates, Liza is also my post-Chorale/pre-Advanced Drama smoking buddy.

"I think I'm gonna pass," I decide, even though I can't believe the words just came outta my mouth. Mind you, I'm not a Burn-Out myself. I don't partake in the whole Mötley Crüe, knee-high moccasin boot worn over tucked-in tight jeans-wearing culture. I just love to smoke.

"Your loss," Liza sighs, sauntering away.

For a second, I think about running after her as she heads down the hall and out the side doors. For the life of me, I can't figure out who started calling the spot across the street from HPHS *Skid Row*. They didn't see *Little Shop of Horrors,* I guess. Me and my friends used to always call it *The Log*. Until we discovered it's really a downed telephone pole laying on its side. Regardless, it's in front of the Blue Building, and where all the badass Burn-Outs go to do their thing.

Unfortunately, I got other business to attend to.

"This seat's saved!"

My fellow fire-haired Senior, Audrey Wojczek, just tried to join me in the third row of recently reupholstered auditorium chairs, complementing the newly painted walls: maroon and gray, respectively.

"Who you hoarding it for?" she asks, as if it's any of her business.

"Um . . ." I start to say. "Somebody."

Aud turns her head slightly to one side, furrows her brow, and purses her lips. "Somebody who?"

Thank God I'm saved by the ringing bell, freeing me from having to succumb to this infernal interrogation. Only I don't see Rob Berger anywhere.

What the fuck?

Audrey takes a seat beside Tuesday Gunderson, a slightly overweight Senior girl with stringy black hair, just as our Drama teacher calls out, *"Dayton!"*

"Right here, Dell."

I give a wave in case Mr. Dell'Olio can't pick out my Howdy Doody hair in this low-level light from where he sits on the lip of the stage, scratching his receding hairline.

"Where's your scene partner, Mr. Berger?"

I look around the auditorium again. Finally, the place is starting to look like a real theatre. My first year in Drama, you should've seen it . . . Torn curtains, lights that didn't light, graffiti spray-painted on the backstage wall by some Class of '86 breakdancer dudes.

"Not sure," I sadly report. "I seen him at lunch."

How am I gonna make it thru the next fifty-eight minutes when I'm wracked with worry?

"Right here, Coach!"

All heads turn towards the deep bass reverberating thru the room. I don't know why Rob insists on calling Dell *Coach.* Maybe because he plays a lot of sports. If you ask me, it's fucking charming as all get-out.

"You're late, Berger!" Dell shouts, taking on a tone only a Varsity football player could relate to.

I can't say I'm attracted to Mr. Dell'Olio—he's at least thirty-five. But whenever he talks to Rob, it's like he becomes a totally different person. Like maybe when he was in high school, he always wanted to be a jock, but instead he got stuck being a Drama Queer. I never realized it before, but it's sorta hot the way he butches it up.

"Sorry, Coach." Like an embarrassed little boy, Rob's cheeks burn bright red. "It won't happen again."

When I see him looking around for somewhere to park his

totally hot ass, in my best stage whisper I hiss, "Berger. . . . I saved you a seat."

Rob nods and smiles.

Scootching in beside me, he puts an arm around my shoulder and gives it a manly squeeze. "Thanks, Bradley."

I think I'm in love.

Let's Hear It for the Boy

"Maybe he's no Romeo
But he's my loving one-man show . . ."

—Deniece Williams

The only thing *worse* than being a Band Fag is . . . Being a Drama Queer.

At least according to the Hillbilly High Handbook.

I see why being in Band can be viewed as sorta lame. I mean, there you are, wearing this wool uniform along with this funny plumed hat and spats, stomping around the football field while all the Cool Kids sit up in the stands enjoying the game. Not to mention having to wake up at the butt crack of dawn for practice. Plus giving up your weekends to march in some stupid parade somewhere.

But how can Drama possibly be considered geeky? You perform plays in front of an audience of admiring fans. What person in their right mind wouldn't enjoy the applause? I know I do. Why does everybody think *movie* stars are totally cool, but not the ones on stage?

Back in 10th grade when I decided I wanted to be an actor,

I didn't realize this would be the case. I totally thought cheerleaders such as Shelly Findlay and Betsy Sheffield or Vikettes like Lynn Kelly and Angela Andrews would be trying out for Drama Club. Maybe even a few football players like Tom Fulton. I remember he seemed to enjoy himself performing in this play we presented back in 7th grade in Ms. Lemieux's class.

Well, it wasn't so much a play as it was a skit, but I did have the lead opposite Tom's then-girlfriend, Marie Sperling. I guess maybe it wasn't *real* acting since I didn't have any lines or anything—it was a silent skit. I did get to soft-shoe to Scott Joplin's "The Entertainer" as this strobe light flashed around us the entire time, making everything look all Charlie Chaplin-esque.

Don't bring this up to Max. Originally, Ms. Lemieux cast him in the lead, but after a few rehearsals, she decided he didn't quite cut it. Not to brag or anything, but once I took over the part, she told me I was a natural talent. Did I mention she was our hot-to-trot Enriched English & Social Studies teacher and her first name is Cinnamon?

Wanna know who showed up to try out for *Okla-homo!*—I mean, *Oklahoma!*?

When I walked into the auditorium that afternoon in March '86, I seen none of the kids I expected to see. Instead, there sat Pee-wee Herman's #1 fan, Charlie Richardson, and the slightly overweight stringy black-haired girl I mentioned before, Tuesday Gunderson.

"You slumming or something?"

Outta nowhere, the only person I recognized as being remotely acquainted with appeared, her bright red locks falling past the bottom of her purplish pink striped sweater.

"Hey," I said, happy to see Audrey Wojczek for the first time in my life.

We may seem like pretty good pals now during Senior year, but at the time, I barely knew her. I mean, we went to junior high together and all, but we weren't exactly friends, you know what I mean? Audrey only transferred to Webb during Freshman year, after spending 2nd thru 8th grades at St. Mary Magdalen's. Judging from the mouth on her, you'd never know it!

"What the fuck are *you* doing here, Dayton?"

Audrey served as treasurer of Drama Club. She also played the mother in *The Skeleton Walks,* the fall play first semester. Her performance came as a bit of a surprise to me when I seen the production, but as the recipient of the Class Clown mock award, I guess Audrey has never been much of a wallflower.

"I'm trying out for the play," I remember telling her. "What do you think I'm doing?"

Back at Webb, me and Audrey constantly fought whenever we found ourselves together. She loved picking on me, saying my hair would fall out someday just because our Health teacher, Mrs. Strong, said that most redheaded men eventually go bald. Shit like that.

"The word is *auditioning,*" Audrey corrected. "And it's a *musical,* not a play."

Whatever . . .

The spring play—I mean, *musical*—that year, like I said, was none other than *Oklahoma!* You know, *"where the wind comes sweepin' down the plain,"* and the *"shiny little surrey with the fringe on the top."* By the guys who wrote *The Sound of Music,* Rogers & Hammerstein. Well, I never seen it before, but I knew the movie version had the mom from *The Partridge Family* in it, who happens to be the real-life mother of my very first crush ever. No, not David, but *Shaun* Cassidy.

Growing up, we never had much money. Evidently, James Dayton didn't make a whole lot working as a cop in Troy while getting his degree in Physical Education from Wayne State. And once Laura Victor married him, she gave up the job she had since turning Sweet Sixteen working as a secretary in the tissues and pathology lab at Detroit Osteopathic Hospital to stay home with me and my sisters, Janelle, Nina, and Brittany.

Yet every so often, Mom found a little extra cash stashed somewhere. Her (quote-unquote) mad money, she liked to call it. I used to think so because she spent it whenever Dad made her mad, which seemed a lot more frequent the longer they stayed together and the older me and the girls got . . . No wonder their marriage ended in D-I-V-O-R-C-E in 1983.

I'll never forget this one time my parents were out bowling on their bowling league . . .

After we put on our footie pajamas, me and Janelle gathered in front of the television with our babysitter, Sheryl Killian. Nina and Brittany must've both been in bed because they were still babies. I'm pretty sure I was in 1st grade at the time, so they were like three and two.

"Ooh, he's cute!"

I'm sure *I* thought it first, but Janelle beat me to saying it out loud. After all, she is two years older.

"That's Shaun Cassidy," Sheryl informed us when *The Hardy Boys* came on channel 7 at 7:00 PM. "Isn't he a fox?"

At the time, we were living in Center Line. The Killians lived down the block from us on Sterling, and Sheryl went to high school at St. Clement's. I remember her being very glamorous in her bell-bottom jeans with her long blond Bionic Woman hair. Me and Janelle liked to sit on the back of the couch and braid it for her while we all watched TV.

"Is he your boyfriend?" I asked, feeling a tad jealous that Shaun Cassidy just might be.

Sheryl laughed. "I wish!" Then she told us, "He sings 'Da Doo Ron Ron.'"

How could I not know that? I loved "Da Doo Ron Ron"! Except I always thought it was "Da Doo *Run Run.*"

Every time we took a ride somewhere in Dad's car, me and

Janelle would hear it on CKLW, so we knew all the words by heart. Boy, did I wish *my* name was Jill!

Thus began our weekly ritual . . .

Every Sunday night while our parents were up at Pastime Lanes, Sheryl would pop the Jiffy Pop, melt an entire stick of *("Everything's better with . . .")* Blue Bonnet on it, while me and Janelle waited patiently in the family room, counting the seconds till show time.

From the moment Frank and Joe appeared in twelve-inch black and white, we sat glued to our seats, not even getting up to pee unless we absolutely had to. This was back before they invented the VCR, you know what I mean? And even if they'd been around, the Daytons certainly couldn't have afforded one.

Wanna know what I remember most about *The Hardy Boys,* other than how cute Shaun Cassidy looked in every episode?

That creepy music from the opening montage! And all the various book covers appearing one by one: *The Clue in the Embers, While the Clocked Ticked, The Hidden Staircase.*

Back then, I didn't know the Hardy Boys and Nancy Drew were literary characters that had been around for fifty years, but oh how my 6-year-old heart skipped a beat when Shaun Cassidy began clapping his hands high above his head, wearing that groovy striped sweater with the scarf draped around his neck.

My favorite episode of all time had to be "The Last Kiss of Summer." 'member, the one where Joe got married? I'll never forget when I first heard about it, I was devastated. Joe Hardy couldn't have a wife. It would ruin the show!

Sure enough, the scene opened with Joe and that girl, Jamie, driving down the coast in Joe's convertible, staring lovingly into each other's eyes, the wind blowing both their long blond hair while that romantic '70s song played in the background.

"If a picture paints a thousand words . . ."

After Joe and Jamie professed their undying love for each

other and shared a passionate kiss, they walked along the beach, arm in arm.

"If a face could launch a thousand ships . . ."

I remember thinking how beautiful Jamie looked in her cut-off jean shorts and blouse tied in a knot in front, but I couldn't take my eyes off Shaun Cassidy's smile. I remember wanting to press my face against the tiny screen—and kiss it. Imagine how confusing that must've been for a 6-year-old boy. Especially one who spent so much time surrounded by his sisters, he sometimes felt more like one of the girls.

"Joe Hardy is sooo cute!" I gushed, scootching closer to the TV set.

"I like Frank better," Janelle decided, even though I couldn't understand how she could think such a thing.

Obviously Sheryl Killian didn't realize how things worked in the Dayton household. "Joe is a boy," she took it upon herself to point out. "You *can't* think he's cute, Bradley."

I turned to Janelle.

She turned to Sheryl. "It's okay . . . Sometimes Brad thinks boys are cute."

To Janelle, it was totally no biggie. She even let me play Barbies with her.

And then tragedy struck.

I knew there'd be trouble the second Joe and Jamie got into their car after the wedding rehearsal and we cut to that jerk, Jocco. Coming from the opposite direction, there he was driving drunk with his bimbo girlfriend. Only I never expected Joe and Jamie to get run off the road.

"Look out!" Me, Janelle, and Sheryl cried out in three-part harmony.

I covered my face with my hands, the way Mom taught me to do whenever there was a scary part, like when Bugs Bunny met Dr. Jekyll and he turned into Mr. Hyde. Yet I couldn't help sneaking a peek thru my tiny little fingers the second I heard that horrible sound.

"Oh, my God . . ."

I started crying soon as I seen Joe slumped over the steering wheel and Jamie laying against the dashboard . . . blood on her shoulder. Thank God that other car with them two guys in it pulled up. How could they just drive away without stopping to help?

Poor Joe . . . He took one look at his soon-to-be wedded wife and knew there was nothing he could do. Holding her tight, he sobbed, "Jamie . . . Jamie."

Leave it to the Hardy Boys to go undercover and catch the killer!

I particularly loved the part when Joe befriended Jocco and they threw that party out at their fancy beach house. I immediately recognized the Muzak version of "How Deep is Your Love?" from the *Saturday Night Fever* soundtrack playing in the background . . . God, I wanted to see that movie sooo bad!

I remember being confused when Frank arrived and Joe acted like he didn't recognize his brother. Really, it was all just part of the plan to set Jocco up and bust him for selling stolen goods. Until Jocco got wise to Frank posing as a big-time surfer, and sent him out on his board in shark-infested waters . . . I'll never forget the sight of Parker Stevenson in that wetsuit, even though my heart would always belong to Shaun Cassidy.

The only other part of "The Last Kiss of Summer" that I remember comes at the very end. After being haunted by her memory the entire episode, Joe spots Jamie walking down the beach in her bikini bathing suit. He runs up to her, touches her on the shoulder, and says, "Excuse me . . ."

"If the world should stop revolving, spinning slowly down to die . . ."

She turns around—and it's some other girl.

How Joe could've been mistaken, I never understood. This broad looked nothing like beautiful Jamie. In fact, wasn't she kind of a dog, if I recall correctly?

"Mommy!"

Later that evening when Laura returned with Jim, she reached into her purse. Besides watching *The Hardy Boys* on TV, this was always my favorite part of the night.

"Hold out your hands and open your eyes . . ."

Mom always brought us a special treat on bowling night. I don't know why, but no matter what kind, candy *always* tasted better coming from a vending machine. This time, I got a Hershey bar and Janelle got a Kit Kat. Nina and Brittany were already asleep so they were shit outta luck.

After we took our bath, Mom tucked us both into bed together.

"Next time you go shopping," I whispered, so as not to wake up Nina or Brittany in the bed beside us, "will you buy me a Shaun Cassidy record?"

Mom sat down next to me, looking like she didn't know what the hell I was talking about. "I might . . . If you tell me who Shaun Cassidy is."

"He's just this boy on TV," I replied, adding, "Janelle thinks he's cute."

Mom smiled, looking at my older sister. "Then how come Janelle isn't asking for his record?"

Coming to her baby brother's rescue, she replied, "We can share it."

Mom kissed my forehead. "Don't forget to say your prayers." She pulled the blanket up so that it barely covered my ear before turning out the light, making sure to leave the door open a smidge.

Dear God, I prayed, eyes closed, hands folded together beneath my chin. *Bless Mommy and Daddy and please don't let them fight anymore . . . Bless Janelle and Nina and Brittany . . . And Grandpa and Grandma Dayton and Grandpa and Grandma Victor . . .*

Who else?

Bless my teacher, Miss Langton, and all the kids in my class at Miller Elementary in Center Line, Michigan. Even Jeffy Morgan who picks on me sometimes.

Now for the important stuff . . .

And please God, if you think about it, next time Mommy goes to Kmart's, maybe you can remind her to buy me a Shaun Cassidy record. The one with "Da Doo Run Run"—I mean, "Da Doo Ron Ron—*okay? I promise I'll be extra good and I won't fight with my sisters anymore. Especially when we're in your house . . . In the name of your Son, amen.*

Lo and behold, a few days later when I got home from school, guess what I found?

Propped up on my pillow, the full-sized face of Shaun Cassidy stared back at me from the cover of his self-titled debut album, hand behind his head, a smile upon his lips, wearing the cutest little white hat cocked to one side. Hard to believe that was over ten years ago . . . God, I'm getting old!

How fitting was it that the first part I'd be auditioning for at Hazel Park High would be Curly McClain, opposite the role of Laurey Williams, first made famous in *Okla-homo!*—I mean, *Oklahoma!*—by Shaun Cassidy's mother, Shirley Jones?

"What've you got for us today?"

Us being Mr. Dell'Olio and his Sophomore Student Director, a girl I knew from Ms. Lemieux's 7th grade Enriched English & Social Studies at Webb, Claire Moody. They both sat scrutinizing me from the front row of the auditorium. First I had to perform a monologue I prepared on my own, and if Dell liked what he saw, he'd ask me to sing and/or read from the script.

"I'll be doing a monologue from my fav-rid—I mean, *favorite*—movie," I told him, hitting the *T*, my voice trembling with fear. I wiped my sweaty palms on the front of my khaki pants, hoping they didn't leave a stain.

"Good, good," Mr. Dell'Olio replied. "What is it?"

With the utmost confidence, I answered, "*Somewhere in Time,* starring Jane Seymour and Christopher Reeves—I mean, *Reeve.*" I always get that wrong!

Dell nodded and smiled, making a note on his clipboard. At that point, I never had him for a teacher, but he seemed like a nice guy. And *The Skeleton Walks* turned out pretty good earlier that fall so I been wanting to work with him ever since.

"Whenever you're ready."

I stared down at my topsiders, took a deep breath, in and out. I closed my eyes for a moment. When I opened them, I imagined myself as Jane Seymour, with Christopher Reeve (no *S*) watching me from the audience.

"The man of my dreams has almost faded now . . ."

Personally, I gave an awesome audition. And I must have, because after I finished my monologue Mr. Dell'Olio asked, "What're you gonna sing?"

"Um . . ."

The only song I could find the sheet music for was "Too Young" by Jack Wagner. You know, Frisco from *General Hospital.* Because I never been in a musical, I didn't know the first thing about auditioning for one. All I knew was I needed to prepare sixteen bars.

"Sounds good," Mr. Dell'Olio said all smiles. "Liza will play for you . . . Again, whenever you're ready."

Sporting her signature spider, Liza Larson smiled at me from behind the piano down in the pit. Back then, I didn't know her very well. Like I said, we would later become buddies once I got brave enough to smoke out on Skid Row.

"All set?" Liza asked me.

I took a deep breath and listened as her fingers began working their magic.

"Hello, love, it's been way too long . . ."

Boy, did I sing my butt off! I reached notes I never hit practicing in my bedroom. My pitch was perfect. Sad to say, I didn't get the part.

At least not the lead, Curly.

This guy, Jake Czyzyk, got it just because he was a *Senior*—and he was totally hot.

Wanna know what role I did get cast as?

Curly's sidekick, Will Parker, opposite Audrey Wojczek as Ado Annie. Thank God by the time the show went up, we totally got along. The cool part was . . . I got to sing two songs, "Kansas City" and "All Er Nuthin'," twirl a rope, *and* do a tap dance in cowboy boots. I looked pretty cute doing it, too, if I do say so myself.

Not bad for a Sophomore who never *really* acted before, huh?

Never Let Me Down Again

"I'm taking a ride
With my Best Friend . . ."

—Depeche Mode

"Your *other* left!"

The following Wednesday, me and Rob Berger are up on stage, during 5th hour. We're working on a scene from a play called *Brighton Beach Memoirs.* You know, by Neil Simon. He's the guy who wrote *Barefoot in the Park* with Robert Redford and Jane Fonda. Dell picked it out for us. I didn't realize the play starred Ferris from *Ferris Bueller's Day Off* when it premiered on Broadway in 1983. Until I opened up the script, and there he was: Matthew Broderick as Eugene Jerome . . . So much for stage actors not being stars!

"For Pete's sake . . . This isn't rocket science."

I watch as Mr. Dell'Olio literally slaps his furrowed forehead. Meanwhile, all the other Drama Queers stare at us in silence.

"You said 'move to the left' didn't you?"

Poor Rob Berger . . . He looks like he's gonna bust a nut he's so confused right now.

"My left, your right!"

Rob looks at me.

I look at Mr. Dell'Olio for clarification. "You mean, *stage* right?"

Stage left. Stage right. Up stage. Down stage.

Sounds easy, huh? Try being the one up there taking direction. Especially when your director is screaming out your blocking at you.

"Just *move*, Berger," Dell orders, "and say your line while you're doing it . . . Got it?"

Rob mumbles softly, "Got it."

You'd think Mr. Dell'Olio would know what he's doing by now. He's been teaching Drama for how many years? And prior to that, he worked as a professional director Off-Off Broadway in New York City. It's not our fault some Russian guy, Stanislavsky, decided back in the late 1800s that *stage right* meant the actor's right and not the director's.

"Is it Christmas Break yet?" Dell asks aloud, to nobody in particular.

"Seventy-eight more days," a voice responds from somewhere in the void.

"Thank you, Audrey!"

"No problem, Dell."

That's Aud, always being a smart-ass!

I look out to see her slumped down in her seat next to Tuesday Gunderson, both girls trying not to chuckle at mine and Rob's expense.

"Whenever you fellas are ready," Mr. Dell'Olio says to us now. "Preferably sometime before I retire in the year 2007."

In the scene, me and Rob play brothers: Stanley and Eugene. Stanley's eighteen and Eugene is fifteen, which is perfect casting if you ask me. I don't look the least bit my real age (seventeen) and Rob looks like he's at least twenty. Must be the mustache . . . and the fact that he's had pubes since he was twelve!

The only thing is, Stanley and Eugene are *Jewish.* Not that I got a problem with Jewish people, I just don't know any. The closest thing you get to a Jewish anything in *The Friendly City* of Hazel Park is when the cross-country team has a bagel sale.

"From the top?" Rob asks, looking in my direction.

"You got the first line," I remind him.

"Oh . . ."

Not that he's not a cool guy, but you can probably imagine why Rob Berger's a Varsity athlete. As hot as he may be, he isn't the brightest bulb in the bunch, you know what I mean? Surprisingly, he's a fairly decent actor—for a jock.

We been in Dell's Drama class together since Junior year. This past spring, he played the role of Dr. Orin Scrivello, DDS in *Little Shop of Horrors* to my Seymour and Liza Larson's Audrey. Picture Rob in a black leather jacket sucking on that nitric oxide. H-O-T!

Poor Audrey . . . She desperately wanted to be Audrey, but Dell decided to go with a blond, like in the movie. Not to mention the fact that Audrey is more of a character actress. This is why she ended up playing Chiffon, one of the three street urchins.

"What are *you* doing here?"

I remember asking Rob this when I saw him at the auditions.

"You think I can't act just because I'm a jock?" he joked.

The second he flashed that fucking grin of his, I was smitten.

Of all people, I never expected to see Rob Berger trying out for a play, least of all a musical. Back in junior high, he never did anything artistic. He didn't sing in Choir or play an instrument in Band or even take Creative Academics with Ms. Lemieux. Now of all a sudden, there he was . . . From Total Jock to Drama Queer!

Only Rob Berger is far from being a queer of any kind as far as I can tell. Sure, he's popular, and we already established how hot he is, but like I said, he's a Varsity football player. How come he doesn't have a *girlfriend*? In fact, I've known Rob for over five years now, and in all that time I can't remember him ever going with anybody.

He did bring this one girl, Katy Griffin, to the 9th grade Carnation Dance. She used to play trombone and sat next to me in Band all three years at Webb, but I always thought Katy might be a lesbian so she doesn't count.

"Hold!"

The second we finally get rolling, Mr. Dell'Olio starts screaming at us again. Personally, I thought the scene was going good. So far I didn't drop a single line.

Too bad I can't say the same for Rob.

"Are we doing something wrong?" he asks, more to me than to Herr Director.

"Yeah, Dell . . . What's up?" I wonder. "Do we totally suck or something?"

"You're fine, Dayton," Mr. Dell'Olio replies. "I can't say the same for your partner."

Rob's face goes raspberry-beret-red. "Sorry, Coach." Frustrated, he kicks at some nonexistent fuzz on the lip of the stage.

What's happening in the scene is . . . Eugene is playing with his football when Stanley enters, all freaked out. He just got fired from his job for disrespecting his boss, this German Nazi-type guy who naturally must *hate* Stanley since he's a Jew, and vice versa. Being a comedy, it's pretty funny shit, even though Dell's taking it super seriously.

"Berger," he says to Rob, sounding like a dad about to have the (quote-unquote) talk with his firstborn son. "Tell me something . . ."

Rob looks up without saying a word.

"What's your motivation?"

After a slight pause Rob asks, "What do you mean?"

Dell loses it. He throws his arms up in defeat. "How many days till Christmas Break?"

"Seventy-eight," Audrey pipes up from the Peanut Gallery. "You already asked."

I can't help but laugh when I see Dell shaking his head, looking like he can't take much more. Really, he's not a crabass. He just can't resist acting all dramatic. In fact, he's just as much a Drama Queer as the rest of us. Except he's not a homo, he's totally married.

"In the *scene*," Mr. Dell'Olio says slowly, trying a new tactic, "what is your motivation?"

Rob repeats, "What's my motivation in the scene?"

I think he thinks if he stalls, the answer will come to him.

Poor Rob . . . I can't stand to see him suffer. Not with Audrey and Tuesday and all the other Drama Queers sitting in their seats scrutinizing him as he starts to sweat. Where's Mr. Fish with his rag when you need it?

"He means, what do you *want?*" I whisper, trying to talk without moving my lips, à la Laverne DeFazio from *Laverne & Shirley.*

Rob's face lights up. "Oh! What do I want?"

"What does *Stanley* want?" Dell corrects.

"What does Stanley want?" Rob repeats, like it's finally starting to sink in. "Beats the hell outta me."

Thunderous applause!

Finally, the bell rings, signaling the 2:00 PM end of Advanced Drama, putting both me and Rob outta our *Brighton Beach Memoirs* misery . . .

"Good scene, you guys."

Audrey approaches from the aisle, her long red hair swaying behind her back. I can't tell if she's being sarcastic or not.

"Seriously," Tuesday snorts, bringing up the rear. "You're a really good actor, Berger."

"Thanks," Rob mutters, avoiding eye contact with the ladies.

Tuesday looks at me, forgetting I'm also standing there. "You too, Brad."

Rob hops off the stage. "Later," he tells us before making his way towards the box office in the back corner.

I can't help but notice the way Aud watches Rob's every move. In fact, Tuesday practically drools down the front of her maroon Flaggots—I mean, *Flag Corps*—windbreaker till he disappears thru the EXIT doors into the front lobby.

"Lucky you," Audrey sighs, "getting to work with Mr. Varsity Football."

"Yeah," echoes Tuesday. "You sure are lucky."

I agree, "Yeah . . ."

What else am I supposed to say in response to their remarks? *Now if he'd only make out with me.*

After an awkward moment of silence, Audrey asks, "Wanna help me and Tuesday with our scene sometime?"

"I'm free on Saturday," I offer, since I don't have to work at Big Boy's till the evening and I got nothing else going on during the day.

"Awesome!" exclaims Audrey.

I never noticed she's got a space between her teeth when she smiles, just like a certain football-playing Lesbian—I mean, *Thespian*—we know.

Tuesday parrots, "Yeah, awesome!"

The girls are working on *The Effects of Gamma Rays on Man-in-the-Moon Marigolds.* Back in the '60s, it played Off-Broadway. They also made a movie version with Paul Newman's wife, Joanne Woodward, which I never seen.

Audrey plays the crazy mom, Beatrice, and Tuesday is the daughter, Tillie, who's all into science and shit. So far they're doing a pretty good job, but if you ask me, the play's totally fucked up. The mom *kills* the daughter's pet rabbit for chris'sakes, you know what I mean?

"We can hang at my house," Aud informs us. "My mom'll be at work."

I'm about to follow my classmates' lead and get my ass moving to 6th hour French III Independent Study when Mr. Dell'Olio stops me on the stairs leading down from the stage.

"Good work today, Dayton."

I can feel my face matching my hair as I humbly tell him, "Thanks."

I don't know why, but I'm a little embarrassed by Mr. Dell'Olio's praise. I mean, I certainly wanna do a good job. I live for the day others will laud me for my acting ability. Except right now, I don't know what else to say. So I just stand there with a stupid smirk.

"You're a natural," Dell flatters, patting me on the back. "I'll see you at auditions, won't I?"

This semester we're doing *A Christmas Carol.* You know, by Charles Dickens. Same guy who gave us *A Tale of Two Cities* and *Oliver Twist.* The first one, we read in Mrs. Malloy's English Lit, the other, I seen the musical years ago. Auditions are coming up the second week of November.

"I'll be there," I confirm.

I can't say I read the script yet, but I watched the movie of *A Christmas Carol* on TV when I was little. I heard the boy who played Tiny Tim is now Artistic Director at Meadow Brook Theatre out in Rochester . . . God, he must be ancient!

I'm still not sure what part I want. Sure, Scrooge has got the most lines, but I don't see myself playing an old man. Being that I'm a Senior, I'm sure Dell will cast me in one of the leads . . . Why wouldn't he, if I'm such a natural?

"What's up, Fox?"

In the commons outside the auditorium, I run into Shelly Findlay—I mean, *Shellee* Findlay. I keep forgetting her and a bunch of the other Varsity cheerleaders officially changed the spelling of their first names. Karla Carlson is now *Karlah* and Melody Carnes is *Mellowdeigh.*

Don't ask!

Me and Shellee go way back to 7th grade at Webb. We used to be in Band together, but like a lot of the junior high Band Fags, Shellee dropped out once we got to high school, which is a damn shame if you ask me because she was a very talented *flautist.*

I don't know why, but a lot of people don't like our HPHS Band teacher, Mr. Klan, just because he's a Total Fag. Well, we don't know if he is for sure, but he *is* over thirty-five and he's never been married, so the odds are in favor. Not that I want him to be or anything. I don't find him the least bit attractive. In fact, he reminds me of my dad, which is totally bogue!

"What's up?" I wonder.

Shellee hands me one of the mimeographed flyers she's been Scotch taping to the glass doors outside Principal Messinger's office. Her brunette head bobs back and forth as she cackles at me. "Duh! It's all right there."

Sure enough, so it is.

Don't forget to Vote!
Homecoming "Top 25"
10/1/87

Ah, yes . . . "Top 25."

The yearly ritual to pick the twenty-five Seniors at Hazel Park High School most deserving to be elected to Homecoming Court.

Personally, I'm pretty bic-cited (excited).

Back in 10th grade, I had these two Senior friends, Alyssa Resnick and Cheri Sheffield. They were both on "Top 25." I remember thinking what an honor being singled out by your peers must be. Not that I need validation or anything. For the most part, I already know that people like me . . . And if they don't, fuck 'em!

I wish Shellee "Good luck!" even though she's a shoo-in. She was always Most Popular Girl at Webb Junior High and continues to be to this day.

"You too, Fox!" she replies, waving with pinky, forefinger, and thumb extended. Then she gathers her flyers and moves on to the display case next to the library.

This is where, along with the VFW award, the American Legion award, and the prestigious Erickson Cup, sits the coveted "Thespy." At least twice a day since Sophomore year, I stop by to stare at it. I imagine how the gold (plated) statuette will feel held in my hot little hand, how my name—BRADLEY JAMES DAYTON—will look engraved on the metal plate marked "1987–88." What it will *mean* to be honored as Thespian of the Year.

For those not up on their Drama Queer terminology . . . Thespis is credited as being the first actor ever to appear on a stage in something like 600 BC. According to Aristotle, Thespis was a singer of *dithyrambs,* which were songs about mythology that featured choral refrains. He also invented the style that became known as tragedy (as in "comedy and . . ."), where one single actor performed *all* the characters in a play, using different masks to differentiate.

Hence the creation of the International *Thespian* Society by a group of college and high school teachers in Fairmont, West Virginia, in 1929.

"Act well your part; there all the honor lies."

This is the motto of the ITS, taken from Alexander Pope's *Essay on Man.*

I won't presume I'm gonna get the "Thespy," but I *am* President of Troupe #4443, so I know I'm in the running.

But first things first . . .

"Top 25."

I can't say everybody shares my attitude. Especially my Best Friend, Jack Paterno. Perhaps I should say, my *other* Best Friend, considering I already referred to Max Wilson as filling that spot. Jack spends sooo much time worrying about what other people think of him. In fact, he even dropped outta Band this year because he was sick of being called a Band Fag.

Or so he said.

Like Carrie Johnson, I met Jack in 7th grade Varsity Band over at Webb. Well, we didn't *really* meet in Band, we met in the cafeteria during lunch. Jack was sitting with Carrie and Ava Reese and Katy Griffin (the girl I think might be a lesbian), going thru some stupid Sign-In Book: *"Calvins or Jordache?"* Well, I walked right up to the table, sat myself down, and was all like, "Fuck those! I like Sergio Valentes better 'cause they make your ass look hot!"

At least that's what Jack says I said.

I seriously doubt I'd say something like that—not in front of a group of girls. Of course, knowing me, if I *did* say it, I was trying to get a rise outta Jack . . . Talk about a Persnickety-Persnick!

If it wasn't for our junior high Band teacher, Jessica Clark Putnam, encouraging us to attend Blue Lake Fine Arts Camp the following summer, we would've never become Best Friends. I remember us bragging to all the other Band Fags about how cool we were and how swanky the whole thing was gonna be. Twelve days in the lap of luxury at an exclusive Summer Band Camp.

Or so we thought.

Imagine the expressions on our faces when Jack's parents dropped us off in the middle of the woods in Bum Fuck Muskegon. Boy, were we surprised!

What the fuck?

I remember this being my first thought as me and Jack stood there, clad in our regulation robin's egg blue BLFAC polo shirts and navy blue shorts, mouths totally agape.

This is what you get for $300?

Nothing but dirt roads and trees for miles . . . So much for being exclusive!

You should've seen poor Jack when we checked in with our counselor over in the Broadway unit at Cabin Cabaret. Try saying that three times. Right next door to Brigadoon, Carousel, and Okla-homo!—I mean, *homa!*

"Where are the walls?" he wondered, suitcase and pillow in hand.

"Maybe they can't afford them," I guessed, even though we were paying a shitload of money to be standing there. Somebody at BLFAC must have thought exposed beams were all the rage in early '80s décor.

I realize when you're little time goes by a lot slower, but they were the twelve longest (and poop-free) days of my life. Up at the butt crack of dawn for breakfast. Followed by Band practice. Followed by lunch. Followed by sectionals. Followed by dinner. Followed by whatever damn evening activity they had planned for us.

This one time they brought in this guy, Slim Goodbody, to put on a show. He wore this skintight bodysuit, painted to look like his skin was removed so you could see all his organs . . . Bogue!

Nobody wanted to sit and listen to good old Slim sing these stupid-assed songs about "Food is Fuel" and "Healthy Habits" and "Bones, Bones, Bones." All the guys in our cabin thought Mr. Goodbody was a Total Fag, you know what I mean? Including me and Jack.

That was the one thing I noticed most about being at Blue Lake. Back at Webb, we had a tendency to get picked on—nothing major. We never got our asses kicked in the parking lot after school or anything, but people (guys mostly) would call us *fag*, just because we were friends with girls and liked to dance at the Fun Nights. Yet the entire twelve days we spent at BLFAC, the guys there were totally cool to us.

Even this one guy, Greg, who elected himself cabin leader.

"Hey, Dick Shine!"

Greg picked on everybody in Cabin Cabaret. He came from Kalamazoo, played alto sax, and was a year older than me and Jack. I'll never forget he had bangs that hung in his eyes and hair on his legs . . . God, he was cute!

"Who, me?" asked Paul, a cellist from Southfield. He kept a stash of apricot nectar buried beneath his bunk. Greg nicknamed him "Berf."

"No *you*, Faggot Ass!" Greg scowled at "Scooter."

"What did *I* do?" Scooter wanted to know. His real name was Jay. He wore thick glasses, played baritone, and hailed from Milford. Or did he go to school at Mumford? I forget.

Scooter—I mean, *Jay*—was hilarious! Somewhere, I got a photo I took of him drying his tube socks with a blow dryer on the steps outside Cabin Cabaret. He had this totally nasal voice and he used to crack all of us up with the dumbest jokes.

This one was my favorite: "So there's this lady, see? And one day, she sends her husband and kids off on a hunting trip . . ."

"Why, Jay?" I'd interrupt, even though I already heard him tell it a dozen times.

"Because," Jay would answer. "She's had *enough*."

"So what did she do?" I'd prompt.

Causing Greg to yell, "Shut up, Dick Weed!" before he tossed a pillow at my head from his bunk beside mine and Jack's.

"So," Jay continued, "she makes a spot of chamomile tea, and she sinks herself into a hot tub. Just as soon as she's all relaxed, there's a knock at the door . . ."

Knock knock!

"The lady's like, 'I'm sorry, I can't come to the door, I'm in the tub.' And the guy at the door is all like, 'Telegram . . . It's important.'"

Meanwhile, I'm about to pee my pants!

"So the lady says, 'Well . . . Could you just sing it?' And the guy says, 'But *lady . . .' 'Sing it!'"* (pause) "'Dum dum dum dum dum dum . . .' (singing) 'Bob and the kids are dead.' The End."

Anyways!

Wanna know what Greg's nickname for me and Jack ended up being?

"Brad the Nad" and "String Sucker."

Wanna know why?

Well, Brad rhymes with nad, and Greg swore up and down he woke up in the middle of the night and caught Jack sucking on the strings of his sleeping bag in his sleep. But I didn't believe him. By that point, I knew Jack for almost an entire year, and not once did I ever know him to suck on *anything.*

I don't know why, but being picked on at Blue Lake never felt the same way as it does here in Hazeltucky. At BLFAC, if somebody called you *fag,* it was like a badge of honor. It didn't mean they *really* thought you were one, even though I totally was—I mean, *am.*

You know I'm gay, right?

As in I like *boys.*

Just checking.

Please, Please, Please, Let Me Get What I Want

"So for once in my life
Let me get what I want . . ."

—The Smiths

Today's the big day!

Basically what happens is . . . Around 12:30 PM, two representatives from the Junior class come into the Choir room with ballots containing the names of all two hundred eighty-three Seniors of the HPHS Class of '88 so that we members of Chorale can cast our "Top 25" vote.

"How have you been?"

One of the girls, Tracy Cardoza, I'm happy to see for the first time since school started a month ago.

"You know," she shrugs, "hanging in there."

I can't believe how much Tracy's changed since junior high at Webb. We weren't ever really friends, but her sister, Lydia, has known my sister, Janelle, since we first moved to Ferndale. Back in 9th grade, Tracy went with Jack Paterno to the Carnation

Dance. I'll never forget she wore this totally Madonna "Like a Virgin" get-up, complete with long gloves and matching scarves in her hair. Now three years later, I barely recognize her.

First of all, she's super skinny. Not that Tracy was ever fat or anything, but I bet she's lost at least twenty pounds. And now she's a Total Punk. She's traded her blond bob for a totally dyed-black, sticking-up-on-top/short-on-the-sides 'do—save for the long wisps coming down by her ears like sideburns. You should also see the way she's dressed . . . Tight black tank top worn with black tights and black rubber bracelets cascading up and down her arms. She must have her ears pierced six or seven times on each side.

Good-bye Book Worm, hello Sex Kitten!

"What's up?"

This I say to the other girl, a short, cute Vikette named Diane Thompson. She looks very Preppie sporting a beige cardigan with a brown turtleneck, pegged pants, and brown leather Bass loafers.

Diane replies, "Oh nothing." She avoids looking at me like she thinks I totally hate her or something, just because she dumped Jack's sorry ass after dating him during Junior year. Yet she asks, "Have you talked to Lou lately?"

Uh-oh, here we go!

I knew I wouldn't be able to avoid this forever.

Where do I start?

'member the two Senior girls I mentioned being friends with during Sophomore year? The ones who both made "Top 25"? Alyssa Resnick and Cheri Sheffield. Well, like Diane, Alyssa also dated Jack. And like Diane again, it only lasted a couple months.

Wanna know why?

I probably shouldn't say anything. It's none of my business, really. But the fact that I barely seen him since school began because of it is starting to piss me off, you know what I mean?

Jack Paterno is gay.

At least *I* think he is, and I been his Best Friend since 7th grade, so I should know, right?

To make a long story short . . .

Me and Jack met Alyssa and her other Best Friend, Luanne "Lou" Kowalski on a Marching Band bus trip at the beginning of Sophomore year. Well, Jack and Alyssa hit it off and started going together, which totally pissed Lou off because Lou is a lesbian, and she was in love with Alyssa at the time.

Fast forward to Valentine's Day 1986 . . .

This totally hot guy, Joey Palladino, moved back to Hazeltucky after his parents got a divorce. Him and Jack were Best Friends back in elementary school at Longfellow, I guess. Seeing Joey again made Jack realize he was in love with him, and probably had been since they were in like 4th grade.

That's about the time I had my *Okla-homo!* audition.

"You're really gonna go thru with that?"

Jack immediately asked me this question when I mentioned I planned on trying out.

"I already told you, it's what I wanna do with my life."

Ever since Mrs. Malloy assigned us the *What I Want to Be When I Grow Up* paper earlier that year in 1st hour English, I made up my mind . . . I, Bradley James Dayton, will be a famous actor someday!

Wanna know what Jack said when I confessed I'd be doing the Jane Seymour speech from *Somewhere in Time?*

"But that's a girl's monologue."

"So what?" I snapped, sounding totally defensive. "I like it and that's all that counts." Plus I can do an awesome Jane Seymour impression: *"Is it you?"*

"Aren't you gonna care what other people think?"

Didn't I say Jack spends all his time worrying about other people? Me, I don't give a shit what they think. The fact that I was auditioning for *Okla-homo!* already made me a Total Fag in most people's eyes, you know what I mean? They don't call 'em Drama *Queers* for nothin'.

And that was the moment I first told Jack I'm gay.

He claims he never knew. That he never once considered it, even though back in 9th grade he helped me steal a copy of *Playgirl* from my sister, Janelle, and conduct a séance to resurrect the then-recently departed Jon-Erik Hexum from *Cover Up* and *Making of a Male Model* with Joan Collins. I can't believe that after being my Best Friend for over three years, Jack didn't suspect I could be (quote) a little light in the loafers (unquote).

Somehow, I managed to get him to admit that he thought he *might* be gay, too. So me and Lou took Jack out to this (gay) bar down on Woodward called Heaven. It's a Total Dump, but we always had a good time.

For a while things were fine. Jack and Lou finally started getting along. When he wasn't spending all his time with Joey Palladino, the three of would take drives in Lou's Escort out I-94 to Algonac, listening to Echo & the Bunnymen. Or we'd go to Elias Brothers (Big Boy's), and Jack would sit while me and Lou drank coffee and smoked. After sooo many years of thinking I was the only gay person alive, now I had *two* friends who were both like me.

That's about the time Jack got the letter.

Dear Jack,
I know you're a fag.
Love, Mom

Okay, Dianne Paterno didn't exactly go that far, but she did say she was pretty sure Jack was (quote-unquote) in love with Joey Palladino. She also said she'd support him no matter what, which was totally cool if you ask me. But Jack totally freaked out.

Next thing I knew, no more gay Jack.

That summer, we barely saw each other, between me getting a job at Big Boy's and working every night, and Jack taking Driver's Ed and spending every day with Betsy Sheffield who he decided he was now (quote-unquote) in love with ever since the whole scan-jul with Joey caused them to stop being friends.

Not that she's not nice, but Betsy can be a little stuck-up. I don't know if it's because she went to the other junior high, Beecher, and lives over in The Courts or what. Sometimes she gets this attitude like she thinks she's better than everybody else, you know what I mean? It makes perfect sense that her and Jack would totally get along since he's always acted this way, too. Did I mention that Betsy is Cheri Sheffield's younger sister?

She's also a Senior and happens to be sitting across the Choir room from me in the alto section at this very moment. I don't know if anybody's told Betsy, but it's the first week of October and she's got on khaki shorts worn with a navy sweatshirt turned inside out, matching socks, and penny loafers. She's always prided herself in being totally Preppie.

Betsy is also a totally popular cheerleader. This is part of the reason I think Jack is friends with her in the first place. Ever since he dropped outta Band, Jack has been bound and determined to infiltrate the popular crowd. If you ask me, it's totally lame. It's not like he's a loser or anything. Jack's already friends with all the popular girls—it's the *guys* who won't give him the time of day.

Once we returned to school in the fall of '86, Lou became drum major. Being in Marching Band under her direction totally sucked! Let's just say, we didn't call her "Baby Hitler" for nothing. To make matters worse, Jack decided to ask out Diane Thompson, even though he knew Lou totally had a thing for her and it would totally piss Lou off. Sure enough, it worked, and soon after, Lou started telling everybody (including Diane Thompson) that Jack was a Total Fag.

Even *I* thought this was true because it had been.

At least for a while.

I guess not anymore.

Poor Brad . . . I totally got caught in the middle. Between Lou dragging me out to the bar with her every Friday night after the football games, and wanting to stay Best Friends with Jack who I hardly seen now that he worked as a bagger at Farmer Jack's, I didn't know what to do.

I certainly wasn't gonna lie about who I *really* am—certainly not to myself. Besides, it's not like I went around advertising I'm a fag or anything. I just continued to act the way I always did.

So Diane eventually dumped Jack, making Lou a happy camper, even though she wasn't gonna get her carpet munched anytime in the near future, since no sooner than Diane and Jack broke up, guess who she started going with next?

None other than the former love of Jack's life: Joey Palladino.

Speaking of . . .

Back in the Choir room on "Top 25" day, I look over to see Diane hanging all over Joey while he's trying to fill out his ballot. I can't say I blame her. Like I said, he's totally hot!

You should see him . . . He's like 6' tall, dark hair, dark eyes, totally muscular. He lifts weights at least five times a week. He always dresses super sharp in Guess? jeans, pegged at the bottom, and penny loafers sans socks. Again, I'm a sucker for bare ankles! He also wears this totally cool navy pea coat, and looks just like a Dago Donny Osmond when he grins.

"Who's Jens Andersson?" I hear Joey ask.

"Got me hanging," Audrey replies from where she sits with the sopranos. The way she's chewing her pencil calls to mind the expression *oral fixation.*

Our Senior class president, Jamieleeann Mary Sue Good, fills us in. "He's that new guy from Sweden." Jamie should know—she's friends with everybody.

For the first time since the '70s, Hillbilly High has not one, but *two* foreign exchange students. One of them is the aforementioned Jens Andersson. He's something like 6'4" and totally blond, so he sticks out like a sore thumb.

I met him briefly when we were both out smoking on Skid Row at the beginning of the school year. Standing there in his Varsity football jersey puffing on a Parliament, I remember him saying in his accented English, "All de kids are allowed to smoke in Sweden, ya!"

Joey tells Jamie, "I think I'll vote for him . . . He seems cool."

It's a good thing Jack isn't in Chorale to hear a comment like that.

Ever since this whole "Top 25" thing started, he's been up on his soapbox preaching to everybody how it's nothing but a big popularity contest. How the people who end up getting picked are the ones who do *nothing* for our school and have *no* spirit. If that guy Jens gets elected after being at HPHS for all of a month, Jack is gonna be sooo pissed!

"What about Maria Torres-Padilla?" I ask the girl sitting next to me, Tonya Tyler.

"She's the foreign exchange chick from Bolivia," Tonya answers, bare footsies up on the chair in front of her, flats on the floor beside it.

"Brazil," Jamie Good announces, correcting her friend.

"She's kinda hot, isn't she?" I hear Joey say, joining in on our conversation.

"Hey!" Diane Thompson hisses. She hits him hard upon the massive shoulder.

"Don't worry," Joey replies. "You're hotter." Then he puckers up and plants one on her.

Personally, I always thought Joey's gay.

Not that he acts like a fag or anything. But the only explanation I could come up with for his sudden interest in Diane Thompson after she broke up with Jack stemmed from Joey wanting to get back at him . . . But why?

This one time I came right out and asked Jack if him and Joey ever messed around back in 10th grade. He claimed they never did, which if you ask me, is totally lame on Jack's part. If I had a friend who was half as hot as Joey Palladino and I suspected he *might* be the slightest bit faggy, I'd totally be all over him.

Anyways!

The next day we have an all-school assembly . . .

I'm sitting with Audrey, Jamie Good, Tonya Tyler, and the rest of Chorale. I don't know why, but we always have these gatherings during 4th hour. Since it immediately follows lunch, everybody's supposed to report directly to the auditorium. For the most part, people take it as an opportunity to skip. Especially the ones who got Mrs. Carey for French.

"Will the following Seniors please rise when I call their name?"

Up on stage behind the podium stands our Senior class advisor, Mr. Verlander. The thing only comes up to his waist, the man's so tall. He must be at least 6'2". As per usual, he wears a permanent-press shirt with a throwback-to-the-'70s wide tie. The second he speaks, his two-pack-a-day voice makes me totally wish I stopped by Skid Row prior to coming here. Instead, I arrived early to grab a good seat.

One by one, Mr. Verlander announces the "Top 25" for Homecoming '87 . . .

"Stephanie Adams."

Co-captain of Vikettes, of course she made it. Stephanie is totally beautiful with long blond hair, green eyes, and legs for days.

"Kimberly Aielli."

Another Vikette and Stephanie's brown-eyed Best Friend.

"Jens Andersson."

The Foreign Exchange student from Sweden.

What the fuck?

I look over to where Jack sits with Max in the center section of seats. They both got Consumer Ec this hour with some teacher I never had before, Mrs. Ireland. From the expression on Jack's face, I can tell he's pissed. Meanwhile, Jens doesn't know what's happening as he's cheered on by his fellow Varsity football teammates to stand up.

"Angela Andrews."

Yet another Vikette.

I can't believe she was Max's first girlfriend back in 7th grade. I don't know how he ever scored her. She was (and is) still totally hot.

"Robert Berger."

No surprise there!

As a Varsity football player, how could he lose?

"Mitchell Bloodworth."

Another Varsity football player.

"Derrick Brown."

And another.

I wipe my sweaty palms on the front of my pants. With the announcement of each name, my heart pounds harder in my chest. I mean, it's not like I'm gonna die if mine's not called . . . I'm a Band Fag *and* a Drama Queer, what can I expect?

"Karla Carlson . . . Melody Carnes . . . Walter Cieslak."

Varsity cheerleader . . . Varsity cheerleader . . . Varsity wrestler.

I hope I'm not too overdressed.

Most of the football players got their jerseys on. Maybe I should have worn jeans like them? Here I am in brown slacks, a tan dress shirt, and matching cardigan I stole—I mean, *borrowed*—from Jack. The last thing I want is to look like I'm anticipating my name being called.

Finishing up with the C's, Mr. Verlander moves onto the D's . . .

"Natalie Davis."

Co-captain of girls' Varsity basketball.

"Kenneth Daw."

Co-captain of boys' Varsity basketball.

"Bradley Dayton."

Band Fag *and* Drama Que—

Oh, my God . . . He fucking called my name!

Audrey whacks me on the shoulder. Like a dork, I stand up, trying not to look too enthused, yet wanting to convey how honored I am to be recognized.

Wanna know the totally stupid thing I do next?

I *wave.*

Not like a small see-somebody-in-the-hall sorta motion, but a grand Queen Elizabeth-out-on-the-palace-balcony-greeting-the-peons gesture.

Audrey rolls her eyes.

Thankfully Verlander moves on to the E's and F's . . .

"Rochelle Findlay."

Told you so!

"Thomas Fulton."

Varsity football *and* basketball co-captain.

From what I heard, Tom's also Betsy Sheffield's date for the Homecoming Dance next Saturday night.

Personally, I can't stand the guy. Him and Max used to be all buddy-buddy when we were at Webster and early on at Webb. In fact, this one time in 7th grade, me and Max and Jack went over Tom's house, and we called this phone-sex party line pretending we were *girls.* If I remember correctly, Tom did a pretty good job talking-the-talk to the guys on the other end . . . Hmmm?

I'd be lying if I didn't admit Tom's a decent-looking guy.

Now that he's traded his horn-rims for contacts, started lifting weights, and dressing designer. Right now, he's got on a heather lamb's wool sweater over a white Polo shirt with button-down collar, and snug-fitting charcoal slacks. I see he's also got a new haircut—sorta long and flippy in front, short around the sides and wedged in back. And of course, beautiful blue eyes, a totally perfect smile, square jaw and dimples . . . See why I hate him?

Now for the G's . . .

"Stacy Gillespie."

Woo-hoo!

Stacy is my very good friend from French III Independent Study. 'member the girl Mrs. Carey gave her teacher's edition last year with all the answers? If I wasn't a homo, I think I'd totally be in love with her. She's sooo tiny and cute with her short dark hair and chestnut brown eyes. Not to mention she's super stylish and super smart. Except I don't think either one of us is gonna learn much taking French III as an Independent Study. Since Mrs. Carey's not there to preside over us, most of the time we end up sitting around shooting the shit.

By the time I finally spot Stacy amongst the student body, Verlander's telling us to "Quiet down, people," so he can move on to the next name . . .

"Jonathan Glowicki."

Another Varsity football *and* basketball player.

"Jamieleeann Mary Sue Good."

Like I said, Jamie is Senior class president. Not to mention Varsity cheerleading captain, secretary of National Honor Society, and don't forget Chorale. She's got a beautiful voice. Last year we did a duet at the spring concert, "Friends & Lovers," by Gloria Loring and Carl Anderson—Liz Chandler-Curtis from *Days of our Lives*, and the original Judas in *Jesus Christ Superstar*.

Jack doesn't notice me watching him, but I can totally tell he's sweating bullets waiting for Mr. Verlander to get to the P's.

He's all dressed up in his navy blue slacks, matching cardigan over gray mock-turtleneck shirt. I know he's expecting something to happen soon. For his sake, I hope his name gets called. I know how much Jack wants this.

"Fay Keating."

The other co-captain of girls' Varsity basketball.

Very sporty and very popular, Fay's another Freshman-year-transfer from St. Mary's back at Webb. She's a totally great girl, but her taste in guys hasn't always been the best. I'll never forget she went to the Carnation Dance with Guy Huckabee, this Total Jerk. When I stopped them on the dance floor to take a picture, Guy just gave me this look like, *She's with me, you fag!*

Whatever . . .

I still have the photo. I just tore Guy outta it.

"Pamela Klimaszewski."

You can bet Max is drooling all over himself when Pam (and her tits) stand up in the row right behind me. I look over my shoulder and give her a wink. I can't help but notice she's got her arms folded across her chest—to hide her rack, no doubt!

Poor Pam . . . I totally love her. I just think she's got a thing about her boobs. I guess maybe she's sorta shy. I mean, she sings alto in Chorale, but I don't think I ever heard her actually *sing* anything. Since I first met her in Mrs. Malloy's Sophomore English, she's always reminded me of a dishwater blond Molly Ringwald. Her boyfriend is this big cross-country champ, Stan Blume. He graduated from HPHS this past June, and is off at Michigan State on a scholarship.

Next, the L's, M's, N's and O's . . .

"Donald Olsewski."

Another Band Fag?

Well, wonders never cease!

Don plays drums and he also DJ's at most of our school dances. I don't know him too well, but he seems like a good guy. I'm pretty sure him and Jack were friends back at Longfellow. In fact, Don and his mom live right down the block from the Paternos on Shevlin in Hazel Park. He's not bad looking, either. He reminds me of Christopher Reeves—I mean, *Reeve*—from *Somewhere in Time*. Only Don's got shoulder-length hair and isn't nearly as built as Superman.

Now for the P's . . .

"Penelope Page."

I'll never forget Penny. She's the girl I smoked my first cigarette with. A Marlboro Red, back in the winter of 8th grade, in the Jehovah's Witness parking lot. I felt like a bad ass!

"Joseph Palladino."

Based on his looks alone, Joey's gotta be a contender for Homecoming King. Except if he wins, Jack will just die.

Speaking of . . .

His name should be next.

Fingers crossed!

"Nathaniel Richelieu."

What the fuck?

I mean, I'm happy for Nate—he's got great hair and awesome ankles. But what happened to Jack Paterno? Mr. Verlander must've made a mistake and skipped a name. Or maybe the alphabetical got outta order?

"Elizabeth Sheffield . . . Marie Sperling . . . Tonya Tyler."

Varsity cheerleader . . . Vikettes co-captain . . . Chorale.

Finally, Mr. Verlander concludes with the U's, V's, W's . . .

No Class Clown, Audrey Wojczek?

And the X's, Y's, and Z's.

Outta all my friends, *I'm* the only one to make "Top 25"?

I can't fucking believe it!

And from the looks of it, neither can Jack.

Across the auditorium, I see him slump down in his seat, looking like he's gonna cry . . .

So am I.

What the fuck is wrong with the fucking people at this school?

Jack Paterno is the smartest guy in our class. Not to mention he's cuter than most of the so-called popular boys. Not that *I* think he's cute—he's like the brother I never had. But there's no denying Jack is attractive.

So what if he's not *hot,* like Rob Berger or Joey Palladino? He's still my Best Friend.

Kiss Him Goodbye

"He'll never love you
The way that I love you . . ."

—Bananarama

You are *not* gonna believe what happened.

'member how I was supposed to go over Audrey's house to help her and Tuesday Gunderson with their scene from *Gamma Rays*? Well, I did. As per usual, the three of us wound up talking more than we did working on anything. In fact, the girls ran thru the scene all of once, I gave them some notes, and they called it quits.

"Who do you think's cuter: Will Isaacs or Allen Bryan?"

It never failed. All Tuesday Gunderson ever wants to do is talk about guys. Maybe because she's never had a boyfriend a day in her life.

"Definitely Allen Bryan," Audrey answered from the kitchen, popping open a bottle of pop.

Tuesday called out from the couch, "You think so?"

"No question," Aud replied. She poured Diet Dr Pepper into

a plastic cup as she entered the room. "Will Isaacs is fat." She handed the half-empty bottle to Tuesday, who took a swig.

"So is Allen Bryan." Tuesday belched low and resonant.

Audrey grimaced. Frantically she put thumb to forehead, wiggled her fingers, and shouted, "Skobie!"

Tuesday wiped her mouth and mimicked her friend, mere seconds behind.

"Brad ate it!"

They both informed me of this fact when I didn't move a muscle, choosing to sit in my comfy armchair next to the fireplace, refusing to play along. I gave them each a look and kept on petting Patches, Audrey's orange and black and white calico.

"But Big Al plays football," said Audrey, picking right back up where she left off.

This seemed to be her justification for just about everything lately. If a guy played sports, he could have three heads on his shoulders and Audrey would still find him hot. I think it's her secret desire to feel a boy's Varsity jacket wrapped securely around her shoulders.

"Yeah, but Will plays trom*bone,*" Tuesday interjected, making a slide-like gesture.

I gotta say, she shocked me with her apt use of sexual innuendo. I always considered Tuesday a Total Nerd, you know what I mean?

"So . . . ? *Brad* plays trombone," Audrey reminded.

Hearing my name enter the conversation, I looked up. "What's that got to do with anything?" I wanted to know. "Are you saying I'm not hot or something?"

"That's exactly what I'm saying."

Scratching the inside corner of my eye with my *middle* finger, I cried, "Right here, Wojczek!"

I used to think Audrey's last name was Wo-check, since it's

Polish and all. Once we became better friends, she beat the proper pronunciation into me: Wo-*seck*.

Whatever . . .

Go eat another paczki, Wo-seck*!*

Tuesday piped up. "It's okay, Brad . . . *I* think you're hot."

"Thanks," I replied, even though the feeling wasn't the least bit mutual. Again, not that Tuesday's not a nice girl. She's just not my type—male.

Speaking of . . .

Across the room, I noticed a framed photo of a rather cute red-haired guy wearing a #63 maroon and gray HP Vikings football uniform. I gave Patches a gentle nudge, and he (she?) climbed down from my lap. I moved towards the photo of Audrey's brother for closer inspection. He looked familiar to me, even though I never met him . . . Boy, do I *want* to!

"What about Rob Berger?"

You can bet this coming from Tuesday caught my ear.

"What about him?" I asked, focusing my attention on the new topic at hand.

"I asked Aud who she thinks is cuter," Miss Gunderson reiterated. "Allen Bryan or Rob Berger?"

"That's like saying, 'Who's cuter: Andrew McCarthy or Anthony Michael Hall?'" I said with an air of superiority.

"Who's Anthony Michael Hall?" asked Tuesday, totally serious.

"You know," I answered, "Rusty from *Vacation* . . . As in *National Lampoon's*." Only one of my favorite movies ever.

Tuesday's dark eyes filled with light. "You mean Farmer Ted from *Sixteen Candles*? I think he's totally cute."

"Shut the fuck up!" I scowled. "You can't tell me you think Rusty is cuter than Blane."

Another blank look beamed from Tuesday.

"Blane from *Pretty in Pink*," Audrey informed her, coming to my rescue.

Tuesday admitted, "Never seen it . . . Sorry."

I found that hard to believe. "Weren't you at Ava's party when we watched it on video?"

"What party?" Tuesday wondered in confusion.

"'member, right before Halloween last year? Jack called in sick to work. He came with with Diane Thompson, and Joey Palladino was there . . ."

Audrey shot me an icy stare.

Oops! I forgot Miss Gunderson wasn't invited.

At that moment, I realized I desperately needed a cigarette. I grabbed my Marching Band windbreaker from the hook near the front door and rummaged around in the pockets in search of my Marlboro Lights.

"Your mom's not home, is she?" I double-checked with Audrey.

"Nope . . . Pat's at work."

That said, I shook out a cig, held it firmly between my lips, and fired it up.

Much better!

A few months ago, Mrs. Wojczek got a job manning the counter at Dunkin' Donuts across from Universal Mall on Dequindre. Sometimes, I'll go up there with Audrey and we'll sit at the counter drinking coffee and eating chocolate cream-filled donuts talking to her mom for days. She's gotta be close to fifty, but she's totally awesome. She even goes out on dates sometimes. Mr. Wojczek died back in like '77. In fact, I'd totally set her up with *my* dad, if he wasn't such a deadbeat.

"Can I bum one of them?" Audrey reached for the half-empty pack and helped herself to one of my smokes.

Chivalrously lighting it for her, I warned, "Don't forget the New Year's Eve incident."

Audrey made a face, exhaling. "Don't remind me."

'member Luanne "Lou" Kowalski, the lesbian who was in

love with Jack's ex-girlfriend, Alyssa? Well, back in 10th grade, Lou had a party at her house, and Audrey totally singed her bangs trying to light a cigarette on the stove . . . I since advised her not to wear so much Aqua Net aerosol.

Tuesday coughed. "If all you guys are gonna do is smoke," she hacked, "I'm going home."

I kicked back in my favorite chair, feeling totally mellow. "See ya!"

Sure, she'll sit around talking about boys and *sex,* but a little underage nicotine abuse enters the picture and Tuesday Gunderson goes all Goody Two-Shoes. She should pal around with Jack "Persnickety-Persnick" Paterno.

I guess I should probably feel sorry for the girl. I remember Jack telling me how when he went to elementary school with Tuesday back at Longfellow, the second their teacher walked outta the room, all the kids would say, "Whoever talks loves Tuesday Gunderson!" Right in front of her . . . Isn't that bogue?

"I thought she'd never leave."

Once Audrey's scene partner made her exit (stage left), she plopped down on the couch across from me and began practicing her French inhaling. There's a rumor we're doing *Grease* as the spring musical and Aud *really* wants to play Didi Conn—I mean, *Frenchy.*

I stubbed out my cig and reached for another. There's nothing quite like that first puff. The taste of the nicotine on your tongue, the smoke filling your lungs, blowing out a beautiful blue-gray plume . . . Heaven!

"You never answered the question," I reminded Audrey.

She flicked an inch-long grandma-ash into an amber ashtray. "What was it?"

I watched as she worked her jaw, sending smoke signals about her redheaded head.

"Allen Bryan or Rob Berger?"

Audrey gave me a look, head titled, brow furrowed, lips pursed. "Is there even any doubt?"

Obviously there was on my part or I wouldn't be asking.

"So you think Berger's cuter?" I said, wanting to make sure I read her correctly.

"Oh, my God . . . Have you taken a look at his ass?"

I couldn't tell if this was a rhetorical question or what. As far as I'm aware, Audrey doesn't know I'm gay. At least *I* never told her, so I don't think she was implying anything by asking this. As it stands, the only friend I got that even knows about me (the *real* me) is Jack Paterno, and how that came about is a whole 'nother story!

Not that I'm ashamed of who I am or anything, but I don't think it's anybody's business whose ass I choose to check out or who I have a crush on. Besides, even though I've known Audrey for over three years now, I don't *really* know her.

What if I admitted, *Yes, I've taken a look at Rob Berger's ass on* many *occasions,* and she went and told everybody? I only got eight more months left in that godforsaken school of ours . . . Why make trouble now?

Somehow, I don't think Aud would care if she knew. In fact, by asking me this, I wondered if maybe she was giving me the opportunity to finally come clean . . . Still, I couldn't do it.

So I said, "I'd probably think Berger is cuter than Big Al . . . If I was a *girl*."

Audrey asked, "If you were a *girl?*" as if she didn't need me to clarify.

Damn!

There she sat, practically giving me the go-ahead, and I blew it. I don't know what my problem was. I guess being true *to thine ownself* is harder than I thought.

"What the fuck's up with Berger not having a girlfriend?" Audrey pondered next.

"Who the hell knows?" I replied, having thought the exact same thing myself for a long time now.

"All the Flaggots have been trying to figure that one out . . . Including Rakoff."

Rakoff is Zack Rakoff, another Senior in our class. I don't know why, but after playing piccolo in Marching Band since Sophomore year, Rakoff went and became the only male member of Flaggots—I mean, *Flag Corps.* He's a bit of an odd bird the way he's always talking about *Monty Python* and *Doctor Who.*

I'll never forget the first time I seen him . . . Like I said, I went to elementary school at Webster with Ava Reese. Well, Rakoff went to Roosevelt, same as Carrie Johnson. The spring of 6th grade, a bunch of us got invited to participate in this all-city Honors Band. We met twice a week after school for X number of weeks, the end result being a concert we put on for our parents up at Hillbilly High.

Well, when you spend seven years going to school with the exact same people, being around a group of new kids is totally bic-citing, you know what I mean? So the night of the concert, I seen this girl I saw for the past X number of weeks sitting in the flute section. A little chubby, but not fat by any means, she had short brown hair, and wore glasses—the kind with the lenses that darkened whenever you went outside. She also wore braces, but she was still pretty cute.

I don't know why, but I remember thinking how much I *really* wanted to talk to her. Maybe because when I originally signed up for Band, I also wanted to play flute. Until our teacher, Mrs. Isaacs (Will Isaacs's mom), convinced me I should maybe try trombone because there weren't any brass players yet.

Finally, I worked up the nerve to go over and introduce myself. She was standing by the punch bowl at this long table full of cookies and cold cuts and three different kinds of Jello (with and without fruit) in the commons outside the auditorium. Looking back, it doesn't even seem like the same place I spend every day during 5th hour. It feels sooo different now. Much smaller.

"Hi, I'm Brad Dayton . . . What's your name?"

I remember thinking how cool it was that this particular little girl's mother didn't make her wear a dress to the concert like all the others. Instead, she had on dark slacks and a sweater along with matching suede GASS shoes . . . I'm sure you can see where the rest of the story is going.

Anyways!

Coming up with what I thought was a totally brilliant idea, I said to Audrey, "I know one way we can find out for sure," regarding the question of Rob Berger's hetero or homosexuality. "Somebody should ask him to the Homecoming Dance."

I looked at her, eyebrows raised for added emphasis.

"You can't ask another guy to Homecoming!" Audrey declared, totally missing the mark.

"Not me, you stupid Polack!" I yowled, trying not to laugh in her face.

"Watch it, you Band Fag!" she shot back, daggers in her eyes.

"Flaggot!"

"Drama Queer!"

It may appear me and Audrey don't respect each other, the way we're constantly hurling the insults. It's totally not the case. Sure, when we first met at Webb, we used to argue all the time. Back then, we seriously meant every nasty word we said. Yet on that early October afternoon, sitting there in her house just the two of us, I realized we're practically becoming Best Friends.

That must explain the idiotic thing I did next.

"I meant *you* should ask Rob Berger to the Homecoming Dance."

Audrey replied, "He doesn't already got a date?" Again, like she didn't believe me.

"I asked him the other day after rehearsal . . . He said no."

She looked at me like I was certifiably insane. "Rob Berger is a Varsity football player . . . He's not gonna go to Homecoming with some lard-ass Flaggot–Drama Queer."

Part of me was being selfish for putting Audrey up to the task, but I *really* wanted to find out which side Rob likes to "butter his bread on," as Grandma Victor always says. And *I* sure as hell wasn't gonna ask him to Homecoming. If it turned out Rob isn't gay, he'd totally kick my ass!

"First of all," I started to explain, "Rob Berger is a Drama Queer himself . . . Secondly, you are not a lard-ass. You're *curvaceous*, like Marilyn Monroe." One of my favorite actresses, by the way, along with Lana Turner, whose 14-year-old daughter once went on trial for killing Lana's mobster ex-boyfriend . . . Talk about scan-ju-lous!

"I'm 5'7" and I've got child-bearing hips," Aud informed me, hands upon them for added emphasis.

"So what?" I quipped. "Some men like a woman with meat on her bones."

Sure, maybe Audrey wasn't cheerleader or even Vikette material, but she's got a pretty face and beautiful auburn hair flowing down to her waist. And she's got an awesome personality. That should count for something, you know what I mean?

"I can't ask a guy to a dance," she retorted, giving up the ship. "I'll look desperate."

"Well, aren't you?" I only half joked. "Pretend it's Sadie Hawkins."

Speaking of . . .

If we don't end up doing *Grease* in the spring, I hope Dell honors our second request, *Li'l Abner*. My role of choice would be Abner, of course, but I'm sure Rob Berger (and his bod) would look much better in a pair of overalls. I'll settle for Maryin' Sam.

"I'll think about it," Audrey concluded.

"No . . . You'll *do* it."

She trailed after me as I headed into her kitchen. "Get back here, Dayton!"

I picked up the black rotary dial phone from where it hung on the wall since 1960-something. Handing it to Audrey, I dialed Rob Berger's number, which I totally had memorized: 544-3616.

She bobbed and weaved, trying to dodge me like a Detroit Piston. "Get the fuck outta here!" Aud howled, having a giggle fit.

I could tell she totally wanted to ask Rob to be her Homecoming date. She just needed a little encouragement.

Thru the end of the phone, I could hear the hollow ring . . . Once, twice, thrice.

Who the hell ever says thrice?

"Hello?"

From across town in Ferndale, Rob picked up. His family lives on Edgeworth, over by Edison Elementary where he went with Shellee "What's up, Fox?" Findlay.

"Talk to him," I hissed, hoping Rob wouldn't hear me. The last thing I wanted was for him to think I was in on anything, even though I totally was.

"Hello?" Rob said a second time, sounding mildly annoyed. "Anybody there?"

Audrey thrust the phone in my direction.

I ducked.

It hit the papered wall.

"Now look what you've done!" I scolded. By the time I retrieved the receiver from where it plopped in Patches's litter box, Rob already hung up. "Call him back . . . Now!"

"*You* call him back!"

I hesitated for maybe a second, then redialed: 544-3616.

Rob picked up after half a ring. "Who is this?" he demanded, skipping the customary salutation.

"Hey, Rob . . . It's Brad Dayton."

I tried my best to sound nonchalant.

"Hey, Bradley . . . What's up?"

I love it when he calls me Bradley!

"Nothing much," I lied, feeling totally deceitful. "I'm over Audrey's helping her and Tuesday with their scene for Drama . . ."

I started babbling about how Tuesday had a fit and went home, so me and Aud were just hanging out, wondering what he was up to.

"Just got home from football practice."

And are you all hot and sweaty and in need of a sponge bath?

Then Rob surprised me by saying, "Did you just call here a minute ago and hang up?"

"Wasn't me," I lied again, shooting Miss Wojczek my best look of spite.

I didn't know what to say next.

Hey, Rob . . . You should totally go to Homecoming with Audrey. Unless you're a Big Fag. Then you could just skip the dance altogether and fool around with me instead.

At that moment, Rob said, "I'm glad you called."

"Oh, yeah?" I asked, feeling a little light-headed knowing he was happy hearing from me.

"Is Audrey there with you?"

I looked over at my accomplice. "She's standing right here."

"Can I talk to her for a sec?" Rob asked, catching me off guard.

I relinquished the phone.

Audrey said, "Hello?" She paused a moment, nodded and smiled. "Um . . . Okay." Finally, she hung up, reporting, "He's definitely not a fag."

I had a feeling I wasn't gonna like her response, but I needed an answer. "How do you know?"

Audrey's face lit up like the Fisher building. "Rob Berger just asked me to Homecoming."

What the fuck?

To quote Crystal Bernard from *High School USA* with Michael J. Fox and Nancy McKeon talking about her boyfriend, Beau Middleton: "I would eat maggots for him."

That's how totally in love with Rob Berger I am.

Just because Audrey's a *girl,* she gets to go to the dance with him, and do God-only-knows-what-else in the backseat of his Pinto afterwards?

No fucking fair!

All I can say is . . . I am *not* teaching her how to give a blowjob.

The Final Countdown

"I guess there is no one to blame
We're leaving ground . . ."

—Europe

Time for the big announcement!

12:00 PM. 4th hour. The auditorium.

On stage right, sit the "Top 25" girls. On stage left, the "Top 25" guys. Standing at the podium in the center, Mr. Verlander, wearing what I think is the exact same permanent-press shirt and throwback-to-the-'70s wide tie he wore to the all-school assembly last week.

He promises, "We're gonna make this short and sweet," addressing the members of the Hillbilly High student body who actually cared enough to come back from lunch for the ceremony.

I look out from where I sit in alphabetical order between boys' Varsity basketball co-captain Kenny Daw and Varsity cheerleader Raquel Easterle. But nowhere in the crowd do I see my so-called Best Friends, Jack Paterno and Max Wilson. I hope this doesn't take too long. This gray aluminum folding chair is killing my ass.

"Quiet down, please . . . Boys and girls."

Okay, Verlander . . . I realize you're almost as old as Methuselah, but come on! Just because we're still in high school doesn't mean we're babies. Most of us have already had *sex*, you know what I mean? Not that I'm gonna go graphic with all the gory details or anything.

"As you know," Verlander continues, "we're here to announce the winners of the 'Top 5' Homecoming . . ."

I think he means, "Homecoming 'Top 5.'"

Finally, in the fifth row center off the aisle, I spy Jack sitting with Max. No matter how disappointed he may be, I knew he'd be here for what could potentially be the biggest day of my life. Not that I'm expecting to make "Top 5" or anything.

Mr. Verlander taps his front shirt pocket. We can all see a plain white envelope tucked safely inside. "The names I'm about to read," he tells us, "represent ten of the best students we've ever had here at Hazel Park High School . . ."

Spare me! He says that every year.

"Among them are cheerleaders . . ."

Like Jamieleeann Mary Sue Good and Shellee Findlay.

". . . football players . . ."

Like Tom Fulton and Rob Berger, maybe?

". . . members of Vikettes . . ."

Marie Sperling or Angela Andrews?

". . . members of girls' Varsity basketball . . ."

I'm thinking, *Fay Keating.*

". . . and boys' Varsity basketball . . ."

Gotta be Kenny Daw! He's the cutest basketball player HPHS has got.

"As in years past," Mr. Verlander drones on, "we're proud to have a member of the Viking Marching Band among our Homecoming Court for 1987."

Two years ago, the Hillbilly High-ons elected Freddy Edwards, a totally hot sax playing Band Fag who happened to also be captain of Varsity wrestling, as Homecoming King. Freddy served as our Band Aide back in 7th grade Varsity Band at Webb, and all the girls thought he was a Total Babe . . . Okay, so did I.

You can bet when I hear this, I look up from the spot I been staring at for what seems like forever. Still, there's no way in hell Mr. Verlander can be talking about me.

He's gotta mean Don Olsewski . . . *Doesn't he?*

"Without further ado . . ."

The auditorium falls pin-drop quiet as Mr. Verlander pulls out the number ten envelope. Breaking the seal with a slide of a finger, he looks over his shoulder. The twenty-five "Top 25" girls sit perched, each one dressed in her Sunday best, hair freshly permed with crown-bangs sprayed to full height.

"Beginning with the ladies," Verlander says, addressing them en masse. "When I call your name, please stand." Turning back to the peons in the pit, he advises, "Let's hold our applause till the end, shall we?"

Fingers crossed at my side, I say a silent prayer for my good friend, Stacy Gillespie. She's just gotta make "Top 5." She's like the cutest and nicest girl in all of HPHS.

"In no particular order," Mr. Verlander stresses, "first up we have . . . Rochelle Findlay."

I told you she's Most Popular Girl!

Shellee stands, giving her "What's up, Fox?" wave. Despite strictly being told *not* to succumb, a spatter of applause spouts from her adoring fans. Mr. Verlander ignores the ruckus and returns to his list.

"Jamieleeann Mary Sue Good."

Senior class president, Varsity cheerleading captain, secretary of National Honor Society, and don't forget she's in Chorale.

"Fay Keating."

The very sporty and very popular girls' Varsity basketball co-captain.

Like I said, I been friends with Fay since she came over to Webb from St. Mary's, so I'm totally psyched for her. Did I mention how awesome she looks since she cut her hair super short and added a few blond highlights?

"Marie Sperling."

Co-captain of Vikettes . . . *Surprise, surprise!*

Don't get me wrong, I love Marie. In fact, she was my first costar when we did that silent movie skit back in Ms. Lemieux's 7th grade Enriched English & Social Studies . . . 'member? Thank God she finally broke up with that jerk Tom Fulton. He did not deserve her!

With only one more slot left to fill, I can't help but worry, who's it gonna be?

Natalie Davis?

Betsy Sheffield?

Please, God, don't let it be her, *let it be . . .*

"Stacy Gillespie."

Woo-hoo!

Stacy stands. She brushes a strand of her brown bob behind an ear, forcing a shy smile as she catches my eye.

"Congratulations," I whisper, hoping Stacy will soon have reason to reciprocate.

Mr. Verlander nods, pleased that he's made these five particular girls' day. "Ladies, please remain standing while I announce the names of the 'Top 5' gentlemen . . ."

Today!

He looks over his other shoulder towards us guys. Since I'm

sitting in the front row, I can't speak for those behind me, but I feel Kenny Daw's leg tense up as it touches mine. I get the feeling he's as fucking nervous as I am.

"Fellas . . . When I call your name, please stand." And to the peons in the pit, Verlander says, "Again, let's try to hold our applause."

Fingers still crossed at my side, I say another silent prayer—this time for *myself.* I may act all devil-may-care, like being on "Top 5" is totally no biggie. To be honest, it's something I been dreaming of since the day I first heard of its existence during Sophomore year.

"Again in no particular order," Mr. Verlander insists, "first up . . . Thomas Fulton."

Varsity football *and* boys' basketball co-captain.

I'm just glad Tom is sitting in the row behind me so I don't have to see the smug look on his face when he stands and takes in the thunderous applause that erupts from the Peanut Gallery. I mean, why can't these people pay attention to anything they're told? "Hold your applause" means "Do *not* clap!" Clearly, Tom Fulton is the Hillbilly High Homecoming King favorite for 1987 . . . I think I'm gonna puke!

"Jonathan Glowicki."

Varsity football *and* boys' basketball player.

"Kenneth Daw."

Despite doing his best to act all cool, I can tell Kenny's totally psyched. So much so, he reaches out and High-Fives me, which comes as a surprise. It's not every day the co-captain of boys' Varsity basketball fraternizes with this Band Fag-turned-Drama Queer.

"Mitchell Bloodworth."

Yet another Varsity football player.

Five seats over, via my peripheral vision, I see a white-blond head nodding up and down on a pair of linebacker's shoulders. Mitch rises and joins the rest of the '87 Homecoming Court.

Shit!

That means there's only one name left.

In his intro, Mr. Verlander clearly stated that one of the names on the list belonged to a member of Marching Band. That means no Rob Berger or Joey Palladino on "Top 5." I'm totally shocked.

Could it be . . .?

What about Don Olsewski? He's in Marching Band . . .

But so am I!

Time slows to a standstill, like in that moment from my favorite movie, *Ice Castles,* with real-life skater Lynn-Holly Johnson, and Robby Benson, from *Ode to Billy Joe.*

After skyrocketing to the top of the circuit, Alexis "Lexie" Winston has become everybody's darling, prompting her to freak out because people wanna *touch* her all the time. At a rooftop party, Lexie goes out for a breath of fresh air. What better way to relax than by skating some laps? As a slew of party guests look on, along with her coach, Deborah Machland, and new boyfriend, the sleazy-but-oh-so-cute newscaster Brian Dockett, Lexie makes her way around the ice.

Up to this point, she's been working on landing the triple, but Coach Deborah keeps telling Lexie she's not good enough—the bitch! Faster and faster, the music builds. Until everything starts moving in slow-mo as Lexie prepares to make the leap . . . One. Two. Three.

Clunk!

The blade of Lexie's skate catches on some stupid chain wrapped around some stupid outdoor patio furniture set up alongside the skating rink. Down she tumbles, smacking her head—hard! Thus causing Alexis Winston's whole world to come crashing to a halt.

I won't ruin the rest of the plot. All I *will* say is . . . It's totally tragic.

"And last, but certainly not least," Mr. Verlander concludes, "the final name on the 1987 'Top 5' Homecoming is . . ."

Please, God, don't let it be Don Olsewski, let it be . . .

"Bradley Dayton."

Oh, my God . . . He fucking called my name . . . Again!

Like a dork I stand up, trying not to look too enthused, yet wanting to convey how honored I am to be recognized. Only this time, I keep my hands at my side. No more waving like fucking Queen Elizabeth!

Unfortunately, I can't tell you what happens after this.

Next thing I'm aware of is the blinding flash of a flashbulb flashing in my face. I'm standing beside Shellee Findlay. All the "Top 5" girls have been paired up with a "Top 5" boy and we're having our pictures taken.

"S-H-E-L-L-*E-E.*"

Miss Findlay reminds the photographer this as he writes down her name with pad and pencil.

"And yours?" I hear a voice say. "Would you prefer Brad or Bradley?"

I blink a few times, hoping to dissipate the fog from inside my head.

"Whatever," I reply, not even sure if I heard the question.

For the first time, I notice who the guy with the camera standing in front of me is.

None other than the Editor-in-Chief of *The Hazel Parker*, and my Best Friend since 7th grade: Jack Paterno.

He looks at me, says nothing. Then he walks away.

Somehow, I just knew *Jack would be be pissed!*

Three days later, I write the following . . .

October 9, 1987

Jack,

I'm sitting in Adv. Gram/Term Paper totally bored out of my mind. You should see the tarp Mrs. Mayer's wearing this morning! Right now she's up there giving one of her "Sugar High" lectures, threatening to ban all candy sales, even though we keep telling her we gotta raise money for Marching Band's trip to Disney World over Spring Break. (Wish you were coming with!)

I'm writing to ask if you changed your mind about coming to the Homecoming Dance tomorrow. I know it totally sucks what happened, but everybody would like to see you there (me, Audrey, Ava, Carrie, etc.) As we always say, "It will be fun!"

It's our *SENIOR* year, Jack. I'd hate for you to miss out on this night. Promise me you'll think about it, *please?*

Your Best Friend forever,

Brad

PS—Write back and let me know what you decide.

Either Jack never got the letter or he intentionally ignored my request. Thirty-three hours later, I still haven't heard from him.

On my way up to the high school, I stop by his house. Maybe I can talk some sense into him in person. At least I hope I can.

Standing outside the door to Jack's bedroom, I dread what's about to happen next. How many times in the past have I knocked, thrown back the accordion-fold, and found my Best Friend happily waiting inside? I don't know why, but I feel this won't be the case.

"Like sands thru the hourglass . . ."

On the other side, I hear the voice of Macdonald Carey reciting his *Days of our Lives* spiel. Rather than giving Jack the opportunity to ask who it is and tell me to get the fuck out, I open the door. The familiar scent of the room hits me full force, making me a tad melancholy.

Jack sits up on his bed, looks over his shoulder. He says nothing once he realizes it's me.

We exchange some casual pleasantries . . .

"Hey, Jack . . . I was in the neighborhood so I thought I'd stop by."

"Nice suit."

"I borrowed it from my sister Janelle's fiancé, Ted . . ."

I'm not complaining, it's a nice navy blue suit with pinstripes, but I'm swimming in it. Lord knows I can't afford to buy my own, just to wear to some stupid dance. Especially since I didn't get crowned Homecoming King at the football game last night.

That honor went to my favorite person: Tom Fulton.

Surprise, surprise!

Wanna know who his Queen was?

None other than my Chorale partner: Jamieleeann Mary Sue Good.

Add another credit to her resumé!

Standing in Jack's room feels foreign to me, even though I spent sooo much time here the past five years. I notice he moved his bed from where it used to rest against the side wall to over beneath the window. The same one we once climbed out on the night Jack went with me and Luanne down to Heaven.

For a second, I consider asking him why he never wrote me back, but I decide to be the bigger man. "I was wondering if you might wanna meet me after the dance . . . I thought maybe we could go down to the bar together or something."

Jack asks if I think Shellee Findlay's gonna get pissed at me for skipping out early. I remind him she's my "Top 5" partner, *not* my date. Besides, Shellee's got a boyfriend, Kyle Henke. He graduated in '87, drives a Corvette, and thinks he's LL Cool J, even though he's Caucasian.

"I don't think I'm up for the bar tonight," Jack declines.

"Okay . . . Maybe we can go out next weekend instead?"

Again he refuses. "I shouldn't be spending a lot of money."

We stand in silence a moment.

"You're not still pissed about the whole 'Top 25' thing, are you?" I ask, taking a seat on his bed. "Why are you letting it bother you so much, Jack?"

He gives me a look, like I just asked the dumbest question ever.

"All I ever wanted since we got to high school was to be on 'Top 25,'" he informs me, even though I already knew this. "God knows I deserve it a lot more than those other guys . . . But because they're all popular, people vote for them."

"Would you stop whining for a minute and listen to yourself?" I ask, interrupting his rant. "You know 'Top 25' doesn't mean anything . . . Nobody cares if you're on the list or not."

"Easy for you to say," he spits. "You're the one wearing the sash."

In the five years me and Jack been Best Friends, I think this is the meanest thing he's ever said to me. What did I do to deserve this treatment?

"You know I had nothing to do with the votes, Jack," I calmly remind him. "I just about shit my pants when they called my name for 'Top 5'!"

Jack rolls his eyes. "You weren't the only one."

Okay, I tried.

I get up and head towards the door. As I reach out for the

handle, I decide to make one final attempt at patching things up. "I thought you'd be happy for me," I say, turning back. "But you don't even think I deserve to be on 'Top 5,' do you?"

Jack responds with something about the movie *Carrie*. Does he really think I'm gonna get pig's blood dumped on me at the dance? No wonder he took up writing . . . Jack Paterno has got the most overactive imagination of anybody I know!

"Just because people don't like *you*, Jack," I snarl, "doesn't mean they don't like me . . . We're not the same person."

His jaw drops. "You think those Jock Jerks at school really like you? Wake up . . . The only reason they're even nice to you at all is because your sister Janelle is totally hot and they all wanna fuck her!"

Like the woman in the "Bob and the Kids are Dead" joke, I've had *enough*.

"Fuck you!" I shout, temper rising. "It's one thing to insult me—I'm your Best Friend, I'll forgive you . . . But do not talk that way about my sister, okay?"

I barely comprehend what Jack says next, I'm so pissed. Something about the reason he won't ever go to parties is because Tom Fulton and all the other Jock Jerks hate him.

Defeated, I throw my arms up. "What reason could anybody have not to like you?"

"That's what I wanna know!" Jack explodes. "What have I ever done to deserve being treated like this? It's not like *I'm* the one going out to gay bars all the time."

Now we're getting somewhere!

So that's what this is *really* about? The fact that I'm a Big Fag so I can't possibly deserve to have any friends or even be considered for Homecoming King?

"Your being the way you are has nothing to do with this," Jack answers, after I confront him.

"Yes, it does!" I snap. "You're jealous because people like me, even though I'm gay."

At this point, Jack starts rambling on about me wanting to be a famous actor someday and aren't I afraid people will find out I'm gay? Not to mention what happened with Rock Hudson dying from AIDS, which is the dumbest thing I ever heard! Until Jack mentions something about spending the last five years of his life busting his ass to convince people he's (quote-unquote) normal.

I repeat, "Normal?" This is the biggest insult yet. "You think I'm not normal?"

"That's not what I meant . . . But it's your choice."

Strike three!

"Being gay is not a 'choice' you can make." For a straight-A student, I'm surprised by Jack's ignorance sometimes. "You either are or you aren't."

I realize he's been going thru a rough patch ever since the whole Joey Palladino/letter from his mom incident. But that happened like a year and a half ago . . . Get over it!

Remembering what Mr. Dell'Olio told us in Drama the other day about trying new tactics to get what we want, I attempt a new approach.

"I'm not saying this to be mean," I say softly. "But I'm your Best Friend, Jack, and I really think you are."

G-A-Y.

He looks away from me, chewing on the inside of his cheek. What I wanna do is reach out and give him a hug, even though I know Jack won't go for that. Not since what happened between us back in 11th grade happened, but that's a whole 'nother story!

"I know you better than anybody else," I remind him, "but until you can admit the truth about who you really are—not just to me but to *yourself*—I don't think we can be Best Friends anymore."

And with that, I fling open the accordion-fold and walk out the door.

Forever . . . ?

Dress You Up

"All over, all over
From your head down to your toes . . ."

—Madonna

I *love* dressing up.

As far back as I can remember, it's always been a thing with me.

Not just like in costume, but like playing Dress Up.

Being the only boy in a family of four kids, you never got much of a choice in the games you played growing up. At Dayton's Depot, there weren't a whole lot of toys back in the '70s. Or in the '80s, for that matter. Like I said, Dad worked for peanuts as a Troy cop, and Mom didn't earn squat as a stay-at-home housewife. I guess when you got four mouths to feed in less than six years, food becomes more important than Fisher-Price.

Hence the Tickle Trunk.

Mom totally stole the idea from *Mr. Dressup*. When we were little, me and my sisters watched the show every morning at 10:30 AM on channel 9 from across the Detroit River in Windsor,

Ontario. *Mr. Dressup* is sorta like *Sesame Street*, except it's just this one guy named (what else?) Mr. Dressup. He's probably in his 50s, and he's got a couple puppet friends—a boy named Casey, and a dog, Finnegan.

Mom used to say I looked like Casey because he's got red hair, too. If you ask me, the kid always creeped me out since he's just this plastic head with a mouth that doesn't move attached to a cloth body. For the longest time, I thought Casey was a *girl.* He sure as hell sounded like one. And poor Finnegan is a fucking mute, so that was even freakier!

But Mr. Dressup is an awesome guy. He's always telling stories and cracking corny jokes, and singing songs like "Down by the Bay," and "Wheels of the Bus."

This is where the Tickle Trunk comes in . . .

Every once in a while, Mr. Dressup would break out this huge red-orange trunk decorated with these '60s-style decal flowers. From inside, he'd pull out these costumes (a bear, a snowman, maybe a dragon), and he'd *dress up* in them, putting on a show for Casey and Finnegan and all the little girls and boys out in TV Land, like me and my sisters.

Maybe I got my desire to perform from watching *Mr. Dressup*, now that I think about it.

Maybe he's the reason my life has taken this turn down Drama Queer Lane.

Maybe Mr. Dressup is the reason I started dressing up in my mom's clothes whenever I got the chance.

That didn't come out right, did it?

What I'm taking about is the Tickle Trunk—I mean, o*ur* Tickle Trunk. The one my mom made for me, Janelle, Nina, and Brittany.

Janelle I already mentioned a few times. She's nineteen and she's got a boyfriend—I mean, *fiancé*—Ted Baniszewski. He's twenty-one, drives a Camaro, and works up at Country Boy's on 9 Mile. In fact, Ted got me my first job working there as a busboy back in 9th grade, even though I hated it. He's a good guy, that Ted. In fact, he looks a little like Robby Benson from *Ice Castles.* Him and Janelle started shacking up after she graduated from HPHS in '86, much to our Southern Baptist church-going mother's dismay. Did I mention Janelle's got big boobs and she's totally hot?

Number two sister is Nina. She's not a redhead like the rest of us, lucky her! She gets her coloring more from Mom's side of the family. Nina's fourteen and a 9th grader at Jardon, the Special Ed school in Hazel Park next to Webb. I guess technically they're both in Ferndale, but that's a whole 'nother story!

Yes, it's true, we do go to Hazel Park Schools, but we do not (repeat, do *not*) live in Hazeltucky. Like I said, the Daytons live in Ferndale, which is almost just as bad, but not quite. At least it's not Detroit, you know what I mean? Still, it's close enough since Dayton's Depot is only four blocks north of 8 Mile on the corner of Wanda and Webster. Back in the day, it used to be a store. Not like a Party Store-store, more like a small grocery store.

I'll never forget the first time Dad took us to see it back in the late '70s after our house in Center Line burnt down. I remember thinking it was sooo glamorous because the huge, sunken-in family room, which used to be the main part of the store, has super-high ceilings with these great old chandeliers. And three bedrooms—two downstairs, one up. Thank God I got my own. Being the only boy outta four kids doesn't always suck.

God bless her heart, Nina was born premature with a slight trace of cerebral palsy. She's been in and out of the hospital for years, and had a ton of operations to replace the shunt in her head from having water on the brain. I love her to death! Sure, she's a tad slow, which makes things hard for her, and for Mom.

This is why *Mr. Dressup* was such a great show for us all to watch together.

Number three sister, Brittany, is in 8th grade at Webb, so that makes her thirteen. Talk about cute! “As a bug’s ear,” like Grandma Victor always says. Maybe I’m prejudiced because she’s my baby sister, but Brittany Dayton is bound to be a real heart-breaker someday. How can she not? She totally looks like our mom, except she’s got our dad’s red hair and freckles, same as me and Janelle.

Back to the Tickle Trunk . . .

Mom knew how much us kids enjoyed watching Mr. Dressup get dressed up in the costumes he pulled out from his Tickle Trunk. So one day, she goes up to the Goodwill or the Salvation Army or some other secondhand store in Royal Oak somewhere. This is like 1979–80, and remember, the Daytons are dirt poor. We can’t even afford to shop at SS Kresge’s, let alone Kmart’s.

And what does Laura Victor-Dayton find at the thrift store?

This huge trunk that not only does she buy, she also paints red-orange and decorates with these ’60s-style decal flowers she got from God-only-knows-where.

Somehow, a good portion of Mom’s own wardrobe wound its way into the Tickle Trunk where me, Janelle, and Nina, and Brittany (once she got older), would fight to the finish over the finest. Of notable mention: the white cotton Country Girl peasant dress accented with embroidery, the groovy orange and blue horizontal-striped mini-dress with mini-belt, and the beige two-piece polyester pantsuit. Of course, none of these fit any of us in the least. This is why I always preferred the mini-skirts since they came all the way down to the ground on me.

And don’t forget the shoes.

My favorites included: a pair of avocado open-toed sling-back pumps with matching leather bows on the front, and these rust-colored cloglike platforms with a cork sole that had to be at least three inches thick. On more than one occasion, I almost killed myself making my way down the steps into our sunken-in family room wearing them!

Or how can I forget the bright red faux-leather knee-high Wonder Woman boots? All shiny with thick wedge heels and full-length zippers running up the inseams. Me and Janelle used to take turns pretending we were Princess Diana sporting those things . . . And each and every item magically appeared from inside the Dayton family Tickle Trunk courtesy of Laura Victor-Dayton herself.

Thanks, Mom!

So tonight I'm going to a Halloween party.

Not a party-party, like the ones Jack used to have in his parents' basement where we'd always end up playing Spin-the-Bottle and Truth-or-Dare. In fact, this isn't even a real party.

Me and my friends are getting dressed up and going to see *The Rocky Horror Picture Show.*

Wanna know who I'm going as?

Columbia.

The tap-dancing groupie-friend of Dr. Frank-N-Furter, and alleged lover of Meat Loaf—I mean, *Eddie*—originally played by Little Nell.

Imagine how difficult it is finding a gold sequined tailcoat with black sequined, unnotched lapels, and matching top hat with black scrunched hatband. Thank God there's this costume shop, Lynch's House of Sequins, up on Dequindre and 11 Mile. You can bet the nondescript middle-aged woman working behind the cash register thought I was a Total Freak asking if she could sell me a black sequined bustier with flat sequins (not cup) in a *man's* size 38 . . . Luckily, I don't have to wear a wig since Columbia's got the same haircut as me—short in back, longer on top, and red.

One day about a year ago, Jack called me up and was all like,

"Oh, my God . . . We must see this movie!" He started rambling on and on about how his 28-year-old coworker (Corrine? Collette, maybe?) told him all about this totally great musical from the '70s. "Everybody in the audience gets up during the middle of it and acts it out."

Well, when I heard that, I knew I had to see it. I wanna be an actor, don't I? I should experience these things. Too bad Jack could never get his friend (Colleen!) to take us. We had to wait till we were seventeen and could purchase the tickets ourselves. So I decided to celebrate my birthday on September 4th of last month by going to see *Rocky Horror* out at Lakeside Mall.

So far I seen the *Picture Show* seven times—once a week for the past two months, except on the night of the Homecoming Dance. That's the problem. They only show it on Saturdays at midnight, which is part of the reason Jack only went with us the one time for my birthday. He always works till 11:00 PM on weekends, so he's too tired to do anything. (Persnickety!)

"Be careful driving."

Mom kisses my cheek, after Nina snaps a Polaroid of me and her and Brittany with the camera we bought Mom for last Mother's Day.

"I will," I promise, checking my lipstick one final time in the side of the toaster.

Brittany cries, "I wanna see!" when Nina starts shaking the photo into focus.

"No fighting," Mom warns. "Or it's off to bed."

Good luck! These girls are pumping so much glucose thru their veins from all the Mary Janes and SweeTarts and candy corn they scored tonight, they ain't never gonna sleep.

The four of us gather in a small circle, awaiting the finished product.

"Don't you look pretty?" Mom beams once our image has materialized. She's not even the least bit embarrassed to be observing her 17-year-old son looking like a transvestite from transsexual Transylvania.

Personally, I think I look good as a girl. Sizing myself up in the white plastic square, I'm amazed at what a little lipstick and mascara can do to transform a boy. Not that I'm one of them gay guys who wants to be a *woman* or anything. I'm perfectly content with what I got between my legs.

"You look pretty too," Nina tells Mom, who blushes.

"I look *old*," she groans, even though it's not at all true.

At forty-one, Mom is as gorgeous as ever. Sure, she's gained some weight since my favorite picture of her with the cat's eye glasses and bouffant hairdo was shot back in 1964 when she graduated from the other HPHS—Highland Park High School. That's what happens when a woman has four kids before she turns thirty!

"No drinking," Mom warns. "You hear?"

Feeling the flask of fuzzy navel strapped to my freshly shaved thigh, I secretly cross my fingers. "Never." Boy, do I hate lying to my mother!

It's been a while since I walked in three-inch heels and I forgot the degree of difficulty. As I stumble down the back porch steps, I almost crash into the cream-colored '68 Valiant parked in our driveway. Leave it to my dad to give me a car that's two years *older* than I am. I can't complain, I'm just happy I finally got my driver's license. Surprisingly, it only took me three tries to pass my road test.

Climbing inside, I take care not to snag my stockings in the process. Leave it to my dad to give me a car with a busted dome light. With my key, I feel around for the dashboard ignition. After finding the hole, I fire up a glamorous Virginia Slim Light 120 that I bought special for tonight's festivities, and away I drive.

First thing I do once I buy my movie ticket is hit the concession stand . . . Well, the second thing, after I look around the empty mall for the rest of the Drama Queers I'm supposed to meet here by 11:45 PM.

My heart races for the finish line as I step up to the register. Why am I so nervous about buying a stupid pop? Because I got a bit of a crush on the dark-haired Chaldean guy with the bulging biceps working behind the counter, that's why! His name tag says: JERRY, even though I'm pretty sure that's not his *real* name. I think it's Ahmed.

Wanna hear the funniest thing?

Jerry looks up from behind the cash register where he stands in his cute little uniform: dark polyester vest over white dress shirt with matching bow tie. I can't see the pants, but I imagine they're super tight and his ass looks totally hot.

He says to me, "May I help you, *miss*?"

I'm about to reply, *Thanks, Jerry . . . But I'm a* guy. Until a glimpse of my reflection in the mirrored glass behind Jerry's head reminds me that I'm totally unrecognizable. In fact, from the way he's drooling over the 36Ds I "developed" by stuffing one of Janelle's bras with plastic L'eggs eggs, I get the distinct impression Jerry thinks I'm a *real* woman. So I decide to have a little fun with Mr. Concession Stand Man.

"I'd like a small Coca-Cola . . . Pretty please."

I don't know where the voice coming from my body comes from, but all of a sudden, I'm Scarlett O'Hara from my favorite movie of all time, *Gone With the Wind.*

"Anything else for you, miss?" Jerry asks politely, putting his English into practice.

I notice the tiny gold Camel imprinted on the cigarette tucked behind his right ear, which a lot of people in Hazeltucky might find *à propos* since the assholes are constantly referring to the Arabs as (quote-unquote) Camel Jockeys . . . Isn't that bogue?

"Why yes," I reply, still the Southern Belle. "Popcorn, please . . . With loads of butter."

Jerry smiles slyly. "What size you like?"

Licking my lips, I respond, "Whatever's the *biggest*."

As he's counting back my change, Jerry suavely brushes my hand with his, holding it a moment. His brown eyes meet my blues, and immediately all the blood in my entire body heads south for the winter. Luckily, my dick is smashed down and tucked between my legs or else I'd look pretty funny standing here with a hard-on popping out from my panties.

For a split second, I consider proposing that we step into the back storage room where I'll show Jerry a thing or two . . . If only he wasn't working and my friends weren't on their way!

"You are very beautiful girl," this guy who's gotta be at least twenty-five tells me. "How old?"

"Twenty-one," I lie, again just to see if I can get away with it.

"I would like to buy you drink sometime," Jerry offers. "Would you like?"

Fuck yeah! I nod and smile, not sure how exactly to answer his question.

"What is your name, please?" my Middle Eastern lover wonders, still holding my smooth hand in his hairy one.

"Brad!"

Quickly, I tear myself away and scurry over to where my friends have just made their entrance from the lamppost-lighted parking lot . . . Talk about good timing—not!

"You better wise up . . ."

This I sing to Liza Larson as the ever wholesome Janet Weiss. I love her pink dress with Peter Pan collar and white cardigan. What a drastic change from her usual all-black wardrobe.

"Hey, Asshole!" I shout at Zack Rakoff as Brad Majors.

He's not quite as tall as Barry Bostwick, but he's got the costume down: tan jacket worn over a blue V-neck sweater vest with blue and white striped shirt beneath and light gray pants with permanent-press crease. Don't forget the tortoiseshell glasses, which are actually the ones he wears every day.

I almost don't recognize Tuesday Gunderson in drag as Riff Raff. The bald cap and stringy blond wig covering her own stringy brown hair throws me. Even Audrey surprises me sporting an authentic-looking maid's uniform.

"Don't tell Dell," she says after I ask her where she got it. "I found it backstage from when we did *The Skeleton Walks.*"

"You're lucky," I reply, knowing she was having a hard time finding a costume.

Doing her best Magenta impersonation, Aud cries on cue, "'You're lucky, he's lucky, I'm lucky, we're *all* lucky!'"

"'The banister's lucky!'" the rest of us shout, quoting the official *Rocky Horror* response.

Again, I'm glad my dick is smashed down and tucked between my legs or else I'd totally pop a boner when I see Rob Berger, as Rocky, take off his raincoat to reveal nothing but a pair of gold briefs. By the way, I don't think they're padded.

Behind my back, I hear somebody say, "You're with me, baby."

I turn to see Will Isaacs dressed in a black Elvis wig, black leather sleeveless jacket, and dark blue Levi's, carrying somebody's saxophone. He makes a pretty convincing Meat Loaf—I mean, *Eddie.* For the first time, being fat *isn't* his downfall!

All we need now is a Frank-N-Furter and we'd be all set . . . Too bad Jack's not here.

I think the reason he won't come see *Rocky Horror* again is because the guy who plays Frank reminds him of his dad, and it totally freaks Jack out to see him wearing a dress and corset. Not to mention watching him do the things he does with Rocky.

It could also have something to do with the fact that ever

since Jack decided he doesn't *want* to be gay, he also doesn't wanna be my friend anymore. It'll be two weeks tomorrow since we had our pre–Homecoming Dance argument. I probably shouldn't have told him I think he's a fag, even though I totally do. Luckily, now that Jack dropped outta Band and we don't have any classes together anymore, it's not that difficult to avoid each other.

I suppose I should explain *why* I think Jack's a fag.

Again, I probably shouldn't say anything. Again, it's none of my business. But like I said, Jack *is* my Best Friend. The fact that I haven't talked to him once in almost fourteen days is starting to piss me off, you know what I mean?

The reason I think Jack is gay is because I know for a *fact* that he is, based upon personal past experience.

To make a long story short . . .

Back in 11th grade during Winter Break, Ava Reese had some people over her house. All the Usual Suspects showed up: me, Max, Jack, Carrie, Audrey. I don't know how, but Max got a case of beer, and we sat around Ava's kitchen table playing this stupid drinking game, Thumper. I totally sucked at it.

Suddenly, the doorbell rang, and who showed up to crash?

None other than . . . Joey Palladino.

With Diane Thompson off in Florida with her folks, I guess he felt like slumming. Eventually, we moved the party into Ava's front room. Or the *French* room, as Max Wilson calls it. We were all sitting around drunk, with Jack and Joey practically on top of each other. Pretty soon, one of the girls suggested we play Truth-or-Dare. Next thing we knew, everybody's French kissing Joey Palladino . . . Including Jack!

That same night, Jack stayed over my house since it's only like ten blocks away from Ava's on College. Being that he's a Total Persnickety-Persnick, he doesn't drink and drive, so we *walked* all the way home.

Wouldn't you know? Dayton's Depot was an icebox.

"What the fuck?" I remember Jack saying, upon entering my moonlit abode. In the quiet of our kitchen, I could hardly hear the hum of the refrigerator over his chattering Chiclets.

"Thank the deadbeat!"

It was totally Dad's fault Mom couldn't afford to pay the heating bill that month. He was late with the child support (again), and we hadn't seen him since his annual Christmas visit six weeks prior. Grinning and bearing it, I stripped down to my BVDs.

So there we were, sitting around my room talking when Jack started freaking out . . . What was everybody gonna say about him kissing Joey Palladino come Monday in school? Now people were *really* gonna think he's a Total Fag.

Da-dah da-dah.

You can bet I took this as an opportunity to press the issue and find out whether or not Jack might still have feelings for his former friend. Especially now that they swapped some serious spit. And when Jack admitted he was even more confused because he *did* sorta like kissing Joey, it didn't surprise me at all.

Now I don't know if it's because we were both drunk or what, but next thing I knew, Jack asked me what it feels like to fool around with another guy. I didn't know how to describe it other than you just gotta do it to find out.

Fast forward fifteen minutes . . .

There's me, wiping myself off with an old T-shirt before stepping back into my underwear. I mean, it wouldn't have been so bad if it only happened the *one* time. Unfortunately, this sorta thing became a regular recurrence for the next several weeks.

The big problem became that whenever me and Jack fooled around, he never seemed to enjoy himself. Sure, he totally got into it while he was down there doing his thing, but not once did he ever get off in the end. And never once did he ask me to reciprocate, which seemed sorta odd, you know what I mean?

I mean, this was fine by me. Like I said, I never felt anything more for Jack than the love of a brother. The last thing I wanted to do was give him the impression I was into him or anything. Still, I couldn't help but feel guilty watching Jack put his clothes on and head home in the cold, like somehow I sucked as a human being because (to be blunt) I enjoyed getting sucked!

"You sure you're okay?" I asked him every single time.

"I'm fine," he always answered, avoiding my eye.

The next day at school, Jack barely spoke to me. I think he feared our friends could somehow tell we were having a scan-ju-lous affair. Or whatever you wanna call it. Yet come the following Saturday night, he'd drop by Big Boy's when I got off, offer me a ride home . . . Where I'd promptly get off all over again!

If it hadn't been for the herpes (simplex two) outbreak right before MSBOA Band Festival, things may never have ceased between Jack and me. Thank God Ava's mom came up with the baby butt rash remedy to heal the cold sore on Jack's lip. This he totally got from *kissing* me—not because of the reason you might think!

That's about the time Jack informed me he wanted to drop outta Band because he was sick of being a Band Fag. Or so he said. Our friendship hasn't been the same ever since.

Who's That Guy?

"Everybody wants you when they don't know who you are
If you're a man of mystery, it really takes you far . . ."

—Maxwell Caulfield

Wanna know the best movie *ever*?

Grease 2.

Not the original "Grease is the word" *Grease* with Olivia Newton-John and John Travolta. I'm talking about the sequel starring Michelle Pfeiffer and Maxwell Caulfield. You know, that totally hot guy who's married to the old lady from *Nanny and the Professor.*

Well, *Grease 2* happens to be one of my favorite movies, right up there with *National Lampoon's Vacation, Ice Castles,* and *Somewhere in Time* with Jane Seymour and Christopher Reeves—I mean, *Reeve.*

I'll never forget the first time I seen it back in 7th grade . . .

Me and Max were spending the night over Jack's house, and we were downstairs in his basement. Jack's dad is all Mr. Fix-it, and he's got one end done up with carpeting, a couch and chairs, and a color TV with cable. On the opposite side, there's this old pull-out sofabed that's uncomfortable as hell. But me and Max used to sleep on it all the time because Jack wasn't about to give up *his* bed upstairs. In case I haven't mentioned it, Jack has always been a tad bit spoiled.

Not that I'm saying he's a brat or anything. He just always seems to have whatever I don't—an Atari, his own phone, a VCR *and* color TV with cable right in his room, you name it.

So the three of us were flipping thru the stations looking for something to watch on Skinemax—I mean, *Cinemax*—when we came across what looked like the T-Birds and Pink Ladies bopping around a bowling alley singing a song about *scoring* tonight.

"Put on MTV," Max ordered. "41."

He seized control of the remote and flipped back to the previous channel.

"Turn it back!" I hollered. "I wanna see what that was."

We returned to Rydell High circa 1963, courtesy of Showtime. How come I didn't know there was a *Grease* sequel? Me and Janelle totally loved the first one. In fact, whenever our babysitter, Sheryl Killian, babysat us and we weren't watching *The Hardy Boys,* we were playing *Danny & Sandy.*

"I don't wanna watch this musical crap!" Max whined. "Put something good on."

"I thought you liked *Grease,*" I said to Jack, hoping he'd come to my defense.

"I do," he admitted. "But I heard *Grease 2* sucks."

Suddenly, Max shouted, "Leave it on . . . That chick is hot!"

This time he wasn't talking about Boy George from Culture Club. Thankfully I was allowed to partake due to Michelle Pfeiffer's big-screen break out as Stephanie Zinone . . . You know, I still haven't seen *The Witches of Eastwick* yet.

From that day on, I was hooked. Whenever I'd see in *TV*

Guide they were showing *Grease 2* on cable, I made sure I got an invitation to spend the night over Jack's house.

"But you've already seen it ten times!" he'd remind me, wanting to watch some crap TV show like *Joanie Loves Chachi* or *Square Pegs*.

"Twelve," I'd correct, "but who's counting?"

I was!

Sure, compared to the original, *Grease 2* is a tad cheesy, but I totally loved it.

That summer when me and Jack went to Blue Lake for Band camp, I practically had the TV schedule memorized. Anytime I knew *Grease 2* was being shown, I'd be like, "I can't believe I'm missing *Grease 2* right now!" You can bet Jack was totally sick of hearing that by the end of those twelve days, you know what I mean?

This one scene I particularly enjoy takes place at the Bowl-a-Rama where all the Rydell High kids hang out on Friday nights, bowling, and smoking cigarettes, da-dah da-dah.

Basically what happens is . . . Paulette's little (lesbian) sister, Dolores, shows up on her skateboard. She rushes inside to tell T-Bird leader Johnny, "Balmudo's out front and he's all alone." Johnny, Goose, and Louis take this as their cue to kick some Crater Face butt.

They whip out their combs, light up their smokes, and make their way outside, pursued by the Pink Ladies. Only right before they arrive, the entire gang of Scorpions shows up, prompting the T-Birds to beat a hasty retreat. Except Dolores is busy dragging Davey to the parking lot, promising him, "action out front . . . Balmudo's gonna get his face mangled."

As the youngest T-Bird flies outside looking for the rumble, Davey discovers he's been ambushed, and Balmudo's gonna kill him . . . When all of a sudden, outta nowhere, this Cool Rider shows up on a motorcycle, flames spray-painted all over the body, dressed in black leather, wearing a helmet and dark goggles, and looking totally H-O-T.

Of course, nobody realizes he's Michael Carrington, aka Maxwell Caulfield, but the T-Birds and Pink Ladies and Scorpions are all floored enough to break into song. "Who's that guy?" they sing while he cruises his cycle around the parking lot and up onto the roof of this '57 Chevy. Once the sirens of cop cars can be heard in the distance, Michael hightails it outta there. Johnny decides it's time for everybody to bowl, and the T-Birds and Pink Ladies head back into the alley.

Well, Stephanie is smitten. She can't stop thinking about the Cool Rider she sang about earlier. Paulette (played by Judy Garland's real-life daughter, Lorna Luft), Sharon (aka Doris Finsecker from *Fame*), and Rhonda "Yo, Ritter!" (who I never heard of before or since), bring up the fact that there's been some doubt concerning Stephanie's (quote) loyalty to the Birds (unquote).

Stephanie, caught off guard, informs her Pink Ladies pals that maybe she's (quote) tired of being somebody's chick (unquote). Paulette tells her pal to relax and offers her a ciggie. As she's trying to get the crappy matches to light, a leather-gloved hand wielding a Zippo pops into frame. Stephanie graciously accepts. When she looks up to thank her knight in shining armor, he's none other than . . . The Cool Rider himself.

"Wanna ride?"

But it's too late. The police have arrived.

Cool Rider takes it upon himself to jump over the cop car, making his escape into the night, leaving an even more intrigued Stephanie in his wake. Later, when she's pumping gas at her father's service station, Michael appears a second time to totally whisk Stephanie off her toes. They spend a romantic evening riding around on his Harley, and end up totally making out before a blazing sunset, the instrumental version of "Cool Rider" playing in the background. The only thing is Stephanie still doesn't know who the guy is.

This brings me to the whole point of my analogy . . .

Today after school, I meet Audrey at her locker. She asked me to help her look for a monologue for our *A Christmas Carol* auditions, even though they're only three days away. Nothing like waiting till the last minute, huh, Aud? I can never remember what number hers is, so I always just look for the door wrapped in GO GREEN! GO WHITE! Spartans paper . . . I suspect maybe Audrey's college of choice is Michigan State.

"I gotta stop by the Band room and pick up my Flaggot shit," she informs me, approaching from the far end of the empty hall between the gym and the pool.

It's only 3:15 PM and everybody's already cleared out, either on their way home or off to some kind of practice. At moments like this, when I get a whiff of chlorine, I realize how much I miss being on the swim team. Especially now that I truly appreciate the male form in all its Speedo-ed glory.

"Why didn't you stop by there first?"

I sidle up closer to Audrey's locker as she spins its dial. I'm not trying to scam her combination or anything. She's got a great collection of Chippendales cards on the door inside, and I can't resist sneaking a peek whenever she opens it. There's this one body builder-type, all oiled up and flexing in nothing but a bow tie . . . Hot!

"Because, dipshit, I had to say good-bye to Berger before he went to work."

It's official . . . Audrey Wojczek and Rob Berger are an item.

Hard to believe, huh?

"Well, smart-ass . . . Why didn't you say so?"

Now that football season is over, Rob's got an after-school job working up at Bray's "Home of the Ass Burgers" on 9 Mile and Dequindre. We call it that because of the giant donkey perched on top of the roof, holding a huge hamburger up with his hooves. I can't say I ever had one, but I hear they're sorta like the sliders at White Castle's.

Years ago, me and Jack used to joke that one day we'd steal the ass from on top of Bray's and hold it hostage. Maybe now that Rob's their official burger flipper and we know somebody on the inside we can come up with a plan. Only Jack still isn't talking to me! It's been a month since I stopped by his house before Homecoming and we had it out. Again, I probably shouldn't have told Jack I think he's a fag, even though I still totally do.

The other day, I wrote a Letter to the Editor of *The Hazel Parker* (Jack) telling him how much it hurts my feelings when other kids call me a Band Fag because I literally am one. I also went on to say that I know for a fact there's at least one other gay kid at HPHS (hint-hint, Jack) who's afraid to be himself all because of what the other (quote-unquote) popular kids will think, and how sad I been since this kid (Jack) dropped outta Band because I miss him.

I'm sure Jack won't print the letter, which is fine, just so long as he knows I wrote it.

"Where the fuck is that *fucking* book?"

I watch as Audrey shuffles around a bunch of shit on her top shelf, finally fetching her homework for Parenting—I mean, *Everyday Living*.

"Just wait till the baby comes," I joke.

Starting next week, Mrs. Ireland is making Audrey and all the girls in her class carry an egg around with them 24/7 like it's a baby. And if anything happens to it, say it cracks or God forbid *breaks*, they fail the entire project, forever an unfit mother.

"You're so funny I forgot to laugh," Audrey groans, closing her locker with a slam.

Bye-bye, Mr. Body Builder!

If you ask me, Everyday Living is a totally lame class. But here in Hazeltucky, where 90% of the girls graduate, get married, and squeeze out a litter of kids by the time they're twenty-two, I suppose it's pretty valuable. Lord knows my sister, Janelle, should have taken that course during *her* Senior year. Did I mention she just found out the other day that her and Ted are expecting? Six months from now on May 4th.

You can bet Mom was livid, but I'm pretty psyched. Janelle's not only my older sister, she's also a friend. All I want is for her to be happy . . . Besides, how cool will it be being Uncle Brad?

"Have you talked to Jack lately?" I ask Audrey when we pass by locker #1427 en route to our final destination.

"Not since Senior Breakfast."

Last week, our entire class got together at the Kingsley Inn, this fancy-schmancy hotel out in Bloomfield Hills, for the first of many Senior Events. Me and Audrey sat at a table with Rob, Carrie, Ava, and Tuesday Gunderson. Directly across from us sat Jack and Max with Jamie Good, Shellee Findlay, Betsy Sheffield, and Tom Fulton, aka the Popular People . . . Now that Max also works at Farmer Jack's, I guess he's Jack's new Best Friend.

"You didn't tell me that," I say, stopping at the porcelain water fountain outside the girls' bathroom to slurp a lukewarm drink.

"He came up to me in the the lobby . . ." Audrey takes a turn, pulling her long hair back. "Me and Rob were waiting in line at the coat check."

"Did you say anything?"

I intentionally choose not to comment on what looks like could either be a curling iron burn on the inside of Aud's neck . . . or a *hickey*.

"No fucking way, the fucker!" she snarls, wiping her face. "We should totally TP his house."

As much as I don't wanna piss Jack off any more than he already is, it's about time he becomes the target of an ambush. You know how many times I been dragged outta bed by my irate mother, after Audrey, Ava, Carrie, Jack, and/or Max decided the apple trees in our side yard make for a perfect place to wrap several dozen rolls of Charmin or Cottonelle or whatever brand Big Boy's or Country Boy's happen to be stocking in their johns that evening? More than I can count!

"Every time I see him lately," Audrey goes on, "he's always with Little Miss Cheerleader."

"I know," I can't help but agree, because it's true.

It seems odd that Jack still spends so much time with Betsy Sheffield. I mean, last year they sorta went together, but now they're just friends. Besides, Betsy's been going with Mr. Homecoming King, Tom Fulton, for over a month. Yet just the other day, I seen Jack and Betsy heading out to lunch together in Jack's 1979 pea green Dodge Omni. Sure enough, when me and Max got over to BK, we saw Tom with some of his Varsity football teammates, but Betsy and Jack were nowhere to be found.

I realize that Tom never got along with Jack back at Webb, but I know if *I* had a girlfriend (in my case, boyfriend), I wouldn't be letting her (him) take off to the Universal Mall food court with some other girl (guy).

"I don't know what he sees in her," Aud mutters as we continue down the Choir/Band hall across from the auditorium. "Why the fuck did I bother joining Flag Corps if Jack was just gonna drop outta Marching Band?"

"I know," I agree again. "It totally sucks without him."

To top it all off, the other day Mr. Klan announced that we're going to Florida to march in the Disney World Main Street USA parade. At first, I sorta thought it might suck wasting my Senior Spring Break with all the Band Fags, but most of my friends will be there (Ava, Carrie, Audrey, Liza Larson), so why shouldn't I go?

"Just let me just grab my flag from the back!"

We enter the Band room proper where it's totally impossible to hear anything over the deafening rendition of Van Halen's "Jump" being belted out by Don Olsewski on drum kit, and his two cohorts, Curt Chaplin on alto sax, and Thad Petoskey on synthesizer.

"Take your time!" I holler back.

Audrey heads towards the practice room where the Flaggots store their flags and rifles and other shit they twirl—batons, hoops, (whips and chains). For a split second, I contemplate taking my trombone home. The thought of lugging it all the way out to my car in the back parking lot is just about enough to kill me.

"Brad!"

A tap on my shoulder scares the bejesus outta me. After I extract my heart from my throat and return it to my chest, I turn around to find Ava and Carrie joined at the hip like Siamese Twin sisters. You know, like the ones who appeared in PT Barnum's Freak Show, but later wound up working as checkout girls in a supermarket somewhere . . . Violet and Daisy something or other.

"What are you guys doing?" I ask them, even though I already know the answer.

Every day after school, Ava, Carrie, and a bunch of the other girl Band Fags like to hang out in the Band room watching the guys practice. Last I heard, Don, Curt, and Thad are forming a band named Too Rad, and the girls are gonna be their official groupies . . . Lame!

"You know," answers Carrie. "Hanging out."

Gawking at Curt Chaplin!

Carrie Johnson's had a thing for the guy since Sophomore year. Not that I can blame her. How come sax players are always the hottest guys in Band? First Freddy Edwards (Homecoming King '85), then Kent Bowman (Class of '87), now Curt Chaplin. With his dark curly hair, mustache, and athletic yet non-jock bod, Curt is right up there in keeping with this rule. The faces he makes when he's blowing that horn . . . H-O-T, hot!

"What are *you* doing?" Ava asks, habitually twirling a lock of her dark curly hair, a hint of a smile gracing her lips.

"Waiting for Godot."

"Who?" asks Carrie, totally perplexed.

"Forget it."

Being non–Drama Queers, neither girl gets the Samuel Beckett reference. We read his play in Dell's class this past week. Personally, I didn't like it. The characters keep waiting and waiting and Godot never even shows up.

At first, I think maybe they think I'm also there to gawk at Curt. Like Audrey, I haven't told either Ava or Carrie that I'm gay. Again, Jack is the only one who knows, other than Luanne Kowalski, who I barely see anymore since she went away to college at Eastern. Again, I'm not ashamed. It's just not something I go around announcing to everybody, you know what I mean?

"Miss me?"

I totally jump a mile as Audrey gooses me with the end of her big-assed Flaggot flag pole.

"Where you two off to?" Ava questions, a hint of innuendo in her voice.

Aud expertly winds the maroon and gray nylon flag around its staff. "Wouldn't you like to know?" she says, all sassy.

I don't know how the hell those Flaggots can twirl those things without getting them caught on something or poking somebody's eye out.

"I'm telling Berger," Carrie teases.

I roll my eyes. "Please!"

I can't believe anybody would ever think there's anything romantic going on with me and Audrey Wojczek. Plus the racket in the room is starting to give me a splitting headache . . . Thank God the Too Rad boys stop at that point to take a pee break.

"Mr. Star Thespian is helping me with my monologue for auditions on Thursday," Audrey explains. "Not that it's any of *your* business."

That's when I hear from behind me the sound of a guy's voice I can't say I recognize.

"Oh, my God . . . You guys are Drama Queers?"

I'm about to turn around and say, *Yeah . . . What the fuck's it to you?* Except as I do, it takes everything I got in me *not* to lose it when I see the totally cute Sophomore—holding a *saxophone.*

A bit taller than me (5'9"), he's got blondish hair that's short on the sides, and sorta long and flippy in front. A tiny cleft sits in the center of his chin, below a perfect set of pearly whites. He's a little on the thinner side than I usually find attractive, but he does fill out a pair of Girbaud jeans rather nicely. I also like his leather K-Swiss tennis shoes.

"I'm Brad Dayton."

"I know."

The guy looks thru me with piercing eyes, perfectly matching the pale blue script on his Blue Lake Fine Arts Camp hooded sweatshirt . . . Definitely a Band Fag.

Normally, I'd be all like, *Who the hell are you?* Only I'm a little stumped. Is he just being an asshole . . . or is he flirting with me?

I honestly can't tell.

All I can manage to do is say, "Hi." Then I just stand there with this totally dumb expression on my face. Like I flunked Special Ed or something. Meanwhile, Audrey, Carrie, and Ava are of no help once Don Olsewski and crew return from the restroom.

"Play 'Panama'!"

Somebody shouts out. Probably Ava. She loves Van Halen and has been devastated ever since their breakup.

"I'm thinking about trying out for the play," Cute Sophomore Guy informs me, a smirk on his flawlessly complexioned face.

"You mean *auditioning?*" Audrey interjects from atop her high horse.

"You totally should," I encourage. At least he'd give me something to look at during rehearsal. "If you need a hand . . ." I offer, meaning with his audition. Until I realize my words could be totally misconstrued, and red I go.

Open mouth, insert foot!

"Thanks," Cute Sophomore Guy replies graciously. "Gimme your number. I'll call you."

Wouldn't you know? I can't find my spiral notebook in my duffle bag. Instead, I open my World Lit book and tear off a corner from the Russian section. Only to discover, I don't have anything to write with.

"Um . . . You don't happen to have a pen, do you?" I ask, feeling like a Total Loser.

CSG loans me a red Papermate Flair. I jot down: 398-5836, and hand him the tiny scrap.

Just when things are starting to get good, Audrey decides, "We gotta go, Dayton . . . Now!"

As I'm practically dragged into the hall, I call out to Ava and Carrie, "Have fun!"

And to Cute Sophomore Guy, whoever he may be . . .

Call me!

Heaven Is a Place on Earth

"When you walk into the room
You pull me close and we start to move . . ."

—Belinda Carlisle

Tonight I'm going on my first *real* date.

I mean, with a guy.

His name's Larry, he lives Downriver, and he's twenty-four.

I know, between the Larry part and the living Downriver, not so great, but the twenty-four is pretty cool, huh? We met this past Friday night at The Gas Station. I mean, the bar, not a real gas station. I would never go picking up a guy at like Gas 'n Go or Mobil. Unless he was hot, then I *might* consider it.

"Just wait'll you see him . . ."

My new friend, Miss Peter, couldn't stop gushing the second I sat down for a drink.

Oh, my God . . . I just realized I haven't mentioned Miss Peter yet!

Miss Peter is this guy named (what else?) Peter. I don't know why, but everybody calls him *Miss* Peter, and refers to him as *her* and he as *she*. And believe me, she is fabulous!

I'm sooo glad the Homecoming Dance last month sucked donkey balls. I ended up cutting out early and heading down to my usual haunt, Heaven, even though I don't usually go out on Saturday nights anymore. Normally, I'd be at *Rocky Horror*, but all my cohorts were back at Hillbilly High "Dancing on the Ceiling."

That's when I met Miss Peter for the very first time.

Waiting in line to pay my cover, I spotted him—I mean, *her*—right away wearing black capri pants with a black and white striped top that reminded me of something outta *The Pirate Movie*. You know, with Christopher Atkins of *The Blue Lagoon* fame, and the bad ass chick from *Little Darlings*, Kristy McNichols—I mean, Mc*Nichol*.

"You do *not* wanna go up there," the big-haired middle-aged man warned when I was about to fork over my five bucks. "The place is D-E-A-D."

I had no other choice but to take his (her) word for it and follow him (her) into the bar downstairs. To be honest, I never even knew there was a second bar, let alone the fact that The Gas Station is also gay. Until I met Miss Peter and she filled me in. She says the fags are the only ones in Detroit willing to drive south of 8 Mile for a little fun and frivolity.

I remember commenting, "I like your sandals."

"They're espadrilles," he (she) informed me, making a beeline for the bar. "Come along, Opie . . . I'll buy you a Shirley Temple." Did I mention Miss Peter's got a voice that's reminiscent of a cross between Brenda Vaccaro and Bea Arthur from *The Golden Girls*?

We spent the rest of the night hanging out and talking till 2:00 AM. That's when Miss Peter first told me about her friend Larry, and decided we'd make a perfect couple.

A month later, she finally got around to introducing us.

"I'm telling you . . . He looks like Fred over there."

With her cigarette, Miss Peter gestured to the black-and-white framed poster of a totally hot half-naked guy holding a pair of Goodyears.

"Who?"

I couldn't fathom any guy looking like the Greek god hanging on the opposite wall above the dance floor—fondly known as The Pit. Not because it's nasty or anything, even though it totally is, but you have to take a few steps down to get to it, with the tables overlooking the area on all sides.

Miss Peter rolled her eyes. "Who have we been talking about?"

"Larry?"

I couldn't help but wonder what a hot guy like that would want with a pipsqueak like me.

"Bradley," Miss Peter said sincerely, sucking on her Parliament, "You're a baby . . . Would I lie to you?" She stubbed the butt out in the ashtray. "Now bum me a ciggie, I'm out."

The other cool thing about Miss Peter is she likes to smoke—a lot. In fact, I started calling her The Once-ler. 'member that Dr. Seuss special, the one with the Lorax? He's that whiny little orange guy with the bushy yellow mustache who's out to save the Truffula trees from being cut down and turned into Thneeds. And all you see is the arm of The Once-ler sticking out the window.

Well, one night after the bar closed, a bunch of us went back to Miss Peter's apartment over in East Detroit. She sat there the entire time in this big old Papasan chair, buried in pillows, smoking up a storm . . . And all you saw was her arm reaching out every once in a while for the ashtray!

Hence the nickname.

"Who's this Larry guy, again?"

I had to have Miss Peter remind me prior to her hot friend's arrival, because truth be told, I was a little crocked the first time she ever mentioned him.

She daintily sipped her Captain Morgan's and Diet Coke thru a candy cane–striped stir stick/straw before elaborating. "He's the kid brother of my high school girlfriend."

I almost choked on my fuzzy navel.

I wouldn't wanna insult Miss Peter in any way, but I can't imagine her ever having an interest in a woman, you know what I mean? Minus the 5 o'clock shadow, you might think she was one herself. I almost asked where and when she went to high school, but something warned me against it.

"You said his name's *Larry?*"

I couldn't help but make a sour face. I totally pictured McLean Stevenson from that sitcom *Hello, Larry.* 'member, he was a friend of Mr. Drummond's from *Diff'rent Strokes,* and his two daughters were played by the girl from *Escape to Witch Mountain*, and the chick from *Jaws 2.* You know, the one Chief Brody saves at the end when he electrocutes the shark.

Miss Peter advised, "Don't judge a book by its cover . . . Unless it looks like *that.*"

Sure enough, when I glanced over my shoulder to observe Larry making his entrance, I almost choked on my fuzzy navel for the second time . . . 'member what I said about not picking up a guy at a gas station? In Larry's case, I'd definitely make an exception. He's SWB, dark hair, dark eyes, not the least bit gay acting at all, i.e., totally my type. Did I mention he wears plaid flannel and works in a body shop?

"Larry, this is Bradley," said Miss Peter, making the formals. "Bradley, Larry."

Larry reached out and shook my hand, something I'm discovering a lot of gay guys do, which I sorta like. His grip was sooo strong, I thought he was gonna crush my fingers.

" 's up?"

I'm not complaining or anything, but Larry sounded more like a Dumb Jock than a Total Fag. Now if only I could do the same. The last thing I wanted was for him to think I was a little girly-boy. Unless that's what he's into, then he could think whatever he wanted.

Miss Peter drained her drink, slurping loudly. "Like my tired old pussy," she reported, "I'm dry."

"Rum and Coke?" Larry offered, ready to make his way to the bar.

"You two stay here," Miss Peter ordered. "I'm not an invalid, for chris'sakes!"

We watched as she stumbled away.

Shortly thereafter, a lull fell over the high-top table. I honestly didn't know what to say. Guys like Larry never give me the time of day, let alone wanna *talk* to me.

"How do you know Peter?" he shouted over the wail of Donna Summer, surprising me when he didn't say *Miss*.

"From here!" I leaned in closer so he could hear my reply.

Larry smelled of Polo, which normally, I loathe. Fucking pine tress, you know what I mean? My cologne of choice for a man is Drakkar Noir. Not for myself. I always wear Lagerfeld.

"So how old are you?" he asked, between sips of bottled Bud Light.

Wanna know what popped into my head and found its way outta my mouth?

"Eighteen."

Larry smiled, showing a chipped front tooth, which I totally found to be hot. I wanted to reach across the table and run my finger along its sharp edge . . . But I resisted.

"I remember eighteen," he sighed, like it was years ago. "So when did you graduate?"

Either he caught me off guard or I had way too much peach schnapps (or both), but I instinctively replied, "I still got another year."

Larry gave me a quizzical look.

Quickly, I covered. "My mom held me back in kinny-garden."

This is how I sometimes say *kindergarten*, mostly when I been drinking.

I guess I got worried Larry wouldn't wanna go out with me if he knew I'm Jail Bait. Not that we're gonna have *sex* or anything on our first date. Unless he wants to, then I'll consider it.

"Where d'you go to high school?"

I watched him swig his beer, wrapping a thumb and forefinger around the longneck bottle in a way that reminded me of Luanne Kowalski. Only when Larry did it, it made me melt.

For a second, I considered saying somewhere glamorous like Huntington Woods or Pleasant Ridge. But I figured if we ever become boyfriends, Larry might wanna pick me up from school one day in his *truck*, and if I lied, then what would I do?

So I hesitantly replied, "Hazel Park."

He responded, *"Hazeltucky,"* the way most people do.

So I made sure to point out, "But I live in Ferndale."

Larry laughed. "Don't apologize . . . I grew up in *Taylor*tucky."

Once we established we had the white-trash element in common, we continued chatting for the next hour or so. Miss Peter completely disappeared, and I completely forgot I planned to have *a* drink and head upstairs to Heaven.

"I don't wanna keep you," said Larry, giving me an out.

"Please . . . I'd much rather stay down here."

He flicked the tip of his tongue at the hole in his beer bottle. "Why's that?"

I blushed. "No reason."

Larry reached out and tousled my curly locks. "Wanna go up together?" Unlike Miss Peter, I didn't complain. In fact, this guy could manhandle me all he wanted!

"We don't have to," I decided, giving him an out. "It's a dance bar."

I couldn't imagine Larry being the type of guy who actually *danced.*

"You kidding? I'm a regular Deney Terrio." He flashed me his dopey chipped-tooth grin, took my hand, and led the way.

I don't know how I ever made it up those rickety steps. The next thing I remember is hearing a song that reminded me of The Go-Go's, and feeling a pair of hands firm upon my hips. Sure enough, Larry stood behind me swaying to the music, my head against his massive chest.

My first *real* dance.

I mean, with a guy.

Named Larry from Downriver.

"Pardonnez-moi . . ."

Round about midnight, I found myself seated at yet another table, this one tucked away in a dark corner beneath a framed picture that looked exactly like the Duran Duran *Rio* album cover.

When I looked up with bleary eyes, who did I see standing before us?

None other than the Matchmaker herself . . . Miss Peter.

I managed to mumble, "Hello," my belly full of too much liquid. Nearby, a couple of lesbians played pool. For a second, I thought one of them was Luanne . . . Thank God it wasn't.

All smiles, Miss Peter cooed, "I saw you out on the dance floor . . . Looks like you're hitting it off."

Larry squeezed my hand. "He's a cutie, isn't he?"

"Why do you think I introduced you?" Miss Peter bragged, taking full credit for the setup.

I couldn't remember how or when mine and Larry's fingers became entwined or which one of us took the initiative, but it sure felt nice being in the presence of somebody like him. He's totally the type of guy I could walk around the mall with and nobody would ever suspect we were anything more than friends. Not that we are just yet, but you know what I mean?

"How you feeling?" Larry asked Miss Peter.

"Sober." She toasted us with her empty rocks glass. "How 'bout another?"

I declined the offer, thinking how totally hungover I was gonna feel the next day waiting tables at Big Boy's from noon till 8:00 PM. "I'm good, thanks."

Miss Peter sneered, "Not you . . . I mean, *me*."

Larry swirled the swills around the bottom of his bottle before draining them. "I'll fly, you buy."

Like the Pope offering his ring to be kissed, Miss Peter handed him a crisp, folded lengthwise fifty. "Bring me back the change."

"Rum and Coke?" Larry double-checked.

"Captain Morgan's and *Diet,*" Miss Peter specified. "*Avec une* lime, *si vous plaît.*"

I told you she's fancy!

My eyes focused on Larry's legs stepping down from his stool. The muscles in his quads bulged beneath torn light denim jeans, supporting all 165–170 pounds of pure man. At 140, I made a mental note to make sure Larry didn't crush me when the time came for us to make out . . . Notice I didn't say *if*?

"That boy's got an ass on him," Miss Peter observed as Larry made his way across the room. *"Hello, gorgeous!"* Suddenly, she sounded like Barbara Streisand as Dolly Levi.

We watched from afar as Larry chatted with the Mike the bartender, another guy I been drooling over since day one. Between the bare buff torso, the army fatigues worn with combat boots, and the six-inch dyed-blue mohawk, I don't know what I found hotter. Again, I marveled at what a regular guy Larry was. How many fags wear work boots out to a bar and could care less what their hair looks like?

Speaking of . . .

Did I mention Miss Peter works in a *salon*? You can totally tell from the way she's got a new style every time you see her. Like I said, our first meeting found her looking like Robert Smith from The Cure, all ratted up and big. This week, it's more demure—parted on one side, with a long bang drooping down over her left eye.

"You're a very lucky boy," Miss Peter sang. "Don't you go breaking Larry's heart."

"Oh, I won't!"

If anything, I was sure it would be the other way around. I couldn't imagine what a 24-year-old guy saw in a 17—I mean, *18*—year-old boy like me. I realize some guys like them younger, but with me, it's never been the case.

I heard the flick of a Bic as Miss Peter lit yet another Parliament. She must've got more from the vending machine, even though I can't believe anybody would ever pay $3 for a pack of cigarettes.

"I am *pooped!*" Miss Peter sighed. She set the smokes down on the table, perched herself on the vacant stool, and crossed one leg over the other, teetering a tad.

"I should probably get home."

Mom was probably wondering why I was out so late again on a Friday night. Now that football season ended, I couldn't use going out to the Tombs after the game as my weekly excuse.

Miss Peter placed a well-manicured hand on mine. "You can't drive," she informed me when I stumbled. "Not till you sober up a little."

There was no point arguing. I flagged down the nearest waiter, a prissy little thing by the name of Aryc. If you think I'm a girly-boy, you should see her—I mean, *him*—in his hot pink spandex biker shorts and off-the-shoulder teal tank top, with his posh British accent.

Polite as punch, I asked, "May I have a glass of wa-dir?"

This is how I sometimes say *water,* mostly when I been drinking.

Aryc rolled his fake-blues. "I'm a bit busy at the moment."

"Don't be a bitch," Miss Peter scolded. "Opie asked you nice."

Aryc and his flippy hair flounced away.

"I can *not* stand her," I grumbled.

"She thinks she's the Princess of Wales," Miss Peter mused before picking up where we left off. "You can't leave without saying good-bye to your new boyfriend."

"Larry's not my boyfriend," I insisted. "We just met . . . It's not like we been on a date or anything."

Miss Peter raised a perfectly arched eyebrow. "What do you call this?"

I scoffed. "I mean, a real date."

A dish-spotty glass landed on our table with a thud. Miss Peter picked it up with an examining eye. "They never heard of Cascade?"

I didn't bother thanking Aryc since he already scurried away like the weasel he is . . . Remind me to slip a Correctol in his cocktail next time I see him with a drink!

"Why don't you ask him out?"

I took a nasty sip just as Miss Peter suggested this. Again, I almost choked. "I'm not asking Aryc to go anywhere!"

Miss Peter whacked me with the *Metra* magazine sitting on the table. "Not him, stupid . . . You *must* be wasted!" She glanced at the shirtless guy on the cover, commented, "Yum!" then came right back at me. "Who have we been talking about for the last fifteen minutes?"

Feeling totally put on the spot, I began giggling like a girl. "I'm not gonna ask Larry out, either!"

Miss Peter gave me a look. "You've got a dick between your legs, don't you?"

"Yeah, but . . ." I wondered what *that* had to do with anything!

She stubbed out her cigarette. "So . . ." She lit another. "That's the good thing about being a faggot. None of them stupid boy-girl rules apply."

I guess I never thought about it before: I'm a guy, Larry's a guy. Somebody's gotta make the first move. Why couldn't it be me?

So that's what I did.

The minute he returned with Miss Peter's drink, I took a deep breath and said, "Hey, Larry . . ."

"What's up, cutie?" He put an arm around my shoulder and nuzzled my ear.

"You wanna go to a movie or something sometime?"

Larry furrowed his brow. "You mean with *you?*"

"No, with me," Miss Peter snapped. "I'm a barrel of laughs on a date."

"Well, in that case . . ." Larry moved to pull Miss Peter into a passionate embrace.

She cried, "Careful, the coif!" shielding herself like a chrysalis in a cocoon. Luckily, she had this huge black shawl wrapped around her shoulders to ward off a chill. Once outta harm's way, Miss Peter droned dryly, "No offense, Larry, but you can't even remember *My Mother the Car.*"

He gasped at the blatant rejection. "So you're saying I'm too young?"

"Have you ever seen *Valley of the Dolls*?"

Larry stood speechless.

Miss Peter shrugged her shoulder pads. "I rest my case."

"What about you?" Larry turned back towards me. "You wanna go out sometime?" Again, he flashed his dopey chipped-tooth grin.

How could I refuse?

Four days later . . .

"Br-a-a-dley . . . Telephone!"

I'm standing in my bedroom in nothing but a towel when my mom pounds on the door.

"Who is it?"

Rifling thru my underwear drawer, I pray I'll find a clean pair—just in case.

"Who do you think it is?" says Mom, sounding somewhat annoyed.

"I mean, who's on the phone?"

My mother asks, "Who's calling, please?" Followed by a moment of silence. Followed by: "He says his name is Larry."

The mere mention and I swear I'm sprouting wood.

"Tell him I'll be right there!"

Grabbing a pair of maroon striped briefs from the pile, I hold them up to my nose, sniff. Passing inspection, I quickly put them on, push my dick down, and reach an arm out the door.

" 's up?"

I'm ear-to-ear smirk the second I hear Larry's voice. "Getting dressed . . . You?"

"Just took a shower."

Great!

Now I can't get the image of him, dripping wet, outta my mind.

Sure enough, my dick is stiffer than a British upper lip.

Goddamn sexual peak!

"Who's Larry?"

Mom's on my heels as I'm practically out the door.

Again, I hate lying to her. So I simply say, "He's a friend."

She looks me up and down. I can tell she's wondering why I'm wearing my best Guess? jeans, the ones that took an entire month of Big Boy's tips to pay for, just to see a movie with a (quote-unquote) friend. But she lets it go.

"Try not to stay out too late . . . It's a school night."

Mom kisses my cheek, and away I go!

We meet at Larry's house in Taylor. He drives us to TGI Friday's in his brand-spanking-new '87 Dodge Dakota. Larry orders the fish and chips and a beer. I have the sirloin steak *au jus,* which comes with this huge-ass onion ring I decide not to eat. Who knows what's gonna happen later? The last thing I want is bad breath.

Next, we go to a movie at Southland Mall, where I can't say I ever been before. Larry pays for the tickets. I can't believe they cost fucking $4.75 each. Something called *Less Than Zero,* starring Andrew McCarthy and the other guy from *Pretty in Pink.* Not Duckie Dale. The one who played the asshole, Steff. Too bad I can't recall what the movie's about, I barely pay attention.

The entire time I keep thinking, *I'm out on a* date *with a totally hot guy* . . . And worrying about what's coming next.

"Now what?"

Once we're back at Larry's house after the show, he asks the $1,000 question.

It's close to 11:00 PM on a Tuesday night in Detroit, so I can't imagine there's much else going on. Standing outside by my piece-of-shit car, which Larry thinks is totally cool and calls an *antique,* I'm freezing my ass off. What can you expect from November in Michigan? I'm sure there'll be snow on the ground soon enough.

"I don't know . . ."

I try acting coy, but between the knocking of my knees and the chattering of my teeth, all I want is to get inside someplace warm.

"You wanna come in for a nightcap?" Larry asks, like we're on an episode of *The Love Boat.* "Or do you need to go home? It's a school night, isn't it?"

"Watch it, mister," I tease. "I may be a Drama Queer, but I'll fuck you up!"

"Oh, yeah?" He gives me a sly and challenging look. "I'd like to see you try."

Like I said, I'm not a virgin. Well, I never did the deed, but I had sexual relations before, and I'm not totally naïve about these sorta situations . . . I know exactly what's about to follow.

Larry opens the front door to his apartment. We get all of three steps inside, and BAM! His tongue is down my throat. My coat is off, my pants down, my harder-than-a-rock pocket-rocket launched.

Then I think about my mom.

She would *not* approve of what I'm doing.

Inside my head, I hear Miss Horchik's haunting refrain: *"To thine ownself be true."*

Despite how good it all feels, and how long I dreamed of having hot S-E-X with a hot G-U-Y like Larry, I immediately lose my hard-on.

"'s up?" Larry asks, tugging on my limp dick to no avail.

Obviously not me!

"You sure you're a fag?" he snickers—and into his mouth I go.

I throw my head back, falling thru the void. I don't *want* him to stop, but . . . "It's late."

Larry hesitates. "You gotta be fucking kidding?" He looks up at me like he can't believe what he's hearing.

All I can do is say, "I'm sorry," and hope he'll understand.

I used to joke around with Jack that I wish I'd been born a girl. They can be Total Whores and have sex with whoever they want whenever they want. Yet here's me, pants down around my ankles, with this 24-year-old mechanic trying to get me off, and I'm asking for a rain check!

"I'll call you tomorrow," I swear.

When it comes down to it, I like Larry. Sure, I've only known him a few days, but . . . I don't *love* him. Call me old-fashioned, but I'm sorta saving myself. Not for marriage or anything silly like that.

For the right guy.

And like I said, technically it's illegal for Larry to do *anything* with me. Until next September, at least, when I turn eighteen for real. The last thing I want is for anybody to get arrested all because I'm a horndog.

As promised, the next day when I get home from school, I dial Larry's number.

Too bad he doesn't answer.

Looking for a New Love

"Gonna get over you
A new boy I'm gonna choose (You'll see) . . ."

—Jody Watley

I hate play tryouts—I mean, *auditions!*

Imagine what it's like getting up in front of everybody and being judged. Not just for who you are, but based on the way you look, the way you talk, and how well you work opposite others. Lemme tell ya, it totally sucks!

Mais ç'est la vie d'un acteur.

You'd think by now Mr. Dell'Olio could just *give* me a part without putting me thru the whole excruciating process. It's not like this is Broadway, for chris'sakes, it's goddamn Hillbilly High School. Shouldn't being a Senior count for something? It's bad enough I gotta prepare two contrasting monologues (one contemporary, one classical) for my Juilliard audition coming up in January. Now I have to worry about *A* goddamn *Christmas Carol.*

Did I mention I finally decided where I wanna go to college next fall? Up till recently, I been torn between Wayne State University in Detroit, and Juilliard School of Drama in New York

City, which is *the* (as in thee) best Drama School in the entire country.

The thing about WSU is they got this four-year tuition-free scholarship, as opposed to Juilliard, which costs several thousand dollars per year. Not that I'd qualify for a free ride since my grades totally suck, and not that I'd automatically get accepted into Juilliard because the competition is fierce. Plus if I did get in, I'd have to move away from home. And leaving my mom and my sisters and all my friends would totally suck, you know what I mean?

But like my junior high Band teacher, Jessica Clark Putnam, once told Jack when he contemplated not going to Blue Lake Fine Arts Camp by himself just because I couldn't afford to go: "Friends hold you back."

So to help me make up my mind, I had a meeting with my guidance counselor the other day, Mrs. Ellis . . .

"It's *your* education, Bradley," she reminded me.

Again, another adult telling me something I already know.

"Christopher Reeves went to Juilliard," I informed her, even though I meant to say Christopher *Reeve* (no *S*). Most people don't realize the Man of Steel is a classically trained actor.

"And Casey Kasem went to Wayne State," Mrs. Ellis reasoned.

No disrespect, but how the hell could she sit there in that goddamn butterscotch-colored plaid blazer she wears practically every goddamn day comparing Richard Collier from *Somewhere in Time* to Shaggy from *Scooby-Doo?*

Gimme a fucking break!

As much as I wanted to shout, *Thanks for nothing, Bitch!* I minded my manners as Mom always taught me and politely replied, "So you can see it's a tough decision."

Mrs. Ellis forced a smile. "If it's any help, I got *my* Bachelor's from Wayne, and I ended up with a good job."

Working as a guidance counselor in Hazeltucky, Michigan.

Did I mention she barely looked up from her lap, engrossed in my permanent record? Until she noticed my ACT scores.

"Have you considered Oakland Community College?"

Fuck Mrs. Ellis!

After that total waste of time, I decided to get Mr. Dell'Olio's opinion. For the past two years, he's worked with me as an actor. His judgment I trust on how I should go about pursuing my future career.

Yesterday after school, I stopped by the Drama room . . .

'member Zack Rakoff, the only male member of Flag Corps? Back in elementary school all-city Honors Band he wore GASS shoes and I thought he was a girl. Well, I popped my head into Dell's class and found Rakoff and Flaggot co-captain Claire Moody sitting at one of them trapezoid-shaped tables, deeply engrossed in debate.

"It wouldn't surprise me," I heard Moody saying to Rakoff. "He hasn't had a girlfriend since What's-Her-Name."

Rakoff replied, "I haven't had a girlfriend *ever.*"

"Maybe you're gay too," Moody mocked, half joking, half not.

"Thankth a lot!" Rakoff lisped, totally insulted.

"Who're we talking about?" I politely interrupted. Around these hallowed halls, there's nothing quite like good gossip—unless it's about *you.*

Like salmon ready to spawn, Rakoff and Moody stopped midstream. They looked at me like I had two heads sprouting outta my mock-turtleneck. Like I couldn't be trusted with such classified information.

"Wouldn't *you* like to know?" Moody snapped smugly.

I felt like saying, *Fine, Bitch . . . See if I care.*

I thought we used to be friends back at Webb and during *Okla-homo!* when Claire was Sophomore Student Director. Evidently not! So I laughed her off, reminding myself, "Claire's a fat girl's name." Not that I'm saying Claire Moody is fat, even though she sorta is.

"Brad can back me up," boasted Rakoff. "He's Jack's Best Friend."

I wanted to say, *I* was *Jack's Best Friend,* but I had a feeling this was one conversation I'd rather stay out of.

What was I gonna say? *The fat girl's right, Rakoff . . . Jack is a Total Fag.*

I couldn't do that to the poor guy, even though Mr. Paterno's made it perfectly clear he wants nothing more to do with me because *I'm* one.

So all I said was, "People have been saying that about Jack for years."

Moody said, "Precisely."

I reminded them, "You should never believe gossip, you know what I mean?"

Quickly, I changed the subject, asking if either knew where I could find Mr. Dell'Olio.

"I haven't theen him thince 5th hour," Rakoff reported.

Moody speculated, "He's probably in the *Parker* office," meaning *The Hazel Parker.* "I know he's on deadline." She rolled her eyes. "Chances are Jack's in there with him, editing the H-E-double-L out of one of my stories."

Did I mention that Dell also serves as faculty advisor for the school newspaper since he minored in English up at Northern? Evidently, Claire's a tad bitter that he made Jack Editor-in-Chief of *The Hazel Parker* when he only joined the paper Junior year, and she's been reporting since Sophomore. Maybe it's true that he did it because Jack is the only guy on staff. Or maybe it's because Jack is a better writer than Claire.

Who the hell knows, and who gives a flying fuck? Not me.

"Brad!"

I was about to head back out the door when Rakoff called. Stopped in my tracks, I asked, "What's up?"

"Claire and I are writing a thort film thcript . . ."

Moody added, "For second semester Mass Media," like Rakoff was an idiot for not specifying.

"For thecond themethter Math Media," he echoed, "and we were wondering if you wanna be in it."

I hesitated a moment. Not because I didn't welcome the opportunity to work on my craft, but back in 10th grade, me, Jack, Lou, and Alyssa had a saying: *"Dare to be different—but not like Rakoff."*

Not that they're not nice people, but did I *really* wanna spend time outside of school with Zack Rakoff and Claire Moody? I could just imagine what Jack would say if he heard I was hanging out with them. Only I remembered that me and Jack are no longer friends, and my acting career is the most important thing right now.

So I said, "Fuck yeah, I do!"

Geek #1 and Geek #2 gawked at me, all perma-grin.

"We'll get you a script by Christmas," Moody promised.

Rakoff added, "We thoot over Winter Break."

"Bitchin'," I replied.

Where did that *come from?*

Claire looked at me with puppy-dog eyes. "You wanna know what it's about before you sign on?"

"Not really." As long as I got to act, I didn't care what the project was.

"Well, it's called *Faded Flowers,*" Rakoff went on.

Moody interjected, "After the Shreikback song," even though I just got thru telling her I didn't need to know anything else.

"'These eyes are blind, this is a pure thing . . .'" Rakoff started singing. "'These hands I kiss, tragic as anything.'"

I realize he's in Chorale and all, but I didn't need a vocal demo.

"Whatever . . . I said I'll do it."

What the hell is a Shriekback, anyways?

"Mr. Dayton . . . What can I do you for?"

Sure enough, I found Mr. Dell'Olio sitting behind his gray metal desk around the corner in *The Hazel Parker* office. I don't know why, but I expected him to be wearing a PRESS visor and chomping a big cigar. Instead, he chewed a red felt tip, checking over what looked like an article written by one of his staff reporters.

"Would you mind doing me a favor?" I asked, a bit apprehensively, barely using my voice.

Dell tucked the wet pen behind an ear. "Depends on what it is."

I didn't mean to be nosey, yet I couldn't help but notice a few of the black words typed on the white piece of paper: *cops, tickets, smoke.*

There's been a heated debate in the pages of *The Hazel Parker* between the Preppies and the Burn-Outs over whether smoking should be banned on Skid Row. The Preppies being pro, the Burn-Outs con. If you ask me, the whole thing's totally lame. If people wanna kill themselves, why should anybody else give a shit?

"Would you mind writing me a letter of recommendation for my Juilliard application?"

Dell took one look at the forms I held out in front of him, and without the slightest hesitation replied, "You got it . . . When's the audition?"

"Sometime in January." I mentally calculated the number of weeks I had left, realizing it wasn't many. "I gotta go to New York for it and everything."

I caught a glimpse of my reflection in the windowpane separating the main part of the classroom from the back office area, where I assumed Jack was, editing the H-E-double-L outta some reporter's article, if not Claire Moody's. I had on what Pam Klimaszweski calls my poet outfit: black pants, black mock-turtleneck, black cardigan. The second I seen my curls sticking out from beneath my black beret, wilder than ever, I made a note to self: *call Lydia Cardoza about a haircut.*

Dell flipped thru the pages outlining the entire audition procedure. On top of the two monologues, and the letter of recommendation, I had to write a Statement of Purpose, i.e., *Why I Want to Go to Juilliard* by Bradley James Dayton . . . Lord help me!

"This is exciting."

"Totally," I agreed. "Too bad I don't know how I'm gonna afford a plane ticket."

My deadbeat dad still hasn't paid a cent of child support, and with yet another Christmas around the corner, there's no way I can ask Mom for any money. What sucks is no matter how many hours I bust my ass at Big Boy's, I'm barely making any tips. I might seriously have to get a second job over the holiday break. I heard the Gap at Oakland Mall is hiring, but the last thing I wanna do is fold goddamn sweaters all goddamn day.

Dell looked up and smiled. "I'm sure you'll work something out."

I could've sworn I seen him wink.

"Bonne chance!"

Today after French III Independent Study, me and Stacy Gillespie spent ten minutes speaking with Mrs. Carey, even though I don't think she understood a word either of us were *parlez*-ing. 'member what I said before about her major in college being Latin? I got a feeling at this point in time, me and Stacy both *comprendre* more *français* than Mrs. Carey ever will.

I'm guessing she got the part about me going to my audition since she wished me good luck . . . I should probably find out the French translation for "Break a leg!"

"What time's your appointment?" Stacy asks, after we bid Mrs. Carey *"A demain!"*

"Not for another half hour," I answer, "but I wanna get down to the aud a little early to check out the competition."

I decided I *am* gonna read for Scrooge, even though I don't think I'm right for it. I mean, I'm what can be considered boyishly cute, not an old-man-type. But it's acting, right? It's all about transforming yourself into something/somebody you aren't. Besides, I figure that out of the Senior guys, I got the most experience. Dell's gonna wanna cast somebody he knows can handle playing a lead.

"Well, I hope you get a good part."

Stacy stops by somebody's locker, slips a folded-up piece of notebook paper into the slats on the door. It must belong to her boyfriend, Luis Sánchez. His family's Cuban or Puerto Rican or from some Spanish-speaking place. He's very cute with dark hair and dark eyes and skin that always looks tan, and he always dresses super sharp . . . Too bad he's only a Sophomore.

"What are you doing now?" I ask before moseying on my way.

Stacy rolls her eyes and groans. "Shellee Findlay wants me to go to the mall with her, and Jamie Good, and Betsy Sheffield."

"So . . . ?"

"So . . . The last time I hung out with those *cheerleaders*," Stacy spits, "I wanted to kill them!"

Something major must've happened if she's getting this heated. Stacy Gillespie's usually such an easygoing person, I can't imagine what Shellee, Jamie, and Betsy did . . . So I ask her.

Wanna know what she says?

"They called me *Killer.*"

I can't help but laugh, she's sooo fucking cute!

Hard to believe how much Stacy has changed since Sophomore year. When I first met her in French I, she was a Total Punk. She used to sit in the back of Mrs. Carey's class with a can of Aqua Net in one hand and a Bic lighter in the other, trying to set the curtains on fire. She had this haircut that was super short in back and long on top and it stuck up and off to one side. Jack used to say she looked like she got hit on the back of the head with a board.

Looking at her now, all dressed up in a long black skirt with a charcoal gray turtleneck and these gorgeous pearls draped around her neck, Stacy Gillespie has become a mature young woman. In fact, all my friends are growing up. I stopped at 7-Eleven the other day to buy a pack of cigarettes and I ran into Max Wilson . . . I barely recognized him without a single zit on his face.

"Try not to let those cheerleaders get to you," I say, offering my best advice.

"Just to be on the safe side," Stacy replies, "I think I'll get high first."

I wish I had time to join her, but it's off to the auditorium I go!

AUDITIONS IN PROGRESS—DO NOT ENTER

Despite the sign posted on the double doors, I sneak inside, making my way into one of the back rows. My eyes take a moment to adjust, the only light coming from on stage where I look up to find none other than . . . Cute Sophomore Guy.

I see he's chosen to dress for the occasion. Pressed khaki pants worn with a pale blue Polo shirt, perfectly matching his eyes. You should see the way they sparkle. Like sapphires.

Be-stilling my beating heart, I listen as CSG's about to begin his audition.

"What've you got for us today?" Dell asks from his usual spot, front row center.

Sitting beside him must be this semester's Sophomore Student Director, a slightly chubby girl with curly brown hair and glasses who I think I recognize from somewhere.

"I'm gonna be doing a scene from *The Breakfast Club,*" CSG informs Dell and the dozen Drama Queers scattered about the auditorium. Instantly, we perk up since we all love this (and every other) John Hughes movie ever made.

At first, I think CSG means *monologue,* even though he called it a *scene,* since he's probably never acted before. Sure enough, when he begins, I can tell he's totally doing Brian "the Brain," talking about how he doesn't like what he sees when he steps outside himself and looks in. Only he switches character, becoming *both* Claire "the Princess," and Allison "the Basket Case," responding to what he's just said as Brian. Then he goes back to Brian talking about getting an F on his elephant lamp, before becoming Bender "the Criminal," having a back and forth conversation with himself over Trigonometry versus Shop.

If you ask me, it's fucking brilliant!

The entire auditorium is pin-drop silent for one hundred twenty seconds, clinging to CSG's every word. Even I can't take my eyes off him, the kid is sooo fucking cute! There's no denying he's got talent . . . He just better not get *my* part.

Obviously Dell thinks CSG's done a good job, judging from the way he's grinning like a Total Geek. "Take a look at the Scrooge/Cratchit scene, would you?"

All smiles, CSG steps down from the stage to receive the sides from our Sophomore Student Director, who he must know since they're in the same class and all.

Again, I follow his every move.

Nice butt!

I hear him say, "Thanks, Miranda."

That's when I realize that SSD is Alyssa Resnick's younger sister.

One time back when Jack and Alyssa were still going together, me and Luanne stopped by Alyssa's house, to check up on them. The four of us were hanging out upstairs in Alyssa and Miranda's bedroom, and I remember thinking how mature Miranda was—for an 8th grader. Did I mention she reminds me of Liza Minnelli?

"Next!"

Mr. Dell'Olio stands up to stretch, surveying the room for his next victim.

I call out, "That would be me," before making my way down the aisle, and hopping up on stage. Boy, do I feel schlumpy in ripped jeans, my Cure concert T-shirt, and slip-on shoes sans socks!

Note to self: start taking these auditions more seriously.

"Find your light!"

From down below, Dell advises me this.

A few of the older Drama Queers chuckle at my expense. Somehow, I can't help but think Audrey and Tuesday are out there instigating. Ignoring them, I move to my right, feeling the fresnels fall on my face. I take a deep breath, ready to introduce myself the (quote-unquote) professional way Dell recently taught us.

"Hello, my name is Bradley Dayton," I begin, even though everybody already knows this. "My selection is from *Tea and Sympathy* by Robert Anderson, the character of Tom."

Dell reacts with a quick nod of the head, rubbing his chin. "Excellent choice."

After I finished working on my *Brighton Beach* scene with Rob Berger, Dell decided I should find a decent monologue. Not only for this audition, but to have in my back pocket once it comes time to head out into the Real World. He suggested I head downtown to the DPL and see what scripts they got there. He told me I should look for a role I could easily be cast in (age, type, etc.), and even suggested a few different titles.

The second I came across *Tea and Sympathy,* I knew I found the perfect fit.

Here's a brief synopsis . . .

Tom Lee is a 17-year-old student at a boys' prep school in the 1950s. But he's having trouble fitting in with the other guys. They all like sports, talking about girls, and listening to "pop" music. Tom prefers classical, he likes to read, he enjoys *theater*. In general, he seems more comfortable in the company of women . . . Sounds perfect for me!

Of course, all the other guys tease him about liking these things. They call him "Sister Boy," and even Tom's father treats him like a jerk. His jock roommate, Al, is the only one at school who's ever nice to him. Al tells Tom that just because he's different, it doesn't make him a homo.

Enter Laura Reynolds, the sexy young wife of the House Master. It seems that Tom reminds Laura of her first husband, killed in World War II—and possibly also a homo. So she befriends the boy, and eventually falls in love with him . . . I won't spoil the rest, but that's the basic jist.

I don't know if Dell meant to tell me something by suggesting I work on this play, but I'm totally grateful he did. I never connected to a piece more and felt like I was acting less in my life.

Once my two minutes are up, I tell everybody, "Thank you."

"No, thank *you,*" Dell replies. "Another fine performance, Mr. Dayton."

His trusty assisant, Miranda Resnick agrees. "Very nice."

The way she smiles at me, I can tell she remembers who I am . . . I have to make sure I talk to her at some point and find out how Alyssa's doing.

"Do me a favor, would you?" Dell says to me now. "Take a look at the Scrooge/Cratchit scene . . . I'll pair you up with somebody in just a sec."

I jump down from the stage to accept the sides from Miranda.

Giddy, I tell her, "Good to see you," partly because it's true, and partly because I'm about to kick some Thespian butt.

"As they say in showbiz," Dell calls out, "'Time is money.'" Followed by, "Next!"

"Hold your horses!" I hear Audrey Wojczek howl just as I slip into the hall between the auditorium and Choir room to get a little privacy while I look over my lines.

After all of about five seconds, I hear somebody sneak up behind me.

"Hey."

I'm about to turn around and say, *Who the fuck do you think you are, interrupting an artist at work?* Except as I do, I realize the voice belongs to none other than . . . Cute Sophomore Guy!

All I can manage to do is say, "Hey, yourself." Then I just stand there with this totally dumb expression on my face. Same as I did the first time I seen him three days ago.

"Mr. Dell'Olio says he wants us to read together," he informs me, holding up the Scrooge/Cratchit sides.

After we run thru the lines a couple times, Cute Sophomore Guy pays me a compliment. "Nice scene, Brad."

Feeling like a dork, I say, "You, too." Mouth agape, the mind boggles. "I'm sorry . . . What's your name again?"

CSG regards me a moment. "You don't remember me, do you?"

Talk about being totally put on the spot!

I nod like one of them old-fashioned bobblehead doll thingies. "From the other day in the Band room . . . Sure, I do."

This guy is *not* about to let me off the hook. "I mean, from before."

Before when?

I give him a hard look up and down, hoping *I* don't get hard myself in doing so. "Um . . ." Again, blushing!

It looks like he's about to say something, but hesitates. Then he replies, "You were my Band Aide."

I stop to think, so hard I can almost smell wood burning. "At Webb?"

CSG smirks. "Unless you were a Band Aide someplace else."

Okay, now he's definitely flirting.

Why can't I figure out who—?

I look at him again . . . This time directly in the eyes.

No fucking way!

"Richie Tyler?"

The faggy little 7th grader who played flute in Prep Band and carried his books like a *girl* . . . He certainly isn't *little* anymore.

"It's Rich now," he declares proudly, in a voice an octave lower than the one I remember.

Wait till Jack gets a load of this!

To make a long story short . . .

During Freshman year, both me and Jack served as Band Aides to Jessica Clark Putnam of "Friends hold you back" fame. We worshiped the ground she walked on since day one. To be bestowed with the honor of being at Mrs. Putnam's beck and call, I can't convey what that meant.

Jack lucked out and got 2nd hour Varsity Band. Me, I got stuck with 3rd hour Prep, which might as well have been *remedial* as far as talent is concerned, and is where faggy little Richie—I mean, *Rich*—Tyler played flute, and afterwards would carry his books like a girl. You know, clutched tight against his chest, as if some bully was gonna come by and snatch them away.

Well, I don't know how it all started, but soon after the school year began, me and Jack decided to make him our whipping boy for the next nine months. I mean, it's not like we were ever mean to him. We never actually said anything bad about him to his face. Both our moms taught us better than that.

I just think for once in our lives, it felt nice to see somebody running around who was faggier than we were, you know what I mean? I don't even know if Rich knows what went on or how, whenever me and Jack used to mention him in a letter, we'd write his name all cursive-y with little hearts and flowers and rainbows all around it . . . I'd feel like a Total Asshole if he did!

"Nice seeing you again," I say, friendly as can be.

And judging from the feeling down yonder in my nether regions . . .

I mean it.

I Hate Myself for Loving You

"Daylight, spent the night without you
But I've been dreamin' 'bout the lovin' you do . . ."

—Joan Jett & the Blackhearts

"There are no small parts, only small actors."

Wanna know what bugs the shit outta me?

When somebody tells me something they think will make me feel better.

Case in point . . .

The morning after auditions, Mr. Dell'Olio posts the following list on the door outside the auditorium.

A CHRISTMAS CAROL

—CAST—

Ebenezer Scrooge..Rich Tyler
Bob Cratchit ....Brad Dayton
Fred, *Scrooge's nephew* ....Charlie Richardson
Peg, *Fred's wife*.............................Darlene Ellington
Solicitor ....Will Isaacs
Marley's Ghost...Keith Treva

Ghost of Christmas Past..................Audrey Wojczek
Ghost of Christmas Present.......Tuesday Gunderson
Ghost of Christmas Future...................Zack Rakoff
Ebenezer, *the boy*.................................Ron Reynolds
Fan...Michelle Winters
Ebenezer, *the young man*............Charlie Richardson
Fessiwig...Will Isaacs
Mrs. Fessiwig ....Darlene Ellington
Belle...Liza Larson
Mrs. Cratchit ....Clarissa Moody
Peter Cratchit......................................Ron Reynolds
Martha Cratchit..............................Michelle Winters
Tiny Tim ....Billy Paterno

Happy fucking Friday the 13th!

Thank God I made a point to get to school early so I could check the cast list in private. If anybody saw the expression on my face when I discovered Richie—I mean, *Rich*—Tyler's name above mine and next to *my* role, I would've diiieed! I mean, what the hell is Dell thinking? Casting a Sophomore in the lead when he's never acted a day in his life.

What the fuck?

"Mr. Dayton!"

When I enter the auditorium for 5th hour Advanced Drama that afternoon, Dell attempts to greet me with his usual smile and sparkling personality . . . But I ain't having it! In fact, I don't even say as much as hello. Instead, I take a seat in one of the furthest rows away from the stage, and keep my mouth shut the entire class.

"I'm sure most of you saw the *Christmas Carol* cast list on your way in," Dell says, all happy and shit, as if nobody has a right to be irked about anything. "For those of you in the show, congratulations. I think it's going to be a good one."

He tries catching my eye, but I look down at my spiral.

I begin doodling Richie Tyler sucks! Because it's totally true . . . God, I hate him!

Call me a bitch, but what can you expect? Here it is my *Senior* year. I got two chances left to perform on stage at this fucking school, and I'm stuck playing Bob-fucking-Cratchit to Richie-the-fag-Tyler's Ebenezer Scrooge? I don't think so.

I'd be lying if I didn't admit the guy gave a damn good audition, but still . . . Everybody knows you gotta pay your dues.

When I auditioned for my first play during Sophomore year, I didn't get cast as Curly in *Okla-homo!*, even though I was the one with "natur-al-ly curly hair," à la Frieda from *Charlie Brown.* There's no way in hell a Senior like Jake Czyzyk would've settled for second billing below a *Sophomore.*

I don't think I pointed out the final name on the cast list belonging to Billy Paterno, Jack's baby brother. I guess I shouldn't call him a *baby.* He's nine-going-on-ten, which makes me feel sooo old!

I still remember Billy as this chubby little 4-year-old dragging around a Cabbage Patch doll, getting in mine and Jack's way whenever I'd spend the night at their house back in junior high.

When Mr. Dell'Olio told us he wanted to find a real kid to play the part of Tiny Tim, I immediately thought of Billy. Back when me and Jack were still Best Friends, I went with him and his mom and his sister, Jodi, to see Billy in this play called *Stone Soup* over at Longfellow. He played the part of the Narrator and he was totally awesome.

So many Drama Queers just memorize their lines, get up on stage, and say them. Billy Paterno isn't afraid to *act.* Plus he looked sooo cute hobbling around on his tiny Tiny Tim crutch at auditions.

I spend the entire weekend telling everybody who'll listen (my mom, my sisters, my manager at work) about the travesty that's occurred, coming to the conclusion that I am *not* gonna waste my time working on a play I'm barely in . . . Therefore, I Q-U-I-T, quit.

"I'm sorry to hear that."

I don't know what I thought Mr. Dell'Olio would say when I break the news to him on Monday afternoon. I sure as hell hoped he'd put up a fight to keep me in the show. I mean, I didn't expect him to take away Richie's role and give it to me. But how about trying to convince me why I shouldn't walk?

I guess what I wanna know is . . . Why did Dell cast the show the way he did? Does he think I'm not good enough to play the lead? Have I not proven myself in all the other plays I been in? And if he honestly lacks faith in my ability, why's he so gung-ho about recommending me for Juilliard?

"Not every actor can play *every* part," Dell tries explaining when I work up the nerve to confront him. "There are some roles you're going to be right for, and others you're not . . . Because of who you are."

I don't get what he's saying. "Isn't that why they call it acting?"

"Yes, but . . ." He shakes his balding head, totally at a loss. "Rich Tyler's a different *type* than you are."

"But I'm older," I reason. Shouldn't that count for something?

Dell nods. "But Rich is *taller*."

"So . . . ?"

"So on stage, he plays older."

Da-dah da-*fucking*-dah.

Maybe I'm wrong, but I was always under the impression that being an actor means I can be whoever I wanna be. I don't have to settle for being just Bradley James Dayton, 17-year-old gay-boy. I can be a nerd like Seymour Krelborn. Or a cowboy like Will Parker. Or an old man like Ebenezer Scrooge. All thru the magic that is Theatre.

"Besides," Dell concludes, "You know what they say: 'There are no small parts, only small actors.'"

What's that *supposed to mean?*

"There are no small parts, only small actors."

I mean, I know what it means: no role is insignificant, a character wouldn't even be in a play if it wasn't important, be a team player. This I am and have *always* been. I don't need some middle-aged, failed-Off-Off-Broadway-director giving me advice, you know what I mean?

"How do you think *I* feel?"

Ultimately, Audrey is the one who convinces me to stay in the show.

Later that night, I call her up to ask her opinion. I have to give Dell an answer ASAP so he can recast my part if necessary.

"At least you weren't beat out by a *Sophomore,*" I remind her.

Poor Audrey . . . She desperately wanted to play Belle, Young Scrooge's love interest. But once again, Dell decided to go with a blond, namely Liza Larson. Unfortunately, I can totally see where he's coming from. Even in *Mr. Magoo's Christmas Carol,* this is the way it was drawn. Yet another case of typecasting.

All the way across town, I hear Audrey sigh. "Well, if you quit, I quit."

"Please . . . Don't let my humiliation stop you from having fun."

This is what it comes down to: what a loser everybody is gonna think I am when they come see the play in December, and there's me (a Senior) bowing before Richie Tyler (a lowly Sophomore).

Audrey does her best to be the voice of reason.

"It's bad enough my own boyfriend's not doing the play . . ."

Rob's new job flipping ass burgers at Bray's conflicts with rehearsals, and therefore his dad decided making *money* is more important than playing pretend. "You're my Best Friend . . . The least you can do is share in my suffering."

"But Bob Cratchit," I whine. "He's a Total Wuss!"

All the guy does is say, "Yes, Mr. Scrooge," and "No, Mr. Scrooge," with the occasional, "Very good, sir," thrown in for good measure. Plus the last thing I want is Claire Moody playing my wife.

Ever since the day I ran into her and Rakoff in Dell's room, she's constantly bugging me about whether I know if Jack Paterno's gay or not, and what a great scoop it would be for her column in *The Hazel Parker*. I keep telling her she should stick to fashion and leave the investigative reporting to somebody else. Besides, it's none of her fat fucking business!

"Yes, but . . ." Audrey considers my argument a moment, coming up with: "In the Disney version, Mickey Mouse played Bob Cratchit."

I'm like, "So . . . ?"

"So . . . Everybody knows Mickey Mouse is the star of Disney, and even he took a lesser role for the good of the show."

"Yes, but . . ." I consider Audrey's argument a moment, coming up with: "You think *Scrooge* McDuck would get cast as anything less than Ebenezer *Scrooge*?"

I can't believe we're having this conversation.

"Please!" Audrey pleads. "You can't leave me alone with Will Isaacs and Keith Treva."

Notorious for their backstage antics, those two are "trouble with a capital T," as Professor Harold Hill sings in *The Music Man*. Like last year during *The Miracle Worker*, they booby-trapped the set and the poor girl playing Helen Keller almost fell right off the stage into the orchestra pit. Thank God it wasn't a musical or she would've gotten a bassoon up her butt.

"And Tuesday Gunderson," Audrey adds. "I'll fucking kill her!"

This much I know is true.

Despite them being so-called friends, I can tell Audrey can't stand Tuesday. Any day now, she's gonna do something drastic. Like telling her to take a fucking shower. Or at least wash her fucking hair. Lemme tell ya, that girl put the BO in BOD—what we call Student Council here at HPHS, aka Board of Directors.

"Fine . . . I'll do the fucking play," I reluctantly give in. "But the second anything else comes my way," like the opportunity to pick up an extra shift at Big Boy's or God willing, I meet a hot guy at the bar and he asks me out after school, "I'm skipping rehearsal and Dell can deal."

And no matter what, I am *not* being nice to Richie Tyler!

The following Monday . . .

At our first read-thru, The Sophomore comes rushing into the auditorium all hot and sweaty and totally pumped up, after an intense workout during Miss Phelan's 6th hour Gym. Did I mention she may or may not be a lesbian, but who cares because she's totally cool? Back in 10th grade, she used to let me and Jack hang out in her office instead of forcing us to play volleyball or run laps around the track with the rest of our classmates.

"Sorry I'm late," Richie huffs and puffs, totally outta breath.

But does Dell'Olio get pissed and give him the old, *"If you're not fifteen minutes early, you're late"* spiel that he got from his playwright friend in New York, David Mamet?

N-O!

He simply says, "That's okay, Rich . . . We were just about to get started."

In actuality, the entire cast had already assembled on stage in a circle of chairs, filled out our contact sheets, and finished hilighting the scripts given to us by our SSD, Miranda Resnick.

"Have a seat next to Brad," she tells Richie, indicating the empty metal folding chair on my right.

He plops down beside me. "Hey, Brad . . . What's up?"

Doe he *really* have to lift up his shirt, exposing his happy trail, in order to wipe the sweat from his upper lip? And what's he doing wearing a fucking tank top in the middle of November? How about putting on some real clothes?

Jesus!

For the next week, I do everything in my power *not* to so much as look at Richie, let alone talk to him. If it's not Bob Cratchit interacting with Ebenezer Scrooge, I want nothing to do with the boy.

Even if we're taking a break between scenes and he says something like, "Nice sweater . . . It totally matches your eyes," all I do is accept his compliment, but pay him none in return. No matter how hot his ass looks in his new Girbaud jeans!

It doesn't take long for The Sophomore to get the hint that I'm a little peeved.

"Are you pissed at me?"

The day before Thanksgiving Break is about to begin, he corners me backstage by The Cage. There's literally this caged-in area stage left with this totally ancient light board with all sorts of switches and giant levers, like something outta *Young Frankenstein*. Every time I'm back there I just wanna scream, *"It's alive!"*

"Not at all," I lie, avoiding Richie's piercing blue gaze. "I'm just wiped."

We spent the last hour working on the final "God bless us, every one!" scene, and having the entire cast up on stage at the same time can be totally chaotic.

"Well, that's good to know . . ."

"What?" I ask, suspecting something's up.

"Oh, nothing . . ."

"What?" I repeat. "Tell me."

The Sophomore flashes me a devilishly dimpled grin. "Audrey

invited me to come with you guys to the parade," he confesses. "I wanna make sure you don't mind."

Audrey what?

A few weeks ago, Audrey and Rob, Ava and Don, and Carrie and Curt decided they wanna go downtown to see the Hudson's Thanksgiving Day parade. Of course, I felt a tad envious. My dad used to take me and my sisters all the time when we were little, and I haven't been since like 1982.

"You can totally come with," Aud assured me.

Despite Ava and Carrie both saying they're just friends with Don Olsewski and Curt Chaplin, I'm not stupid. The whole thing sounded like a triple date to me and I wasn't about to crash.

I politely thanked her for the invite. "I am *not* gonna be your seventh wheel."

She was like, "So bring somebody."

And I was like, "Somebody who?"

"I don't know . . . There's gotta be *somebody* you like!"

Right off, I noticed Audrey didn't say, *some* girl *you like.*

This was fine.

Like I said, my plan is to eventually tell her about me. If she figures it out first and I don't have to say anything, I'm not gonna complain. But who the hell was I gonna bring to the parade as my so-called date?

Looks like Audrey went and decided for me.

"Thanks a lot!"

On the way out to my car after rehearsal Wednesday evening, I'm totally pissed.

"It's for your own good," she insists, sounding more like my mother than one of my Best Friends.

Digging thru my pocket for my keys, I pray my piece-of-shit car will start in this cold. It's not even 6:00 PM and it's already totally dark outside. Did I mention how much I hate it whenever we *fall back* in the fall?

Audrey shivers audibly. "Just hurry up and open the goddamn door!"

I do as ordered, and we crawl inside.

I jam the key in the dashboard ignition. Thankfully the engine turns over.

"Oh, my God . . . I love this song!"

I turn on the radio, hearing one of my new favorite tunes: "Cow Cow Boogie" by The Judds.

Audrey gives me a look like I'm outta my mind. "Since when do you like Country?"

"Since my mom's from Alabama," I answer, cranking it and singing along. *"Comma ti yi yi yeah . . ."*

Ever since me and my sisters were little, Mom's always listened to WCXI and W4. Tammy Wynette, Dolly Parton, June Carter Cash. These are the songstresses we were reared on. Sure, I love Cyndi Lauper, but nobody sings a better story than Loretta Lynn. I can't even remember how many times I seen *Coal Miner's Daughter.*

Audrey reaches across the dash, lowering the volume. "How about some heat, for chris'sakes?"

"It's broke," I apologize. What can you expect when your car's two years *older* than you are?

Audrey pulls her hood up over her head in a huff. "Your scenes are only gonna suffer."

"Comma ti yippity yi yeah . . ." I continue crooning. "What scenes?"

"Would you focus here?" she demands. "Your Scrooge/Cratchit scenes!"

The one good thing about staying at school late for rehearsal is *not* having to deal with traffic in the back parking lot. Pedal to the metal, I pull out onto Felker in a squeal of steel-belted rubber.

"They are *not* gonna suffer."

Audrey rolls her eyes. "If you keep on hating The Sophomore, they will."

I say, "Bob Cratchit hates Scrooge," staring out my driver's side window. No smokers out on Skid Row at this hour.

This reminds me . . . I lean forward to push in the lighter.

"He does not," Audrey insists, again sounding just like my mom.

Whatever . . .

The second I'm about to light my cig, the B-I-T-C-H snatches it from between my lips.

"Listen to me, Dayton . . . I'm in this goddamn play, too, you know? I'm not about to let it turn into a piece of shit," she hisses, "just because you got a bug up your ass!"

I totally scoff at what I'm hearing. "I don't have any bug up my ass . . ."

Do I?

Thanksgiving Day morning . . .

First of all, it's fucking fuh-reezing.

Thirty-two degrees and a light snow.

Time to break out the long johns!

One thing I don't remember from when we were little is getting up at the butt crack of dawn just to find a place to watch the parade. It doesn't even start till 10:00 AM, but by the time we get downtown around 8:30 AM, there's already a ton of people lined up along Woodward eagerly anticipating Santa's arrival.

"Coffee," I mutter thru clenched teeth. "Must . . . have . . ."

"You wanna go and get some?" asks Richie, the only one who seems to care about my frostbit fingertips.

"Nah."

I'd hate to lose our perfect spot in front of the DIA or risk having Richie think I'm not still pissed at him . . . Because I am.

"Now what?" The Sophomore asks after about all of a second of standing around.

Time for a smoke!

"We wait," answers Ava, still half asleep.

Struggling to fish out a fresh cigarette, I take note that for the first time, Ava is actually *not* twirling her hair. Instead, she's got her hands buried deep in the pockets of her Viking Marching Band Varsity jacket, complete with Drum Major embroidered across the back.

Carrie asks Richie, "Haven't you ever been to the Thanksgiving Day parade before?"

I'm just about to rip off my gloves when Richie palms my pack of Marlboro Lights.

"Smoking kills, you know?"

I know. "But it sure tastes good . . ."

Giving up, he extracts a cig, slips it between my lips, and flicks my Bic.

Ahhh . . . Nothing like your third cigarette of the day at only 9:00 AM!

Richie winces, batting his baby blues. "I could never kiss a smoker."

I'll keep that in mind.

"Hey, can I bum one of them?" asks Don Olsewski, helping himself to my stash.

Audrey chimes in, "Me too, me too."

I'm like, "Get your own, people!"

As they take turns blazing up, Richie wonders, "Does *everybody* smoke?"

For the first time in a while, I can't help but notice he sounds a little faggy . . . But he's still cute as fuck!

"Not me," Carrie answers, disgusted. "Smoking is g-ross!" She gives Curt a glance that says, *Don't even* think *about starting!*

Ava says, "We're in Band," in case we all forgot. "We can't afford to go polluting our lungs." She looks at Don.

He grins, taking a good long drag. "That's why I play drums."

"I'm a Flaggot," Audrey reminds us. "My lungs got nothing to do with twirling."

By the time the festivities kick off, I can barely feel my feet. I knew I should've worn my snow boots! Instead, here I am looking all stylish in my brown faux-leather deck shoes sans socks.

"Brrr!" I tremble. "Fucking Michigan weather."

"Body heat," I hear somebody mutter.

When I look over, Audrey and Rob, Ava and Don, and Carrie and Curt are all paired off in couples, huddled together keeping each other toasty. Meanwhile, me and Richie stand shivering like that girl Karen from *Frosty the Snowman* before they finally find that greenhouse . . . 'member? Karen's sneezing her head off, so Frosty takes her inside to get warmed up, but then that mean old "messy, messy, messy" magician, Professor Hinkle, comes along, closes the door, trapping them in. Leaving poor Frosty to piddle away into a puddle. Until Santa shows up on his sleigh all "ho, ho, ho" and saves the day.

Finally, I'm like, *Fuck it!* Next thing I know, me and The Sophomore are clinging to each other like Saran Wrap on leftovers . . . He smells fucking delicious!

"What are you wearing?" I ask, attempting to sound oh-so nonchalant.

"Cologne," he states, staring straight ahead as the NBD float floats by. "Drakkar Noir . . . Does it stink?"

"On the contrary," I disagree, blushing.

Richie gives me a look like I'm outta my mind. "Who the fuck says 'contrary'?"

Oh, my God . . . He's totally flirting with me!

Well, I am *not* gonna fall for it.

Like I said, I hate Richie Tyler.

Don't I?

If that's the case, why do I find myself writing him the following note the following evening?

November 28, 1987

Hey Rich,

What's up? Not much here. It's Saturday night and I just got home from work. I'm smoking a cig (sorry!) in my room and trying to relax.

How was the rest of your Thanksgiving? After the parade, I went to my Grandma's for dinner in Highland Park. All in all it was an okay time. I ate a shitload of turkey, yams (yum!), cranberry sauce, green bean casarole, and pumpkin pie. I thought for sure I was totally gonna puke!

Thank God I finally got a day off tomorrow. I'm thinking about going to see "Dirty Dancing" up at the Berkley. I hear it's pretty good. It's got that guy from "North and South" (mini-series) and the chick from "Ferris Beuller's Day Off." The one who played the sister with the schnoz. It's only $1.50. Give me a call if you want to come.

Brad
398-5836

Before I can change my mind, I get in my car and drive the almost two miles over to the Tyler's house on Brickley, two blocks south of 10 Mile and two blocks over from where the Paternos live on Shevlin. Only on the opposite side of John R.

What the hell am I doing?

When I see Burgers & Kreme on the corner, I almost do a U-y right in the middle of the two-lane road.

It's only a fucking letter, Bradley.

I write them to my friends all the time. No biggie!

Except if that's how I *really* feel, why do I start freaking out the second I slip the sealed envelope inside the Tyler's mailbox?

Oh, my God . . . I just asked The Sophomore out on a date!

I Think We're Alone Now

"Look at the way
We gotta hide what we're doin' . . ."

—Tiffany

"Strawberry waffle."

Have you ever seen the episode of *Laverne & Shirley* where Lenny hires L & S to run the greasy spoon diner he inherits from his dead Uncle Laslo, and he and Squiggy rename it *Dead Laslo's Place*? Only for whatever reason, Laverne (the cook) takes to calling Shirley (the waitress) by the name *Betty*.

It all starts when Miss DeFazio's manning the grill. She's cracking eggs onto it, and throwing the shells over her shoulder, all the while wearing this white poufy chef's hat. Every time she gets an order, Laverne leans over and talks into this silver microphone attached to this bendy microphone stand-thingie.

"Betty, please . . ."

She drones this over and over, till finally Shirley's like, "Why are you calling me *Betty*?"

And Laverne's like, "I don't know . . . Betty sounds so much better than *Shirl*."

Well, eventually the place becomes packed. Laverne's in the kitchen, boiling spaghetti and flinging it against the wall before drenching it in ketchup. Out front, Shirley's bopping between tables taking orders from a gang of bikers. When she gets one for chicken tetrazzini, Laverne doesn't know how the hell to make it, and ends up cramming an entire plucked *poulet* into a pot!

But the *pièce de résistance* has gotta be the pancakes.

Not realizing what she's done, Laverne douses the entire grill with batter. She leans over into the mic and croaks, "Lucky, lucky, lucky . . . For the next ten minutes, everything comes with *free* pancakes."

Meanwhile, the male customers start groping Shirley. She's screeching and screaming, and getting totally pissed because everybody keeps calling her Betty—including Laverne, who uses a dustpan to flip the flapjacks prior to loading Shirl down with a dozen plates, shoving one directly in her mouth.

One by one, the natives get restless. They're banging on the tables, brutally chanting, *"Betty . . . Betty . . . Betty."* Until finally Laverne gets on the horn and begs them, "Please don't harass Betty, please."

Now for my point . . .

At Big Boy's, we have a similar microphone system, complete with bendy microphone stand-thingie. Whenever I have to use it, I can't help but think of Penny Marshall as I call out my order to Tony (the cook) in the kitchen.

"Strawberry waffle."

Picture a guy with fat forearms, wiry whiskers, two teeth in his head, and you'll get Tony. I'm sure he's got a MOM tattoo somewhere. Lemme tell ya, the guy thinks he's Mel Sharples from *Alice.* All he needs is the beanie. Any day now I expect him to bang the bell with his spatula and shout out, "Dingy!"

Plopping a side of fries onto a plate, Tony bellows, "Couldn't hear ya!"

Oops! I forgot to hit the ON switch.

So I repeat the order, using my best stage speech. "Strawberry waf-fle."

The menu may read: *Our scrumptious Belgian waffle made with farm fresh eggs, served with succulent strawberries and creamy whipped topping*. But when you boil it down, *strawberry waffle* says it all.

"Somebody sure could use a drink."

Around 7:00 PM, me and my manager, Shir, pop into the back room to take our break together.

I ask, "You or me?" thinking how fun it would be to knock back a few fuzzy navels right about now.

All day at work I haven't been able to concentrate. Richie's parents went to Chicago for the weekend to bowl in some tournament. So he invited me to spend the night.

"What are we gonna do?"

This I asked him yesterday when he asked me yet again if we were still on for our Saturday sleepover.

"I don't know," he replied sheepishly. "Play pool, watch a movie, hang out."

I been giving The Sophomore a ride home from play rehearsal since the Monday after Thanksgiving, two weeks ago. I figured it was the least I could do to pay him back for keeping me from freezing my ass off at the parade. Plus I feel terrible for being such a jerk to him these past few weeks. It's not Richie's fault that Mr. Dell'Olio gave him *my* part in the play, you know what I mean?

By the way, we didn't end up going to see *Dirty Dancing*. Nobody in Richie's family bothered to check the mailbox because it was a Sunday, so he didn't even get my letter till that Monday *after* he got home from school.

"I gotta work till ten."

I reminded him this, thinking it might be too late to play pool, watch a movie, and hang out by the time I finally got over his house.

Richie replied, "So . . . ? I'll be here all by my lonesome waiting for you." Did I mention he looked totally cute all bundled up like an Eskimo about to brave the December cold?

Like me, The Sophomore's got three sisters, but his are all older and either married or moved out. He claimed it'll be a Total Blast having the whole house to ourselves. I think he's a Total Baby and is terrified of staying home alone.

"Sounds cool."

This I concluded after realizing I been wanting to see what the inside of Richie's house looks like and not just the front.

Back in the Big Boy's break room . . .

"Fuck!"

I fish into my shirt pocket, and discover I'm totally outta cigarettes.

"Have one of mine," Shir offers, extending her half-full pack in my direction.

Normally, I admire the fact that she partakes in the Virginia Slim Menthol Light 120. 'member, I had those exact same ones (minus the menthol) on Halloween night when I dressed up as Columbia and went to see *Rocky Horror*? But right now, I can't bear the thought of accepting such a girlie gift. Instead, I get a pop from the vending machine.

Shir lights her smoke and takes a seat. "Somebody's got something on their mind."

Sure enough, Shir is right.

All evening I been wondering what is gonna happen once I get over Richie's. I mean, I won't assume anything will happen, but let's face it . . . Why is he so keen on having me spend the night at his house while his parents are away if he doesn't have something planned?

Tempted as I am to bear my soul to Shir about my man troubles, I decide I'd rather not get into the whole Richie thing.

As all *"To thine ownself be true"* as I'm trying to be, I still haven't told anybody I work with that I'm gay. Not even Shir, who's like my second mom. I mean, I know she'd totally be cool with it. I just haven't found the right time, and refilling the Heinz 57 bottles with Del Monte at Big Boy's certainly isn't the right place. Besides, I don't even know if there *is* a whole Richie thing to get into.

Looks like I'm about to find out . . .

Ka-thunk!

The second the time clock strikes 10:00 PM, I punch my card. As quickly as I can, I make my way to the men's room where I wash my pits, put on some Speed Stick spice, and a splash of Lagerfeld. Next, I change outta my black-and-white waiter uniform into a pair of Downy-fresh Guess? jeans, along with my new favorite Gap sweater. Did I mention I applied for a part-time/over-the-holidays job after all?

Wish me luck getting it because I am B-R-O-K-E!

Nauseous is the word to describe the feeling I feel fumbling with my keys out in the parking lot, trying to open my car door. I don't know why I bother locking it, the piece of shit!

"Sorry, Val."

Once inside, I apologize. Nope, nobody's with me riding shotgun. Val is what I call my car—short for *Valiant*, get it? Originally I thought about calling it Prince, as in *Prince Valiant*, but I feel that she's a girl. Plus people might think I'm talking about Prince, as in *The Revolution*, and get confused.

Truth be told, Val's a bit temperamental, but what can you expect? She's almost twenty years old! In the months we been together, I found she responds better when I give her a little love and affection. And if I wanna make it the almost-mile over to Richie's, I know I better treat her right.

Pulling outta the Big Boy's parking lot, I cut across the I-75 overpass before making a "Louie" on the northbound Chrysler service drive, taking me past the Holiday Inn. I can't believe I lived in Hazel Park/Ferndale my entire life, and the first time I set foot in the joint was just last year. "Call me Hal" booked a Chorale gig in the banquet room for some club of some kind—Elks, K of C, Kiwanis, maybe? I don't know what I was expecting, but it sure as hell wasn't fancy.

At the 9 Mile stoplight, I think of Jack. Probably because of the Farmer *Jack's* on the corner where his dad works. The other day, my mom made me run in to pick up some milk, and I totally avoided cutting thru the Produce department just in case Mr. Paterno might happen to be chopping broccoli or something. I don't know what I was afraid of. It's not like Jack's dad is gonna be rude just because me and his son are no longer friends, you know what I mean?

In a way, I sorta hoped I *would* see Mr. Paterno. If I did, I could've inquired as to how Jack is doing. Last I heard he's been hanging out with Betsy Sheffield and Tom Fulton in all his free time.

Whatever . . .

Knock knock!

I guess I should've called first before coming over The Sophomore's, but I didn't wanna waste any more time than I already did fucking around with my hair in the bathroom. I swear every time I take a shower, the drain is more and more filled with my locks. Lemme tell ya, the day I go bald, I'm shaving my head.

Peeking thru the tiny cut-out window in the Tyler's front door, I see a cozy room, complete with couch and matching love seat. A leather La-Z-Boy rests in one corner, a Windsor rocker in the other. Except for the light coming from a small lamp on the table between the two, the house looks dark.

Great!

I bet Richie got sick of waiting for me and decided to go to bed . . . So much for our sleepover!

This time I ring the bell.

Ding dong!

Thru the archway separating the family and dining rooms, I catch a flash of something furry leaping from the pedestal table onto the oval-ringed rug below.

I coo, "Kitty-Kitty," thinking that the Tylers' cat might actually open the front door and let me inside.

Wanna know what the stupid Siamese does?

She (he?) sits there in the middle of the floor, licking her/himself inappropriately.

"Go tell Richie that Brad's here," I whisper, not wanting to wake him, but also not giving up the fight just yet.

The cat turns and bolts in the direction from whence it came.

Down the block, bright headlights from a passing car. I'm sure I look totally suspicious standing on the Tylers' porch, peering inside. It's only a matter of minutes before the HP PD will arrive to arrest me for B & E, you know what I mean?

In the words of Shellee *What's up, Fox?* Findlay: Looks like I won't be "getting some gravy" anytime soon.

Jesus!

From outta nowhere, a face pops into frame, scaring the bejesus outta me.

"It's about time . . ."

Richie flings open the front door, giving me a heart attack—and a hard-on.

'member how much I'm into bare ankles? There he stands in nothing but a skimpy pair of Champion short-shorts. His practically hairless legs lead down to white Adidas hi-tops worn with matching footies.

"I thought you were never gonna get here," says The Sophomore, beckoning me inside.

I explain what a nightmare my entire day has been, and how it took me forever to get the fuck outta Big Boy's and over here. "Sorry . . ."

"That's okay," he replies. "I just didn't hear the door . . . I was downstairs lifting weights."

As if the sweat dripping down your totally bare-chested bod didn't tip me off!

Richie leads the way thru the family room, dining room, and kitchen to the basement where he's got a black aluminum weight bench set up. A plethora of plastic donuts in various sizes clutters the carpeted floor. From a boom box sitting atop the billiards table, I recognize the voice of former Wham! front man, George Michael, belting out one of my new favorite tunes.

"I swear I won't tease you
Won't tell you no lies . . ."

Richie picks up a dumbbell, plops down on the bench. Holding the weight in one hand, he lets his forearm rest against his meaty thigh, proceeding to crank out a set of twenty reps. Meanwhile, I try not to gawk at the blue vein bulging from the center of his bicep. Lemme tell ya, for somebody I once considered to be *thin,* Richie is pretty ripped.

"You look like you could use a drink," he observes.

Thinking I couldn't agree more, I reply, "What've you got?"

Continuing his silent count, Richie jerks his head towards the far end of the room.

An assortment of bottles and other paraphernalia adorn the counter top: a set of frosted *"Down the hatch!"* shot glasses, a miniature street lamp with the word BAR printed across its globe, a strong man sporting a handlebar mustache and a red one-piece bathing suit holding up a pint of Beefeater. On the brick wall behind, a framed mirror advertising Stroh's as *America's only Fire-Brewed Beer.*

Let's see . . . Vodka. Rum. Whiskey. All the Usual Suspects.

Something in a Mrs. Butterworth's-shaped bottle looks interesting: *Frangelico.*

I read the story of its legend printed in Olde English on the label. Something about some guy living three centuries ago in a hilly area by the right bank of some river. So long as it tastes sweet, and it does (like hazelnuts), that's all I care about.

"I need a beer," says The Sophomore, toweling himself off. Much to my chagrin, he throws on a "Who's that Girl?" '87 World Tour concert T-shirt and some sweats.

"Oh, my God. . . . Did you see Madonna at the Silver Dome?" I gush.

"Fifth row center," he boasts, reaching into the circa 1950s Frigidaire for a bottle of Black Label . . . Bogue!

Lucky bastard. I been dying to see Motown's own Material Girl since the tour of the same name in '85, but still haven't had a chance.

Richie lets out an *"Ahhh!"* like his hops totally hit the spot.

Personally, I don't know how anybody can stand that shit! Whenever I used to hang out with Jack and Max back in the day, that's all they ever wanted to drink. Me, I always preferred sloe gin and orange juice. Or at least 7-Up.

Richie calls me, "Sloe poke," sipping my *liqueur* from a snifter. "Wanna see what's on cable?"

The Tylers' basement isn't exactly what you'd call *finished,* with exposed beams on the walls and ceiling overhead. Past the pool table, there's a color-console TV, sorta like the one the Paternos have downstairs at their house, with a tan two-seater sofa in front.

Richie's dad works for Chrysler's so they got all the movie

channels: HBO, Showtime, Cinemax. To be honest, I don't care what we watch so long as we're sitting side by side as we flip thru the stations.

"Oooh . . . What's this?"

The Sophomore stops on a scene of a woman getting banged from behind in what looks like an English country garden. I immediately recognize it as *Young Lady Chatterly Two,* starring some chick whose name I don't remember, and "Nick the Dick" from *Bachelor Party.*

'member the scene where Tom Hanks's fiancée and all her girlfriends, including fat Wendie Jo What's-Her-Face from *Bosom Buddies,* go to that Chippendales-style strip club for their bachelorette party, and Tom and his all friends sneak in and pay the totally hot waiter to sandwich his schwantz between those hot dog buns? That's the guy I'm talking about.

Me and Jack used to watch *YLC2* whenever I spent the night at his house back in junior high and they were showing it on Skinemax. If I remember correctly, the premise has something to do with Young Lady Chatterly II feeling neglected by her husband, so she seeks love and affection elsewhere. In this particular scene, she finds it with her Cockney-accented gardener, Thomas. Talk about a Total Babe! Lemme tell ya, I passed many a moment fantasizing about this guy, you know what I mean?

Stemming from the fact that I'm totally wasted (and totally horny) off two sips of Frangelico, I ask Richie, "If you were a *girl,* would you think that guy's hot?"

He turns to look me directly in the eyes. "Why would I have to be a girl?" Then he says, "What about you? Would you think he's hot if *you* were a girl?"

I hesitate. "I asked you first."

Richie pulls me into a headlock, quoting *The Breakfast Club:* "'Just answer the question, Claire.'"

In my mind, I hear Miss Horchik: *"To thine ownself be true."*

Looking up at him, head in his lap, I confess, "I totally would."

The Sophomore responds, "I thought so," a shit-eating grin gracing his gorgeous face.

What's that *supposed to mean*?

Hungry Eyes

"I've been meaning to tell you
I've got this feelin' that won't subside . . ."

—Eric Carmen

"Another openin', another show . . ."

Only this one's right here in good old Hazeltucky. Not "in Philly, Boston, or Baltimo'."

That's a reference from *Kiss Me Kate,* a factoid I wasn't privy to till earlier this year when Mr. Fish forced us to sing a *schmedley* of show tunes featuring such classics as:

"The Sound of Music" from *The Sound of Music.*

"Fiddler on the Roof" from *Fiddler on the Roof.*

And "Camel-cock"—I mean, *"Camelot"*—from *Camelot.*

Every time we got to "Anything Goes," from (what else?) *Anything Goes,* Hal would be all like, "Give it up for La Merm!" All the while wiping his pits with his sweaty sweat rag . . . Bogue!

After about the bijillionth time, we were like, *"Who?"*

Of course, Hal looked at us like we were all on drugs, and

not just the Burn-Outs. "Don't tell me you kids don't know Ethel Merman?"

Soon as I heard the name, it called to mind my favorite episode from *The Love Boat.* 'member the one where Julie's aunt, Doc's ex-mother-in-law, Isaac's mom, and Gopher's mom come aboard the *Pacific Princess* to perform in a musical revue? Except each one of the old bags thinks *she's* the star of the show. So backstage, it's nothing but barbs and diva fits the entire time they're together.

Well, it turns out Julie's aunt was played by Carol Channing, the original Dolly in *Hello, Dolly!,* Doc's ex-mother-in-law was Ann Miller, star of some Broadway show, *Sugar Babies,* with Mickey Rooney, Isaac's mom was Della Reese, a native Detroit gospel singer, and Gopher's mom was none other than . . . Ethel "Everything's Coming Up Roses" Merman.

Anyways!

Tonight is Opening Night of *A Christmas Carol,* adapted by Lynn Stevens, based on the novel by Charles Dickens. The tension backstage is cut-it-with-a-knife thick. It's been that way with each and every play I acted in since second semester Sophomore year. Picture a bunch of Dickensian-dressed Thespians running around exclaiming, "My lines, my lines . . . I can't remember my lines!" from the old Detroit Zoo commercial . . . 'member?

"Next!"

In addition to serving as Sophomore Student Director, Miranda Resnick graciously offered to help us with hair and makeup at each performance.

"Try not to make me look too old," Richie begs Madame Artiste.

"You're playing *Scrooge,* aren't you?"

"I know . . ."

"Well, Scrooge is an old dude," Miranda reminds her victim.

The Sophomore sighs. "I know . . ."

I can totally see where the guy's coming from. Call me vain, but no matter what part I'm playing, I still wanna look attractive. And I totally think I do in my 19th century waistcoat and ascot. At least one good thing came out of not being cast as Scrooge.

I can't tell you how glamorous I feel surrounded by all the lights, sitting at the makeup counter, waiting my turn while perusing the program—I mean, *TheatreGoer.* Who the fuck ever decided to name it that?

Time to check out the bios . . .

Oh, look who's first!

BRAD DAYTON *(Bob Cratchit)* is no stranger to the HPHS stage. Previous roles include Will Parker in *Oklahoma!,* Seymour in *Little Shop of Horrors,* and James Keller in *The Miracle Worker.* A Senior, Brad is President of Thespian Troupe #4443, 1st chair trombone in Wind Ensemble, and a member of Chorale. He dedicates his performance to his mom, Laura.

DARLENE ELLINGTON *(Peg, Mrs. Fessiwig)* is a Sophomore. She plays JV tennis and is making her stage debut in *A Christmas Carol.* "Thanks, Dell!"

TUESDAY GUNDERSON *(Ghost of Christmas Present)* made her acting debut in 4th grade as the Narrator of "Casey at the Bat." HPHS roles include Gertie Cummings in *Oklahoma!,* a blind girl in *The Miracle Worker,* and Mrs. Luce in *Little Shop of Horrors.* She is a Senior member of Chorale and Flag Corps, and serves as Treasurer of Thespian Troupe #4443. "Pasquale's!"

After Opening Night of every show, the Drama Queers always end up at Big Boy's, something they been doing since long before I ever became one. I don't know why, but all thru *A*

Christmas Carol rehearsals, Tuesday's been bugging us to try some new place up on 13 Mile and Woodward.

Well, we ain't going to Pasquale's, Gunderson . . . So get over it!

WILL ISAACS *(Fessiwig)* is a Junior. He plays trombone in Wind Ensemble, and sings bass in Chorale. Last year he played Dr. Anagnos in *The Miracle Worker.* He is a proud member of Thespian Troupe #4443. "Bang your head!"

LIZA LARSON *(Belle)* has been singing since age five and playing piano since age nine. She is happiest when performing on the HPHS stage. Past roles include Audrey in *Little Shop of Horrors.* Liza is a Senior member of Chorale and plays flute in Wind Ensemble. "For Gus."

Liza's been going with the same guy since like 7th grade at Beecher. I don't *really* know him, but Gus graduated from HPHS in '86 with my sister, Janelle. He seems totally cool, and Liza dedicates every song she ever sings in Chorale to him. I'm sure they'll eventually end up married with a kid, if not several.

CLARISSA MOODY *(Mrs. Cratchit)* appeared as Anne Sullivan in the HPHS production of *The Miracle Worker.* She also served as Sophomore Student Director on *Oklahoma!* She is co-captain of Flag Corps, Secretary of Thespian Troupe #4443, and writes her own column, "Fashion Faux Pas," in *The Hazel Parker.* Clarissa is thrilled to be graduating from HPHS this June. She plans to pursue a career in Journalism. "Spiffy!"

BILLY PATERNO *(Tiny Tim)* is a 4th grader at Longfellow School. He enjoys acting, singing, playing *Star Wars, Transformers,* and chess. "For Mom, Dad, Jackie, and Jodi."

ZACHARY RAKOFF *(Solicitor, Ghost of Christmas Future)* has no idea how he got talked into being in this play! He is a Senior member of Flag Corps, Thespian Troupe #4443, and he plays piccolo in Wind Ensemble. Someday he hopes to make the big bucks selling a screenplay to Hollywood. "Thanks for the mayonnaise cake, Mom!"

Okay, here's the story . . .

Back when we were in 7th grade Enriched English & Social Studies with Ms. Lemieux, we had a Christmas party. Well, Rakoff decided he wanted to make his mom's special mayonnaise cake. Only instead of actually asking her for the recipe, he bought a box of Duncan Hines and added Hellman's to it . . . Talk about bogue!

RON REYNOLDS *(Ebenezer, the boy, Peter Cratchit)* is a Sophomore. *A Christmas Carol* is his first play. He hopes to join Thespian Troupe #4443 in the spring if he's invited. "Thanks, Dell!"

CHARLIE RICHARDSON *(Fred, Ebenezer, the young man)* returns to the HPHS stage after playing Bobby Embrey in *The Skeleton Walks,* a bum in *Little Shop of Horrors,* Percy in *The Miracle Worker,* and Ike Skidmore in *Oklahoma!* He is a Senior member of Chorale, and Thespian Troupe #4443. "I know you are, but what am I!"

KEITH TREVA *(Marley's Ghost)* is a Junior. He sings baritone in Chorale, plays JV basketball, and is a member of Thespian Troupe #4443. One day he hopes to become a professional actor and change his name to Frank Booth. "For Debbie!"

When I turn to the next page, what I see there totally warms my heart . . .

RICH TYLER (*Ebenezer Scrooge)* is proud to be making his HPHS stage debut in *A Christmas Carol.* A Sophomore, he enjoys playing alto sax in Symphony Band, singing with Varsity Choir, and lifting weights. "To B. Thanks for showing me the ropes!"

I didn't know The Sophomore was gonna mention me in his bio.

The question is *why*?

It's not like I did something special and he owes me. So I took him under my wing, and taught him the difference between stage left and stage right. No biggie!

To be honest, I can't figure out what's up with this kid.

All week I been thinking about what he said to me last Saturday night: *"I thought so."*

Obviously he wasn't surprised when I all but admitted I'm a Total Fag, but it's not like he said he *cared*. And he sure as hell didn't say he's a Total Fag, too! In fact, he just changed the channel and sat there sipping his beer.

Until finally I was like, "I'm tired," totally faking a yawn.

"You wanna go to bed?" Richie asked, not taking his eyes off Whitney Houston dancing about the screen looking for somebody who loves her . . . Is it just me or is the hair she's sporting in that video totally a wig?

"Where am I sleeping?" I wondered.

"Upstairs."

We climbed the steps leading to The Sophomore's room.

"Upstairs where?"

"Where do you think?"

Okay . . .

At first, I thought maybe Richie had bunk beds, the way Jack used to at his house. This was *not* the case. Once we got up to his U of M shrine, I seen a single twin bed.

"We both can't fit on that thing," I decided, not wanting to put him out. "I'll sleep on the couch."

He insisted, "There's plenty of room," giving me a sly look. "I won't bite you."

What if I want *you to?*

The Sophomore stripped down to his short-shorts.

I was about to get undressed myself. Until he started doing push-ups.

The knobs of his shoulder blades.

The curve of his lats.

The hollow of his spine spilling down to his . . .

"Be right back."

I realized I should excuse myself to the bathroom. Not because I'm shy or anything, but . . .

"What's-a matter?" Richie jumped to his feet, huffing. "You got a hard-on or something?"

How the hell did he know?

Needless to say, I didn't get a whole lotta sleep that night laying in bed beside him. And not just because I was smashed up against the wall with his ass in my side!

Back in the HPHS dressing room . . .

"What are *you* staring at?"

Richie totally catches me gawking.

"Nothing," I lie, thinking how totally fucked up this situation is . . . And how hot the tops of his pecs look poking out from his V-neck undershirt.

"Just sit there and read your program," Richie teases. "And keep quiet."

"Fuck you!" I spit, totally sarcastic.

He responds, "'No, Dad . . . What about you?'", à la Judd Nelson, and we both burst into hysterics.

"Hey, hey, hey!"

For a second, it's like we forgot there's somebody else here in the room with us.

"Sorry."

Miranda stares down her nose over the top of her tortoise-shell frames. "Time is money," she spouts, even though nobody's being paid anything to be here.

Richie's eyes meet mine.

Those beautiful blue eyes!

Like a game, we hold our gaze.

Why is he teasing me like this?

With Miranda here, the last thing I wanna do is sprout wood.

I can't take it anymore!

Immediately, I focus my attention back to my program—I mean, *TheatreGoer.*

MICHELLE WINTERS *(Fan, Martha Cratchit)* is a Sophomore, making her stage debut. She sings soprano in Varsity Choir and plays flute in Symphony Band. "Dedicated to my parents, and my sister Mary."

AUDREY WOJCZEK *(Ghost of Christmas Past)* was last seen on the HPHS stage as Chiffon in *Little Shop.* Other roles include Mrs. Embrey in *The Skeleton Walks,* Ado Annie in *Oklahoma!,* and Kate Keller in *The Miracle Worker.* She is Vice-President of Thespian Troupe #4443, and a member of both Chorale and Flag Corps. "I love you, Rob!"

MIRANDA RESNICK *(Sophomore Student Director)* is a Sophomore (duh!) She enjoys singing in Varsity Choir, and is very active in her church, Calvary Baptist. This is her first time being involved with Drama, but hopefully not her last. "Ministry Rules!"

"What are *those* for?" Richie whines, causing me to look up and over at him again.

Obviously Miranda's not done working her magic yet. With an eyebrow pencil, she draws a line from Richie's nostrils down each side of his mouth.

"They're nasal-labial folds," she declares with the utmost confidence.

Sure enough, according to *Stage Makeup* by Richard Corson, which Miranda's got open on the table beside her, that's indeed what they're called. Of course, I can't help but cringe when I hear the word *labial* . . . Bogue!

After tracing each dark line with a light one "to create highlight and shadow," Miss Resnick gently powder-puffs Mr. Tyler's face, making sure everything sets, and *voilà* . . .

I barely recognize the old man I see before me.

"*Now* you're done," Miranda confirms, closing the book with a snap.

The strands of long gray and white hair poking out from beneath the old-fashioned top hat on Richie's head add the finishing touches to his costume. I didn't think it was possible, but he really *does* look like Ebenezer Scrooge.

Miranda hugs us both, adding the customary "Break a leg!"

"You, too!" I say, even though I don't know if it's something one tells the Sophomore Student Director or not.

Richie replies, "Bah, humbug."

To quote Sally Brown from *Peanuts: "Isn't he the cutest thing?"*

I can't help but feel sorta jealous watching The Sophomore about to go on stage as the star of the show. I mean, I'm totally happy for him and proud of the work he's doing. Yet at the same time I keep thinking, *I wish it was me* . . . Does an actor ever get over this feeling?

"Father!"

At that moment, Billy Paterno bounds into the dressing room looking for his stage dad—namely me.

I ask, "Is your family here tonight?" after we do a quick run-thru of our lines.

Billy adjusts his little newsboy hat. "Just my mom and dad, and my sister." Next, he checks himself out in the mirror, tightening the scratchy scarf around his neck.

"Where's your brother?"

This is what I *really* been wondering.

"He went with our uncle Roy to see Judy Tenuta," he replies, acting like it's no biggie, yet sounding a little hurt.

Okay, now I'm pissed!

I don't care if Jack doesn't consider me his Best Friend anymore. Or if I got a show tonight so I totally couldn't go with him anyways . . . He knows how much I (capital) L-O-V-E Judy Tenuta! Why the hell wasn't *I* invited?

Of course, I'm not gonna let on to Billy that I'm mad.

Calmly I question, "Where's Judy Tenuta performing?"

Jack's uncle is a comedian, too, and I know he sometimes works at The Comedy Castle in Royal Oak.

"Someplace called Ann Arbor," Billy reports.

To tell the truth, I'm surprised he even knows who Judy Tenuta is!

Not that it's any of my business, but I ask, "Did they go by themselves?"

Billy hops up onto the makeup counter, his short little legs dangling in their navy blue britches. "Jackie took some guy with him."

"You mean Max?"

I thought Max had to work at Farmer Jack's tonight. That's what he told me when I invited him to come see the play.

"Nah . . . Some guy, Tim."

Tim?

As far as I know, Jack doesn't know anybody named Tim . . . And then it hits me.

"You mean, *Tom?*"

"Maybe," says Billy. "He wears a jacket with a letter on it."

He's gotta mean Tom Fulton.

What the fuck?

Since when is former Band Fag Jack Paterno, hanging out with Jock Jerk Tom Fulton? I mean, I know Tom's going with Betsy Sheffield and she's friends with Jack and all, but last I knew, Jack (capital) H-A-T-E-D Tom, and vice versa.

Like I said, ever since we were in 7th grade, Tom Fulton's been nothing but a Total Asshole to Jack and me both. Except for that one time we went over his house with Max and we got him to call the phone-sex party line pretending he was a girl . . . Now that I know Tom is hanging around with Jack, it makes me call his heterosexuality into question even more.

"Red-leather-yellow-leather."

Time for some warm-ups!

"Rubber-baby-buggy-bumpers."

Luckily, I'm not the only one making a fool of myself.

"She-sells-sea-shells-by-the-sea-shore."

Oh, the cacophony backstage, with thirteen teenaged actors plus one 9-year-old, all dispersed in various corners, running thru an array of tongue twisters and other vocal exercises.

"Five minutes!"

Miranda pops her head around the flat I'm standing behind, scaring the bejesus outta me.

"Thank you, five . . ." I reply, holding my racing heart.

Why is it that *every* time I'm about to go on, I gotta pee?

Hopefully we got a big house tonight. The non-musicals are always a harder sell, you know what I mean? From what I can hear beyond the curtain, the auditorium sounds pretty full. I can't make out any specific voices, but I know Mom, my sisters, and Grandma Victor are all out there, probably in the front row. They never miss an Opening Night. My dad, on the other hand, is a totally different story. He hasn't been to a play of mine since I started my Drama Queer career . . . I didn't bother inviting him to this one.

Both Ava Reese and Carrie Johnson said they were coming tonight, and afterwards they're gonna join me and Audrey up at Big Boy's for the post-show celebration. Normally, I wouldn't wanna hang out someplace I work, but Shir always saves us our usual tables in the smoking section by the salad bar, and she always treats us right no matter how rowdy we may become.

"Places, please!"

Why is it that *every* single time I'm about to go on, I crave a cigarette?

Crossing stage right, I take a seat at my (Bob Cratchit) desk. I say another silent prayer, hoping I don't forget my dialogue, and more importantly, that none of my fellow actors do!

Richie follows suit, taking his place center stage. Only he doesn't look at me as he's now totally in-character. Did I mention how hot he looks, even as a crotchety old geezer?

Squeak!

The squelch of the sound system sends a shiver up my spine.

Tap-tap-tap!

Below the hem of the curtain, I see a familiar pair of brown suede shoes. Once I regain my hearing, I recognize the sound of Mr. Dell'Olio's voice on the mic . . .

"Good evening, ladies and gentlemen."

I can picture Dell standing out front in his standard gray plaid suit, balding head nervously nodding, giving his customary curtain speech. I do my best to tune it out. Until he gets to the part where he reminds all the friends, family and faculty, "This is what our kids *should* be doing!"

Meaning, staying outta trouble by putting on plays, as opposed to off somewhere smoking cigarettes (no comment!) and/or doing drugs or God-only-knows-what-else . . . Having S-E-X, maybe?

Da-dah da-dah.

A thunderous round of applause indicates that Dell has at last stepped out of the spot.

Lights fade.

Here we go . . .

Cue music.

"Hark the herald angels sing . . ."

Curtain up.

God, I gotta pee!

Last Christmas

"This year, to save me from tears
I'll give it to someone special . . ."

—Wham!

My dad hates me.

Okay, maybe he doesn't *hate* me (I hope not), but I always felt this way, ever since I was little. In fact, sometimes I think I'm the reason my parents ever got a divorce, you know what I mean?

Maybe it's because at age two, I wet the bed.

Maybe it's because at age four, I was scared of the dark.

Maybe it's because at age six, I wanted to be a girl.

I mean, I didn't necessarily *want* to be a girl. But being the only boy in a family of four kids, I tried my best to fit in. I'd be lying if I didn't admit it was confusing sometimes. When you see your three sisters all asking Santa Claus for a giant Barbie head, why would you possibly care about GI Joe?

When Dad wasn't busy walking his beat, he spent all his time down at Wayne State studying for his degree in PE. At home, it was always just me, my mom, and my sisters. *Bradley and the girls.*

This one time, when I was like nine or ten, Dad was off at either work or school, leaving poor Mom stuck at home with me, Janelle, Nina, and Brittany . . .

"Let's play Beauty Parlor!"

Guess who unanimously decided this for everybody else?

I'll never forget the hair dryer Mom used to have. Not a blow dryer, like by Conair, but an actual *hair* dryer you put on top of your head and sit underneath in rollers. Made out of a light bluish purple plastic-y material, the thing reminded me of a shower curtain. It wasn't big or bulky like the ones Wilma and Betty use on *The Flintstones.* It was totally collapsible, with its own little matching faux-velvet carrying case.

Of course, *I* got to sit there and watch my three sisters take turns getting their hair Wella Balsamed, and wound in pink plastic sponges, before Mom placed the purply-blue hair-dryer-hat on each of their curlered heads. I distinctly remember crying out at the injustice of being a boy, watching Mom tuck the hair dryer away on the tippy-top shelf of the hall linen closet.

"I want a turn!"

Wanna know what Mom said?

Not *Bradley, you're a* boy . . . *Boys don't put curlers in their hair or sit under hair dryers.*

In typical Laura Dayton fashion, she looked down at me, all smiles. "Honey," she said, "You've already got curly hair."

"So does Janelle *and* Brittany!" I wailed, pointing out the obvious.

As far as I was concerned, Nina was the only one with hair in need of enhancing . . . And she was only like six or seven, so who cared what *she* looked like?

Next thing I knew, there I sat, hair dryer crown atop my tiny head. The thing weighed a ton, and the motor on top roared in my ears.

I watched Mom disappear a moment, returning with her Kodak Instamatic 126 camera. She removed her wire-framed glasses, held it to her face, and told me, "Say cheese!"

This is what I *assume* she said. I still couldn't hear her.

A spectrum of stars shot out with the pop of the Magic Cube. Patiently, I waited for the timer on the Amana Radarange to ding so I could witness my results.

I looked exactly the same.

At least *I* thought I did.

Mom had a different opinion.

"Don't you look beautiful?" She held her pink plastic hand mirror-mirror up where I could see myself. "Doesn't Bradley look beautiful?" she beamed, turning to my siblings.

I remember 5-year-old Brittany suppressing a giggle. "He looks like a *girl*."

"He does!" Nina agreed, totally cracking herself up.

That's okay, it didn't bother me. I thought I looked glamorous.

Mom turned to Janelle. "Go find your church dress . . . The red one."

Next thing I knew, there I stood, looking exactly like Little Orphan Annie.

"The sun'll come out . . ."

I knew all the words by heart and sang the entire song for them.

I remember thinking Andrea McArdle was sooo cute when I seen her the year before on *The Captain Kangaroo Show*. When Christmas rolled around, you can bet I asked Santa to bring me the *Annie* Original Broadway Cast recording on 8-track.

"You're only a day a-way!"

My audience of four burst into applause. Mom snapped another picture, first of me solo, then one of her *four* girls, fresh from their Beauty Parlor makeover.

We gathered around the full-length mirror in Mom and Dad's bedroom, posing as Annie and the other little orphans living "The Hard Knock Life" in 1930s "NYC." Too bad Mom could never afford to take us to see the show when it played the Fisher Theatre downtown.

Just then, we heard the back door open . . .

"Honey, I'm home!"

Immediately, me and the girls ceased our infernal singing. We looked at Mom all like, *What do we do?*

Without saying a word, she ushered her only son into the bathroom, closing the door behind us, locking it. Looking down at me, she held a finger to her lips, giving me the international sign for "Shut the fuck up." I'm kidding! Mom would *never* say the F-word, she's a Christian.

On the other side of the wall, we could hear Dad's footsteps as he made his way from the back door, past my vacant bedroom, and into our orange *Brady Bunch* kitchen.

"Laura!"

He called from just outside his and Mom's room where Janelle, Nina, and Brittany still remained, awaiting his arrival.

"Daddy!" they cheered in gleeful unison.

I could picture the girls throwing themselves at our father, wrapping themselves around his thighs, pleading to be picked up and coddled, all the while helping their only brother bide his time while their mother stripped him of his Little Orphan Annie dress.

Mom spun me around and went to work on doing just that. I could sense her frustration as she tugged forcefully on the stubborn zipper.

"Damn!" she cursed under her breath.

You can bet this was the first (and last) time I ever heard Mom swear.

Knock knock!

"It's locked," Mom told Dad, even though he could obviously tell since the door wouldn't budge no matter how hard he jiggled the handle.

"What are you doing in there?" Dad demanded.

"What do you think I'm doing in the bathroom?" Mom gave another yank on the YKK, but to no avail. She twirled me back around, whispering, "Arms up."

I obeyed her instructions, feeling quite the whirling dervish . . . Whatever the hell that is!

"Laura?"

Mom sighed, sounding totally frustrated. "Give me a second, okay?" Like a banana, she peeled the dress over my head with one quick motion. "Inside," she ordered, pulling back the pink shower curtain.

I loved the sound the plastic rings made when they clinked together. But I still had my Superman Underroo bottoms on, the ones I wore to the Central Freewill Baptist Halloween party, my red bedspread tied around my neck. Imagine the horror when Lefty Kerr (the bully) noticed the little flap in front and informed everybody, "Bradley's wearing underpants!"

As much as I wanted to protest, I followed Mom's lead. I knew the second she turned on that tap, the water would come cascading down, totally flattening out my Little Orphan Annie 'do . . . Too bad I had no other choice than to hop on in.

"Damn it, Laura!" Dad swore loudly from the safety of the other side. "What are you doing taking a shower *now*?"

The world around me darkened as Mom shut me in. The

water felt a tad too hot, I looked like I peed myself, but still my big concern was not quenching my coif.

"All right, James . . ." Mom unlocked and opened the door. "You can take your turn."

"Why is the shower still running?" Dad's voice grew louder as he stepped inside the room. "You know how expensive our water bill's gonna be?"

This was a constant *discussion* between Mr. and Mrs. Dayton as of late. If it wasn't the H_20, it was the heat. If it wasn't the heat, it was the "electricity, e-lec-tri-city!" (*School House Rock*)

"Little Brad is taking a shower," Mom reported. She used to call me this sometimes, since my grandpa Dayton is also named Bradley.

I heard my dad cry out, "Son!" He used to call me this sometimes, and still does . . .on the rare occasions that I see him.

I tilted my head back. The warm water splashed against my bare body. I wasn't sure if I was supposed to be taking a shower for real or what.

"Hi, Daddy!"

I picked up the blue bar of slippery soap. I loved how fresh and clean it smelled, and the fact that they called it (quote) the eye opener (unquote).

Beyond the pink plastic, my parents' shadows put on a show.

"I'll leave you to your business," Mom told her husband.

He replied, "I'll wait till Little Brad is done . . . A man needs his privacy."

Next thing I knew, they departed, leaving me to myself.

Looking back, I'm not sure if Dad meant that I needed *my* privacy while taking a shower or that *he* needed his in order to pee. I hate to think my own father would think I might try to sneak a peek at his willy while he took a whiz.

It didn't help when six weeks later, Mom asked Dad to pick up the pictures she recently dropped off for developing at Perry's . . .

"Aren't your daughters beautiful?"

From behind her post at the film-processing counter, the saleslady complimented Dad. One by one, she flipped thru the photos of James and Laura Dayton's wonderful family: Christmas morning . . . Easter morning . . . The Hazel Park Memorial Day parade.

"They most certainly are," Dad boasted with paternal pride.

"Oh, my . . . I didn't realize you had *four!*"

Neither did Dad.

Sure enough, there they were in full Focal color after a night of playing Beauty Parlor with their mother. Janelle, Nina, Brittany, and . . .

Who's that other one in the middle wearing the red dress?

You can bet Dad let Mom have it when he got home.

"Damn it, Laura!" he cursed. "What do you think you're doing?"

Upstairs, me and the girls played with our giant Barbie heads. We had a pair. One, Santa brought the girls two Christmases ago. The other, Mom got special for me—much to my father's dismay. I shared mine with Brittany.

"You can't go dressing our son up like he's a goddamn girl!*"*

As per usual, we pretended we couldn't hear our parents fighting down below. Instead, we continued with our Barbie makeovers, unable to take in Mom's response. She always argued in hushed tones.

Whatever the outcome of that particular fight, it didn't stop Mom from reading the headline in the *Free Press* a few weeks later:

HOLLYWOOD SEARCHES MOTOWN FOR LITTLE ORPHAN.

Yes, it seemed somebody was making a movie version of *Annie*, starring Carol Burnett as "I love you, Miss Hannigan," and some guy I never heard of, Albert Finney, as Oliver "Daddy" Warbucks. They were coming to Detroit as part of a nationwide casting call, looking for the star.

"I think we should go," Mom told me, not even aware that I had any aspirations of becoming an actor one day, because I don't think I did at the time.

"But Annie is a girl," I remember telling her, even though she already knew that.

"So . . . ?" Mom replied, ever the positive thinker. "It's acting . . . What difference does it make *who* plays the part as long as they can sing?"

I loved Carol Burnett! Me and Janelle used to watch her TV show with Mom every Saturday night, cuddled up together on the couch. My favorite episode of all time has gotta be the one where they spoof *Gone With the Wind* . . . 'member? *Went With the Wind,* featuring Carol as Starlett O'Hara, Harvey Korman as Rat Butler, Tim Conway as Brashley Wilkes, and Vicki Lawrence as the maid, Sissy, with special guest star Dinah Shore as Melody Hamilton.

I'll never forget the first time we saw Starlett swoop down that staircase wearing a curtain rod round her shoulders. We were cracking up sooo hard, we almost peed our pants.

The thought of having the chance to work with Carol Burnett would be like a dream come true.

But what about Dad?

Thankfully, on the day of the audition, I came down with a bug of some sort.

"Mom, I'm sick . . ."

"No you're not," she informed me in typical Laura Dayton fashion.

Why did she always think I was lying whenever I made this claim?

"Feel my forehead," I insisted, not faking it.

Mom clicked her tongue and fetched the thermometer. Five minutes later, she retrieved it from my mouth and sure enough, my temperature was Rod-Stewart-103 . . . Another song I love-love-love!

As much as I wanted to go, as much as I knew I could totally play Little Orphan Annie in the movie version starring Carol Burnett and Albert Finney, I kept thinking about how pissed Dad got when he saw the pictures of his only son all dolled up in a little red dress.

The expression of disappointment on Mom's face was too much to bear. The last thing I wanted to do was let her down. Yet somehow, I think she realized we probably shouldn't take our chances at making Dad even madder.

"Maybe next time."

The reason I bring all of this up pertains to what happened last week after Opening Night of *A Christmas Carol* . . .

As you probably know, by the end of the story, Scrooge is redeemed. The Three Spirits show him the way and all is fa-la-la-la fine and dandy come Christmas morning. Even if the Ghost of Christmas Present did skip an entire page of dialogue in scene five.

In the moment (as we say), I sorta felt sorry for Tuesday Gunderson. I mean, she's a Total Geek and all, but she's still a nice girl. Once she realized what happened, the look of panic on her pimply face was punishment alone for fucking up.

Thankfully Richie is a pretty good ab-libber—I mean, *ad-libber*.

All he had to do was look at Tuesday and say, "Do you mean

to tell me, Spirit . . . ?" And then he just fed her the line she forgot and got everything back on track. What can you expect from amateurs?

Once Tiny Tim chimed in with his "God bless us, every one!" and Miranda Resnick cued music and lights, the curtain closed. Immediately, Will Isaacs and Keith Treva (who else?) started hooting and hollering the way they always do after a performance has concluded.

"Today!"

As the soon-to-be elected Thespian of the Year, I knew I had to take charge of the situation and get everybody in line for curtain call.

The Sophomore stepped center stage, extending his hands to either side.

Audrey took the left. "One down . . . Two to go!"

I must say she looked awesome in her flowing white Ghost of Christmas Past gown, but the baby powder she put in her hair made me wanna hack up a lung.

Suppressing a cough, I stepped up to Richie's right.

"I'm not holding your hand," he wailed in disgust. *"Psyche!"*

He took my palm, gave it a firm squeeze, then flicked his middle finger against it a few times: the international sign for "Wanna fuck?"

I felt a rush of exhilaration, coupled by confusion.

What the hell was that kid up to?

I could *not* wait for Christmas Break to come so I could get away from him for a while.

The rest of our castmates joined us in two single-file lines across the stage—principals in front, peons behind. Once the curtain parted, all eyes looked to Richie in the middle for the signal. He raised his arms at the elbows. We all followed, gently bowing from the waist.

Leave it to the idiots (Will Isaacs and Keith Treva) to knock everything off-kilter. Is it that difficult to step forward and bend over? I'm sure we looked like a bunch of paraplegics up there, like we were trying to do the wave or some sort of Vikette kick-line ripple effect. Why can't these so-called actors be proud of the performance they just gave and take pleasure in the applause?

The way I do.

As happy as I was for Richie, there was a part of me that still felt totally jealous. I wanted to be the one standing in the center with everybody focusing on *me,* not slightly off to one side. And how come I had to share my final bow with Claire—I mean, *Clarissa*—Moody, and all our Cratchit kids?

"Good job, good job!"

"Thanks," I told Ava and Carrie, giving them each a big hug.

Once we take off our costumes, it's customary to greet our guests down front of the auditorium near the edge of the stage. Stage left, that is. Like going to Big Boy's on Opening Night, I don't know how this tradition got started. But it's what we Drama Queers have done after every show I been in since *Oklahomo!*

"Can I get your autograph?" asked Ava, handing me her *TheatreGoer* and a pen.

"Me too," Carrie insisted, practically shoving her program in my face.

These two did this after every performance. Silly as it seems, I always comply. I gotta get practice pleasing my adoring fans, don't I?

"You're coming to EB's, aren't you?" I asked, just making sure.

"You mean *Big Boy's?*" said Ava, giving me a look.

"Yeah," added Carrie. "Get it right."

I don't know why they hate it whenever I refer to Big Boy's as EB's. That's the official name, isn't it? Elias Brothers' Big Boy.

Maybe it's because I used to call it that when I was friends with Luanne back in the day, before I started hanging out with

Carrie and Ava on a regular basis. Neither of them ever liked Lou, least of all last year when she was "Baby Hitler"—I mean, *drum major.*

Still, I apologized. "Sorry . . . Are you coming to *Big Boy's?*"

"I thought Tuesday wanted to go to Pasquale's," Ava replied sarcastically.

"Fuck Tuesday! Me and Richie are going with everybody else."

Carrie shot me a suspicious glance. "Richie Tyler?"

"Yes, Richie Tyler," I answered defiantly. "You got a problem with that?"

"But he's a Sophomore . . ."

"He came to the Thanksgiving parade with us," I reminded her.

"Wasn't *my* idea."

Years ago, Carrie went to elementary school at Roosevelt with Richie, and she still can't think of him as anything but the faggy little flute player he used to be. Just because he was totally driving me crazy with his mixed signals (and totally hot body) didn't mean I wasn't gonna bring The Sophomore along for our traditional Opening Night at EB's—I mean, *Big Boy's.*

"We'll see you guys over there," Ava chimed in, twirling her locks once again.

I was surprised to see Carrie drop the subject. "Let's go see if Aud needs a ride."

"Where's Berger?" I wondered, thinking of all people, he'd be here to see our performance.

Both girls informed me, "Work," in perfect unison.

"Damn ass burgers!" I brayed. (Get it?)

I just about shit my pants when I heard a familiar voice: "Son, watch your language."

My father was the last person I ever expected to see standing in the HPHS auditorium after one of my productions. What the hell—I mean, *heck*—was *he* doing here?

"Hi, Dad . . ."

We stood in silence a moment, both trying to figure out what to say. The last time we seen each other, he gave me the car, two months ago. We hadn't talked since. Not that I had anything to say to him, and I'm sure the feeling was mutual. It sorta sucks when you're staring at the man responsible for giving you life, the man you realize you're starting to look like more and more each day (with your *thinning* hair), and there's absolutely nothing you can talk about.

"I enjoyed the show," said Dad, finally.

This made me happy to hear. "Thanks for coming."

"I saw the article in the *Daily Tribune*," he admitted. "That's how I heard about it."

Now I felt like a jerk for not inviting my own father to come see my play. What kind of son am I? A terrible one.

I was just about to apologize when we were rudely interrupted.

"Hello, Superstar!"

I could *not* believe who I seen weaseling her way thru the throng at that very moment, wrapped in a fucking full-length fox fur, hair wilder than ever.

None other than her Highness herself . . . Miss Peter.

Of all nights, why did she have to attend the exact same performance as James Bradley Dayton, patron saint of conservatives?

"I am sooo proud of you!" Miss Peter gushed, totally not even seeing the older version of me standing by my side. I prayed she wouldn't lean in for a kiss, the customary greeting in the gay bar world. Instead, she enveloped me in Aramis, speaking into my ear. "You *must* introduce me to that Scrooge boy!"

Of course, Miss Peter is the only one I told what happened *Chez Tyler* the previous week.

"Later," I muttered without moving my lips.

I couldn't help but notice my dad clench his jaw, totally tense.

He averted his eyes, pretending not to notice anything *wrong* with this person who was clearly my acquaintance. I knew he wouldn't be rude to Miss Peter if I introduced them. He'd just stand idly by, silently judging her.

Dad cleared his throat. "I'll leave you to your friend," he politely offered.

For the first time, Miss Peter noticed him next to us, all bundled up in his tan overcoat and matching scarf. "I am sooo sorry!" she sang, apologizing for her *faux pas.*

"Good seeing you," I told Dad, because it was, no matter how awkward.

"Make sure you get to church on Sunday," he advised me before blending into the crowd and slipping out the side EXIT door.

I couldn't help but think this was Dad's way of sending Miss Peter a silent signal, to let her know he was onto her. That no matter how hard she tried, she would never get his good Christian son to choose her way of life.

Too bad I'm discovering it's not a choice.

"Slow down, Brad!"

At this very moment, me, Nina, and Brittany are on our way out to Grandpa and Grandma Dayton's in Lake Orion where we're having dinner with our father.

"Please don't tell me how to drive!" I beg, nervous enough as it is about taking the freeway so far north.

"I'm telling Dad you were speeding . . ."

Did I mention tonight is Christmas Eve?

"Go right ahead, Nina," I retort. "See if I care!"

Mom's going to Grandma Victor's and then we're meeting them later at church with Janelle and Ted.

Speaking of . . .

Tonight they're telling our grandparents and our father that they're getting married in February on account of they're (quote) in a family way (unquote).

If the expression on Dad's face when he witnessed Miss Peter at my play was priceless, just wait till Janelle drops her baby-bomb over eggnog and bread pudding.

Merry fucking Christmas!

I'm Falling in Love Tonight

"Moving together as one
'Til the first gentle rays of the sun . . ."

—The Judds

Where the hell is everybody?

On a good night at Big Boy's, I can take home anywhere between $50 and $75.

This is *not* the case, however, the day after Christmas.

I don't know if it's because people have gorged themselves leading up to the holiday or what. Maybe they're tapped out from spending all their savings on Super Mario Brothers for their kids' Nintendos. Who knows? But they sure as hell weren't coming out for Slim Jims and Brawny Lads on this fucking fuhreezing Saturday night!

After counting my measly tips (a whopping $32), I make my way to the men's room where I change outta my uniform. Well, just the special sauce–stained shirt. I spent my entire shift keeping my pants pristine so I can wear them out in public. The last thing I wanna do is carry a bag into the bar filled with my stink!

Keeping my black slacks on, I slip my new white-and-black houndstooth sweater over my head, taking care not to muss (what's left of) my hair. Not to sound arrogant or anything, but I love the way this sweater makes my chest look. Like I actually have one. Janelle gave it to me for Christmas, even though with the new baby on the way, she and Ted are sooo broke they can barely afford to pay attention.

By the way, Dad totally broke down in tears after Janelle and Ted made their big announcement after Christmas Eve dinner. In all my 17-going-on-18 years, the only memory I have of my old man crying was the time he had a kidney stone.

Wanna hear the kicker?

The reason Dad lost it wasn't because he's ashamed of his oldest daughter for disgracing the Dayton family name, but because he's always wanted to be a grandpa so he can make up for being such a terrible father . . . Isn't that sweet?

"Somebody smells good."

Shir catches me coming outta the bathroom, clean as an Irish Spring whistle.

"What's her name?" Tony chimes in from behind his post in the kitchen, scrubbing a pot.

"Um . . ."

I *really* don't wanna have this conversation.

If I say, "*Her* name is . . ." I'm a liar. If I say, "*His* name is . . ." I'm a fag.

Not that I'm ashamed of who I am or anything, but I'm only gonna be working at Big Boy's for another six to eight months. Then I'm off to Juilliard (God willing), and I'll never see any of these people ever again. Why should I bother getting into something so personal? Besides, it's already after 11:00 PM and optimal bar time is ticking away.

To avoid having to lie, I reveal, "I'm meeting a friend."

Tony cackles like a clown. "Wear a rubber!"

Shir shoots him a look before telling me, "Be careful, y'hear?"

Sometimes I think maybe Shir suspects something's up with me. Not that I think she'd care if she knew I'm gay or anything. She's totally cool—for a 40-year-old. In fact, if it wasn't for Shir, I would never have gotten my driver's license. She's the one who loaned me the $350 to enroll at the U-Drive driving school. She even drove me up to Secretary of State on 9 Mile and Ryan when it came time to take my road test, after letting me practice in her Ford Taurus up at the Oakland Mall parking lot.

Thank you, Shir!

Outside, I almost fall flat on my face coming down the slippery slope of a sidewalk. It's times like these I could use a pair of GASS shoes! I'll have to find out where Rakoff got his. I'm guessing Pickway's probably.

"Ready, Val?"

Thank God the roads are pretty much deserted. Maybe that's why nobody came into the restaurant tonight. They all stayed home after Sonny Elliott warned them about the weather. Fine by me! Like I said, I hate driving as it is, particularly on the highway with other cars.

"Here we go . . ."

Whenever I take I-75 south towards downtown, I think about the time me and Lou convinced Jack to come to the bar with us back in 10th grade. We had sooo much fun that night, dancing on the dance floor, flirting with the cute guys. I honestly thought it was the start of something special for us. No more lying about who we *really* are. No more hiding our true feelings. Finally, we could talk to each other about whatever it was we had on our minds.

I can't believe it's almost 1988—the year me and Jack have been waiting for forever. We should be celebrating the fact that we're *finally* graduating in less than six months. Instead, I don't know when (or if) I'm gonna talk to my Best Friend ever again . . . Life totally sucks!

And it's about to get worse.

S-N-O-W.

The second I cross 8 Mile, like magic, the flakes begin to fall.

"Easy there, Val . . . Don't you worry your pretty little head."

Of course, Val has no control over what Mother Nature decides to do. And from the looks of the way the snow is starting to come down, she must be pissed! 'member the Chiffon margarine commercial circa 1970-something? *("It's not nice to fool with . . .")* Why's she always such a bitch?

Like in *The Year Without a Santa Claus.* 'member when Mrs. C pays Mother N a visit, accompanied by that buck-toothed kid, Ignatius Thistlewhite, and Santa's trusty elves, Jingle & Jangle Bells? All they want is for Momma to make her spoiled-brat sons, Heat Miser and Freeze Miser (or is it Snow Miser?) get along for a second so that Santa can get his holiday day off . . . 'member?

Mother Nature's got that bird's nest hat on her head with the real-live red-red-robin bobbin' along above it. When she summons her selfish sons, they start crying and carrying on like Total Babies. So she zaps 'em with a bolt of lightning. Talk about some mother! If Laura Victor-Dayton-Victor ever did that to me, Janelle, Nina or Brittany, they'd call Child Services on her behind.

"No need to panic . . ."

Okay, now I'm talking to myself.

I'm getting a little nervous here, what with the snow coming down now in buckets. Or however snow comes down when it's really, *really* hard. To calm my nerves, I light a cig and jack up the radio full blast. Singing along with my favorite girls always helps keep my mind off imminent catastrophe . . . Tonight it's Miss Reba.

"Oh little rock
Think I'm gonna have to slip you off . . ."

I knew I should've listened to Dad and bought those snow tires. And a new pair of windshield wiper blades would've made a good stocking stuffer. Not to mention, I should have also gotten the heater fixed. Again, that's what I get for driving a car that's two years—

Oh, F-u-u-ck!

Somewhere south of State Fair, poor Val totally bites it.

Outta nowhere, she hits an icy patch.

"Round and round she goes . . ."

In a state of panic, I can't remember if I'm supposed to turn the wheel in the direction of the spin or the opposite. Again, like in that triple axel/Lexie goes blind scene from *Ice Castles,* everything starts moving in slow-mo. Next thing I know, I'm on the side of the road, with good old Val smooching a light pole.

Happy Fucking (six days till) New Year's!

Soon as I make sure I'm still alive, I get outta the car to check on Val. Sadly, her front fender is all banged up and bent inward against her left tire. No way is she driving away from the scene of this accident . . . This means neither am I.

"Now what?"

Again, me talking to myself.

Okay, let's consider my options: turn around and walk all the way back to Ferndale in the fucking fuh-reezing *cold.* Continue walking to the bar thru the burnt-out *ghetto.* Flag down the next passerby and accept a ride from a total *stranger.* Honestly, I don't know which is the lesser of three evils.

Thank God I won't have to decide.

After twenty minutes of standing on the side of the road,

watching car after car (after car) whiz by while smoking four cigarettes, here comes a cop. Like a dork, I start waving him down, up on my tippy toes, in case he can't possibly see me standing beneath the street lamp in this blizzard. The only thing missing is my white hankie.

Oh, shit!

What I thought looked like a cop car turns out to be an old beat-up, painted-shit-brown Volaré that used to be one. The flashers have been removed from the roof, but it's still got the light-thingie on the sideview mirror, which is what made me think it was a police vehicle in the first place.

As the driver pulls up, he shines it right at me.

Oh, my God . . . I'm gonna die!

Trying to identify the person behind the wheel who could potentially be my murderer, I shield my eyes. I inch my way towards the idling vehicle, maintaining enough distance should somebody jump out unexpectedly and I have to make a break for it.

Wouldn't you know? Tinted windows.

Again, let's consider my options: remain calm, and be ***killed.*** Run for it, and be ***killed.*** Beg for mercy, and be ***killed.*** Again, three evils.

I don't know what possesses me, but I reach for the silver handle and pull the door open.

"Hello?"

Shivering from fear as much as the snow flying in my face, I greet my captor.

Wanna know what happens next?

From inside the dark interior, I hear the sweet sounds of Naomi and Wynonna, better known as The Judds. Followed by, "Hey, Brad-licious!"

What the—?

"Sean?"

Before I go on, maybe I should backtrack a little . . .

'member how I said I might need to get a second job over Christmas Break? Well, I did. Up at the Gap in Oakland Mall, just what I said I didn't wanna do. You should see me fold a cable knit—like a pro!

Unfortunately, I didn't have much of a choice. I got my Juilliard audition coming up at the end of January, and I finally bought my plane ticket to New York City. To the whopping tune of $229! Luckily, Mr. Dell'Olio offered to put it on his credit card and told me I could pay him back.

Hence my fall into the Gap.

For the most part, the job is pretty easy: stand around, greet customers, make sure nobody shoplifts. I work five days per week, eights hour per day, and they pay me $5.15 per hour for a total of $41.20 per day, $206.00 per week. Except by the time they take taxes out "it's a tired feeling, really." (Paula Poundstone)

So I started the Gap this past Monday, 12/21. On Wednesday, 12/23, when it came time for my break, I wandered next door into Harmony House. I had to get outta that shoebox of a store and all its pastel Gap glory. Plus I wanted to buy a cassette to stuff in Mom's Christmas stocking.

"Can I help you find something?"

It used to bug the shit outta me whenever me and Jack and/or Max would come up to the mall just to look around, and the goddamn salesclerks jumped all over us the second we walked into a store. Merry-Go-Round was always the worst! Now that I myself was working in retail, I totally sympathized.

I gave my usual "I'm fine" response, hiding the tape I just picked up from the rack behind my back . . . But it was too late.

"What-cha got there?" the sales guy asked with a tilt of his blondish brown head. His nametag said: SEAN.

"Where?" The last thing I wanted was for the very New Wave sales guy to catch me browsing thru the Country section.

"There . . . In your hand." Before I could stop him, Sean reached an arm around my back and snatched the cassette from my clutches.

Truth be told, I was a little worried he thought I was trying to steal it. So I said, "I work next door . . . At the Gap."

He replied, "I know . . ." Followed by, "Your name's Brad, right?"

At first, I was like, *How does Sean the New Waver guy know* my *name?*

Maybe we met somewhere before.

Maybe he's a regular customer at Big Boy's.

Maybe he read the stupid Gap tag I still had pinned to the stupid Gap sweater they force me to wear every goddamn day. (Duh!)

"Sorry . . ." I felt like a Total Dork. I'm sure I sounded even more like one when I began to laugh uncontrollably outta embarrassment.

"Don't apologize . . . I love The Judds."

Sean returned the tape, and I breathed a sigh of relief.

"Oh, my God . . . You're kidding?"

"*Heartland*'s an awesome album," he declared when I asked if I should buy it or not. "Totally."

I said, "Thanks," confessing, "It's for my mom . . . For Christmas."

Sean dropped his chin to chest in disappointment. "So you're not a Naomi and Wynonna fan yourself?"

"I am," I admitted, impressed that he called mother and daughter by their first names. "I just don't meet many guys my age who even know who The Judds *are* . . ."

"What can I say?" Sean modestly replied. "Occupational hazard." Then he asked, "So what *is* your age, anyways?"

'member what happened the last time I lied to Larry the mechanic from Downriver? Keeping that fiasco in mind, I stated, "I'll be eighteen on my next birthday."

Sean grinned. "Look at you . . . Not even legal yet."

I blushed. "I know . . . It sucks, right?"

"I don't know . . . Does it?"

I was just about to say, *You should know . . . You already been there.*

And then I got it.

This guy is totally gay and he's totally flirting with me!

"H-h-how old are *you?*" I stammered, not knowing how to answer his question.

Sean replied, "I'll be twenty-one next August," as if he had one up on me just because he was older. Followed by, "I'm a Virgo, by the way."

Like a dork, my face lit up. "So am I!"

"The 29th."

"September 4th."

I don't know why, but whenever I meet somebody with the same sun sign as me, it's like I immediately bond with them. Like somehow, our being born between the same thirty-day span connects us in some spiritual way or some shit. Why is that? It's not like I'm a firm believer in astrology or anything, even though I totally read Joyce Jillson every day!

"So what're you doing Saturday night?"

"I don't know . . ." I played it coy. "Why do you ask?"

Now here's the thing about being gay: it's like it's this secret society not just *anybody* can join. You gotta be a certain type of person, you gotta dress a certain way, use certain expressions to let others know you're a member of The Club.

Up till this point, I didn't know for sure if Sean carried a card. I had a stinking suspicion he did, from the way his eyes held mine when he looked at me, from the proximity of his (male) body to my (male) body as we stood together between Country and Classical.

Then he gave me the signal. "There's this bar downtown called Heaven . . ."

That's where I knew him from!

A few weeks back, I was standing in line, waiting to pay my cover . . .

"How's your *boyfriend*, Nancy?"

I couldn't help but overhear the guy in front of me talking to the girl in the Sally Jessy Raphael glasses who works the door. An inch or so taller than me, he had on a black leather biker-style jacket, black jeans slightly cuffed at the bottom, and black leather boots with two buckles on each. He wore his hair slicked back on the sides, and sorta poufed up on top, in a style reminiscent of *Grease* or The Stray Cats. I couldn't quite see his face, but I had a feeling he was pretty cute. Sometimes you can just tell, you know what I mean?

Nancy answered, "Steven is good," taking the man-in-all-black's five bucks.

"Tell him we got the new Madonna twelve-inch at Harmony House . . . I'll give him my employee discount."

"Stop it!" Nancy ordered. "Steven is *not* gay."

And Nancy isn't fat . . . "She's big-boned!" (Judy Tenuta)

She's also got very large teeth. Rumor has it her uncle owns Heaven, so she can totally let in whoever she wants for free. Too bad she never does.

"You know what they say," the guy in front of me said. "Takes one to know one."

From the way he cackled, I had a feeling he was already wasted. I heard him say something about JP's, which I'm told is a gay strip club in Canada where the guys go *nude*. Can't say I ever been!

With her black magic marker, Nancy marked an *X* on the top of his hand, meaning N-O drinking. "I want my *Powertool* tape back," she bellowed. Then she shouted, "Next!" and the guy, who I now realize was Sean, turned over his shoulder to smile at me before disappearing inside.

Back to the future . . .

"What the fuck were you doing out there?"

Sean asks me this once I climb into the safety of his (former) cop car and we're back on the road.

"Freezing my ass off!"

Despite the heat being cranked full-blast, I can't get warm.

"You're lucky I recognized you . . . I almost didn't stop."

"You totally freaked me out . . . I thought you were a psycho killer!"

"Qu'est-ce que çest?"

Sean taps the wheel with a leather-gloved hand. I almost don't get the Talking Heads reference, I'm so frostbit. I pray I don't catch pneumonia from being out in the cold for so long.

Wouldn't it be just my luck with New Year's Eve coming up next week? I'm supposed to go to a party at Shellee Findlay's house and I wanna ask Sean to come with . . . I'm *really* starting to like him, but I can't tell if the feeling's mutual or not.

"Drive faster," I order. "I need a hot toddy!"

Sean gives me a look. "Too bad my name's not Todd."

Guess that answers my question!

As per usual, the lot behind The Gas Station is packed, so we find a spot on the street halfway down the block. The worse thing about going to a gay bar in Detroit is the parking situation. Lemme tell ya, there's been many a time I had to literally *run* from my car outta fear of getting shot by a passerby. Or at least called *Fag!*

I turn to Sean, about to make a break for it. "You ready?"

"Hold on a sec." He places a hand on my shoulder, stopping me from opening my door. "There's something I wanna do first."

And then, as the song says . . .

He kisses me.

New Year's Day

"I want to be with you
Be with you night and day . . ."

—U2

Splat!

Wanna know what that was?

The sound of 13-year-old Jodi Paterno puking all over Shellee Findlay's kitchen floor at her house in Ferndale . . . I knew tonight was gonna be a trip.

It all began around 11:35 PM with me and Sean practically getting ourselves killed by a shit-brown boat of an Impala as we rounded the corner on 10 Mile looking for a place to park.

"Did you see the way that guy was swerving?" my passenger asked, climbing outta the car into a three-foot snow bank.

"Fucker!" I hissed. "I hope he crashes and burns."

Why do all the crazies come out on New Year's Eve?

And better yet, what are they doing out on the roads *driving*?

We started crunching our way up Shellee's street. She lives on Harris, two blocks east of Hilton, and down the road from Edison Elementary.

Sean asked, "Which house?" not knowing where the Findlay family lived.

"Can't you tell?"

To me, it seemed pretty obvious: the beige one-story aluminum-sided number on the right with porch light aglow and all the cars parked out front.

"Is that a Rabbit on the lawn?" Sean asked, sounding totally shocked.

No, he didn't mean a bunny as in Bugs. An actual VW found itself parked in the middle of the Findlays' front yard. If I knew my Hillbilly High classmates, this was probably the handiwork of Tom Fulton and/or his jock friends, who have nothing better to do than get all drunk and act disorderly.

"Guess they didn't party like this at Fraser, huh?"

That's where Sean went to high school, Class of '85.

Stepping up to the Findlays' single step of a porch, I recognized the routered wooden *Home Sweet Home* plaque Shellee made in Mr. Bowdoin's 7th grade Wood Shop, back when she was still Shelly with a Y.

Knock knock!

I figured nobody could hear me over the obnoxious blare of some new band I can *not* stand, Guns N' Roses, rattling the window panes . . . 'member when '80s music was actually good?

"I say we just walk in," Sean decided, opening the front door and leading the way. Did I mention how hot he looked?

Dressed in cuffed jeans, wearing his signature leather jacket and buckle boots, his hair slicked back à la his favorite model/musician/singer-songwriter, Nick Kamen. Don't worry, I didn't know who the hell he was either till Sean clued me in.

'member the Levi's 501 commercial circa 1985 where the totally cute dark-haired guy walks into a laundromat looking about for an empty washer? "I Heard It Through the Grapevine" plays in the background as he removes his Ray-Bans. A pair of bratty-faced boys scrutinizes him while he dumps a bunch of rocks into the machine, for that sought-after *stonewashed* effect.

As the mother shoos away her sons, the guy strips off his black T-shirt and black leather belt before unbuttoning his button fly. Nearby, a woman wearing 3-D glasses and her friend giggle like schoolgirls. But the cute guy pays them no mind (hmmm . . . I wonder why), picking up a magazine and plopping a squat between them in nothing but his boxers.

Well, that guy happens to be the guy I'm talking about . . . Nick Kamen.

According to Sean, his debut album, *Each Time You Break My Heart*, came out last year, produced by Madonna . . . Who knew? Maybe it's because he's British, but I can't say I ever heard of him. This seems strange to me, since the guy's a Total Babe, you know what I mean?

"Watch it, Asshole!"

Wanna know who greeted me the second we entered the Findlays' house?

I'll give you a hint . . .

"Oh, it's *you*."

He's the totally hot Sophomore who I totally love—I mean, *hate*.

If you said, "Richie Tyler," you win the prize!

"Sorry," I apologized, even though he's the one who shouldn't be standing behind the door totally blocking the foyer.

Richie grinned. "It's okay . . . Don't let it happen again."

That's when I heard the drunken shriek of a female voice.

"Don't talk to my Chorale partner that way!"

Since we have more girls in 4th hour than guys, I actually have *two* Chorale partners: Jamie Good and Tonya Tyler. And since I just saw the former make her way down the hall with her boyfriend, former boys' Varsity basketball captain Jeff Rhimes, I assumed the denim mini-skirt-clad brunette swigging from a plastic two-liter of Sun Country strawberry daiquiri cooler must be the latter.

"What's up?"

I'd be lying if I didn't admit I was a tad surprised to see such a popular girl hanging out with the likes of a Sophomore. Until I made the connection: Tonya *Tyler* . . . Richie *Tyler.*

"You guys aren't related, are you?" I had to inquire.

Mr. T informed us, "She's my cousin."

"No," Miss T interjected. "You're *my* cousin."

An argument erupted over who's whose cousin, what came first: the chicken or the egg, da-dah da-dah . . . Personally, I couldn't care in the least.

Not because I don't like Tonya, she's a Total Sweetheart, even if she gets a little loud and obnoxious when she boozes. (Who doesn't?) But the last thing I wanted at 11:40 PM on New Year's Eve was to have a conversation with the (former) love of my life when the (hopefully) new love of my life stood by my side. Especially when former love looked totally hot sporting a white turtleneck with black pegged pants and suspenders hanging down around his waist, along with white slip-on shoes without socks.

On anybody else, this outfit would make the wearer look like a waiter. Or a penguin. Richie Tyler somehow made it work.

Damn him!

Quickly, I said, "Tonya and Richie, this is Sean . . . Sean, this is Tonya and Richie."

Richie reached out a hand. "Actually, it's Rich."

Whatever . . .

I'm never gonna get used to *Richie* Tyler going by Rich.

"Hey."

Sean totally sized The Sophomore up, even though he wasn't

aware I once had feelings for the boy, and therefore had no reason whatsoever to be envious.

Of course, Richie wondered, "How do *you* guys know each other?"

I prepared to launch into my spiel (not that it's any of his business) when suddenly, from a far corner of the room, I heard a familiar shout.

"Dude!"

Max Wilson toasted me with a half-empty bottle of Bud, his close-set blue eyes now glassy and red. He stood chatting with our hostess, smoking what looked like a Capri cigarette.

"What's up, Fox?" Shellee gave us her signature semicircular wave with pinky, forefinger, and thumb.

I excused us from the Cousins Tyler, leaving them to their spat. "See ya!"

Sean called out over his shoulder, "Nice meeting you," then under his breath he sighed, "What a hunk!"

I replied nonchalantly, "You think?"

Nodding and smiling at a bunch of faces I barely recognized, we weaved our way thru the crowd.

Who invited all these children?

There must've been a dozen Freshmen from both Beecher and Webb milling about Shellee's front room, totally wasted. I swear one girl looked like she's ten.

Properly, I introduced Miss Findlay to my guest. "Sean . . . This is Shellee."

"S-H-E-L-L-E-E," Sean spelled, doing his best to impress.

"Very good, S-E-A-N." Shellee nodded approvingly. "Where did Brad find you? You're ca-ute!"

I explained our Oakland Mall connection, how we been hanging out this entire Christmas Break, da-dah da-dah. I didn't go as far as to say that we're (unofficially) dating, however. Not that I'm ashamed of Sean or anything, but I'd rather not run the risk of being judged right now. Especially with a room full of jocks, cheerleaders, and Vikettes who might overhear my confession.

"'s up, Dude?" said Max, smoke billowing in his face, Capri tight between his teeth. In one hand he held his beer, extending the other to Sean. "I'm Maxwell."

Since when?

I said, "Me and *Max* have been Best Friends since 4th grade," even though he's barely spent any time with me this semester now that he's hanging out again with Jack.

Speaking of . . .

"Is Jack here?" I wondered aloud.

"Jackie Paterno?" Shellee's bobbed head bobbed from side to side, crown-bangs firmly fixed in place by a fifth of Final Net. "I thought he was." She made a face. "Ooh, I'm a little dizzy!"

For a second, I thought she said "ditzy."

Speaking of *Jack* . . . Something told me Shellee had a little too much Mr. Daniel's and Coke by that point.

"You just missed him," Max reported. "He left with Tom Fulton."

Figures!

I thought the shit-brown boat that almost ran me and Sean off the road seemed somehow familiar. I had to take back what I said earlier about it crashing and burning. I'd feel totally terrible if anybody I knew ever got killed in a car wreck, let alone my (former) Best Friend.

"His sister Jodi's here," said Shellee, gesturing towards her kitchen, which wasn't very far from where we were standing considering her entire house couldn't be more than nine hundred square feet.

"You're kidding?"

Sure enough, 13-year-old Jodi Paterno stood by the refrigerator/freezer—right beside the washer/dryer—knocking back shots of Southern Comfort with Lynn Kelly, Angela Andrews, and Marie Sperling . . . Something I'm sure hers and Jack's mom, Dianne, would *not* approve of in the least little bit.

"You wanna say hello?"

Sean asked me this, even though he wasn't sure who Jodi Paterno was or how I knew her exactly.

I decided, with the inebriated state she found herself in, it was best to stay away. Until somebody I wished I *wasn't* seeing made his way across the room in my general direction.

"Be right back."

Leaving Sean to the care of Max and Miss Findlay, I beat a hasty retreat from Billy Idol wannabe Bobby Russell. I can't believe he still wears his blond hair all spiked like that, circa 1983.

I made my way over to Jack's sister. The poor girl looked up at me, lips crimson from too many wine coolers. I could tell from the haze in her hazel eyes, she couldn't comprehend who I was.

"What are *you* doing here?" I asked, still not sure how she and her other junior high cohorts managed to crash.

"Jodi's with us," Angela Andrews informed me.

"Isn't she a little young to be partying with the Seniors?"

Lynn Kelly answered, "All the Parkerettes were invited."

Parkerettes are the junior high equivalent of Vikettes.

Sure enough, I looked around the room and saw a bunch of very young, very *drunk* girls being hit on by a bunch of wasted older guys. Thank God my sister, Nina, is (quote-unquote) special so she's not friends with any of the girls in this crowd.

And that's the precise moment when Jodi Paterno completely lost her cookies . . .

Splat!

"Sorry," she sighs, slobber dripping down her chin.

Immediately, I go into big brother/Florence Nightingale mode, leading the girl down the hall to where I'm assuming I'll find the bathroom somewhere.

"Coming thru, coming thru," I warn the crowd, doing my best Marty from *Grease* impression . . . 'member when the Pink Ladies are at the drive-in and Marty thinks Rizzo's prego? And she's like, "Lady with a baby."

Nobody gives a shit, least of all the couple I find making out in the tub once I flip on the light, seashells and sea foam green surrounding us.

"Excuse me . . ."

This I say to Jamie Good and Jeff Rhimes, closing the door behind me. Did I mention Jeff graduated in '87 with Luanne Kowalksi, and used to be a Band Fag baritone player back at Webb? Until he got to HPHS and gave up instrumental music because it was no longer cool.

Jamie tries to pull away, looking a tad embarrassed at being caught, but Jeff forges ahead cramming his tongue down her esophagus. I pull the shower curtain shut, just in time to situate Jodi in front of the toilet, and lift the lid before she blows chunks.

"You're all right," I coo, gently patting her back the way my mom does whenever I ralph. "Can I get you some water?"

Have I mentioned the way I say *water* sounds more like *wadir*, and how much I hate it?

Jodi shakes her head, down on her knees, both fists full of porcelain.

A quick check of my Swatch informs me it's 11:44 PM. Only sixteen minutes till 1988. The last place I wanna be when the ball drops at midnight is holding back the hair of a drunken 13-year-old girl while she literally spills her guts!

"Stay here."

Praying Jamie and Jeff don't take things any further than second base behind the plastic curtain, down the narrow hall I go, hoping Sean is okay talking with Max in the French room—I mean, *front* room. I'm sure Mr. Wilson is rambling on about some stupid movie he saw on Skinemax with some big-boobed broad in it . . . Why is Max sooo lame sometimes?

"Yo, Dayton!"

The door to what I'm guessing is Shellee's bedroom opens. The sweet fragrance of something familiar seeps out from the dark.

"Hey, Bobby."

Billy Idol Jr. offers me the burning joint he holds between middle finger and thumb. "Wanna hit?"

"No thanks," I decline. Not because I don't entertain the idea of getting high, I just have no desire to do it with Bobby Russell.

"C'mon!" he implores, pulling me inside, totally against my will.

The only thing worse than arguing with a drunk is arguing with a high-on. I *really* don't wanna get into this right now. In fact, if I knew there was the slightest chance Bobby was gonna be here tonight, I wouldn't have even come to this par-tay.

I guess I didn't realize Shellee and Bobby were still friends. Back in 7th grade they went together for something like six months. I'll never forget the time Mr. Grant (the babe Civics teacher) got a hold of one of Shellee's *Dear Bobby* love letters, and read it aloud in the cafeteria in daily installments during lunch.

"What are you doing?" I ask my classmate, my eyes adjusting to the lack of light.

"What's it look like?" Bobby replies, taking a toke. "Want some?"

The glow of the waning moon shines thru the slats of the vinyl blinds, and I try not to sigh too audibly. "I already told you . . . I don't wanna get high."

Bobby extinguishes the joint, slipping it into the front pocket of his hospital scrubs. I can't believe he still wears them things.

"'s not what I'm talkin' about," he says suavely.

Sure enough, I look down to find Bobby Russell standing before me—holding his crotch.

Oh, God!

Next thing I know, Bobby whips it out. Totally flaccid, he begins tugging on himself. "I could sure use some help."

Not from me.

With my right hand, I reach for the doorknob.

With his left, Bobby blocks my way. "What's your rush?"

"It's almost midnight," I remind him. "I gotta get back to my friend."

Bobby sneers. "The faggot?"

I'm about to declare, *He's not a faggot* . . . Yet if I do, I know I'd be lying. Instead, I simply state, "His name's Sean."

Bobby presses himself up against me, his breath a sickly combination of booze and weed.

"'s Sean your boyfriend?"

Like I told Shellee Findlay when she asked me: I been spending a lot of time with Sean over Christmas Break. Still, I don't know where we stand exactly relationship-wise. I guess you could say we're (quote-unquote) dating. I mean, Sean's the first guy I ever made out with on more than one occasion, so maybe that does kinda make him my boyfriend.

Well, this sucks!

Not because I don't want Sean to be my boyfriend, I do. He's a totally great guy. Not to mention a totally great kisser. He does this thing where he sucks on my tongue, kinda hard, like it's some kinda life-saving drug and he's gotta swallow every drop. And sometimes, he'll stick his own in my ear, which you'd think would feel totally bogue, like somebody's giving you a Wet Willy or something.

But it doesn't—it's totally hot.

Now that I think of it, I could totally get used to having him around.

Brad + Sean.

TLF.

True Love Forever.

Yeah, right!

How the hell is that gonna happen when, just the other day, Sean informed Brad he's high-tailing it to LA on account of he can't cut the cold, and dwelling in Detroit for another day will totally depress him?

This is why I tell Bobby, "Sean's not my boyfriend." Because obviously he doesn't *want* to be. Or else he wouldn't up and abandon me without considering our (quote-unquote) relationship.

"Liar."

Bobby leans into me, so close I can feel the tickle of his tiny mustache on my nose and the weight of him growing against my leg.

"Knock it off."

I try to sound casual, even though in actuality, I'm a tad freaked out.

Bobby forces his eight-incher into my palm. "*You* knock it off," he slurs. "Like ya used to."

No, he's not making shit up. What Bobby said just now is totally accurate.

As all *"To thine ownself be true"* as I'm trying to be, I still haven't come clean about me and Bobby Russell. As in what happened between us back in 9th grade—as in *sexually.*

To make a long story short . . .

One day at the beginning of Freshman year, Bobby asked me if I wanted to spend the night over his house. It's not like we were friends or anything, but we knew each other from the swim team and we spent the last two years together in Band.

Bobby played trumpet and sat right next to Jack, so I suggested we invite him along since Jack lives just on the other side of John R from where Bobby lives on Morehouse. Or is it M-O-O-R-house? I always get it mixed up. In Hazel Park, it's spelled one way, in Ferndale, the other.

For whatever reason, Bobby didn't want me telling Jack anything about his invitation, even though he knew I been Best Friends with the guy since 7th grade, and I told him everything . . . Well, not *everything*.

At the time, I never told Jack how hot I thought Bobby was. He used to wear these skin-tight Sergio's with white Nike hi-tops and, he had this one black and gray striped shirt from like Chess King he wore unbuttoned to his navel . . . And he was always going around school talking about what a big trout he had in his trousers.

Of course, I was like, "Hell yeah, I'll spend the night!" Especially when Bobby informed me there was *mari-ju-ana (do you wanna?)* to be had.

I guess this explained why he didn't want Mr. Persnickety-Persnick Paterno tagging along.

Or so I thought.

The first time, I couldn't believe what was happening . . . There we were, sitting around Bobby's basement in our underwear, smoking a doob and listening to Quiet Riot. Due to the bagginess of his boxers, I couldn't tell if Bobby had a big one or not. The fact was finally confirmed when he started stroking it thru his shorts—right in front of me!

At first, I didn't think anything of it. Sometimes a guy's gotta adjust himself, you know what I mean? Until he accidentally-on-purpose let it fall out. It totally touched his belly button when he leaned back.

"Oops."

Next thing I knew, I had mine out, and we were totally beating off together. I couldn't take my eyes off Bobby doing his thing. I never seen another guy do that before, you know what

I mean? The look of intensity on his face, the way his forearm flexed, and he held his breath . . . Totally hot! But something tells me Bobby wasn't nearly as into it as I was. Once he finished, he just sorta sat there with his eyes closed, acting like I wasn't even in the room.

So the next time, I decided to give Bobby Russell something to remember me by. Just as he was about to burst his bubble, I reached over and took him in my hand. Boy, did he respond to that!

Then I was like, *Okay . . . My turn.*

But Bobby was like, "I'm hungry." Like nothing even happened.

Watching as he wiped himself off with his Def Leppard T-shirt, I was like, "Wow . . . I can't believe you're a fag, too."

And Bobby was like, "Just because I let a guy beat my meat doesn't make me a fag."

This might explain why he never did anything back to me . . . *Ever.*

But I didn't care, because I was finally having S-E-X.

Even if it was one-sided.

So began what became a weekly ritual, lasting the majority of our Freshman year and thru most of the following summer. Until we got to HPHS in the fall and Bobby dropped outta Band. Then me and Jack met Luanne and Alyssa, and started hanging out with them all the time . . . The rest is history.

"You know you want it."

Finding myself once again faced with Bobby and his big one, I'm thinking, *I really don't.* And I haven't for a long time. The last thing I want right now is to be used by somebody who doesn't give a crap about me in the least little bit.

"To thine ownself be true."

Thank God there comes a knock on the door.

Knock knock!

"Who is it?"

"Open up . . . Police!"

Sure enough, this party is O-V-E-R.

Turns out, Shellee Findlay's neighbor lady got sick of listening to a bunch of high school (and junior high) kids partying like it's 1999, and she called the cops. Of course, Bobby would be totally busted if the fuzz caught him all high on reefer. So being the kindhearted soul I am, I help hoist him out the window before following happily ever after . . .

How's that for a narrow escape?

—1988—

January–May

Hideaway

"One day the boy decided
To let them know the way he felt inside . . ."

—Erasure

What the—?

Imagine my surprise the first Monday back from Christmas Break when Zack Rakoff approached me after 1st hour Wind Ensemble. Beaming like a *Monty Python* freak in awe of the Holy Grail, he handed me twenty-six typed, mimeographed pages, bound together with shiny brass fasteners.

"Here ya go . . ."

FADED FLOWERS

a short film by
Zachary M. Rakoff
&
Clarissa Moody

© January 1988, Fish Below The Ice Productions

I couldn't figure out why Rakoff was talking to me, let alone giving me a gift.

Then I remembered . . .

"Claire and I are writing a thort film thcript . . ."

"For second semester Mass Media . . ."

". . . we were wondering if you wanna be in it."

It all started that day I was desperately seeking Dell'Olio to ask if he'd write a letter of recommendation for my Juilliard audition, which is coming up two weeks from tomorrow. But I'm not thinking about that right now.

"We'll get you a script by Christmas."

"We thoot over Winter Break."

I didn't think they were serious about making a movie. You know how many times Rakoff's come up with some crazy scheme and never followed thru? Back in 7th grade, he asked me and Jack if we wanted to be in a New Wave band with his friend, "Dragon Horce," called either Third Triple Three or Say Saying Said . . . And did that ever get off the ground?

N-O!

In 9th grade, he made me and Jack help him haul all this camera equipment over his grandma's house in Sterling Heights so he could shoot establishing shots for a videotaped production of *Sorry, Wrong Number* . . . And did he ever finish it?

N-O!

Why should this *Faded Flowers* thing be any different?

"I totally forgot about this," I told Rakoff, who stood there like some Trekkie waiting for Scotty to beam him up.

"Firtht read-thru is tomorrow after thchool in Dell's room."

As much as I wanted to back out, I knew I couldn't. I needed all the experience I could get, and having a short film under my belt would look good on my resumé.

So I said, "I'll be there."

Rakoff let out a sigh of relief. "Thorry it took us tho long to get you a thcript . . . We used the break to make thome latht-minute changes."

"Whatever . . . I said I'll do it."

That night, I crawled in bed beneath my reading lamp, and gave the script the once-over.

—CAST—

Amanda..Clarissa Moody
Mary Beth......................................Audrey Wojczek
Jenn...Ava Reese
Ryan ....Brad Dayton
Noel..Rich Tyler

Oh, no!

I was *not* getting myself involved with anything that would put me in close proximity with The Sophomore. Especially when the new love of my life (Sean) was about to abandon me by moving to Los Angeles the following weekend, leaving me alone and feeling vulnerable.

Maybe I was totally overreacting.

Maybe it wouldn't be as bad as I thought.

Maybe unlike in *A Christmas Carol,* me and Richie wouldn't have any scenes together.

Fingers crossed!

I'd be lying if I didn't admit it shocked me to see Ava Reese's name amongst the cast of characters. Sure, she came to see every one of mine and Audrey's plays, but not since Miss Norbert made us put on a production of Gilbert & Sullivan's *The Mikado* for our parents back in 4th grade had I known Ava to have *any* interest in acting.

Unfortunately, I was totally wiped from my shift at Big Boy's to get past page one. This boy needed his beauty rest. *Faded Flowers* would have to wait till tomorrow . . .

Lemme tell ya, the next day after school, I regretted not staying up.

"Welcome cast and crew!"

Claire Moody greeted me, Audrey, Ava, Richie, and Rakoff, who I guessed must be the aforementioned *crew.*

"Thank you for giving up your time and talent to work on this project with us," added Rakoff.

All of us actors sat around nodding and smiling. Except for Ava.

"I didn't give up anything," she groaned. "I was drafted."

Turns out, Dell decided it would be good for Miss Reese to stay in school an additional semester and take Mass Media, as opposed to graduating in January, which I guess she had more than enough credits to do. Regardless, it made me happy to have her on board.

"Please open your scripts to page one," Miss Moody said, ignoring Ava's wisecrack. "Zachary, would you mind reading camera directions?"

Like a bumbling fool, Rakoff fought with his script. "What page?"

Claire gave him an icy stare. "I *said* page one."

"Thorry . . ." Rakoff adjusted his tortoiseshells, clearing his throat. "*Faded—*" His voice cracked, à la Peter Brady singing "When it's Time to Change."

"We'll wait," droned Claire, à la Total Bitch.

Rakoff read the title page before moving on to the synopsis: "Thet in a thmall thuburban town, *Faded Flowers* focuthes on a group of high thchool thudents, and what happens when one of the girls finds out her ex-boyfriend is homothexual."

What the—?

"Nobody said anything about me playing a gay guy," I piped up.

Claire regarded me with the same cold look she gave Rakoff only moments ago.

"Didn't Zachary tell you we made some last-minute changes to the plot?"

I nodded. "Well, yeah . . ."

"And did you read your script?"

"Not all of it," I lied, knowing I didn't read *any* of it.

"It's all there in black and white," Claire stated emphatically.

Zack chuckled, a dopey grin on his chubby face. "Actually, it's purple and white."

"Don't correct me," warned Claire.

Put in his place, Rakoff turned to me. "Is there a problem with your character, Bradley?"

What was I gonna say? *Of course, I don't mind playing a fag because I* am *one.*

Talk about an easy gig!

Claire attempted to justify the alterations she made to Rakoff's original story. She explained how she felt making the lead male character gay would heighten the controversy factor of the script, thereby garnering attention when submitted to the festival circuit . . . That's not all she had planned.

"Shall we begin?"

FADE IN:

INT. RYAN'S BEDROOM–DAY

Ryan and Noel lie together in bed, torsos bare, bodies entwined, after a passionate session of love-making.

Turns out, not only is my character gay, he's also fucking his Best Friend!

Despite my original apprehension, I was totally geeked at the thought of playing opposite Richie Tyler. Not because I still found him incredibly attractive, even though I did, but because everybody knows he's a very good actor—for a Sophomore.

So long as *he* didn't have a problem playing my secret gay lover, neither did I.

"I'm cool with it," Richie informed Claire when posed with this question.

"Spiffy," she replied, adding, "You two make a beautiful couple."

The script wasn't nearly as bad as I expected. Especially the relationship between my character, Ryan (a Senior), and Richie's character, Noel (a Sophomore), who become involved after Claire's character, Amanda (also a Senior), and Ryan break up.

Too bad Amanda soon realizes she's pregnant with Ryan's baby and wants him back. What sucks even more is when she drops by Ryan's house to give him the news . . . and finds him in bed with Noel!

NOEL

That was the best.

RYAN

No, you're the best.

They share a sensual kiss.

RYAN (CONT'D)

I love you, Noel Jordan.

NOEL

I love you, Ryan—

A KNOCK on the door.

AMANDA (O.S.)

Ryan?

Ryan and Noel freeze, caught in the act.

Busted!

Swallowing her pride, Amanda turns and goes, determined to raise the baby on her own, vowing never to tell Ryan he's the father. To top it off, when she tells her friends, Jenn and Mary Beth, what she's found out, the girls confess they've known the guys were gay and secretly a couple all along, thereby betraying Amanda's trust.

Quelle scan-jul!

I had a feeling this part of the storyline came from Claire. Her writing was always a tad overly dramatic . . . But in a good way!

Years ago back at Webb, Claire collaborated on a short story with Carrie Johnson and Jack about some teenaged runaway who becomes a prostitute and falls in love with her pimp. Too bad their teacher, Miss Shelton, caught them passing it around during Social Studies, and threatened to have Mr. Grant read it aloud in the cafeteria during lunch—same as he did with Shellee Findlay's *Dear Bobby* love letter.

"Nice work, everybody."

After we finished the read-thru, Claire went around the room asking for any questions or comments.

Audrey chimed in. "How does Mary Beth feel when she finds out Ryan is gay and in love with Noel?"

"Good question," Rakoff replied. "How would *you* feel if your Betht Friend came to you and told you the exact thame thing?"

Aud's eyes fell on me a moment. "If Brad came to me and said he was in love with another guy . . . I wouldn't give a flying fuck."

Everybody chuckled, even though we could all tell for once Audrey wasn't trying to be funny.

Rakoff said, "That's exactly how Mary Beth feels about Ryan."

"This is a good script, you guys," Ava complimented them, sounding as if she might actually enjoy acting in it.

"Totally," I concurred. "I can't wait to start filming!"

No matter how much it might suck getting naked with and kissing Richie Tyler, this was indeed the opportunity of a lifetime. How many actors in Hollywood were willing to play gay characters that weren't totally stereotypical? Imagine the kind of praise I would get for taking on such a challenging role.

For the sake of my future career, I had to do it.

This explains why I'm pulling up to Richie Tyler's house at 7:45 PM on a Friday night to pick him up for our date . . .

No, I'm not being facetious. Me and Richie Tyler are going out to dinner—as a *couple*.

Mr. Klan recommended a restaurant down on Woodward called Backstage after Moody and Rakoff suggested we explore the world of (quote) gay male subculture (unquote). Of all people, Mr. Klan would know where we should go. Like I said, the guy's over thirty-five and he's never been married. "Do a diagram, figure it out." (Paula Poundstone)

"You're cool with this?"

Before we head into the restaurant, I ask Richie this question.

"Shut the fuck up . . . It's research, remember?"

He holds the door open, even though I'm older so *I* should be the one doing this for him. Once we're inside and we take our seats at a candlelit table for two, I make sure I pull *his* chair out . . . Who knew gay dating could be so confusing?

The place is actually sorta cool, decorated in a Theatre theme, with posters and *Playbills* covering the walls from various Broadway productions. Above our table hangs a showcard from something called *Torch Song Trilogy.* I can't say I ever heard of it, but some guy named Harvey Fierstein wrote *and* starred in it, along with Estelle Getty, better known as Sophia Petrillo from *The Golden Girls* . . . Did you happen to see her in *Mannequin* with

Andrew McCarthy? I didn't realize she isn't such an old bag for real.

"Would you gentlemen care for a cocktail?"

That voice!

Our waiter sashays up to our table, dressed like a proverbial penguin, wine list in hand. I immediately recognize him and his flippy hair.

"Hello, Aryc."

'member the snotty cocktail server from The Gas Station? The one me and Miss Peter can *not* stand. He sure looks different without his biker shorts and tank top. Like I said, he's a Total British B-I-T-C-H, but once he sees it's me sitting with Richie the Babe, Aryc becomes my new Best Friend.

"Oh, my goodness . . . Opie!"

Richie gives me a look, as if to say, *Who the hell's Opie?*

In return, I shoot him a silent stare, hoping he'll realize we do *not* wanna engage this guy more than we have to. Then back to Aryc, I say, "Actually, it's Brad."

"And who do we have here?" he inquires, fixing his colored contacts on *my* date.

"Richie . . . Aryc. Aryc . . . Richie."

The Sophomore nods and smiles. "Actually, it's Rich."

Aryc squeals, "Oh my! Isn't *he* butch?" Then he turns to me, ear-to-ear grin. "You two aren't dating, are you?"

Great!

The last thing I need right now is Aryc outing me to Richie Tyler.

Not that I'm ashamed of who I am or anything, but this dinner date is all about business, you know what I mean?

"As a matter of fact . . . We are."

Those words did *not* come outta my mouth.

That was all Richie Tyler doing the talking.

I don't know what he's up to, but the expression on Aryc's prissy puss is priceless.

"Tonight's our anniversary," Richie brags. He takes hold of my hand, sending a thrill from my fingers thru my spine. "Two months."

I think back to our first meeting, that day in early November. Richie can't possibly remember the exact date we met, two months and four days ago . . . *Can he?*

"Congratulations," says Aryc, not sounding the least bit sincere. "I'll be back to take your order in a jiff."

After our server slinks away, I attempt to retrieve my hand.

Richie won't let go. "Research, remember?"

My heart goes from zero to sixty in no seconds flat.

Whatever you say!

I can't even tell you what I eat for dinner. Or what we talk about. Or whose idea it is for us to continue the date by moving on to The Gas Station . . .

"You sure they'll let me in?"

"As long as you're with me," I assure Richie after we park my car and make a break for it. I just hope Nancy's working the door tonight.

Sure enough, as we approach the front of the line, there Jabba the Hutt sits.

"Where's your boyfriend?"

I assume she means Sean. "'member? He moved to LA."

A quick glance at Richie reveals he doesn't look the least bit fazed at Nancy referring to my having a boyfriend. In fact, I think all he's concerned with is getting inside where they keep the booze.

Nancy bellows, "I told him I wanted my *Powertool* tape." She takes my five bucks, marking my hand with her Sharpie. "Next!"

The Sophomore steps forward.

"Where's your ID?"

"I don't drive," he confesses, not sure what else to add.

"He's with me," I interject, hoping that'll do the trick.

It doesn't.

"How old are you?"

A true Drama Queer, Richie turns to me for direction.

"Sixteen."

This I tell Nancy, even though I know she shouldn't care that he's *really* fifteen. There's underage kids running around Heaven and The Gas Station every weekend. Why should tonight be any exception?

Mrs. Ed shows us her horse teeth. "Robbing the cradle, eh, Brad?" Nancy accepts Richie's cash, marks his hand with a big black *X*, and says, "No drinking, I mean it . . . The cops catch you in here, I'm pleading the fifth."

Whatever . . .

"Hello, handsome . . . What can I get you?"

'member the totally hot bartender with the bare buff torso, army fatigues worn with combat boots, and the six-inch dyed-blue mohawk? Soon as we belly up, Mike's all over Richie . . . Why do the beautiful people get all the attention?

"What are you drinking?"

Richie looks to me, uncertain. For the first time since I met him, The Sophomore seems outta his element. You wouldn't think so judging by the way all eyes undressed him the second he walked thru the door.

"I'll take a Labbatt's," I answer, even though I can't stand beer so I don't know why I ordered it. Nervous, I guess.

Richie concurs, "Make it two," totally avoiding Mike's eye.

"You got it, Stud."

What the—?

"Somebody sure does like you," I say, feeling a tad jealous. Usually *I'm* the one on the receiving end of Mike's affection.

"You think?"

"Totally."

I watch as Richie watches Mike bend over and retrieve two green glass bottles from the refrigerator, his round bottom aimed in our direction. Is it just me or is Richie Tyler checking out another guy? For my sake, I can only hope!

"Two Labatt's . . ."

Mike pops the caps off and offers us the cold ones. I give Richie three crumpled dollars. He gives the bills to the bartender, along with a few of his own.

"'s on me," says Mike slyly, refusing the money.

How many months have I been coming to this bar, and never got a free drink? From now on, Richie Tyler is coming out with me every Friday night.

"Cheers," I toast. "To *Faded Flowers.*"

Richie remarks, "To Noel and Ryan."

"To *Ryan and Noel,*" I correct, taking a sip . . . Bogue!

Richie shrugs, "Age before beauty." Then he downs his beer in one big gulp.

Smart-ass!

At that moment, one of my absolute favorite tunes starts to play.

"Oh, my God . . . I love this song."

Those words did *not* come outta my mouth.

Again, that was all Richie Tyler doing the talking.

Lemme tell ya, this kid is full of surprises tonight.

I'm like, "You do?"

And he's like, "I got the cassette for my birthday in September."

"September what?"

"7th . . . I'm a Virgo."

I'm like, "You're kidding?"

'member what I said about meeting somebody with the same astrological sign, and immediately bonding with them in a spiritual way? Not only do I find out Richie is an Erasure fan, but he's also born *three* days (and two years) after me.

I have to ask him, "You know what this song's about, don't you?"

"Duh!" Richie replies. "A boy tells his parents he's a fag, and they disown him for it." From the way Richie makes this comment, I can't tell if he's being sympathetic to the boy in the song's plight or mocking it. Regardless, the next words outta his mouth comes as a total shock: "You wanna dance?"

I'm like, "Do *you?*"

And he's like, "Noel and Ryan dance, don't they?"

"At the Prom," I remind him.

This is the most pivotal scene in the *Faded Flowers* script.

After getting caught in bed by Amanda, not only do Ryan and Noel decide to come out, they also make their relationship official by attending the Prom together . . . So what if they're ridiculed as the laughingstock of the school? They still got each other.

"We should probably practice, shouldn't we?" suggests The Sophomore.

He takes my hand, leads me to the dance floor. Disco lights reflect in his crystal blues as we slow-dance the night away—no matter what song the DJ plays next.

Around 2:30 AM, we arrive home at Richie's house in Hazel Park . . .

Luckily, Mr. and Mrs. Tyler are away at another bowling tournament so he won't get in trouble for coming home late.

"Did you have fun?" I wonder, not wanting the night to ever end.

"'That was the best,'" Richie replies, quoting from *Faded Flowers.*

Picking up my cue, I respond, "'No, *you're* the best.'"

And then, as the script says . . .

They share a sensual kiss.

Research, remember?

His lips feel so soft.

His breath tastes so sweet.

His skin smells so sexy.

'member the scene from *Somewhere in Time* when Elise McKenna, aka Jane Seymour, spends the afternoon traipsing about Mackinac Island with her soon-to-be lover, Richard Collier, aka Christopher Reeve (no *S*)?

After meeting on the steps of The Grand Hotel, E & R take a horse drawn carriage ride, waltz arm in arm along the shores of Lake Huron, followed by a rowboat excursion out to the lighthouse. Upon their return to the isle, Richard walks Elise back to room 117, where she attempts to put the brakes on by offering her hand, thanking him for "the most pleasant *ah*-fternoon."

But Richard Collier is having none of it. He didn't travel sixty-eight years not to even make it to first base. Despite declaring she must rest before her performance in the play that evening, next thing Elise McKenna discovers, she's handing over her key and allowing her pursuer to cross the threshold of her boudoir . . . Where they will *talk,* "just for a moment or so."

Yeah, right!

It may be the year 1912, but the look in Elise's eye says she understands full well exactly what she's in for. Still, she plays it coy, remarking, "What did you want to talk about?" in her posh, British accent, once Richard closes the door behind them, shutting out the rest of the world.

Take note how she positions herself, ever so demurely against the doorframe. Imagine the thoughts running thru Miss McKenna's mind as her Superman utters nary a word, his X-ray eyes never losing site of their focus, as he sidles up close.

"Oh, my God . . . What's happening?"

The firm grasp of his hands upon her shoulders.

The tender caress against her cheek.

The delicate way he lifts her chin.

Her words may deny it, but her body burns with a desire she has never known . . . This is exactly how I feel the moment *my* Richard presses his lips to mine.

My life will never be the same.

Welcome to the Jungle

"You can taste the bright lights
But you won't get them for free . . ."

—Guns N' Roses

"Start spreading the news . . ."

Look out New York City, Brad Dayton *est arrivé!*

You can bet Moody and Rakoff pitched a bitch when I told them I wouldn't be around this weekend to rehearse *Faded Flowers.* Like I'm gonna skip the biggest audition of my life when I been planning it for months. Besides, it's not like we still don't got two more weeks before we start shooting.

Wanna know what I love most about NYC so far?

The people.

Like the lyrics to my favorite Sunday School song says, *"Red, yellow, black, and white . . ."* Well, so far I haven't seen any Indians—I mean, *Native Americans*—but I'm sure they're here somewhere.

Outside LaGuardia, I stand smoking a cigarette, waiting for the bus to transport me to Manhattan. I'm surprised how warm it is here. When I boarded the plane this morning at Metro, it was twenty-two degrees and *snowing*. Now it feels a balmy forty with partly sunny skies. I heard somebody say something about it being on account of New York is located on the ocean . . . Who knew?

I'd be lying if I didn't admit I'm a tad freaked out having to find my way all by myself. For the bijillionth time, I reach deep into my pocket for my directions, scratched out on a piece of scrap paper.

Express bus from LAG to GCS
S train to Times Sq
1/9 to Houston

I don't know why I'm worried. If I get lost, I'll just ask somebody. Despite what I been warned about New Yorkers not being friendly, how bad can they *really* be?

"Does this bus go to Grand Central Station?"

After almost getting on the Q33 to Queens, I turn to the Hispanic-looking woman sitting on the bench beside me at the stop. I swear she's carrying as many babies in her arms as she's got bags at her feet, all of them dirty-faced and fat and totally adorable. The babies, I mean, not the bags.

The look she gives me says, *How dare you talk to me, you Midwestern gay-boy?* "No speak English."

Well, how should I know?

Ten minutes later, a bus rolls up, large and blue. With the words GRAND CENTRAL prominently displayed on the light-up sign above the windshield, it's gotta be the right one . . . I hope.

Back in Detroit, we rarely ever take the bus anywhere. In fact, I think the last time I rode one was back in 10th grade when me and Max hopped the SEMTA up John R to see *The Legend of Billie Jean* at Oakland Mall. This was before any of my friends could drive and feels like sooo long ago.

Like Rosa Parks from my native Motown, I make my way towards the back of the bus. There's not a seat to be found amongst the natives and other tourists en route to their final destinations.

Lonely people in a city of millions.

After we pull outta the airport parking lot and onto the highway, in the distance I see it. The City (as they call it), where the neon lights of Broadway are bright and magic fills the air . . .

An *hour* later, I step off the bus.

Back when I was little, whenever our phone rang, Mom would say "Grand Central" before picking it up. At the time, I never knew why. But when I exit the bus and enter the *real* Grand Central Station, I learn the answer . . . The place is a zoo!

In the middle, there's this giant area called the Main Concourse. According to the brochure I picked up . . .

> The Terminal's Beaux Arts interior measures 275 feet long by 120 feet wide. The vaulted ceiling is 125 feet high, and the arch windows are 60 feet high at each end. The walls are covered with a warm buff-colored stone with wainscots and trimmings of cream-colored Botticino marble . . .

In the center sits the world famous rendezvous spot, a round Information Booth with its four-sided clock and pagoda made of marble and brass. I guess there's also a hidden spiral staircase leading down to the lower level. Pretty cool, huh?

Turning back to the brochure, I discover . . .

> The great astronomical mural, from a design by the French painter Paul Helleu, painted in gold leaf on cerulean

> blue oil is the most notable feature of the Main Concourse. This extraordinary painting arches over the 80,000 square-foot Main Concourse, portraying the Mediterranean sky with October-to-March zodiac and 2,500 stars.

Back in the day, the sixty largest stars were lit with forty-watt lights that had to be replaced by hand on a regular basis. There's no way you'd catch this boy climbing up 125 feet just to change a lightbulb! If you ask me, the ceiling looks a little dingy, which is probably why they're about to begin a master revitalization plan with the help of the guys responsible for restoring Ellis Island.

The other interesting factoid I read about is the Whispering Gallery . . .

> Located at the end of both ramps when heading down to the Lower Level, the Whispering Gallery offers a phonic treat to visitors of Grand Central.

Supposedly, if you and your love stand facing the walls in opposite corners, you can whisper sweet nothings to each other and hear every word said. Doesn't that sound totally romantic? Now I *really* wish The Sophomore was here!

Truth be told, I don't know what's going on between me and that kid.

After that first kiss in my car, Richie's been all about getting in-character for this *Faded Flowers* film. Like I said, we start shooting in two weeks, and he's bound and determined we *become* Noel and Ryan, secret gay lovers.

Whenever he calls me, it's "Hey, Ryan . . ." Whenever we hang up, it's "Good night, Ryan . . ." Whenever we have lunch, it's footsies under the table. Not that I'm complaining or anything, I think it's totally cute.

About the only thing we *haven't* done is have S-E-X.

At least not Y-E-T.

But I'm not gonna think about that!

There's no time right now. I gotta find the S train and get myself down to Greenwich Village.

Mr. Dell'Olio's good friend, Christopher, is letting me stay at his place on Houston Street. He's a professional actor. I guess they met back in the day when Dell was working as a director Off-Off-Broadway.

'member the play I seen the show card for, hanging above mine and Richie's table at Backstage? *Torch Song Trilogy* by Harvey Fierstein. Well, apparently Christopher understudied in the original production back in like 1982 when it transferred to Broadway. How cool is it that I get to meet somebody who does what I wanna do for a living, you know what I mean?

"Does this subway go to Times Square?"

Finally, I see a sign leading me to the S train, where I promptly get in line at what I'm pretty sure is the token booth, and address the oh-so friendly looking attendant behind the bulletproof Plexiglas.

The look the guy gives me says, *Are you an idiot, you Midwestern gay-boy?* "Only place it goes."

Determined not to be affected by the nasty attitude of others, I ask, "May I buy a token . . . Please?"

Without any expression whatsoever, Token Booth Guy replies, "One dollar."

I'm not saying he's being a jerk just because he's black and I'm white, but coming from Ferndale/Hazel Park where there's *one* African-American kid in all of Hillbilly High ("but he's nice"), how am I supposed to feel? Ever since I seen that commercial where the little boy tells his grandpa that his Jewish friend, Jimmy, called him *prejudice,* I always make sure I treat people alike no matter who they are.

I slip a $20 bill thru the slot.

"Ain't you got nothing smaller?"

As much as I wanna answer, *If I did, I would've given it to you, now wouldn't I?,* I mind my manners. "Sorry . . ."

Token Booth Guy says, "How long you in town for?" As if it's any of his business!

I reply, "Until Monday." Only because *my* mother raised me to be polite.

"Buy a ten-pack."

"How much does that cost?"

TBG looks at me like I'm a Total Moron. "Ten dollars."

Well, how should I know?

I thought maybe they give you a discount for buying in bulk.

Whatever . . .

Taking the plastic bag of tokens TBG practically throws at me along with my change, I head towards the overhead signs marked S.

At the end of the tunnel, I find *four* different sets of tracks.

"Excuse me . . . What train do I take to Times Square?"

This time I decide to ask a (white) woman wearing Reeboks with her tweed business suit and wool winter coat. She looks at me like I have TOURIST tattooed across my forehead. "Any of 'em."

Well, how should I know?

I thought maybe each of the four different trains went someplace else.

Whatever . . .

Lonely people in a city of millions.

Like a lamb to the slaughter, I follow the herd towards the arriving subway, climbing on board once the car doors slide open. A loud snap-crackle pops above my head.

"This is the shuttle to Times Square," the husky male voice announces. "Stand clear of the closing doors."

For a second, I panic. I'm supposed to be taking the S train, *not* the shuttle, whatever that is. A quick check of the map hanging next to the door informs me I'm indeed on the S (for *shuttle*) and that there's only one stop between Times Square and Grand Central Station . . . So far so good!

Now that I think of it, I can't say I ever rode a subway before. In fact, the only train I ever been on in my life is the one at the Detroit Zoo. Back when we were little, Dad used to take me and the girls at least once a year during the summer. At first sight of the shiny silver water tower rising above Woodward, I just about wet myself I got sooo bic-cited.

Whenever we went, we made sure to follow the white-painted elephant prints along the exact same route: the penguin house, the bird atrium, followed by the reptiles. A quick stop at the polar bear fountain, say hello to the prairie dogs, then work our way back towards the giraffes and zebras in their colorful Egyptian display. I *hated* the Hippo House . . . Talk about a stink!

With my red plastic elephant key, I made sure we stopped at every yellow information box, listening to the facts for each particular habitat. I'm sure this drove Dad totally crazy. But what I loved most about our annual zoological excursion was the end-of-the-day train trip from Africa Station back to the parking lot.

Sure, the cars were tiny, but the trip thru the tunnel made it worth the ride as me and Janelle competed to see who could scream their heads off the loudest. We also begged Dad to buy us one of them giant spiral-colored all-day suckers from the souvenir stand, and he would always remind us he spent enough money already.

"So what brings you to the Big City?"

A middle-aged man with a cheesy mustache and wire-frame glasses shares my subway seat. He reminds me of Mr. Klan, all bundled up in a navy blue faux-fur trimmed parka. You know, the kind with the snorkel hood and orange interior, circa 1977.

My first thought is, *How's this guy know I'm a tourist?* Then I remember the suitcase by my side, which I can tell is totally annoying everybody whose way it's in.

"I'm here for an audition," I confess.

The look he gives me says, *Hello, Midwestern gay-boy!*

Rambling along on its track, the jerking of the train makes conversation tricky. I explain all about how I'm an actor, about Juilliard, how I never been to New York, da-dah da-dah . . . Probably *not* such a good idea.

Not that he looks like a child molester or anything, but I'll never forget what happened when I was five years old and the Oakland County Child Killer struck for the first time . . . 'member?

It all began in February 1976 . . .

With the bicentennial mere months away, the body of a 12-year-old boy from Ferndale was found laid out in a snow bank in a parking lot on 10 Mile in Southfield. He had been strangled and sexually assaulted.

Over the course of the next thirteen months, three more children were abducted and murdered, much in the same way. The second victim, a 12-year-old girl from Royal Oak, ran away from home just three days before Christmas. On the morning after, they discovered her body along I-75 in Troy near 16 Mile, aka Big Beaver. She had been shot in the face.

In January 1977, a 10-year-old girl disappeared from a 7-Eleven in Berkley. A little over two weeks passed when a postal carrier found her, lifeless, laying on the side of a road in rural Franklin. She had been smothered to death.

Finally, an 11-year-old boy from Birmingham went missing in March after buying a magazine at a nearby drugstore. Two teenagers later spotted him in a shallow grave near 8 Mile in Livonia, his skateboard by his side. He had been suffocated after being sexually abused.

What kind of person could do this to an innocent child?

Luckily, when these tragic events took place, my family was living in *Macomb* County, where as far as we knew, no Child Killer lurked. Yet I'll never forget the terror instilled in me and Janelle at the time. Every day we ran home from school, fearful of being snatched up by a stranger. Every evening when the *Macomb Daily* arrived, we prayed they didn't print another headline about another kid gone missing.

Over ten years later, the mystery of the Oakland County Child Killer remains unsolved.

"Next stop Times Square."

Like nails on a chalkboard, the subway screeches to a halt.

Parka Guy informs me, "This is us."

The train doors open, the people pour out, like sardines from a can. I don't know where I'm going, so I keep my eyes peeled for directions to the 1/9 line to Houston.

"Can I carry that for you?"

As much as I wouldn't mind the assistance, I keep thinking how freaked out my mom would be if she knew I was talking to a stranger, let alone accepting help from him. Especially one who may or may not be a serial killer, but *is* most likely gay and clearly into young boys.

"I'm good, thanks."

Turns out, Parka Guy is also going my way, so I have no other choice but to follow. Down and around, in and out, past some kid beating a plastic gallon bucket with drumsticks.

Up ahead and down some steps, I hear what sounds like a subway pulling into the station. Sure enough, on the sign above, I see the word DOWNTOWN and the numbers 2, 3 and 1/9 in white on a red circle. Looks like we made it in the nick of time!

We step in, and stand clear of the closing doors.

"So does this train stop at Houston?" I ask. Only I pronounce the street name the way I been since I got here, like the famous Texas town.

You can bet I feel like an ass when PG replies, "No . . . But it stops at *How-ston.*"

I do a double take. "In Green-wich Village?"

"No . . . In *Gren-ich* Village."

What the fuck?

I thought Detroit was the only place they were dumb enough to pronounce G-R-A-T-I-O-T as *Gra-shit* and S-C-H-O-E-N-H-E-R-R as *Shaner.*

"Well, I'm staying with a friend on *How-ston* and Green-wich—I mean, *Gren-ich,*" I inform PG. Again, probably not such a good idea.

"Get off at Houston," he tells me, "and walk two blocks west."

I'm not sure how exactly I'll be able to tell east from west, but once I get there I'll either figure it out or ask somebody. To quote Paula Poundstone (yet again): "I can't tell left from right without pretending to eat!"

At the next stop, 14th Street, I notice the train has filled up quite a bit since we first got on. An older woman with white hair and wrinkles stands in front of where I'm sitting. Straining to reach the bar overhead, she's weighted down with shopping bags from someplace called Fairway.

"Excuse me, ma'am," I say politely. "Would you like to sit?"

The woman looks down at me and smiles. "I'm fine, I'm getting off."

I have to laugh at the way she pronounces *fine* like *coin.*

"This is the 1/9 to South Ferry," a female voice announces rapidly yet audibly this time. "Next stop Houston . . . Step in, stand clear."

Once again, we're off, the clickety-clack rhythmically rocking me to rest.

It never fails, whenever I get in a car or other moving vehicle, no matter how long the ride, I immediately wanna take a nap. Back when I was little and Mom couldn't get me to fall asleep, she'd make Dad drive us around the block. In two seconds, I'd be out like a light . . . Too bad this guy in the parka keeps yakking my ear off.

"So how long you in town for?" he questions, milking each moment of our time together.

"Just till Monday."

Boy, am I ready to get off this train and be on my merry way all by myself!

"If you need someone to show you around, feel free to call."

Growing creepier by the second, the guy jots down seven digits on a scrap of paper with a pen he pulls from deep within his parka.

Lying thru my in-much-need-of-braces teeth, I reply, "I will."

As if! Not that I'm saying he's a perv or anything, but come on . . . The guy's gotta be at least twice my age. What's he doing offering to play tour guide to a teenager?

Finally, the subway comes to another screeching halt.

"This is our stop," Parka Guy informs me.

Turns out, he's also getting off at Houston.

Just my luck!

Out on the street, once more he offers to assist me with my suitcase.

"I'm good, thanks . . ." The last thing I need is him knowing exactly where I'm staying all weekend, you know what I mean?

"You positive?"

Not sure how else to give him the hint I'm not the least bit interested, I answer, "Positive . . . My *boyfriend* is meeting me here any minute."

Thank God he finally gets it.

Like a weasel, I watch him burrow back beneath the ground. I guess this wasn't his subway stop after all! I can't help but feel sorry for the guy. It must be tough making friends in this town, let alone finding somebody special.

Lonely people in a city of millions.

Hot Child in the City

"So young to be loose and on her own
Young boys, they all want to take her home . . ."

—Nick Gilder

Bradley James Dayton, you're a fool!

I been in New York City for all of ten hours and already I got myself in trouble.

Make that *twelve.*

A glance at my Swatch informs me it's almost 2 o'clock in the morning. Only eight more hours till the biggest audition of my life.

What the hell am I doing wasted off my ass in a gay bar?

Around 3:30 PM, I arrived at Mr. Dell'Olio's friend Christopher's place on *How-ston* and *Gren-ich,* after escaping the evil clutches of Parka Guy the Pedophile.

Buzz!

I pressed the button marked 5-B and waited . . . Nothing happened.

Buzz!

I pressed the button again . . . Nothing happened.

Buzz!

I pressed the button a third time, before coming to the conclusion that all I needed to do was *push* the door open since it wasn't the least bit locked. How's that for feeling secure?

After hauling my suitcase up five flights of stairs to a darkened hall with lead-painted peeling walls and a single burned-out bulb, my gracious host greeted me at the door.

"I see you survived the subway . . ."

Barely!

About 6' tall with feathered-back sandy brown hair and just a hint of hi-lights, Christopher appeared rather stylish for a guy his age—twenty-seven. When I followed him into the apartment, I couldn't help but notice his ass hanging out of a well-placed rip beneath the right cheek of his Bugle Boys. He reminded me of George Michael from the "Faith" video. All he needed was the leather jacket, sunglasses, and some scruff.

"Can I offer you something to drink?"

Dying of thirst, I replied, "I'll take some pop."

Christopher chuckled at my Michigan-ism. "One *pop* coming right up."

I made myself comfortable on the couch, gulping down a refreshing Diet Rite. *"Ahhh!"*

"So when's your big audition?"

"Tomorrow at 10 o'clock."

After months and months of waiting, the big day was about to be here.

I glanced around the living/bedroom. On the walls, an assortment of *Playbills* and Theatre posters reminiscent of Backstage restaurant made me suspect that Christopher most likely was gay. His record collection also tipped me off, comprised of classics such as *Go West* by The Village People, Bette Midler's *The Divine Miss M,* and the brand-new, self-titled *Cher,* featuring "We All Sleep Alone," which I L-O-V-E!

"You've got *plenty* of time," my host assured me with a flounce of his wrist. "Get out and see the sights before the sun goes down."

Truth be told, I couldn't do anything for the next eighteen hours but worry about my audition. This is why I decided to pick up some postcards, thinking I better send one to my mom and my sisters . . . And Mr. Dell'Olio . . . And The Sophomore.

"There's a great little bookstore you should check out called Oscar Wilde's."

I'd be lying if I didn't admit I don't know much about the guy. Other than he wrote *The Picture of Dorian Gray,* which Mrs. Malloy forced us to read in 11th grade English Shit—I mean, *Lit.* I barely remember the story. Something about a guy who is sooo vain he doesn't wanna grow old, so he pays this artist to paint a portrait of him that ages instead.

At the time we read it in class, I didn't realize Oscar Wilde was gay. Until Stacy Gillespie raised her hand and was all like, "Mrs. Malloy . . . Wasn't Oscar Wilde homosexual?"

Flummoxed, Mrs. Malloy was all like, "Why yes, he was."

End of discussion.

The Village (as they call it), is totally cute, but totally confusing!

With tiny crooked streets running all different directions, a person could easily lose his way. At one point, West 4th Street actually crosses West 10th. There's even an aptly named *Gay* Street right across from the Oscar Wilde Bookshop, which Christopher says is like the world's oldest gay bookstore, established in 1967, two years preceding the birth of the Gay Liberation movement.

A few years ago, I begged Jack to come to New York with me to celebrate his 16th birthday, which falls on June 27th, the eve of the Stonewall Riots . . . And do you think he would?

N-O!

"Good afternoon."

A young lesbian-looking woman greeted me from behind the counter as the jingling of bells announced my arrival. Like everything else in NYC, the bookstore was super tiny. I guess there isn't a whole lot to offer in the world of Gay Literature. The fact that such a place even exists totally amazes me. I can't imagine *ever* finding anything gay-owned and operated in Hazel Park. Or even Ferndale, for that matter.

A display marked STONEWALL BOOK AWARD-WINNERS offered such titles: *The Spirit and the Flesh: Sexual Diversity in American Indian Culture, Sex and Germs: The Politics of AIDS,* and *The Celluloid Closet: Homosexuality in the Movies.* Out of curiosity, I wondered if they had a copy of *Now Let's Talk About Music* by Gordon Merrick laying around anywhere.

Years ago, I bought a copy of this trashy gay romance novel up at B. Dalton's in Universal Mall, all about these gay guys, Ned and Gerry, cruising about on the gay *Love Boat,* getting it on with anybody and everybody who comes along. Lemme tell ya, me and Jack read that book over and over (and over) till the cover practically fell off. I can't believe he threw it in a mailbox on his way to school one morning, fearing Dianne would find it when she was snooping about, aka cleaning his room.

"Are you looking for something particular?" Lesbian Lady inquired, a polite smile gracing her fine-featured face. Why do some women look good without makeup and others not?

"Just these, please."

I decided to skip the Gordon Merrick in favor of a few black-and-white NY landmark postcards I found on a rack next to the register: Empire State Building, Statue of Liberty, World Trade Center. The last thing I needed was to start reading *The Adventures of Ned & Gerry* and get all distracted when I had the biggest audition of my life in the morning, you know what I mean?

"Come again," Lesbian Lady told me after I paid for my purchase.

"I will . . . Next time I'm in town."

I couldn't resist letting it slip I was a tourist, as if LL couldn't already tell by my I ♥ NY shopping bag filled with the I ♥ NY T-shirts I bought for my mom and my sisters . . . And Mr. Dell'Olio . . . And The Sophomore.

Before I could depart, LL asked, "Where you visiting from?"

"Detroit, Michigan," I answered proudly, probably for the first time in my life.

"What brings you to The City?"

Her genuine interest took me by surprise.

"Well, since you asked . . ."

I explained all about how I'm an actor here for my Juilliard audition, da-dah da-dah . . .

Wanna know what she said to this?

"I auditioned for Juilliard . . . *Three* times."

This explained why she was working in a bookstore and not on Broadway.

"How did it go?" I wondered if maybe she could give me some insight as to what tomorrow had in store.

"Fine, I thought . . . The last one, I even got a callback."

"Well, that's a good sign." I tried my best to sound encouraging. "Maybe four's a charm."

The woman shrugged. "Being an actor is tough . . . Especially if you're a Friend of Dorothy."

Dorothy who?

Outside, it surprised me to see how dark it was at only 4:30 PM. Maybe because of all the tall buildings blocking out the sun. Or the fact that New York City is on one edge of the Eastern time zone and Detroit the other, closer to Central in Chicago. Either way, it totally depressed me. I thought of Sean living it up in Sunny LA, probably hanging out at the beach with David Lee Roth and all the California girls—and the bodybuilders . . . Lucky!

Down the block, I discovered a lovely little café, *Les Deux Gamins.* Not sure how that translates (The Two Somethings), but I decided to stop in, order a cappuccino and smoke a cigarette while I wrote out a quick note.

1/30/88

Dear Noel,

Greetings from Greenwich Village! Got here a couple hours ago, did some shopping, now I'm pooped. Tomorrow's the big day . . . I think I'm gonna throw up.

Love, Ryan

PS—Wish you were here!

Later that evening, Christopher hailed us a cab and we headed uptown for dinner at this famous restaurant called Sardi's on W. 44th Street right off Times Square. You might remember it from *The Muppets Take Manhattan* when Kermit goes in, disguised as a famous producer or director or somebody, trying to generate some hype about his musical, *Manhattan Melodies* . . . 'member?

All these caricatures of famous Theatre-types cover the walls. Fozzie takes down the one of Liza Minnelli, and replaces it with Kermit's, causing the entire room to start buzzing about the famous producer or director or whoever they think Kermit is. Until the *real* Liza Minnelli shows up. Only to discover she's been replaced by a frog . . . Boy, she's pissed!

"So what advice can you give an aspiring actor?"

Over dinner, I decided to ask Christopher some questions. I figured since he's been there and done it, he could offer an insider's perspective I can't get anywhere else on the Acting Biz . . . *Carpe diem,* and all that jazz.

"You want the honest truth?" He pushed his half-full plate

of pasta aside in favor of a Merit Ultra Light. "It sucks." He lit up, exhaled. "If there's anything else you can think of doing, if there's *anything* that'll make you just as happy . . . Do it."

At first, I thought he was joking around, saying the same thing everybody else keeps telling me: "It's a hard business." "Only a small percentage of actors actually make a living." Da-dah da-dah. Too bad the bitter tone in Christopher's voice made me realize just how serious he was.

"But you been on Broadway," I reminded him, lighting my own Marlboro Light. Around us, the din of pre-show diners made me wonder if anybody would recognize my companion from his *Torch Song* days. Secretly, I hoped they would.

Christopher scoffed, "Five years ago," fiercely sucking on his cig.

Five years? I didn't realize it's been so long.

"Well, what have you done since?"

I watched him stab at the olives in what I think was his third martini.

"Oh," he sighed, "a little temp work here, a little cater-waitering there . . ."

Clearly the man was *not* happy with his current career path.

"What about TV?" I wondered. "Can't you get a job on a soap?" I knew they filmed *Days of our Lives* in LA, but what about all the other shows like *Loving* and *Another World*?

"Sure . . . I'll just give 'em a call and let 'em know I'm available."

"Don't you have an agent?" I assumed a professional actor must.

This was the point where Christopher laid it all on the line.

"I don't know if you know this," he began, "but I'm gay."

Like I said, I had a feeling this might be the case, but I didn't wanna insult my host by being all like, "Oh, yeah . . . I could totally tell you're a fag." Instead, I said, "You are?" doing my best interpretation of surprised.

"In this business, everybody's gay," Christopher confided. "Actors, agents, casting directors, you name it."

"Well, that's cool," I replied, never stopping to consider. I mean, I knew Rock Hudson was gay, and I always assumed that guy from *The $1.98 Beauty Show*, Rip Taylor, had to be a homo.

"The thing is . . . *Nobody* talks about it."

This didn't make sense to me. "Why not?"

Christopher lapped up his last drops of vodka. "Because if you admit you're a fag," he explained, signaling the waiter, "nobody will hire you."

Again, I didn't get it. "Why not?"

Contemplating the bottom of his empty glass, he commented sadly, "That's show-biz."

Boy, was Jack gonna be happy!

This was the *exact* same thing he said Sophomore year when I first told him I'm a homo: "Aren't you afraid people are gonna find out about you?" As far as Jack Paterno was concerned, everybody knows famous people can't be gay and famous.

"What about Rock Hudson?" I remarked. "He was famous *and* gay, and everybody knew it."

"And look what happened to him."

At the time, I thought Jack was totally overreacting, but here was Christopher, a (quote-unquote) professional actor, backing him up.

Now what was I gonna do?

We sat in silence, smoking our cigarettes, waiting for the check.

"I don't mean to discourage you," Christopher said sincerely, after a moment. "You seem like a nice guy."

I nodded and smiled, unsure where this conversation was heading.

"You're cute, you're intelligent, obviously you're talented or Ray wouldn't recommend you for Juilliard."

For a second, I had to stop and think about who Ray was . . . Then I remembered he's Mr. Dell'Olio.

Christopher stubbed out his smoke. "Let me ask *you* a question . . ."

Again, I nodded and smiled.

"You wanna be an actor?"

"More than anything."

"Why?"

I thought long and hard.

Like I said, it all started when Mrs. Malloy assigned us the *What I Want to Be When I Grow Up* paper during first semester of Sophomore English. At the time, I never considered how I wanted to spend the rest of my life. Being a C student, I didn't think I'd get into college, let alone about what I might study.

The only thing I enjoyed up till that point was playing my trombone, and I didn't wanna become a professional Band Fag! Maybe *le français*? Sure, I enjoy speaking it, but what would I do with a degree? Teach high school to a bunch of brats and wind up like Mrs. Carey standing in front of an empty classroom? The only other thing I enjoyed doing was watching TV and going to the movies.

Hence my decision to become an actor.

From that moment, I began to eat, sleep, live and breathe Drama. I checked out and read all the plays in the HPHS library. This didn't amount to many: *A Streetcar Named Desire, You Can't Take It with You, The Matchmaker,* which is the non-musical precursor to *Hello, Dolly!*

I started attending the Theatre on a regular basis. Not the Fisher, downtown, I couldn't afford it. But I took in *Two by Two* at Stagecrafters in Royal Oak, and saw many a show at the local area high schools: *Kiss Me, Kate* at Lamphere, *Guys and Dolls* at Berkley, and *Oliver!* at Ferndale, which was probably my fave.

The lead actors did an okay job, but the girl who played Mrs. Sowerberry, the undertaker's wife, really stole the show with "It's Your Funeral." Her name I'll never forget: Miriam Shor. You can bet she's gonna go far!

Of course, all that happened before I ever even stepped on a stage. Once I got a taste of what it feels like to appear in front of a live audience, to hear their response to something I did, to make them laugh and possibly cry . . . That feeling is nothing short of magic, and one I can *not* live without.

"Then remember what I said," Christopher replied once I told him all of this.

After everything I went thru with Jack, after all the time I spent trying to get him to come out, I promised myself I would *never* live my life in The Closet.

Why do I feel like now, I don't have a choice?

Next, we headed over to this half-price ticket booth called TKTS, located in the middle of Times Square, between the giant Coca-Cola sign seen in all the movies and where the ball drops every December 31st on *Dick Clark's New Year's Rockin' Eve*. For $50 (plus service charge) we got two tickets to see the 1987 Tony Award–winning Best Musical, *Les Misérables*.

Christopher highly recommended we see it since he knows some of the actors in the cast. The story is all about this French guy, Jean Valjean, who goes to jail for stealing a loaf of bread, but eventually rises up to become the town mayor, and adopt this little orphan girl after her whore of a mother drops dead from syphilis or something.

I guess it's based on a book by some guy, Victor Hugo, from like 1800-something. I should probably know this since the story takes place in France, and we know how I like all things French . . . Why don't I play French horn?

I gotta say, it totally surprised me when I found out *Les Miz* (as they call it), is one of the few shows actually playing *on* Broadway. Apparently, the term has nothing to do with the actual road. Most of the theatres are located on various side streets throughout the Midtown area.

Regardless, the show was awesome. Afterwards, we got a backstage tour, so we could see the turntable and barricade up close. Talk about cool! I can *not* wait till I get a chance to appear on a Broadway stage—hopefully sooner than later, you know what I mean?

This is where I met the guy I been hanging out with for the last two hours . . .

"Where'd you go?"

My new friend appears holding two plastic foam-filled cups, which he paid something like $4 for—apiece. Talk about a rip-off! Back in Hazel Park, you can get an entire six-pack up at Kado's Market for less than that.

"Isn't it Last Call yet?"

I do *not* need to be drinking anything else right now. In fact, I can't even remember the guy's name I'm talking to, that's how wasted I am.

"Not in New York," *Les Miz* Guy informs me. "Bars are open till 4 o'clock."

Just what I need to hear!

Actually, he's a friend of—

Shit!

The guy I'm staying with . . . What's *his* name?

Christopher!

The guy I'm at the bar with is an actor friend of Christopher's. Speaking of . . .

"What happened to Christopher?"

I just realized I haven't seen him in like over an hour.

"He wasn't feeling too good," *Les Miz* Guy reports. "He said he'll see you in the morning."

"I hope it wasn't something he ate."

Now that I think of it, I feel a tad sick to my stomach myself. But maybe it's from all the beer I been drinking.

LMG shrugs. "He probably had to take his pills."

This confirms my suspicions: *Christopher has* AIDS.

I had a feeling this might be the case.

When I first arrived at his apartment, before heading out to the bookstore, I excused myself to the little boys' room. Of course, I couldn't help but sneak a peek inside the old medicine cabinet. I don't know why, it's just something I always do whenever I'm in a new home . . . Call me curious!

Sharing the space with the tube of toothpaste, mini-bottle of mouthwash, and cinnamon-flavored floss, I found a collection of amber-colored containers. You know, the plastic prescription bottle kind with the childproof "Keep Out of Reach" caps. Only instead of familiar contents like *penicillin* printed on the labels, these held something called *azidothymidine*.

This immediately called to mind the 1985 made-for-TV movie starring Aidan Quinn, Ben Gazzara and Gena Rowlands, *An Early Frost* . . .

Michael Pierson (Quinn), a successful-but-closeted lawyer, learns he has AIDS after his lover reveals he cheated on him. Soon after, Michael returns home to break the news to his parents (Gazzara and Rowlands), and his bitch of a pregnant sister (some chick from *A Nightmare on Elm Street 2*, Sydney Walsh).

In typical father fashion, Michael's dad does *not* deal well with the disclosure. At first, he refuses to speak to his son, but eventually breaks his silence, telling him, "I never thought the day would come when you'd be in front of me and I wouldn't know who you are." Michael's mother, God bless her, attempts to persuade her family to accept her offspring for who he is. After all is said and done, Michael winds up in a hospital where he eventually withers and dies.

How's that for an *up* film?

Poor Christopher . . . Why does something sooo terrible have to happen to somebody sooo nice? Talk about a buzz kill!

"I should probably get going . . ."

Five hours and counting till it's time to rise and shine for the big day!

My original plan was to head back to the apartment right after the play and go directly to bed, "Do not pass GO, do not collect $200!" Like I said, I got my audition at 10:00 AM up at 66th Street and Columbus Avenue, and I don't know how long it's gonna take me to get there on the subway.

"But it's still early . . ."

If this guy (what *is* his name?) wasn't sooo cute, I would *not* entertain the idea of staying one second longer. Why does he totally have to be my type: dark hair, dark eyes, SWB? I think I remember him saying he's twenty-two, which I suppose isn't that old. Not to mention he's got this totally sexy New York accent, which has gotten progressively thicker (and sexier) as the night's dragged on (and the more he's had to drink).

Bradley James Dayton, you're a slut!

What about Noel/Richie back in Michigan? Not that we're a couple or anything.

And what about poor Christopher, dying of some fatal disease, all because he chose to be intimate with the *wrong* person? Not that *Les Miz* Guy wants to "do" me or anything.

At that moment, one of my absolute favorite tunes starts to play.

"Oh, my God . . . I love this song!"

Those words did *not* come outta my mouth.

That was *Les Miz* Guy doing the talking.

I'm like, "You do?"

And he's like, "I had the album back in 7th grade."

I'm like, "You're kidding?"

I mean, so did I. Well, I had the 45. Only I was in *2nd* grade when I asked Mom to buy me it. At the time, I didn't realize the song was about a teenaged prostitute. I have a feeling neither did Mom or she never would've let me listen to it.

I remember being in Mrs. Stephens's class at Miller Elementary in Center Line at the time, because one day I brought the record in for Show-and-Tell. Like my mom, Mrs. Stephens's first name was Laura, which is why I think I loved her so. She used to read us *Where the Sidewalk Ends* and *The Giving Tree* by Shel Silverstein, and to her I owe my love of *Charlotte's Web*. Unlike Mom, Mrs. Stephens was well aware of the song with its suggestive lyrics, and wouldn't allow me to give an audio presentation for my 7-year-old classmates.

The year after Mrs. Stephens taught my class, she moved to Noblesville, Indiana, with her husband and two sons. For a while, we used to write letters back and forth. Then when I was like nine or ten, they stopped. Probably because we moved to Ferndale and I forgot to tell her . . . Remind me I need to find Mrs. Stephens's address and drop her a line to see how she's doing after all these years.

"Let's Dance!"

Les Miz Guy cries out at the top of his lungs, like he's David Bowie circa 1983.

"I'm sorry . . ."

Thinking of The Sophomore tucked away in his tiny twin bed back in Hazeltucky, and poor Christopher dying of a dreaded disease here in NYC, on top of the fact that my Juilliard audition is now less than eight hours away, I decline the invitation.

LMG says, "You're cute, you know that?" Totally outta the blue.

Even at this late hour, I blush. "Thanks . . . So are you."

Being the actor that he is, he takes that as his cue. Next thing I know, a pair of full lips firmly press themselves against mine . . . And we're totally making out.

Bradley James Dayton, you're a whore!

What I Am

"I'm not aware of too many things
I know what I know, if you know what I mean . . ."

—Edie Brickell & New Bohemians

"If you're miserable, it's your own damn fault."

Wanna know what time I woke up this morning?

9:00 AM.

'member what time I had the biggest audition of my life?

If you said, "10:00 AM," you win the prize!

The second the alarm goes off, I want to kill myself. Or roll over and go back to bed. Luckily, the windows in Christopher's apartment don't have any treatments, so the sun shining directly in my eyes makes it impossible to do just that.

If I said it one time, I said it a bijillion times: I am *never* drinking again!

Hoping not to rouse my snoring host asleep on the fold-up cot three feet from me, I tiptoe into the bathroom. Except that's not where they keep the shower in this particular apartment. Whose idea was it to put a stand-up stall on top of the kitchen counter?

Don't ask me, but there it sits, three steps up. The last thing I wanna do is wake poor Christopher now that I'm aware of his illness. So forgoing cleanliness in favor of practicality and time, I stick my head beneath the bathroom sink . . . Too bad nothing can be done to get that night-at-the-bar smoke stench off the rest of my body.

Great!

Now I want a cigarette.

At already 9:15 AM, my nicotine fix will have to wait.

Quickly, I assemble my audition outfit: brown slacks, tan dress shirt, and Jack's matching cardigan, exact same thing I wore to the "Top 25" ceremony in October. Once I'm dressed, I break out my curling iron and get to work on my mess of hair.

Yes, I did say *curling iron.*

Actually, it's a Clicker. You know, one of them cordless jobs that's basically a giant cigarette lighter filled with butane so you can use it anytime, anywhere. As you can imagine, the access to electricity is always an issue *Chez Dayton*. Back in the day, I used to borrow Janelle's, but soon as I started making money at Big Boy's, I saved up and bought my own.

See, what I do is . . . I use the curling iron—I mean, *Clicker*—to curl back the hair, then I brush it out with a brush, holding the hair in place with a little hairspray for a more feathered look. About a year ago I tried going *au naturel,* but somebody told me I looked like the guy from Simply Red.

The only problem is sometimes I get a little impatient, like when I'm in a hurry, and I—

Motherfucker!

Burn myself . . . The way I did just now.

Across the room I sprint, reaching for the freezer and finding a silver metal ice tray, circa 1972. The second I pull the lever, I think of Grandma Victor.

Crack!

God, I hope that didn't wake Christopher up.

A quick check in the bathroom mirror reveals a nice red mark right above my brow. Looks like today I'll be sporting bangs! At least my sister, Janelle, could blame a neck burn on a hickey and vice versa.

Speaking of . . .

What the fuck is that *thing* just below my left ear? Looks like today I'll be sporting a turtleneck!

What else can possibly go wrong?

Other than the fact that it's now 9:30 AM and I need to travel sixty-six blocks in less than half an hour. To quote Judy Tenuta (once more): "It could happen!"

Down five flights I fly, out the front door onto Houston—I mean, *How-ston*—running west all the way towards the subway. Too bad I'm supposed to run *east.* Next thing I know, I'm shielding my eyes from the warm winter sun, staring across some river at what I think is New Jersey . . . Maybe it's Brooklyn.

"Taxi!"

Sticking my arm up in the air like I seen in the movies, I shout at the top of my lungs.

There's one . . . And another . . . And another.

What the fuck's a boy gotta do to get a cab in this town?

If this was a film, and I was—I don't know—Marilyn Monroe, I'd step up to the curb and flash some leg. Not like that's gonna work for me here in New York City. Especially since I'm a teenaged boy and all the cab drivers are men, you know what I mean?

Errrk!

Lucky for me, standing in the middle of the road works just as well.

"Where to?"

At least I'm *assuming* that's what the driver says.

The guy's got an accent thicker than Jerry the Chaldean from the Movies at Lakeside. 'member the 25-year-old with the bulging biceps who works the concession stand? Remind me I still need to take him up on his offer to buy me a drink sometime.

"Juilliard School of Drama," I say politely, adding, "and step on it," just because it sounds like something a true New Yorker should say.

Twenty minutes later, we arrive at a big white building with five amazingly beautiful arches and an enormous fountain out front.

"Lin-coln Cen-ter," Cab Driver Guy reports, again in his accent.

I can't believe he took me on a wild goose chase.

I'm like, "I need to go to *Juilliard*," adding, "School of Drama," just in case he doesn't comprehend what I'm saying.

Cab Driver Guy repeats, "Lin-coln Cen-ter."

I say, "Jui-lli-ard," thinking even my sister, Nina, isn't this slow.

CDG insists, "Lin-coln Cen-ter *is* Jui-lli-ard."

Sure enough, across the way a sign points out my final destination, up the stairs and on the left. I slip CDG a $20 bill, not even bothering to look at the meter, before bolting out the door.

I would've said, "Keep the change," because I always wanted to, but right now I'm too pissed . . . Not to mention L-A-T-E.

"Name, please?"

A burly African-American female security guard greets me at the check-in desk.

"Bradley Dayton."

With her three-inch, filed-straight-across and painted-red fingernail, she scrolls down her clipboard, shaking her beaded-braided head as she goes. "Don't see no Bradley Dayton on *my* list."

Well, Sunshine . . . Why don't you take a closer look?

"I'm auditioning for Juilliard," I report proudly, the fact that

I'm standing in the actual School of Drama lobby not yet sinking in.

"Well, where do you think you is . . . The Taj Mahal?"

This she says with a smile, cracking herself up at what's gotta be the funniest thing she's ever told anybody.

I say, "I have a 10 o'clock appointment," adding, "Bradley Dayton from Hazel Park High School." Truth be told, I almost said Hillbilly High, I'm so used to calling it that.

"10 o'clock *AM?*" Sunshine repeats, turning back a page on her clipboard.

No, I'm twelve hours early.

"Why didn't you say so?" Down the list the nail goes, stopping halfway. "Bradley Dayton, is that you?"

No, Sunshine . . . My name is Mahatma Ghandi.

I nod and smile, taking note of the time displayed on the digital clock nearby.

9:57 AM.

"Better hurry, Bradley Dayton . . . You gonna be late."

Thru the turnstile I pass, into the elevator, and up to the 3rd floor. A list posted on the wall informs me of the room number I need to report to, where I find what must be at least twenty kids my age milling about, running thru their own equivalent of "red-leather-yellow-leather" and "rubber-baby-buggy-bumpers."

And this isn't the *only* room.

There's another four or five just like it on this same floor, where at least twenty other kids my age are running thru the exact same drills, and will continue to for the next eight hours. Not to mention the ones auditioning in Chicago, Los Angeles, and God-only-knows-where-else across the entire *États Unis.*

I wanna go home. Or at least to the bathroom. Suddenly, I'm not feeling too great.

"Good morning!"

An attractive man in his early-to-mid-thirties enters, calling out to us. Surprisingly, the room falls silent. Back at HPHS the kids keep on talking and talking (and talking) no matter who's trying to get their attention. I don't know if he's a teacher or what, but the guy looks like somebody important. Did I mention he's sorta cute, in a Greg Brady sorta way, with curly dark hair and thick matching eyebrows?

"I'm new to the faculty here at Juilliard," he tells us. "If you have any questions, my name is Richard . . ."

Great!

Now I feel like I'm gonna cry.

I can't believe I cheated on poor Richie. What kind of person does that make me? I'm away for not even a *day*, and already I'm kissing another guy.

"In just a moment, you'll be taken to a practice room," Richard the faculty member continues, "where you'll have time to go over your audition pieces."

That's *all* we did, me and *Les Miz* Guy.

". . . you'll have three minutes to present your two contrasting monologues . . ."

Well, except for the hickey he gave me.

"Any questions?"

I mean, I'm sure we would've done more, if *I* wanted to . . .

"Break a leg!"

But I didn't.

The entire time LMG was sucking on my neck, I kept thinking about how guilty I felt for letting him do it. Finally, I was like, "I gotta pee." Then I snuck out the side door and stumbled my way down 7th Avenue, using the Twin Towers to guide my way south.

I never did find out his name.

I don't know why I let the guy kiss me in the first place. If

I'm sooo in love with Richie Tyler like I keep saying I am, why would I even *look* at another guy? With all the problems my parents had in their marriage, never once did my dad cheat on my mom.

Back in junior high, I remember reading this book called *The Hite Report on Male Sexuality.* It had this whole section on gay men and how they're much more *promiscuous* than their heterosexual counterparts. For obvious reasons, I became fascinated with this fact. I'll never forget this one story about this guy who used to sit on the toilet in a public restroom, picking up men after men (after men). Whenever somebody sat down in the stall next to him, he'd slide his foot underneath as a signal. If the other guy was interested, he'd signal back and BAM!

As hot as that story seemed at the time, I never imagined my life would come to something like that. I always pictured myself falling in love with one guy. We'd buy a house together, and settle down for the rest of our lives, just me and him. Maybe adopt some kids. Or at least a dog.

I mean, that's all I want outta life.

What everybody else wants.

Just because I'm gay doesn't mean I shouldn't have it . . . *Does it?*

"Where you from?"

A totally cute guy in his early twenties shows me to a tiny room where I have ten minutes to run thru each of my audition monologues.

"Michigan," I reply, unable to get over the guilt feeling in my gut at cheating on my boyfriend-who's-not-*really*-my-boyfriend, even though I totally want him to be. Otherwise, I might actually attempt to carry on a conversation.

About 6'1", the boy is rather well-dressed in a button-down Polo worn with a navy blue blazer, pleated khaki pants, and penny loafers. In fact, most of the guys I seen here are all taller than me. This one reminds me of Robert Downey Jr. from *Weird Science.* He also happens to be a third-year in the acting program here at Juilliard, so I should totally be chatting him up just in case he can put in a good word.

"I went to high school in Michigan," he offers casually.

"Oh, yeah?" I reply, feigning interest. "Whereabouts?"

"Interlochen Arts Academy . . . You know it?"

"I thought Interlochen was a summer camp," I admit, remembering some of the kids I met at Blue Lake mentioning they tried getting into Interlochen, but weren't good enough.

Sounding like a Total Snob, he informs me, "It's *also* a four-year performing arts high school with majors in Theatre Arts, Creative Writing, and Dance."

Well, la-dee-dah!

"So where in Michigan are you from?" I wonder. Not that I give a shit now that I know he's got an attitude.

Interlochen Boy replies, "My family's from Connecticut . . . I just went to school in Michigan."

I'm like, "Oh."

Then he says, "Where do *you* go to school?"

I'm like, "Hazel Park," throwing in "but I live in Ferndale," for good measure. When this registers a blank stare, I add, "It's a suburb of Detroit."

Interlochen Boy says, "One of my best friends is from Bloomfield Hills."

I'm like, "Bloomfield Hills is nice."

And full of rich people!

Whatever . . .

I got more important things to worry about right now, like the fate of what I thought was going to be my profession totally going up in flames.

Inside the tiny practice room, we find a simple gray folding chair, and a black metal music stand. There's also an upright piano. Thank God I won't be doing any singing. I barely have a speaking voice after all the cigarettes I smoked last night . . . I *really* gotta quit!

"Need anything else?" my escort inquires before leaving me to my monologues.

I'm about to respond, *Not that I can think of, Dickface.* Then I change my mind.

"Can I ask you a question?" After talking to him, I figure this guy's gotta know the answer. "Are there any gay guys here?"

IB closes the door behind us. For a second, I think he's gonna make a move on me. "Why do you ask?"

"No reason . . . Just curious."

He gives me a suspicious look, much like the one my mom does when she suspects I'm up to something. "You mean like teachers . . . or students?"

I answer, "I don't know . . . Students, I guess."

IB hesitates, chewing a manicured fingernail. "If there is," he quietly informs me, "*I* don't know any—and neither does anybody else."

Whatever . . .

"Hello, my name is Bradley Dayton . . . My selection is from *Tea and Sympathy* by Robert Anderson, the character of Tom."

Shit!

The last thing I wanna do is walk into my Juilliard audition with a *gay* monologue. I'll never get in that way. I wish Mr. Dell'Olio would've warned me, like his friend Christopher did, before I spent the last two months wasting my time rehearsing and rehearsing (and rehearsing) this stupid selection.

Now what?

I think I'll be fine with my classical (Romeo from *Romeo & Juliet*), but the contemporary has sooo gotta go! Unfortunately, the only other piece I got memorized is the Jane Seymour "Man of My Dreams" monologue from *Somewhere in Time.* It looks like I'm screwed either way.

"Good morning!"

From behind a folding table I'm greeted by three adjudicators. I'm sure I should know their names, but for the life of me can't remember due to the nervous state I'm currently residing in. The men are both middle-aged and balding, while the woman looks to be about thirty with short dark hair, parted on the side, and matching tortoiseshell glasses.

"Hello."

This is all I can manage to muster up.

Looking around the room, I gotta say, this isn't exactly the place I envisioned myself auditioning for Juilliard in. I'm guessing this is a dance studio of some sort, with one entire wall covered in mirrors, and a wooden bar running across about waist high. I thought for sure I'd be in an actual Theatre. I mean, this is *the* (as in thee) best Drama School in the entire country, for chris'sakes, you know what I mean?

"You must be Bradley Dayton," the woman says, when I continue standing there, mouth agape, looking like a Total Dork.

"Yes," I nod and smile. "Thank you for having me."

Something about the way the woman takes charge of the situation reminds me of Jessica Clark Putnam, though she looks more like Mr. Drysdale's secretary on *The Beverly Hillbillies,* Miss Hathaway. I wonder if she's a lesbian. I see no cluster of diamonds on her ring finger.

"And what will you be doing for us today?" asks Baldy #1.

Something about the glint is his eye makes me wonder if he, too, is gay.

Clearing my throat, I launch into my spiel. "Hello, my name is Bradley Dayton . . ."

Duh!

Before I can continue, I'm interrupted by Baldy #2. "Where are you visiting us from today, Bradley Dayton?" he wonders, in a voice reminiscent of Paul Lynde, who I adore as Uncle Arthur on *Bewitched* reruns.

"I live in Ferndale, Michigan."

Jane Hathaway's face lights up. "I love Michigan!" she cries, adding, "Are you at Interlochen?"

"I'm afraid I'm not," I reply, trying *not* to let it show on my face how humiliated I am. "I go to school in Hazel Park."

"And where is that?" Baldy #1 wonders.

Holding up my right hand, palm facing out, I point to the base of my thumb on my Michigan hand-map. "It's a suburb of Detroit."

"Ah, yes . . . Detroit." Paul Lynde sighs. "I've got good friends who live in Bloomfield Hills."

Of course you do!

"Well, welcome," Jane Hathaway says warmly, concluding the small talk. "Whenever you're ready . . ."

Now I'm totally thrown off!

Taking it from the top, I begin with, "Hello, my name is Bradley Dayton . . . My selection is—"

Fuck, I forgot there's two!

"My selections *are* . . . Romeo from *Romeo & Juliet.*"

I never start with the classical!

Why I went there, I don't know.

"And . . ."

Wanna know what I say next?

"Bob Cratchit from *A Christmas Carol.*"

From the expression on the judges' faces, I get the impression they weren't expecting that one to come outta my mouth—and neither was I. Especially since there isn't the slightest thing resembling a monologue for Bob Cratchit in the entire play.

Now I'm gonna have to ab-lib—I mean, *ad-lib.*

I don't know why, but in the moment, I kept hearing Christopher's voice inside my head: *"Don't be gay."*

I mean, that's not exactly what he said, but he implied it, didn't he?

"If you're a homo, you'll never become a famous actor."

Despite the fact I'm almost positive the three middle-aged folks sitting behind the brown metal table, holding the fate of my future in the palms of their hands, are *all* Friends of Dorothy (i.e., Judy Garland—Christopher explained it), I can't take a risk by giving them the slightest indication that *I* might be, too.

"To thine ownself be true."

Fuck that shit.

Faded Flowers

"We had some good machines, but they don't work no more
I loved you once, don't love you anymore . . ."

—Shriekback

2-2-88

Dear Brad,

I was this close to coming up to Big Boy's last night to stalk you in person, but I decided to be civil and write you instead. If I didn't know better, I'd think you were avoiding me. Unless Laura's losing it and keeps forgetting to tell you I called. Three times since you got back from NYC on Sunday, but who's counting?

What's up with you quitting Faded Flowers? I walked into rehearsal yesterday after school and saw Joey Palladino sitting in your seat. Rakoff and Claire told us he's taking over your part and I want to know why.

There will only ever be one Ryan for this

Noel. Is there some way I can change your mind and get you to come back? (I can think of one or two!)
Richie

I suppose I don't have to tell you why I dropped outta the film.

But I will.

Two days ago, I got back from New York, and immediately got Rakoff on the phone . . .

"I hate to break this to you," I said casually. "I can't do the movie."

"You mean *Faded Flowers*?" he asked from the other end of the line, totally outta breath. I didn't wanna think about what I might've interrupted . . . Bogue!

"No, Sherlock . . . *Doctor Who Meets Monty Python*."

Rakoff scoffed. "Claire's not gonna like thith."

"Tough shit!" I responded, trying to sound like a Total Bad Ass.

I honestly didn't mean to be a jerk. I just knew I had to get myself as far away from this fag-movie as I possibly could. Of course, I didn't wanna admit the real reason why.

That's exactly what Rakoff asked me about next.

"May I athk why you're quitting?"

"I'm not *quitting*," I answered defensively. "I'm dropping out."

"Forgive me for thaying tho," Rakoff lisped, "but I don't thee much of a differenth."

"Well, there is!" I spat, sticking to my guns. "If you *must* know, Rakoff," I continued, emphasizing the F's, "some of us gotta work for a living. We can't take time off just to shoot a stupid student film."

What did he possibly know about anything? Rakoff's an only

child whose mommy gives him whatever he wants . . . Even if it is just a dumb old mayonnaise cake!

"Is it the thcript? I can rewrite it," Rakoff volunteered. "I just want you to be happy."

No amount of rewriting could save that piece of shit.

I came this close to saying that, but knew I couldn't. Talk about bogue! In fact, just thinking it, I felt so ashamed I had to turn away from myself in the mirror.

"The script is fine," I said sincerely. "It's a great opportunity for an actor to show off his talents . . . But that actor isn't me."

"Well, I'm thorry you feel thith way," Rakoff replied, disappointed.

"Yeah . . . Me, too."

After I hung up, I went in my room where I found a note on my bed.

Welcome Home!
Love, Mom
PS—Call Richie

Normally, I'd pick up the phone and be over the Tylers' faster than a sorority girl can spread her legs, but I knew that just wasn't possible. Not anymore, at least.

All the way back to Detroit on the plane, I dreaded the conversation me and Richie were bound to have once I got home. So I conveniently forgot about Mom's note, and opted for a night over Janelle and Ted's watching the Super Bowl (Redskins vs. Broncos), followed by the premiere of some new TV show called *The Wonder Years.*

Set in the suburbs during 1968, the story focuses on 12-year-old Kevin Arnold, played by some kid I never heard of, Fred Savage. It totally made me think of being that age, growing up with Max and Jack, doing all the things we did together: playing Pac-Man at the party store, ordering pizza from Randazzo's, looking at *Playboy.* Five years later, we're not even friends anymore . . . Why does growing up suck so bad?

You can bet Audrey was pissed when she got the news.

What do you mean you're quitting the movie?

The next morning during 2nd hour Consumer Ec she slipped me a note.

I wrote: Can't do it. Then I folded up the piece of notebook paper and passed it back.

Because my last name starts with *D* and Audrey's with *W*, and Mrs. Ireland makes us sit in alphabetical order, this wasn't an easy feat as there are three rows of desks between us. We had to use several go-betweens, namely Marie Sperling, Fay Keating, and Tom Fulton.

Audrey wrote: Why the fuck not?

I wasn't about to get into this via a note that could possibly be intercepted at any moment by one of my asshole classmates or our crazy teacher. So I wrote back: We'll talk about it later.

Just when I thought the discussion had ended, I felt another tap on my shoulder.

"Dude . . . From Ostrich."

Tom Fulton passed the note my way. I can't believe he was even taking part in my scheme, let alone talking to me. And how did he know Audrey's nickname from back in kinny-garden—I mean, ***kindergarten?*** My guess was Jack told him since he's the one who told me.

I read the note: When?

Hunching over my desk, I scrawled out my response: Lunch?

Tom waited to make his next move. Despite hating me since we were in elementary school, he seemed to be enjoying himself. Anything to put one over on a teacher, I'm sure.

Audrey wrote back: Going to BK with Rob.

Not my problem.

If she wanted to know why I dropped out from the movie, she needed to make the effort, you know what I mean? Not that I was gonna tell her the real reason I quit is because I can't be "tempted by the fruit of another" (man) anymore.

Unfortunately, I knew I couldn't avoid Richie forever. Sure enough, Monday night when I got home from work, I found another note on my bed.

Richie called.
Love, Mom

Again, I ignored it.

The next morning before Wind Ensemble is when I find Richie's letter stuck inside the slats of my locker. Thank God he's only a Sophomore. I don't have to deal with having him in *any* of my classes.

By the time I get to the Band room, all the Band Fags have already started warming up. Luckily, the bell rings just as I'm slipping safely thru the double doors. But that doesn't stop Mr. Klan from crying out, "Mr. Dayton . . . You're late!"

"Kiss it."

This I mumble from the storage room, matching his tone. The last thing I need this early on a day like today is Mr. Klan's shit. This is why I take my sweet old time locating my trombone case in its place on the designated shelf.

The tinny tap of Mr. Klan's wood baton against metal music stand emanates from the Band room proper, and all the Band Fags suddenly fall silent.

"Sweetheart," Mr. Klan says to Ava Reese. "Would you give us a B-flat, please?"

Sliding my slide into place while Ava does her 1st chair clarinet duty, I sneak into my seat in the middle of the third row of risers, next to Will Isaacs.

"You trying out for *Grease* next week?" he whispers.

"You bet I am."

After months and months of begging, me and Audrey convinced Dell to let us put on the musical of *our* choice for once. Tuesday Gunderson pushed for *South Pacific,* but we pretty much convinced her she'll never get cast as Nellie Forbush. Besides, there's a perfect part for her in *Grease* as Jan, the Twinkie-eating Pink Lady.

"Quiet, please!" Klan sings, not looking at me and Will, but we both know he's barking at us. Then he concludes, "A hair flat," with regards to Ava's pitch being monitored by the trusty tuning machine poised on the trapezoid table behind his podium.

"I disagree," Will sniggers, eyes focused on Ava where she sits beside Carrie Johnson in the row beneath us. "Nice sweater."

Ava gives it another go, holding her note (rock) steady.

This time, Mr. Klan practically wets himself. "That's it! Now everyone all together . . ." He gives a wave of his magic wand, uniting each and every Band Fag in the quest for the perfect B-flat concert note.

Fifty-five minutes later, the bell finally rings . . .

Quickly, I spring to my feet, beating a hasty retreat back to the storage room where I toss my T-bone in its case and fly thru the double doors like a bat outta hell.

"See ya!"

Knowing that Richie is now on his way to 2nd hour Sophomore Symphony, sax in tow, I'm hoping to avoid any confrontation that might occur in the hallowed halls of Hillbilly High. Instead, I plan to write him a note during Consumer Ec, which I will ask Audrey to slip into his locker on her way to

Mr. Thomas' 3rd hour Chemistry. Only because it's right there in the exact same hall.

February 3, 1988

Dear Richie,

Sorry I haven't written back sooner. I been super busy since I got home from NYC. I'll call you tonight, I promise.

Brad

"You can't avoid The Sophomore forever," Aud warns, ever the voice of reason.

"I know . . ."

We move down the front hall past the library, where I feel the slap of harsh reality at the handiwork of Shellee Findlay once again on display, taped to the doors outside Principal Messinger's office.

Don't forget to buy your tickets!
VALENTINE'S DAY DANCE
February 12, 1988
7:30 PM

The original plan was for me and Richie to go together, a trial run for the filming of the Prom scene in *Faded Flowers.* Chances are we'd get our asses kicked. Or at least made fun of, but it would all be for the sake of Art.

"I can't believe it . . ."

Rounding the corner by the junk-food stand, the roll-up metal window pulled down and padlocked till lunch, Audrey continues with her train of thought.

"What can't you believe?" I wonder, clutching my books tight against my chest. The second I see some Total Jock coming our way, they find their proper place at my side, resting against my hip.

"Oh nothing . . ."

We pass by locker #1427. I almost forget to think of Jack, it's been so long. I don't know why I even care, but I pray he's not falling for Tom Fulton the way he did Joey Palladino once upon a time.

Tom, I can't speak for, but Joey, I still suspect is gay. Especially now that he enthusiastically agreed to take over my role in *Faded Flowers.*

Wanna know how that whole thing came about?

Basically what happened was . . . Once I quit the movie, Rakoff and Moody got it in their heads to ask Joey to play my part. I guess he's in their 5th hour Mass Media class this semester, and he mentioned he did some acting when he was going to school out in Clarkston. The last thing I want is Joey Palladino kissing Richie Tyler during those hot and heavy love scenes. Too bad there's nothing I can do about it.

Hello, Mr. Body Builder!

We stop at Audrey's locker to pick up her Chemistry book.

Despite my state of irritation, I notice she's added a couple new pictures to her Chippendales collection. I'm not too sure about the earring on the dark-haired guy (too faggy), but the blond with the hi-lights is definitely a babe!

"What can't you believe?"

Pulling myself away from the all-male peep show and getting back to the matter at hand, I implore my friend.

"Forget it," Audrey dismissively replies, rifling thru a mess of papers on the top shelf.

"Fine."

I'm *not* about to beg.

"No skin off my ass."

She slams the locker door shut and continues on past the office of *The Hazel Parker,* leaving me in her dust. Knowing Jack's got class in there this coming period, I can't resist sneaking a peek inside. Sure enough, there he sits hunched over his desk, red correction pencil in hand. Before he has the chance to spot me, I scurry on my way.

"Tell me!"

I catch up to Audrey, dying to know what's got her so concerned.

Brow furrowed, she gives me a look. "Something must be up."

"Nothing's up," I adamantly insist. "Why would you say such a thing?"

"Think about it . . . Mr. Star Thespian gives up a shot at making a *movie.* There's gotta be a good reason."

Now I'm wondering if Aud suspects something's going on between me and The Sophomore, even though there isn't, and yet there totally used to be.

To throw her off the scent, I say, "I already told you . . . I gotta work."

"The entire break?"

"Pretty much."

I can tell she's not buying my excuse, even though it's totally not one.

"Big Boy's or the Gap?"

"Both."

Six nights at EB's on top of weekend mornings at the mall, and I'm still barely getting by. There's no way I can afford to take *any* time off, that's the God's honest truth. My plan is to double my hours at the Gap over Winter Break, and if that doesn't work, I been thinking about either selling my body on 8 Mile or getting a job as a go-go boy at Gold Coast.

"I thought you were quitting the Gap," Audrey continues with her interrogation.

"So did I."

"Let me guess . . . They shriveled up and fell off."

I realize she's quoting *Pretty in Pink*, but I don't get the connection. "What shriveled up and fell off?"

"Your balls."

I make a you're-so-funny-I-forgot-to-laugh sound, and head to 3rd hour Government with Mr. McCain—my *least* favorite class of the new semester.

Talk about old school! The man is the epitome of White Southern Baptist, except he looks like a 60-year-old Oompa-Loompa. Only taller and with white hair instead of green. Lemme tell ya, something about his skin is sooo Fake 'n Bake, I'm wondering if he's hitting the tanning booth in preparation for Spring Break, like most of the girls I'm friends with. I'm sure the guy knows I'm a Total Fag and prays every night I'll burn in hell.

Whatever . . .

Four hours later, me and Stacy Gillespie are walking up Hughes, past the Blue Building, on our way back to HPHS. On this early February afternoon, it's a balmy thirty-three degrees and sunny outside, so we hit House of Beer on 9 Mile and grabbed a pop and some Funyuns. We got Mrs. Carey's French III Independent Study during 6th hour, 'member?

"What are you doing after class?"

Stacy asks me this, casually waving away the cigarette smoke I'm unintentionally blowing in her face.

"Working on my *Grease* audition with Mr. Fish."

I decided to sing "Sandy," even though the stupid play version doesn't include it. Instead, Danny sings this other song called "Alone at a Drive-In Movie," which isn't nearly half as good. I don't know why the play script is sooo different from the movie. The T-Birds aren't the T-Birds, they're the *Burger Palace Boys.* Putzie isn't Putzie, he's *Roger*, Miss McGee is called

Miss Lynch, and there's no "Hopelessly Devoted to You" or "You're the One that I Want."

Lame, huh?

"What part are you trying out for?" Stacy asks, like there's even a doubt.

I tell her, "Danny . . . What do you think?"

She stares down at her feet, flats crunching away in the snow as we cross the street. "Oh . . ."

"Why?" I ask, even though I can totally tell what she's thinking,

"Nothing . . . I just never thought of you as much of a John Travolta-type."

Because I'm gay?

"Why not?"

"I don't know . . . Your hair's red."

I explain to Stacy how Danny Zuko is a *character,* and just because Vinny Barbarino played him in the movie doesn't mean that's the only way he can be portrayed, you know what I mean?

"Well, I heard Joey Palladino is also trying out."

Great!

It's bad enough Joey already took over for me in *Faded Flowers,* and gets to make out with my boyfriend-who's-not-*really*-my-boyfriend, even though I totally want him to be, but now he never will.

Speaking of . . .

When we sneak back into the building, just as the 3:00 PM bell begins to blare, who do I see waiting for me at my locker?

"What's up, Ryan?"

I'll give you a hint . . .

He's holding a saxophone case at his side.

"I'm not Ryan anymore, 'member?"

The correct answer would have to be . . .

"And I wanna know why."

Richie Tyler.

Didn't We Almost Have It All?

"A moment in the soul can last forever
Comfort and keep us . . ."

—Whitney Houston

"There are no small parts, only small actors."

'member that old adage?

Well, here we go again!

The morning after auditions, Mr. Dell'Olio posts the following list on the door outside the auditorium.

GREASE

—CAST—

Danny Zuko . . . . Joey Palladino
Sandy Dumbrowski. . . . . Liza Larson
Kenickie . . . . Will Isaacs
Doody . . . . Brad Dayton
Roger . . . . Keith Treva
Sonny . . . . Allen Bryan

Rizzo . . . . Jamie Good
Frenchy . . . . Audrey Wojczek
Jan . . . . Tuesday Gunderson
Miss Lynch . . . . Ava Reese
Eugene Florczyk . . . . Charlie Richardson
Patty Simcox. . . . . Michelle Winters
Johnny Casino/Teen Angel . . . . . . Ron Reynolds
Vince Fontaine . . . . Richie Tyler
Cha-Cha DiGregorio . . . . Diane Thompson

Perhaps you noticed where *my* name falls?

Fourth one down, after the lead role of Danny Zuko, being played by Joey-fucking-Palladino, who's never been in a play during his entire three years at HPHS! Maybe it's just me, but I can't help think I'm playing Doody because of my Howdy *Doody* hair, you know what I mean?

I guess what pisses me off is . . . All the Drama Queers know it was *my* idea to do *Grease* in the first place. I been pushing for it since the beginning of the school year, you know what I mean? Well, me and Audrey, who at least got the part she wanted.

Ever since I can remember, I wanted to be Danny. Okay, maybe when I was little I wanted to be Sandy, but *Grease* has always been my favorite musical. Me and Janelle weren't allowed to see the movie when it was at the show, but our babysitter, Sheryl "Bionic Woman" Killian, had the record album. Sometimes she'd bring it over when she watched us and we'd listen to it with her.

I remember the cover opened up and it had all them pictures from the movie inside, like they were snapshots laid out on a table at The Frosty Palace, along with a pair of salt and pepper shakers, a malt cup with straw, and a napkin holder. I used to look at it for hours, trying to imagine how each scene played out, based on the different photographs.

Me and Janelle would dance around our family room pretending we were Olivia Newton-John and John Travolta performing "Summer Nights." Most of the time, I played Danny. But every once in a while Janelle would let me be Sandy, since I was shorter, and my voice was higher. And I could dance "You're the One that I Want" in high heels without falling on my face—unlike her.

Never in my wildest dreams did I imagine Joey Palladino would audition for *Grease,* let alone steal the role of Danny Zuko out from under me. How could I possibly beat him? He's Italian, for chris'sakes!

Notice who else's name is on the cast list, second from the bottom? As far as I knew, Richie wasn't even auditioning for the show on account of he can't carry a tune, even with a handle. This explains why Dell cast him as Vince Fontaine, host of *National Bandstand.* 'member, he's the old guy who judges the dance contest when he's not roaming around the gymnasium hitting on Marty?

Speaking of . . .

I just realized Mr. Dell'Olio forgot to include my favorite Pink Lady on the cast list. I don't know who's playing the part of Miss Maraschino. ("You know, like in cherry.") Remind me to find out at our first read-thru this afternoon. I'm also not sure why Dell listed The Sophomore as "Richie" this time around, and not *Rich.* I'd ask Mr. Tyler himself, but he's currently not speaking to me . . . I can't say I blame him.

I suppose I should elaborate on what exactly went down between us last Wednesday after school, huh?

On the last episode of *Life in Hazeltucky* . . .

Our hero, Bradley Dayton, had just returned to Hillbilly High with his partner-in-crime, Stacy Gillespie, after skipping Mrs. Carey's French III Independent Study—yet again. Upon arriving at his locker, Mr. Dayton found himself greeted by his soon-to-be ex-boyfriend, Richie "The Sophomore" Tyler.

"So what's up, *Brad?*"

From the way Richie bit off my name, I could tell he was bound and determined to get an answer outta me as to why I quit *Faded Flowers.* Of all people, he knew how much I been looking forward to filming, so why would I wanna give it up?

"I said I'll call you later," I told him, not wanting to have it out in front of Stacy. Or anybody else, for that matter.

"What's wrong with right now?" Richie wondered, still on the defensive.

In all these months, I never heard his voice sound so harsh. It reminded me of when my mom got mad at me or my sisters over something one of us did. I hated it.

"Now's not a good time," I answered calmly.

If there's one thing I can't stand it's seeing those poor cheerleader girls screaming at their football player boyfriends (or vice versa) while everybody passes by. This was starting to happen as more and more kids filled the hall, ready to get the hell outta HPHS for the day.

But Richie wouldn't back off. "It's good enough as any."

At that moment, guess who wandered by?

Jack.

Our eyes met for only a second, but he looked totally surprised to see me talking to Richie Tyler, the faggy little 7th grader from Webb Junior High. I couldn't help but notice Jack's new Best Friend was nowhere to be found . . . Wonder what's up with him and Tom Fulton, anyways?

Richie snapped, "Let's talk!" drawing me out of my reverie as Jack disappeared.

"I have to meet Mr. Fish," I explained. "He's helping me with my *Grease* audition."

"Fuck your *Grease* audition!"

'member that scene in *Pretty in Pink* where Molly Ringwald corners Andrew McCarthy in the hall by his locker, demanding to know why all of a sudden he's been blowing her off? She's all like, "What about Prom?" and he's like, "I don't wanna talk about this right now," and she's like, "I said, *What about Prom?*"

Finally, she forces him to say he forgot he already asked somebody else. Thus prompting Molly to let Andrew have it with her famous, "You're a filthy fucking liar!" line, screaming and jabbing him in the chest while everybody and their brother (and sister) looks on. That's exactly how I felt right then and there, half expecting The Sophomore to haul off and hit me as a small crowd gathered around us.

Luckily, I still had Stacy to protect me. But not for long.

"Good luck with your voice lesson."

She bid me farewell and went on her way thru the crowd in search of her own boyfriend, Luis Sánchez. I can't believe they're still happily going together after all these months. Why do some people have such lucky love lives?

"Tell me why you dropped out of the movie," demanded Richie, forging ahead.

Before I could think up an excuse, we were interrupted.

"Boys . . . Is everything all right?

I turned to see Miss Horchik's beady brown eyes beaming at me from beneath her Pilgrim's bonnet. I wasn't sure how much of our conversation she overheard.

"Everything's fine," I insisted, hoping Velma would vamoose.

"Is it?"

The Sophomore stared down at me, hands on hips. The last thing I needed at that moment was the Holy Virgin reminding me to be true to mine ownself. I could totally tell she could tell something was up. But for whatever reason, she chose not to pry.

"Please tell your mother I miss having you in my class . . . I always enjoyed sending her my Happy Notes."

From outta the pocket of her long wool coat, Miss Horchik pulled what can only be called a *muff*. She buried her hands deep within its faux-fur and headed out into the cold, the world of Hillbilly High fading to black.

Quickly, I came up with a plan. "What are you doing right now?"

"What's it look like?" Richie scowled. "Having a tea party . . . One lump or two?" He raised a fist and shook it in my face.

"I'm gonna cancel my lesson with Fish . . . We can go somewhere and talk."

"What's wrong with right here?" he demanded, causing more heads to turn our direction wondering what the hell was up.

A month or two ago, I would've killed to have a conversation like this. A lover's spat with my *boyfriend*. Now that it was taking place, it totally sucked.

"Don't do this, okay?" I pleaded. "Please."

Richie softened. "Fine . . . I'll let you drive me home."

Ten minutes later we pulled out of the parking lot . . .

"How about some heat?"

"Sorry," I apologized. "I still haven't got it fixed."

Another reason I couldn't take time off work to make a silly movie. I needed money and I needed it *yesterday*.

The entire ride over to Richie's, I couldn't think of a single thing to say. I tried making small talk: "How was your weekend?"

He replied, "It sucked," not even bothering to ask how my Juilliard audition went. What he did say was: "How come you didn't call me?"

"When?"

"Friday night."

"We went to dinner and saw a show."

I explained all about *Les Miz*, conveniently omitting the part about *Les Miz* Guy.

"What about *after* the show? I was home all evening."

On the corner of Woodward Heights and John R, I noticed a newly built brick wall, the words ST MARY MAGDALEN printed across in silver, a bed of fresh flowers planted in front.

"When did they put that up?"

I couldn't recall it being there before I left for New York.

Richie turned his head slightly to take it in, but said nothing.

"It looks nice," I added, even though I didn't understand what purpose it served.

"Turn right."

Richie gave me this order once the light changed from ruby to emerald.

"I know . . ."

Hand over hand I turned the wheel, allowing it to slide back thru my palms the way I was taught in Driver's Ed. We drove by Doug's Delight, Truba Carpet, and Daisy Petal. Past Annie O's, Hazel Park Food Center, arriving at Burger's & Kreme on the corner of Brickley.

"Left," Richie commanded, as if I never been over his house.

"I know . . ."

Blocking traffic always makes me nervous, you know what I mean? It didn't help that in my rearview mirror, I noticed a line of irate drivers backed up behind me.

When the moment of opportunity presented itself, Richie wailed, "Go!"

This only made me more nervous, freezing my foot to the brake like that kid in *A Christmas Story*'s tongue to the flagpole.

"Please don't tell me how to drive," I requested quietly.

Somebody honked as they pulled around us to the right. If I wasn't so frazzled, I would've totally flipped them off! Taking my time, I completed the left turn on my own terms, waiting till I was good and ready.

"Halfway down the block," said The Sophomore, again as if I didn't know where I was heading. "The blue house on the right."

"I *know* . . ."

This time I added the subtext of *Do you think I'm stupid?* to my tone.

I wanted to talk things over with him, but I wasn't gonna sit back and let Richie Tyler treat me like I'm a moron. In fact, thinking about his catty comments the entire way over his house made me wanna drop him off and forget the whole thing.

"Aren't you coming in?" he asked once we came to a stop, sounding totally snotty.

"Not if you're gonna keep acting this way," I retaliated.

For the first time, Richie looked at me. "Acting what way?"

"Like a Total Baby."

"Fuck you!" he spat. "I don't need your shit."

I spat back, "Then get the fuck outta my car!"

Richie didn't move. He just sat in his seat, staring straight ahead.

So did I.

Wouldn't you know? At that precise moment, Whitney Houston started singing some sappy song on the radio. By the chorus, we were *both* crying.

Years ago, I used to listen to this program called *Pillow Talk* on WNIC. The DJ, Alan Almond, had this totally smooth voice, and he played songs like "When I'm with You" by Sheriff and "Somone that I Used to Love" by Natalie Cole. Tune after tune, it tore my heart out. Except back then, I didn't know what it was to *really* love somebody . . . The way I did now.

How is it that a stupid love song can capture the essence of human emotion? How can some singer/songwriter come up with a bunch of words that describe precisely what so many of us are going thru at a particular moment, when they never even met us before?

After what felt like forever, the both of us freezing cold, The Sophomore said softly, "Please come in."

I wanted to. But I knew I shouldn't. The last thing I needed was for him to get me inside his house, and start getting all *Ryan* on me. I'd never be able to say what I knew must be said.

"I can't," I decided, opting for better safe than sorry.

"Fine . . . Then tell me why you're doing this."

I assumed he was back to wondering why I dropped out of the film.

Did he *really* wanna know?

I can't be in Faded Flowers *with you because I don't want people thinking I'm a fag.*

I care more about my acting career than I do about you.

I don't know what the fuck I want anymore.

"I'm totally broke," I admitted. "I can't be taking time off work like I thought I could."

Apparently, that's not what Richie was referring to.

"I'm not talking about the goddamn movie, Brad . . . I wanna know why you're breaking up with me."

Hold the fucking phone!

Correct me if I'm wrong, but don't you have to actually be somebody's boyfriend before you can break up with them?

"I wanna hear you say it," Richie continued, once again in Molly Ringwald mode. "You're ashamed of me."

I had to laugh. "It's not *your* fault you're a Sophomore."

Obviously, he didn't find my humor funny.

"You don't remember, do you?"

Suddenly, the subject changed. Again, I felt totally lost.

"The winter of 7th grade . . . You and Bobby Russell . . . Green Acres Park . . ."

That's all he needed to tell me.

'member at the beginning of the year when I first met The Sophomore, and I totally didn't recognize him? Then I ran into him at *A Christmas Carol* auditions . . .

"You don't remember me, do you?"

"From the other day in the Band room . . . Sure, I do."

"I mean, from before . . . You were my Band Aide."

'member how embarrassed I was because me and Jack used to refer to Richie as "the faggy little 7th grader who played flute in Prep Band and carried his books like a girl?" But at least we never said anything mean about him to his face . . . I can't say the same for Bobby Russell.

On the day in question back in 1985, me and Bobby were on our way over Bobby's house to smoke some pot (and fuck around after the fact). Richie happened to be lucky enough to cross our path, and Bobby decided to be a Total Dick to him. I remember him saying something like, "Where's your flute, you little fag?" And Richie was like, "I'm not a fag, I'm not a fag," in the whiny little fag voice he had at the time.

Bobby ended up chasing Richie across the I-75 catwalk, and cornering him in the Calvary Baptist parking lot where he was all like, "Shut up, you little fag." And Richie was like, "Make me." Next thing I knew, I was helping Bobby drag Richie to Bobby's house where he proceeded to do just that.

Please don't ask me what went on exactly, just know I wasn't involved *physically.*

"We're not breaking up."

This was all I could say to Richie at that point as he sat silently in my car.

"We're not?"

He sniffled a little, wiping the snot from his nose.

"How can we?" I wondered, masking my frustration with more laughter. "We're not even going together!"

He looked at me point blank. "Then what the fuck's been happening between us for the past month?"

"We been rehearsing for a film."

Richie scoffed. "This is just another part you're playing? None of this means anything *more* to you? It's all about some stupid movie!"

"I never said it was stupid."

He looked at me, puppy-dog eyes pooling. Now it was Richie's turn to plead. "Don't do this, okay?"

As much as I hated it, I knew I didn't have a choice. Especially if what Christopher told me in New York was in fact true.

"I can't be your boyfriend."

Tears flowed.

"Why not?"

I swallowed hard. "I'm not a fag."

Liar!

Only in My Dreams

"Couldn't see how much I missed you (now I do)
Couldn't see how much it meant . . ."

—Debbie Gibson

As if this night couldn't get any worse!

Wanna know where I'm spending *my* Valentine's Day?

Go on, take a wild guess.

"This place is D-E-A-D."

Sitting at The Gas Station with Miss Peter, drowning our sorrows in high-octane, all the while listening to unrequited love songs on the jukebox. Did I mention Janelle and Ted got married yesterday? Their wedding was nice, but just another reminder of how *everybody* but me manages to find their True Love.

"It's Sunday," I say, trying to account for the lack of eye candy and the emptiness of The Pit. "Maybe they're all at Menjo's."

With the exception of me and Miss Peter seated side by side on stools, and Mike-the-mohawked-bartender bare-chested at his post behind, there's a total of *zero* other guys in the entire bar.

"And to think I wasted this outfit . . ."

In honor of the holiday, Miss Peter sports a pink off-the-shoulder sweatshirt, à la *Flashdance* ("What a feeling!"), a big broken heart stenciled on the front. On her feet she wears ballet slippers. Covering her lower extremities, leggings—I made the mistake of calling them *tights*. Big mistake!

"I like your fairy wings."

When she first arrived, I complimented the homemade feather-covered pair she had strapped to her back, along with one of them container-thingies that holds the arrows . . . A quiver, maybe? Thank God the pink tips are only plastic suction cups.

"I'm Cupid," Miss Peter croaked. "Not a fucking fairy!"

No comment.

To quote Rizzo from *Grease* when she turns to Marty after spying Crater Face Balmudo in the Rydell High parking lot, coming up with a plan to score a date for the *National Bandstand* dance contest: "I think our luck just might be changing."

Thru the door walks a very attractive man. Tall, dark, and handsome, you could even call him with his slicked-back hair, parted on the side, and matching mustache. An olive-drab trench coat drapes his broad shoulders. He wears tan slacks, a plaid button-down shirt, open just enough at the collar to reveal a patch of hair sprouting up from his chest. He looks a tad bit like a teacher, but he's definitely a man. As opposed to some 15-year-old *boy*, like the one I been pining away for the entire evening.

"Well, well, well . . ."

Miss Peter becomes an entirely different person the second she spies School Teacher Guy walk past us. Her eyes sparkle, a smile dances its way across her only-moments-before dour face.

Seconding the emotion, I echo, "Well, well, well . . ."

"I could sure go for some baked ham," Miss Peter muses, without taking her eyes off the prize.

"Some baked ham sure would hit the spot," I concur. "Don't you think so, Mike?"

Mike chuckles to himself. "You girls are insatiable." This doesn't stop him taking a break from restocking the refrigerator with Bud Light bottles to peek over his shoulder. "Mmm mmm mmm . . . Baked ham *does* sound good right about now."

Baked ham is one of our code words. Like when one of us sees somebody we like and we wanna make it obvious to the other without coming out and blatantly saying so. Last week it was *casserole*.

School Teacher Guy pulls up a stool about five feet away from us. "Can I get a Bud?"

Miss Peter just about wets herself at the sound of his voice. Not since Jon-Erik Hexum have I heard such a deep, resonant bass.

"So . . . ?" she says, a little louder than usual, even for how inebriated she is.

"So . . . ?" I repeat, trying to pique STG's interest.

Too bad his eyeballs are glued to the TV above the bar where some spandex-clad speed skater does laps around an ice rink in Calgary, Canada. The Winter Olympics only started yesterday, and already I'm sick of them interrupting my regularly scheduled ABC programming. Like tonight, I'm missing Dolly Parton's new variety show, *Dolly.* I only caught a few episodes, but some of my favorite guests so far include Juice Newton, Emmylou Harris, and Miss Piggy.

I'd be lying if I didn't admit I'm a big fan of the Olympic Games, particularly the winter ones. Call me stereotypical, but my favorite event has gotta be women's figure skating. This might explain my passion for *Ice Castles.*

Starting with Dorothy Hamill in '76, I fell in love with the sport, even though I was only six at the time her (and her haircut) took home Olympic gold, so I barely remember a thing. I do, however, recall seeing the commercials the following Christmas for the Dorothy Hamill doll.

It wasn't till four years later that I developed a serious passion for the sport while watching the 1980 Winter Olympic Games held in Lake Placid. I distinctly remember skating around our sunken-in family room in my stocking feet, pretending I was the dark-haired American contender, Linda Fratianne, sporting my sequined skating dress, displaying my perfect axels, triple toe loops, and triple salchows. I was sooo bummed (and outta breath) after watching poor Linda skate her butt off and only win the silver—what a gyp!

"Me thinks I need another . . ."

My cup far from runneth-ing over, I decide I could use a refill.

"Allow me," Miss Peter offers cordially. "It's the least I can do since you were *dumped* on Valentine's Day."

This last part she says at the top of her voice, for the benefit of our new arrival, I'm sure.

"Hey!" I cry, totally taking offense. "I'm the dumper here, not the dumpee."

Miss Peter shakes her head, winking at Professor Studly. "Sure you are . . ."

Reaching for one of her love darts, she draws back her bow and lets her arrow go. Luckily, Miss Peter is already wasted off her ass, not to mention her aim sucks to begin with. The arrow falls to the floor with a thud, missing its mark by a bijillion miles.

"You girls need something?" asks Mike.

I just about cream my jeans watching him suction-cup the toy to his massive man tit.

The only reason Mike's even here tonight is because Heaven isn't open on Sundays and, believe it or not, he's single. Being the good guy he is, he decided to give the regular bartender the night off and come slumming with the rest of us losers. Only thing is, Mike gets *paid* to be here!

"What-choo havin', Opie?" Miss Peter turns to me, slurring her words only slightly.

"Sloe gin fizz."

With the entire bar draped in red, I figured I might as well match my drink to the décor and switched from fuzzy navels. What stinks even more about this whole V-Day situation is . . . I been plotting it out in my head for like the last month as to how exactly I wanted to spend the holiday: alone with Richie as Ryan and Noel.

Mr. and Mrs. Tyler went away for another bowling tournament, and we were gonna have the entire house to ourselves. I specifically requested the night off from Big Boy's, so I only had to work 10:00 AM–5:00 PM at the Gap, allowing plenty of time to go home, shit, shower, and shave, and be over Richie's by 6:00 PM for a romantic candlelit dinner of chicken parmigiana, garlic bread, and mixed-greens salad, which he promised to have ready and waiting on the table.

I even bought a new pair of Calvin Klein undies up at Hudson's for the special occasion, in case we ended up rehearsing any of our Ryan and Noel love scenes, you know what I mean?

"Bottoms up."

Mike returns with our drinks in hand.

His massively large hands, matching the rest of his massively large, totally perfect body.

Why can't I find a boyfriend like Mike?

Because I don't *want* one . . . 'member, I'm not a fag?

Liar!

Making the most sour-looking face I ever seen, Miss Peter lets out a serious moan. "What is in this drink?"

Mike replies, "Captain Morgan's."

"Captain Morgan's and . . . ?" Miss Peter quizzically questions.

"Captain Morgan's and Coke."

This Mike says with a slight trace of uncertainty.

"Well, no wonder if tastes like ass . . . I asked for Captain Morgan's and *Diet*."

"My apologies . . . I'll take it back."

Mike reaches for Miss Peter's glass, but she isn't giving up the ghost.

"Oh, no . . . This one I'm keeping."

Miss Peter slurps her Captain and Coke as Mike makes her another *avec Diète*. She's practically done with the first by the time the second appears.

"Sorry about that."

Reaching into her man-purse, while at the same time firing up a Tareyton, Miss Peter instructs, "Just take it out of this," flinging Mike a $50.

"Your money's no good here, ma'am," her informs Miss Peter, doing his best Wild West barkeep impersonation.

"Since when?"

Mike nods his head towards our not-so secret admirer.

"It's nice to see *somebody* take pity on a couple of single girls," Miss Peter sighs with glee.

"Sorry, guys . . . Wasn't me." STG downs his Bud and signals for another. "Yo!"

Wanna know who we see standing just *beyond* School Teacher Guy?

Go on, take a wild guess!

Both are tall and handsome—one dark, the other fair.

At first, I don't recognize them on account of they're the last two people I expect to find at The Gas Station on a Sunday night, let alone on Valentine's Day.

"Bradley," says the dark one, nodding his gorgeous head of hair my way.

"What's up?" asks the other, shit-eating grin on his beautiful blue-eyed face.

Obviously, Miss Peter doesn't recognize them either.

"Those boys are cute!" she squeals. "Let's go over and say hello . . . We're gonna *starve* if we wait around for some baked ham."

I can't help but follow the fifteen feet to the end of the bar with Miss Peter dragging me along as her human crutch.

"What are you guys doing here?" I inquire, the second we're within speaking range.

"It's Valentine's Day, isn't it?" the older of the two responds. "We're celebrating."

"Isn't that sweet," Miss Peter coos. She raises her glass, offering a toast. "To young love . . . What's your name, bitches?"

"Noel and Ryan," supplies the happy couple's younger half. "I'm Noel . . . This is Ryan."

"Charmed," Miss Peter replies, drunkenly yet still demure.

Before she gets a chance to extend her hand, I cut in. "No . . . You're *Richie* and he's *Joey*."

Miss Peter does a double take. "Richie from Scrooge, Richie? I thought you said your name was Joel."

I explain to Miss Peter that Richie and Joey are working on an acting project for school, in which they portray characters named Ryan and *Noel*—with an *N*. Like a lot of Drama Queers, they sometimes get carried away with playing pretend, so we have to indulge them.

"I'm a big fan of role play," Miss Peter quips. "Care to join Opie and I for a cocktail?"

Now it's Joey's turn to do a double take. "Opie?"

Richie replies, "Don't ask."

As if this night couldn't get any worse!

I properly introduce Miss Peter to my so-called friends, and we take our seats. Luckily, there happens to be two empty stools between us and our stingy new friend, the school teacher. I make sure to grab the one on the far side, keeping as much distance from

Noel and Ryan as I possibly can. My plan is to sip my sloe gin in silence, and let Miss Peter do all the entertaining while I smoke a cig-rette.

This is how I sometimes say *cigarette,* mostly when I been drinking.

"So what are two nice boys like you doing in a dump like this?"

Richie begins, "We were in the neighborhood—"

Miss Peter interrupts, "You mean the *gay*borhood?" She laughs so hard, she starts hacking up a lung.

Note to self: don't smoke for too *long.*

"We were in the gayborhood," Richie continues, "having dinner at Backstage."

You can bet this gets my attention.

"Did you try the chicken parmigiana?" Miss Peter interjects, salivating. "It's to die for!"

I can't believe The Sophomore had the nerve to take Joey Palladino for dinner at *our* special restaurant. Now he brings him to the very same bar we went afterwards . . . What the fuck is up with that?

"Tell me more about this acting project you're working on," says Miss Peter, lighting another Tareyton, legs crossed at the knees, all ears.

"It's a film called *Faded Flowers,*" answers Joey, filling her in.

"After the Shriekback song," adds Richie.

Miss Peter makes a face like she's smelling a fart. "What the hell's a Shriekback?"

That's what I *said!*

"It's a New Wave band," Joey explains, removing his navy pea coat.

I can't help but notice he's all dressed up in super-tight navy dress pants and a super-tight white dress shirt, unbuttoned just enough to show off the little gold chain around his neck, which I'm pretty sure he got from his *girl*friend, Diane Thompson.

Where the hell is she tonight, anyways? It's Valentine's Day, for chris'sakes!

Miss Peter shrugs, exhaling. "If it ain't Donna Summer, Gloria Gaynor, or Teena Marie, forget it . . . What's the movie about?"

"This group of high school kids," says The Sophomore. "One of the girls gets pregnant, two of the guys are gay . . . Your basic John Hughes plot."

Again, Miss Peter shrugs, oblivious. "If you say so."

"We're playing the gay guys," Joey reveals, as if there was any question. "My character is the ex-boyfriend of the pregnant girl."

"Now we're getting somewhere!" Miss Peter gives her full attention. "So you break up with the girl because you're queer?"

"No," answers The Sophomore. "He doesn't realize he's queer till *after* he breaks up with her and falls in love with me."

"Smart boy!"

Miss Peter praises Joey with a squeeze of his bulging bicep. You can bet she's milking the situation for all it's worth. Has she totally forgotten what I told her a mere two months ago?

'member when I spent the night at Richie's house and he totally called me out about being a Total Fag? Not to mention everything I confessed concerning what me and him have been doing together *physically* for the last thirty days, give or take. For all intensive purposes, Richie Tyler is my *ex*-boyfriend, and here he is at the gay bar with another guy! Or is it "all intents and purposes"? I never know exactly which one it is whenever I say it. So I just sorta slur my words together hoping nobody else will hear me say it wrong if I am.

Then Miss Peter says, "Wait a minute . . . This sounds vaguely familiar." She turns to me, confused. "Weren't *you* making a movie with the exact same plot?"

I sit up in my seat, tall and proud. "I was . . ."

The Sophomore insists on slamming me back down. "He quit."

"I didn't quit," I defend myself, refusing to meet his gaze. "I dropped out."

"Same difference."

"I took over his part," elaborates Joey.

"So now *you* two are boyfriends," Miss Peter deduces, finally making sense of the scenario.

"That's right," Richie affirms with a smile. "Opie's out . . . Joey's in."

As ABBA's "The Winner Takes it All" comes to an end, the bar falls eerily silent.

"Be right back."

Sliding off my stool, I dig deep into my jeans pocket, in search of some quarters. If there's one thing I can't stand it's being in a bar without any background music. The challenge is finding something to play on the jukebox that isn't a Golden Oldie.

"Howdy, boys . . ."

Outta the corner of my eye, I see Mike make his way over to welcome the latest addition to our pity party.

"Give these young *men* whatever'll make them happy," Miss Peter orders.

Mike grins, his square jaw working a piece of cinnamon Dentyne. "I can think of a thing or two that might do the trick."

Miss Peter howls. "Get your mind outta the gutter, hooker!"

I choose #A-34: "Only in My Dreams" by Debbie Gibson. To this day, whenever I hear that song, it takes me back to the night I set foot in my first gay bar.

Flashback to the spring of 1986 . . .

Me and Luanne just came out to each other. One night while sitting at Big Boy's drinking coffee and smoking cigarettes the way we always did, we encountered our favorite waiter, Brett. A cute guy in his early 20s, tall and thin with dark hair and dark eyes, Brett always slipped us free fries on account of he knew me and Lou were both poor as dirt.

"What are you guys doing later?" he asked, refilling our cold cups with hot Maxwell House.

We were like, "Nothing . . . Why do you ask?"

Brett was like, "I'm meeting some friends down at this bar on Woodward . . . You should come by."

He reminded me of that guy Robbie from *Dirty Dancing*, which I finally went to see by myself, by the way. 'member, he's the one who knocks up Johnny's dance partner, Penny, so they gotta take her to have that back-alley abortion? What a jerk!

Sadly we informed Brett, "We're still in high school."

"That's okay . . . They'll totally let you in."

That particular night, Lou's mom was on her case (as per usual), and she had to have the car back by 10:00 PM. So after we paid our bill, she took me home.

Well, I got to thinking about how much fun it would be to go Dirty Dancing with Brett at a bar, since I never been to one. Except at the time, I was only fifteen, so I didn't even have a driver's license, let alone a vehicle.

Wanna know what I did?

I dug out the yellow pages and called a cab, which is something you never do in the *Motor* City.

Twenty minutes later, I stood in line all decked out in my favorite jeans and turtleneck/cardigan sweater combo, waiting to fork over my five bucks.

"ID."

The burly Bouncer Guy grunted, looking down at me. This was before Nancy's uncle hired her (and her horse teeth) to be the Crypt Keeper.

"Um . . . I don't drive."

You can bet I batted my eyes, hoping if I looked cute enough the guy wouldn't care that I was underage and would invite me inside.

"How old are you?"

"Um . . . Fifteen." Remembering what Brett said, I figured I didn't need to lie.

"Hand."

The guy grabbed my paw, marked it with an *X*, and up the stairs I climbed.

"Well, if it isn't Chicken Little . . ."

That's the first thing Mike said to me from his post behind the bar. I'll never forget he had on his uniform: military fatigues, combat boots, and no shirt. At first, I thought I couldn't possibly be in a gay bar with a guy that looked like *him* working there.

"How are you?" I asked, trying to focus on my bartender's face and not his bod.

Mike said something like, "What can I get you?" Or maybe, "What's your poison?"

Like I said, at the time, I never been to a bar before, so I didn't know the first thing about ordering alcohol. I knew I wouldn't like the taste of beer. In fact, I only ever drank *one* time at that point in my life, at Luanne's New Year's Eve party a few months prior when me and Jack got wasted on jug-wine.

Wanna know what I ordered?

"I'll have a Tom Collins."

Now I didn't know what a Tom Collins even was, but all I could think of was my favorite episode of *The Jeffersons* where Weezy witnessed a murder one Halloween . . . 'member? The guy who did it was dressed up in a rabbit costume, and when he discovered Louise seen him, he tracked her down and held her hostage. In order to stall, and keep him from killing her, too, Mrs. J offered to make the man a drink: a Tom Collins.

"You want that in one glass or two?"

Obviously my request wasn't too far fetched because my bartender barely batted an eye.

"Um . . ." I responded, uncertain how to answer.

Mike told me, "It's Tuesday," which I thought seemed odd because as far as I could remember, yesterday was *Friday.* Then he pointed to the sign above the bar.

Saturday = Two's-day
2-4-1 drinks
10 PM-2 AM

"Oh . . ."

Boy, did I feel like an ass!

"One glass or two?"

Again, I didn't get it.

"You know what?" I decided to make things simple. "I'll just have a 7-Up."

Mike grinned. "One glass or two?"

Finally, I was like, "I'm sorry . . . I don't understand the question."

And he was like, "It's two-for-one . . . You want two small drinks or one *big* one?"

I laughed, but at the time I don't think I got the sexual innuendo.

Mike replied, "No problem, Chicken Little . . . You're still young."

Not anymore!

Back in 1988 . . .

Mike says, "What'll it be?" turning his undivided attention towards Joey.

"I'll take a beer," Mr. Palladino, the novice bar-goer replies.

"What kinda beer?"

"What kinda beer you got?"

Mike runs thru the list: "Bud, Bud Light, Miller, Miller Lite, Miller Genuine Draft, Labbat's, Coors, Stroh's . . . You name it, we got it."

"I'll take a Bud," Joey concludes after all that.

"Aren't you a butch one?" Mike teases. Next, he turns to Mr. Tyler. "And for you, Chicken Little?"

Okay, that does it!

"I'll take a Labatt's . . ."

There's only room for one Chicken Little around here, you know what I mean?

"You got it, cutie pie."

I hate to say it, but Mike sounded totally gay when he said that. Maybe he's not as hot as I originally thought he was.

"Thanks, dude."

Hold the fucking phone!

First of all, in the four months I've known him, I never heard Richie Tyler use the word *dude,* let alone call somebody one. Secondly, I can *not* believe the way he's blatantly flirting with Mike the bartender, right in front of me—and Joey Palladino. And third, what the hell does he think he's doing bringing Joey to a gay bar? Sure, him and Richie can say they were doing (quote-unquote) research for their movie, but what if Joey goes back to school next week and tells everybody he saw *me* here?

"I just need to see some ID."

A look of panic crosses Joey's face when Mike questions him on this. Until Richie takes charge of the situation . . .

"I don't drive."

"Fair enough," Mike responds. "How about you?" He turns to Joey.

"Me?" Joey replies. "I drive."

"So show me your pretty picture."

From my post at the jukebox, I'm getting a cheap thrill outta watching Joey Palladino squirm, even though I know what's ultimately gonna happen: he'll take out his license, Mike will look at it and see he's not even eighteen, and he's still gonna serve him. He did the exact same thing with me when I first arrived tonight with Miss Peter. It's what they do here at The Gas Station. Checking ID is a mere formality, in case the cops come in unexpectedly.

Speaking of . . .

'member School Teacher Guy? Soon as Joey takes out his license as requested by Mike, STG gets up from his stool.

"While you're at it, let me take a look . . ."

Turns out, STG works for the Detroit Police Department and we are B-U-S-T-E-D.

As if this night couldn't get any worse!

Magic Changes

"I'll be waiting by the radio
You'll come back to me some day I know . . ."

—Sha-Na-Na

"Another Openin', another show . . ."

HAZEL PARK HIGH SCHOOL DRAMA
presents
Grease
A New 50's
Rock'n'Roll Musical
Book, Music, and Lyrics by Jim Jacobs & Warren Casey
Directed by Mr. Ray Dell'Olio
March 17–19, 1988
7:00 pm
Hazel Park High School
23400 Hughes, Hazel Park, MI

Tonight was Opening Night.

Thank God!

The last month has been H-E-double-L, hell.

Ever since I ran into The Sophomore and his new boyfriend, The Dago, on Valentine's Day down at The Gas Station, I haven't spoken a single word to either one of them. Needless to say, it made for some pretty interesting rehearsals, considering Joey's captain of the T-Birds and all. It's bad enough he stole my part in the play and I still have to act with him. Now he knows I'm a frequent frequenter of a homosexual establishment.

What the fuck do I care? I'm just there to do my thing, give a good performance, and get on with my life.

By the way, it turns out the cop who busted us just so happens to be Betsy Sheffield's uncle. You can bet he probably told his niece how he kicked a bunch of her underage classmates out of a fag bar down in Detroit. Lemme tell ya, if word gets around school, I'm kicking the bitch's ass—cheerleader or not.

"Good show, guys!"

After the performance, our new Sophomore Student Director appeared in the doorway of our dressing room. She's a quiet little blonde named Ashley Lott. Turns out, Miranda Resnick got cast in the role of Marty, the Pink Lady who Dell forgot to add to the list. For her first role on the HPHS stage she knocked 'em dead with her rendition of "Freddy My Love," a song that's not even in the movie, as far as I can recall.

"Thanks, Ash . . ." Or should I have said, *"Cendre,"* the French translation of my nickname for her?

Ashley, I'm told, went to junior high at Webb, but I honestly can't say I remember her. I also heard a rumor her family's Mormon—not something you see every day at Hillbilly High. But I know she likes Yaz, so she must be cool.

Next, she told us guys, "Make sure you hang up your costumes, okay?"

After the curtain call, *some* people have a tendency to just run backstage and throw their shit in a pile. I won't name names (Will Isaacs and Keith Treva), but I'm not one of them. Not that you can do much damage to a pair of blue jeans and a white T-shirt, you know what I mean?

Speaking of . . .

I almost forgot my smokes, rolled up in my Doody-sleeve.

The girls are sooo lucky! They get to wear all those great '50s clothes, with the poodle skirts and saddle shoes and scarves around their necks. The coolest thing about my costume is the black leather jacket I borrowed from my brother-in-law, Ted. He didn't want me painting anything on it, so I came up with a solution to use white Johnson & Johnson waterproof tape to spell T-BIRDS on the back. From the audience, you can't even tell.

"You coming to Big Boy's?" I heard Will Isaacs ask Ashley before she left us.

Sadly, she replied, "I don't think I can."

I had a feeling it had something to do with her religious upbringing, but I wasn't about to ask. Leave it to Keith Treva and Will Isaacs!

"Why not?" pried Tweedledee. "Everybody's going."

"Yeah, come on!" interjected Tweedledum, laying on the guilt.

"Don't listen to them," I told the poor girl. "You have a good night . . . Thanks again for your help."

"You're welcome." Then Ashley added, "Your solo sounded great, by the way."

I rolled my eyes.

"I mean it," she insisted. "You were really feeling it . . . I could tell."

It did go okay, I guess. Like I said, the *Grease* play is a tad different than the *Grease* film, which is what everybody knows and comes in expecting to see. In fact, the song I sing, "Magic Changes," is only in the background of the movie at the dance. In the stage version, it sorta comes outta left field near the top of the show in scene three.

Basically what happens is . . . We finish "Summer Nights," then there's a short scene. You know, the one where Rizzo's like, "Danny, we got a surprise for you." Then Danny and Sandy come face-to-face, and he's like, "What are you doing here?" and she's like, "Plans changed." And then he totally blows her off. End of scene.

Next thing we know, the school bell rings. In walks Doody (me), carrying his guitar. Danny's like, "Play something Elvis," and I start pantomiming, and singing:

"C-C-C-C-C-C . . ."

The tune itself is sorta dopey. All about how this guy doesn't wanna hear this certain song on the radio ever again on account of it reminds him of his long-lost love, and how he can't live without her, da-dah da-dah.

All thru rehearsals, it went off without a hitch. Then for whatever reason, when I reached the last verse during the show this evening, I totally lost it. As in, I started bawling. I mean, not like a baby or anything. I got thru it. But there were serious tears in my eyes.

Wanna know what happened?

I started thinking about The Sophomore, instead of just singing the words the way I usually do. I actually thought about what they *mean*, and how I would feel if I was Doody for *real* and I lost *my* one true love . . . Sorta like what's happened in my own personal life, you know what I mean?

Of course, Richie wasn't on stage during that part of the show. He doesn't appear as Vince Fontaine till the dance contest in Act Two. So I don't know if he even heard me singing my heart out for him or not.

I didn't think it would be this difficult. I thought I could push my feelings deep down inside and forget anything I ever felt for the guy. Everything about him that makes me weak in the knees.

The way he lifts his shirt up, wiping the sweat from his lip while he's lifting weights.

The way he sucks on his saxophone, moistening the reed sensuously, before playing a single note.

The way he kisses me, hard and strong as if his life depended on it.

"Dayton!"

Despite it being almost 9:30 at night, I discovered myself daydreaming in the dark.

"I'll see you guys tomorrow," I told Will or Keith, whichever one called my name.

"Ain't you coming?"

It was Keith. For a second, I thought he didn't bother changing outta his Roger costume. Until I realized he just traded his sweaty white T-shirt for a fresh one.

"I think I'm gonna pass . . ."

Early on, I decided I couldn't go out and celebrate, feeling as miserable as I felt. The last thing I needed was to be stuck in a booth at Big Boy's with Richie Tyler staring me in the face, reminding me what I gave up for the sake of my so-called career.

The good news is . . . *Faded Flowers* finished filming at the end of February, so it's not like Richie and Joey are still involved. To be honest, I don't think they ever were, really. I know for a fact Joey's still going with Diane Thompson, who's playing Cha-Cha in the show. I seen them totally making out backstage before curtain. That doesn't mean Joey and Richie didn't do any (quote-unquote) practicing for their onscreen debut that Miss Thompson doesn't know about, you know what I mean?

"Let's go!"

From outside the dressing room door, I heard a familiar cry.

"Brad says he's not coming," Keith told Richie, who popped his head in to see what was taking us so long.

"He is too coming," Richie replied, catching my eye in the makeup mirror.

"Move your ass, Treva!"

From outside the dressing room door, we heard the growl of Tuesday Gunderson. It seems she and her onstage love interest have developed an off stage show-mance. Now Keith's totally *P-whipped,* as all the straight guys say.

"I'll see you dudes over there," Keith told us. Then he called out, "Calm your ass, woman!"

The next seven seconds felt like fifty.

Me and The Sophomore, alone for the first time since we officially broke up.

I had to stop and remind myself we were never *really* going together.

"You don't wanna miss the Opening Night party," I told him, busying myself with the compacts cluttering up the counter, along with other various pencils, brushes, and powders.

"And you do?" asked Richie, burning a hole in me with those piercing blue eyes.

Damn him!

Next thing I knew, I was following Diane Thompson and her passenger west on Woodward Heights. For whatever reason, they got 9 Mile blocked off between Hughes and I-75 due to construction. I think they're finally putting in a much-needed left-turn lane. Lemme tell ya, it's been a pain in the ass getting to school every day. I gotta either take 8 Mile to Dequindre and backtrack or follow the service drive down to Woodward Heights, and cut across that way.

This brings me to where I am right now . . .

A quick pause at the stop sign by Tubby's, then blow thru the yellow light by Mobil, followed by a sharp right at Woodruff, and into the Big Boy's parking lot.

Great!

Wanna know what kinda car I just pulled up next to?

A 1979 pea green Dodge Omni.

This would be the vehicle driven by one Mr. John R. "Jack" Paterno.

What the hell is *he* doing here?

I heard a rumor he was reviewing Opening Night's show for *The Hazel Parker,* but I never expected him to hang out with the Drama Queers post-performance. Especially since we're all still pissed at him. Thank God I stopped at Kayo's and got a brand new pack of cigarettes.

This is gonna be a long night!

Up the snow-covered sidewalk I climb, past the life-size statue of Big Boy himself. He's got a lot of nerve standing there in his red and white checkered overalls, holding that huge hamburger over his head, grinning. Doesn't he realize the doom I'm about to face as I walk thru that door? I feel like Jessica Tate from *Soap* when she went before that firing squad . . . I wonder if they ended up shooting her or not.

"Doody!"

As per tradition, all the Drama Queers burst into applause the second I enter the building.

"Why didn't you guys grab a table?"

Watching Audrey, Ava, Joey Palladino, and the rest of the Rydell High Ringtails huddle en masse near the PLEASE WAIT TO BE SEATED sign, I don't know what they're doing.

"Smoking was full when we got here," Audrey informs me, her now-pink hair still saturated with "Beauty School Dropout" spray.

"Fuck!"

Ava rests a gentle hand upon my shoulder. “Easy there,” she sighs, mocking what she thinks is me having one of my nicotine fits. “A couple tables just cleared out . . . Shir’s setting them up now.”

Truth be told, my cursing like a truck driver has nothing to do with our lack of a place to hang out, even though I don’t know why Elias Brothers is bustling on a fucking Thursday night. I’m pissed because I can see the exact two tables Shir’s cleaning off for us, located directly across from where the Editor-in-Chief of *The Hazel Parker* sits in a booth opposite my favorite Varsity cheerleader—not!

“You kids are all set.”

Shir grabs half a dozen menus from the stack near the register and leads the way, even though none of us needs an escort, on top of the fact that I’m an employee of the establishment so I can handle seating myself. Before I sit, I decide I’ll be the bigger person and say hello to Mr. Paterno and Miss Sheffield. Except just as I open my mouth, the words barely forming on my lips, Jack totally looks away, pretending like he doesn’t notice me.

Bullshit!

I watch as he dumps an entire packet of sugar into his pop, making his stupid “Citron Fizz.” I’ll tell you what he’s making: a mess all over the table as the Sprite erupts volcano-style.

Fuck him!

If that’s the game Jack Paterno wants to play, I’ll gladly return the volley. Or serve. Or whatever the hell sports term applies here.

“Cha-cha . . . Vince Fontaine!”

The Drama Queers burst into applause as Diane Thompson joins us at our table, accompanied by You-Know-Who.

“Sorry we’re late,” apologizes The Sophomore.

“We had to make a pit stop,” Diane slyly discloses.

Joey's face lights up. "You got the supplies?"

"You bet your sweet Dago ass we did!"

You'd think this comment would come from Diane, but it actually belongs to Richie. Cha-Cha's too busy being pulled onto Danny Zuko's lap and having her face sucked off.

A quick take reveals Mr. Paterno acting like he doesn't see any of this either.

Hmmm . . . Is it just my imagination, or does Jack look a tad jealous?

He can't still be carrying a torch for Joey Palladino . . . *Can he?*

Last I checked, he was sooo into Mr. Homecoming King.

Speaking of . . .

I heard a rumor that Betsy Sheffield recently dumped Tom Fulton's ass. But nobody knows the exact reason. I guess this would explain why Jack and Tom are no longer all buddy-buddy.

"Who wants to hit the salad bar?"

Tuesday Gunderson gets up from the table, followed by Audrey and Ava.

"Bring me some soup, would ya?" Keith Treva orders, like Tuesday's his waitress. Or his mother. Or whatever the hell inferior female term applies.

Tuesday fires back. "Get it yourself, *Rump!*"

This would be Keith's *Grease* nickname on account of Roger is the one who sings the "Mooning" song.

"You comin', Rizz?" asks Audrey in her Frenchy/Didi Conn accent.

"Bite the weenie," Jamieleeann Mary Sue Good replies, à la Betty Rizzo. She leaps up from the table where she sits beside Allen Bryan and cries, *"Psyche!"* Then she tags along with the other Pink Ladies, sans Sandy (Liza Larson) who I'm sure is off somewhere with her boyfriend (Gus), and Marty (Miranda Resnick) whose mother won't let her stay out on a school night.

I gotta say, at first I didn't think Jamie would fit in with the Drama Queers, being that she's one of the Popular People. Same goes for Allen Bryan. But it's been sooo much fun having them in the *Grease* family. Plus Jamie sings a heartbreaking rendition of "There Are Worse Things I Could Do," and Allen is hilarious in his "Yes, ma'am . . . No, ma'am" scene with Ava Reese as Miss Lynch, aka Miss McGee (Eve Arden) in the movie. I think some of the other DQs were a tad apprehensive about Dell casting outside the usual DQ circle. But I love Jamie to death and Allen is totally cool—for a jock.

"Let's all hit the salad bar."

Diane Thompson jumps off Joey's lap, takes him by the hand, and leads him across the restaurant like a 2-year-old. Or a dog. Or whatever the hell subordinate term applies here.

"I'll come too," I decide. Not because I'm dying for a cup of clam chowder. But I get the feeling Jack and Betsy are talking about me and my friends, and I wanna eavesdrop as I pass by their table.

The second I do, I swear I hear Miss Sheffield say: "You think he's a fag?"

I got a good mind to walk right up and bash her fucking face in!

How dare that bitch talk about me that way?

I had a feeling her cop-uncle ratted me out.

Of course, maybe she *isn't* talking about me. For all I know, Betsy could be commenting on any number of the male Drama Queer members—from Rakoff to Richie to even Joey Palladino.

By the time I return to our table, soup and salad and in tow, Jack Paterno and bitch-friend are nowhere to be found. I help myself to a few abandoned fries they left laying on their plates . . . "Waste not, want not!" I always say.

Around 11:00 PM, after acting out the entire Frosty Palace scene from the *Grease* movie, with the exception of Jamie "Rizzo"

Good throwing an actual milkshake in Will "Kenickie" Isaacs's face, we wrap things up. I don't know about anybody else, but I didn't *really* need to finish that entire hot fudge ice cream cake.

"Shall we take this party elsewhere?" Mr. Palladino wonders, addressing the entire gang.

"I gotta go," says Rakoff, sounding totally sullen.

After all, it *is* a school night. Us babies gotta get home so our mommies can tuck us in and bid us beddy-bye before serving us our mayonnaise cake.

Surprisingly, Tuesday Gunderson echoes, "I gotta go too." Followed by, "Treva . . . You wanna give me a ride?"

This can only mean one thing: they're gonna go make out in the backseat of WIFEY 1, which is what we dubbed Keith's mom's '84 Dodge Caravan based on the vanity plate his Evil Step-Devil recently bought for it.

"I should scoot," Ava decides. "I told Don I'd call him at 11 o'clock."

"Can you give me a lift?" asks Audrey. "Berger's supposed to stop by on his way home from work."

Somebody brays. Most likely Will or Keith.

Ava hesitates. "But I live around the corner, and you're all the way over by the racetrack."

"I'm not *that* far," Audrey pleads. "I'm closer to the Church of Christ."

"Same dif."

Aud gives Ava the finger. "Fine . . . Be that way!"

"I'll drive you," offers Jamie, who lives down on Davey, behind HPHS.

Will Isaacs says, "I'll take a ride," even though he knows Jamie is still going with Jeff Rhimes, who will kick his ass if he keeps on flirting with her.

After what can only be described as a *mass exodus*, I'm left sitting at the table with Joey Palladino, Diane Thompson, and The Sophomore.

"Where to next?" Richie asks, ready to move on to greener pastures.

I reply, "Bed . . . I'm pooped."

Joey says, "Come on, ya big baby!"

Diane adds, "I got some wine coolers in my car."

The last thing I wanna do right now is hang out with The Sophomore when there's alcohol involved. Even if he does look exactly like James Dean with his hair slicked back, à la 1950s. I totally wanna run my fingers thru it and mess it all up.

I bid my friends a fond farewell. "I'll see you guys bright and early."

"Not me."

Joey looks pleased with the fact that he's neither a Band Fag nor a member of Vikettes, so he doesn't gotta get up for practice at the butt crack of dawn.

"Fucking Klan," I mumble, making my exit.

I can't believe he's got us coming in to rehearse at 7 o'clock in the fucking AM on account of the big Marching Band trip to Disney World coming up in less than two weeks.

Actually, I decided I'm not going. Not because I don't wanna spend my Senior Spring Break stuck in Orlando with a bunch of Band Fags, even though I sorta don't. I'd much rather be soaking up the sun in Daytona, combing the beach looking for *like that* lifeguards. The main reason I can't make the trip is because, truth be told, I can't afford it.

Now all I gotta do is break the news to Mr. Klan.

Ten minutes later, I'm home-sweet-home . . .

Before heading inside, I stop on the back porch to have my last cigarette of the day. How many does that make total? Ten, maybe fifteen. I had at least five while we were at Big Boy's. Again, I gotta quit.

Here's a little secret: sometimes, I like to watch myself smoke.

Like right now, I can see my reflection in the back door window, and here I stand just taking it in. Not because I think I look cool, that's not it. There's something about the act of *observing* myself. Placing the cigarette in my mouth, the way my fingers hold it, the way my cheeks suck in when I take a puff. Particularly, the way the smoke appears, thick and gray, as I send it soaring off into the air.

Seeing it makes it all the more real, you know what I mean?

Sometimes when I'm smoking and I *can't* see myself, I feel like I didn't even do it. Same thing with eating. Like if I have a snack or something when I'm talking on the telephone, after I finish, I'm still hungry. I wonder if that's why people put mirrors over their beds. Maybe it's the same way with making love?

Great!

Now I'm thinking about Richie—again!

Imagine what would've happened if I let them guys come over my house. I can visualize the entire scene . . .

The Sophomore arrives with Joey and Diane. We crack open the coolers and get totally crocked. Joey and Diane end up making out in a corner somewhere, leaving me and Richie alone in my family room together to do what?

Boy, do I need a shower!

A nice cold one.

Tap-tap-tap!

Not more than five minutes after I strip down to my skivvies, somebody bangs on my bedroom window, totally fuh-reaking me out.

Quickly, I kill the lights.

Wanna know who I see standing alongside our house?

"'How 'bout a little Sneaky Pete to get this party going?'"

That's a line from *Grease.* 'member during the slumber party scene when Rizzo whips out a bottle of Italian Swiss Colony to accompany Jan's Twinkies? Only it's not Jamieleeann Mary Sue Good standing in my *boudoir*, a Bartles & Jaymes four-pack in her hot little hands . . .

"What's up?"

Dressed in nothing but a dirty towel I grabbed off the doorknob and wrapped around my waist, I greet my unexpected guest.

"I was just about to ask *you* the exact same question . . . Opie."

Wouldn't you know? Total Hard-on.

Fucking Richie Tyler!

Control

"When I was 17 I did what people told me, uhh! Did what my father said, and let my mother mold me . . ."

—Janet Jackson

'member how I keep saying I need a *new* job?

About a week ago, I came home from my five-hour shift at Big Boy's with a whopping $37.83 in my pocket. As if that wasn't bad enough, when I walked thru the door, I found my mother at the kitchen counter phone in hand, in tears. I thought for sure somebody died . . . When you got three grandparents all in their sixties, you worry constantly.

"How was work?"

Mom saw me, dried her eyes, and returned the receiver to its cradle. She put on her happy face, as if the gray skies were already clearing up.

"It sucked."

"Mind your language," she playfully scolded. Then she reached out. "Can I have a hug?"

Even at seventeen, I'm not afraid to show a little love and

affection every now and then to the woman who gave me life. The second I wrapped my arms around her, Mom broke down.

"What's wrong?"

This was all I could think to say, not even sure I wanted to hear the answer.

She uttered two words: "Your father."

I understood completely. Once again, his child support payment was due. Once again, the deadbeat failed to pay it.

I'm sure you heard of Old Mother Hubbard and her poor dog. Well, you're looking at Old Lady Laura and her two hungry daughters. Me, I'm fine. I eat most of my meals at Big Boy's, which is one of the perks of working in a restaurant. Unfortunately, two teenaged girls like Nina and Brittany can't survive on PB & J and government cheese. Never mind the fact that I don't know where I'm gonna get the money to go to Juilliard in September—*if* I even get in.

I can't believe, for the biggest audition of my life, I pieced together a Bob Cratchit monologue from *A* goddamn *Christmas Carol.* I'll never forget the look on the judges' faces when I concluded with a rousing cry of "God bless us, every one!"

What the fuck was I thinking?

Baldy #1 just sat there staring at me, all Shields & Yarnell.

Baldy #2, aka Paul Lynde, practically held his nose, like I took a dump in the middle of the Juilliard dance studio.

And Jane Hathaway . . . Let's just say, if she'd been sitting before a gong, she would've grabbed the nearest gonger.

But enough already!

At that particular moment, I had more important things to concern myself with.

Like making sure my sisters didn't starve.

"I'll handle this."

I planted a kiss upon Mom's salty cheek, changed outta my uniform, and drove down to Detroit . . .

"If I were you," Miss Peter commented after I conveyed my plight, "I'd go over the old man's house and kick his fucking ass."

If only I could. "He's a cop, 'member?"

I sipped my screwdriver, yet another in the long line of non-beer alcoholic beverages I been sampling in hopes of finding one I actually enjoy.

At that moment, our favorite spandex-clad cocktail waitress rudely interrupted us.

"Would you gents care for anything else?"

"Why yes, Aryc," Miss Peter said smugly. She held up her glass and gave the rocks a gentle roll. "Another round, *si vous plaît . . .*"

"Rum and Coke?"

"Captain and *Diet*," Miss Peter snapped. She turned to me, pleading, "Why can't anybody seem to get it? I'm watching my *weight!*" Then back to Aryc, she ordered, "And bring Opie another screwdriver . . . With some extra screw."

Aryc flounced away, tank top sleeve slouching off his shoulder.

"What I need to do is make some serious money," I said, getting back to the subject, still at a total loss. Until it hit me. "What about wet-Jockey-shorts Tuesdays?"

Every third night of the week, before the maddening crowd, a big old Drag Queen by the name of Zephyr "The Lady Z" dons a one-piece swimsuit and climbs into a kiddie pool, where she hoses down the eager contestants. Despite the enthusiastic hooting and howling, none of the guys are ever very attractive. *Desperate* is the word I'd use to describe them as they (attempt to) strut their stuff. But the prize is indeed $50. Where else could I make that kinda money in ten minutes' time?

Miss Peter reminded me, "You're in high school," as if maybe I forgot this fact. "I will *not* allow it . . . You're only seventeen."

"Not anymore."

Like Angie Dickison wielding her *Police Woman* badge, I whipped out my recently acquired fake ID. I concocted it myself using two number 6's cut out from the phone book (with my mom's cuticle scissors) and glued over the original digits: 7-0. After the scare we had with Officer Sheffield of the Detroit PD, I decided not to take any more chances. Only I wasn't about to abandon my nights out at the bar. I'd die without a social scene.

Two shakes later, Aryc returned with our cocktails held high atop his tray.

"Did I hear you say you're in need of some fast cash?" Aryc may sound all posh, but he was totally eavesdropping. "I believe we're looking to hire another server."

"You mean *here?*"

Never for one second did I fathom actually working in a place like this. It's a bar, for chris'sakes, and a gay one, you know what I mean?

Miss Peter exclaimed, "That's a fab idea! How much money can Opie make?"

"On a good evening?" Aryc answered. "One-fifty, two hundred, maybe."

"Dollars?" I exclaimed, seeing $ signs in my eyes.

"Depending."

Something about the way Aryc said this made me pause.

"On what?" Miss Peter inquired on my behalf.

"Oh, you know . . . How pleasantly he treats the customers."

I heard rumors about things that went on in some of the other bars around town. Like I said, I know they have (quote-unquote) strippers at Gold Coast. But Miss Peter tells me they might as well be *hustlers,* based on the things those boys are willing to do—if the price is right.

"Let's just say," Aryc told us, a twinkle in his Aryan eye, "a boy can earn a pretty penny, and have a bit o' fun while he's at it."

"You got that right!"

Some totally drunk guy I never laid eyes on before chimed in from the table next to ours, giving Aryc's *arse* a hefty swat.

"Watch it, you wanker!" Aryc warned. "Or I'll cut off your drinks, followed by your cock." Then he said to me in a hush, "As you Yanks say, the work's all 'under the table.'"

The next night I gave Shir my notice at Big Boy's.

I started working at The Gas Station that same Friday.

Good Friday, to be exact.

While all my Band Fag friends were en route to Disney, and all the Popular People (plus Jack and Max) found themselves Daytona Beach bound, I set out to begin my career as the employee of a divey Detroit gay bar.

"Somebody's late!"

Just when I thought I might actually get along with Aryc, he goes and proves me wrong. I wasn't even thru the door *three* seconds and he was already on my case.

"Sorry," I apologized. "My piece-of-shit car died on 7 Mile . . . I had to find a pay phone and call a cab."

"Do you know what time it is?" Aryc said sharply.

I wasn't sure why he asked since he clearly wore a watch upon his wrist. A diamond-studded number that I'm sure cost more than your average takes-a-licking-and-keeps-on-ticking.

"8:08," I replied, regarding my humble Swatch.

"And what time does your shift start?"

"8 o'clock."

"You best arrive at least fifteen minutes *before* you begin," Aryc informed me. "You want plenty o' time to change your jumper and trousers." He looked me up and down in my cardigan and khaki pants. Thank God, or I wouldn't know what the hell he was talking about.

"I didn't bring any other clothes," I admitted, suddenly feeling insecure.

Aryc rolled his eyes and let out a huff, scattering his flippy bangs across his forehead.

"What?' I mumbled, not even sure I wanted to hear the answer.

"Never mind."

We headed to the bar, where Mike and his mohawk were *not*. Being Friday, a big night for the Gay Detroit scene, he was tending upstairs at Heaven. Instead, this guy, Sam, held down the fort. While very nice, Sam is no Sam Malone from *Cheers*. Medium everything, you know what I mean?

Basically my duties entail . . . When I arrive for my shift, I immediately hit the bar, where the tender on duty gives me my bank. This is $50 in cash I keep in my pocket. As I work the room, stopping by to check in on customers and take their drink orders, I use the money from my bank to pay the bartender, reimbursing myself with the cash the customers fork over, and keep anything extra as my tip.

The first hour I made twenty-five bucks.

Not bad!

At Big Boy's, I'd have to work twice as long to make that much moolah. And these dollars are all duty-free. I could smell the steak *à poivre* sizzling on the stove back home in the kitchen at Dayton's Depot.

Other duties include: gathering empty glasses, changing the Coke tank down in the cellar, aka Freddy Krueger's furnace, and . . .

"Anything else?"

"When you're finished," Aryc said, answering my inquiry, "I'll show you the dressing room."

This is basically a glorified broom closet with a makeup mirror and chair. Lady Z. Zephyr uses it to prepare herself for wet-Jockey-shorts Tuesdays before whipping out her hose. Aryc tells me she likes the closet kept clean and stocked with the finest amenities: Final Net, Barbasol, and Wet Ones . . . It's the simple things that keep a performer happy, really.

"Come in and close the door."

I followed Aryc inside, doing as instructed. Adorning the edges of the mirror, I noticed an array of photos of Lady Z posing with her favorite Drag Queen cohorts: Vanessa LeSabre, Nikki Stewart, Trixxie Deelite. Talk about glamorous! All done up in full regalia, with lots of big hair and face paint, these so-called ladies looked spectacular.

One particular Queen I didn't recognize. She was a white woman with a Patti LaBelle hairdo, circa 1985. You know, all flat and fanned out, from her "Somewhere Over the Rainbow" Live Aid period. I'd be lying if I didn't admit I'm a tad bit frightened by Female Impersonators. Not *frightened* really, more like intimidated, you know what I mean? Most of them seem sooo secure with who they are, it's hard to imagine they were once little gay boys running around the halls of some high school somewhere.

"Damn, this is good shit."

From the darkness, I heard an unfamiliar voice.

Suddenly, I smelled an old familiar scent.

Wanna know what I seen when I turned around?

Aryc smoking a joint in the middle of Zephyr's closet—I mean, *dressing room.*

"Take a toke?"

He extended the joint, smoke wafting between us. As sweet as it smelled, I haven't smoked pot in probably three years. The last thing I needed was to get caught getting high my first night on the job. So I politely refused.

"Pussy . . ."

I looked at Aryc like he was a post-demon Regan What's-Her-Name from *The Excorcist.* Any second, I expected heads to spin and pea soup to fly. In all the time I knew him, Aryc always had this distinct, upper-crust *British* dialect. Suddenly, he sounded like every other gay guy in Detroit.

"What happened to your accent?"

"I grew up in Grosse Pointe," he confessed. "I got my MFA in Acting from the Hilberry."

I don't know why it surprised me to discover Aryc a Drama Queer.

"'Wayne State . . . Good school.'" He quoted Casey Kasem, sounding like my guidance counselor, Mrs. Ellis, the flake! Then he snuffed out the doob, and picked up one of Lady Z's compacts from the table. "My nose gets shiny," he reported, giving his schnoz a gentle powder.

Lemme tell ya, I felt just like Linda Lavin following Polly Holliday around Mel's Diner the way Aryc showed me the ropes, telling me to shake my titties and show 'em some ass.

"Lose the Preppie look and you'll make better profits."

This was Aryc's advice to me when he caught sight of my stash at the end of the evening. Personally, I thought I looked cute, whereas he looked like a Total Tramp sporting them god-awful spandex shorts. Perhaps he *did* have a point as I noticed a lot more George Washingtons, and even a few Abe Lincolns staring up at Aryc from the pile o' money he pocketed.

Note to self: next time, dress slutty.

"Did you wipe this table off?"

Upon returning from the *loo,* Aryc asked me this.

"I did . . . There was a bunch of dust all over it."

For a split second, I thought I was a dead man.

"That wasn't dust, you *ass,*" Aryc fumed, fire in his eyes. "That was coke!"

As in *caine.*

Well, how the hell was I to know?

The following Tuesday finds me back in action . . .

Only this time, I invested in a uniform, much like Aryc's biker shorts/tank top combo. I feel sooo scrawny, but the tips are a-flowin' so what do I care? Like I said, tonight is the weekly wet-Jockey-shorts contest, hosted by Zephyr "The Lady Z," and the place is packed. Down in The Pit, two shirtless guys spin round in circles, connected by what resembles a torn T-shirt held tightly between their teeth.

"What are they doing?" I ask Aryc in passing. "Some sorta modern dance moves?"

Over the blare of Miss Jackson (if you're nasty) belting out her latest hit, he shouts, "Ethyl rag!"

Ethyl who?

I don't take a break till almost 10:00 PM. Two hours without a cig and I'm *dying*. I sneak into the back for a quick butt. Upon returning, Sam the bartender makes an announcement: "Look what the cat dragged in."

Thru the door walks a grandfatherly gentleman, decked out in a three-piece suit, no tie, open at the collar to expose a rather hirsute chest. I can't help but notice the gaggle of college-aged guys surrounding him.

"Who's he?" I wonder aloud, not recognizing the old fart at all.

Aryc starts humming. *"He's the man, the man with the Midas touch . . ."*

Turns out, they call him "Goldfinger." Just look at the rings on his right hand and you'll understand why. One of them, a chunky rock of a number resembles the MGM lion head, mid-roar.

Me and Aryc spend the night fighting over who gets to care for Grandpa G and be the recipient of his big, fat—tip. Luckily, he likes 'em young, so Yours Truly wins the loot. Each time I bring him his $3.75 Sea Breeze, I'm rewarded with a crisp Andrew Jackson, followed by a firm fondle of my behind.

"Keep the change."

So what if he's a smarmy old man? I make almost fifty bucks alone off the guy.

"The Bitch is back . . ."

Once again, Sam is the first to spot the arrival of The Gas Station's next celebrity guest.

Once again, Aryc starts humming. *"The day my mama socked it to . . ."*

Turns out, one of Lady Z. Zephyr's theme songs is "Harper Valley PTA," which I (Harper Valley) L-O-V-E! I'm told she does a routine where she sings the song all done up in '60s housewife drag. When she's finished, she makes the DJ play the record in reverse, and she strips to it while singing the song a second time. Only *backwards.* She's got the lyrics memorized phonetically, I guess. Talk about a feat!

Sadly, I don't remember the *Harper Valley PTA* movie very much. I only saw it once when they showed it on channel 50 or 20 back when I was little. I remember them turning it into a series in like 1980–81, I think. Mom wouldn't allow me and the girls to watch it—too racy. After all, Stella Johnson was a divorcée, wasn't she? If poor Mom only knew the path her own life would follow.

I'm pretty sure the TV version featured none of the same cast, save for Barbara "I Dream of Jeannie" Eden, who my dad used to have a crush on big-time. Or was it Barbara Feldon of *Get Smart* fame? I know the chubby girl who played Stella's daughter on TV was the fattie from *Little Darlings* and *Honky Tonk Freeway.*

The latter, I totally loved. It's got the best ensemble cast ever in a movie . . . Beau Bridges from *Heart Like a Wheel*, Beverly D'Angelo from *Vacation*, Terri Garr from *Tootsie*, Howard Hesseman from *WKRP in Cincinnati*, and Celia Weston, aka Jolene from *Alice* (among others).

"Lady Z needs assistance!"

Sam bellows, and I run like a bat outta hell.

Being the "new girl in town" with my "fresh freckled face," Aryc sends me to do the dirty work. Honestly, I don't mind. The closest thing I ever saw to a Drag Queen up close is Miss Peter. While she's got the hair down pat, she never wears an ounce of makeup, so she doesn't count.

"What took you so long?"

Somehow, this isn't the response I expect when I knock and enter Lady Z's abode. I mean, sure I know she's a tough broad. I once heard her tell a straight male heckler, "I'm more man than you'll ever be and more woman than you could ever handle."

"Excuse me," I say, not sure whether or not I should throw in *ma'am.*

Zephyr stands at the mirror teasing her dark brown wig into a big old bouffant.

"Well, hello . . ."

From what Aryc told me, Lady Z also favors the young boys. This might explain why her attitude drops the second she sees me standing in the door. Did I mention how tiny she is? 5'2" if even that. Up on stage, she always looks so much taller. I forgot about the five-inch spikes she wears during her act, I guess. You should see the deep-squatted Russian kicks she can do in them things!

"Here's a towel," I say, shyly offering her the pink cloth of terry.

"Thank you, young man." Lady Z dabs at the beads of perspiration on her forehead, calling to mind Ann Bancroft trying to seduce Dustin Hoffman in *The Graduate.* "You're a newbie."

I can't tell if she's asking a question or informing me of a fact. Regardless, I nod and smile. "My name's Bradley."

"Will you be assisting me this evening, Bradley?"

As long as I been coming to The Gas Station, I can't recall seeing Zephyr ever working as a duo. How much assistance could a dress-wearing man need wetting down some other men in their underwear?

Still, I mind my manners. "Not unless you need me to."

Lady Z smiles demurely. "I don't *need* anything."

I'm not sure how to take that comment. So I smile right back before making my departure.

I don't get very far.

"You're a pretty thing, aren't you?"

This I take as a compliment.

"I mean it," Lady Z continues. "Such beautiful bone structure."

Believe it or not, she literally grabs hold of my chin with her surprisingly soft man-hands, turning my face from side to side, inspecting me like a piece of pork she purchased at Kroger's or Great Scott's.

"Have you ever done drag, Bradley?"

I let out a guffaw and almost ask, *Are you nuts?* But I realize the question might come off as an insult to a man who makes his living pretending to be a woman.

"When I was six, I dressed up like a gypsy fortune teller for Halloween."

Lady Z's face lights up. "You started young!"

"And last year I went to see *Rocky Horror* in costume with some friends."

Tip to tip, she clicks her Lee Press Ons together. "Let me guess . . . Magenta?"

"Columbia . . . I even wore my own hair," I state proudly.

Zephyr runs a hand thru my curly locks. "You ever think about giving it a shot?"

"Doing drag?" I inquire incredulously. "Never."

"You got a problem with Drag Queens?" Lady Z sneers.

"Not at all."

The last thing I want is her thinking I have issues with her people.

"How old are you?"

I almost say, "Seventeen." Until I remember my ID indicates otherwise. "Twenty-one," I reply, hoping my voice won't waver as I lie thru my teeth.

"I'm hosting an amateur drag show at Gigi's," Zephyr informs me. "This Saturday at midnight . . . You should come by."

Miss Peter says she used to go to Gigi's all the time back in the day, but I never been. Most likely because of my Drag Queen-a-phobia.

As flattered as I may be, I still have to ask, "Seriously?"

I can't tell if this woman—I mean, *man*—is feeding me a line in order to get in my pants or does she—I mean, *he*—think I truly got what it takes?

"With that face and that hair," she gives each a quick grope. "Pick yourself the perfect song and costume . . . You can't lose."

"But I never performed before," I confess. The last thing I wanna do is make an ass of myself in front of all of Gay Detroit.

Zephyr is bound and determined. "Not even in your high school play?"

Hello!

"Yeah, but . . ."

"So you're a Drama Queer?" Lady Z points to her tits. "Brother Rice Thespian of the Year, Class of '74."

Maybe Zephyr is right.

Maybe all these years of playing Dress Up would finally pay off.

Maybe the transition from Drama Queer to Drag Queen would be a walk in the park . . . Albeit, one in high heels.

Think about it: Drama/Drag. Queer/Queen.

And then Lady Z. Zephyr utters the magic words . . .

"First prize is five hundred bucks."

Where do I sign up?

Through the Eyes of Love

"Please, don't let this feeling end
It's everything I am . . ."

—Melissa Manchester

April 9, 1988.

When I look back on my childhood, this date will mark the moment that Laura Victor-Dayton-Victor and Bradley James Dayton went from being mother-son to faithful friends.

"Which exit should I take?"

Clutching the wheel at ten-and-two, Mom stares straight ahead down the Southfield Freeway. Surprisingly, there's not a lot of traffic at 10:50 PM on a Saturday night here in the bowels of Detroit.

"West Warren," I confirm, heart speed-racing as we draw closer to our final destination.

I could totally use a cigarette right now. Too bad I make it a point never to smoke in front of my mother. I know some kids' parents allow them to partake, but I find it the ultimate in white trash, you know what I mean?

"Bradley . . ."

The subtext to the way Mom just said my name means she serioiusly doubts my navigational skills.

"It's coming up," I promise. "On the right."

We just passed the Greenfield Village billboard with its Independence Hall knock-off, an indicator we're getting close.

Mom puts on her blinker, even though there isn't a car behind us for *miles.*

"Bradley, this is the ghetto," she informs me, as if I can't tell by the burnt-out buildings and abandoned houses flanking either side of the freeway.

"Lock the doors and don't look at anybody."

Damn Miss Peter!

Leave it to her to go on a bender at Backstreet and wind up in bed all day. I begged her *not* to party the night before I'm to make my official drag debut. But did she listen?

N-O!

I would've totally drove myself this evening, but once again, Val up and died on me. This time for good, I'm sad to say. As of this year, she's officially an old girl of twenty, so I should probably put her out to pasture, huh?

Heading home from the Headrest earlier today, she totally conked out at 10½ Mile and John R. I know what they say about too much tanning, but why should I be the only Casper in town once all my classmates return from Florida? Luckily, Jack's Aunt Sonia and Uncle Mark live nearby and were home so I could use their phone . . .

"Brad-ski!"

Sounding happy yet surprised to find me knocking on her door, Aunt Sonia welcomed me into her home, smothering me in *("And they call it . . .")* Charlie. Meanwhile, her hubby sat on the floral print love seat watching *Wide World of Sports.*

"How ya doin'?"

Uncle Mark rose to shake my hand. With his over-the-ear

salt-and-pepper hair and mustache, I often think of Detroit's own Tom Skerritt in his role as Lexie Winston's father in *Ice Castles*, Marcus Winston. Only with a warm Southern drawl.

"Want some pop?" Aunt Sonia offered. As per usual, she made me think of Penny Marshall, only Midwestern. "I got Faygo Rock & Rye or Moon Mist."

I politely refused, opting for a glass of *water*, which I took extra care to pronounce precisely. Then I joined her in the dining alcove. I couldn't help but notice the china cabinet just beyond the table. A small, single-masted schooner made entirely of seashells sat alone amidst a collection of owls. There must've been fifty, if not more, in all shapes and sizes from Great Horned to Woodsy. *("Give a Hoot—Don't Pollute!")*

Aunt Sonia took out her Virginia Slim Menthol Light 120s (in the box), and I saw this as my cue to reach for my Marlboros. "May I borrow your lighter?"

She offered me her pink Cricket, and I proceeded to smoke. Like I said, I make it a point never to partake in front of my parents. For whatever reason, I'm not as concerned when it comes to other adults. Besides, after all these years, I consider Aunt Sonia as more of a friend.

I'll never forget the time I went Up North with Jack's family to his grandpa's cottage in Gaylord. Aunt Sonia and Uncle Mark came along and they spent an entire afternoon trying to teach me and Jack how to drive a stick. Talk about frustrating! No matter how hard I tried, I could *not* remember whether I was supposed to step on the clutch or step on the gas, and at which point to shift the shifter . . . Yet thru all the grinding of the gears, not once did Uncle Mark lose his grip.

I remember being sooo nervous sitting beside him in the front of his Chevy S-10 pickup, complete with cab on the back. Like I said, Uncle Mark reminds me of Tom Skerritt, who I had a crush on since like age ten. He also smelled super good, wearing what I think was Old Spice. Maybe Jovan Musk for Men.

"How come we haven't seen you for a while?"

Aunt Sonia wanted to know this once we were both comfy doing what we did best.

As much as I wanted to tell her, *Ask your nephew,* I opted for something civil like, "Oh you know . . . I been busy with school."

Call me crazy, but I couldn't make my (former) Best Friend look bad in his aunt's eyes, even though *he's* the one who wants nothing to do with me anymore.

Then I asked, "Have you talked to Jack lately?" since my mind was on the subject.

Aunt Sonia sent a menthol plume soaring above her head, nodding. "He called me from Daytona Beach on Monday . . . For my birthday."

"Happy Birthday!"

Aunt Sonia scoffed, stubbing out her cig. "I'm thirty-eight . . . How's that for old?"

And I thought eighteen was ancient!

Despite my insisting I could call my mother, Aunt Sonia made Uncle Mark get off his duff and drive me home. When I arrived half an hour later, I found Mom at the kitchen counter up to her elbows in making meatballs . . .

"I need a favor."

"Well, I owe you one," she reminded me.

That morning, we made a special trip out to Meijer's where I used most of my tip money from the night before to stock the pantry full for a month. Lemme tell ya, the smell of something other than boiling Ball Park Franks found itself most welcome at Dayton's Depot.

Mom turned the heat down to simmer, placing a lid upon the pan. "What is it?"

"I can't tell you," I confessed, contemplating whether I actually could or not.

I mean, sure I *could*. I could tell my mother anything. Learning that her only son's a homosexual would be hard to take, but not harrowing. Finding out he's about to put on a dress and become (Drag) Queen for a Day might not have the same effect.

"Then how can I do you a favor," Mom wondered, "if I don't know what it is?"

"It's no biggie," I assured her. "I need a ride somewhere."

Why didn't I listen to my dad when he encouraged me to take Auto Shop? Instead, I thought, *When I'm a rich and famous actor, I'll just* pay *somebody to fix my car.* Now I *really* needed to win that $500 Drag Queen–tainted pot o' dough!

Mom wiped her hands on a dish towel after washing them in the sink. "Where am I taking you?" she questioned suspiciously.

I paused a moment. "I don't want you to know."

Mom shook her head, regarding me with reluctance.

"Bradley . . ."

Again, she said my name like I couldn't be trusted.

"Please, Mom . . . There's something I gotta do, and I don't want you knowing what it is."

Sounding exactly like Carol Brady grilling Greg, Peter, or Bobby, she demanded, "Are you in trouble?"

"I promise, I'm not."

"Then what are you doing that's such a secret?"

I assured, "It's nothing illegal."

Now that I think about it, being underage in a bar while participating in an amateur Drag Queen competition very well *could* be against the law. But Mom didn't have to know how I'd be spending the last Saturday night of my Senior Spring Break.

I imagined Richie, Audrey, Ava, and Carrie whooping it up with Mr. Klan and all the other Band Fags at the Best Western

Orlando. Or wherever the hell they're staying. Just like we did Junior year when Wind Ensemble went to MSBOA State Band Festival, and afterwards checked into the Holi-dome up in Fowlerville. We spent the entire evening playing Marco Polo in the pool, and watching some godawful movies (*The Fly* with Jeff Goldblum, and *House* with *The Greatest American Hero* guy) on a VCR that Mr. Klan rented in his room.

Mom would just have to take my word for it on this one.

"Turn left, you said?"

At the corner of West Warren and the Southfield Freeway service drive, Mom stops at the red light. I reach into my pocket, fishing out the directions Miss Peter dictated when I called this afternoon to ask what time she was picking me up, just before she bailed.

8 Mile W to S'field
S'field S to Warren
L on Warren, 3 blocks down
Btw. Clayburn + Memorial.

"What's a Gigi's?"

On the left side of the street, plain as day, Mom points out a purplish-color building with a turquoise sign.

"It's where you're taking me," I tell her, adding, "I think it used to be a bowling alley."

There's no way I'm divulging its current business as a *bar.* Drinking alcoholic beverages is strongly frowned upon in the Freewill Baptist faith. I'm almost positive so is being a Drag Queen.

"Would you look at those boys?" Mom says, slowing down for a group of five or six (gay) guys piling out of a Golf parked across the street. "They're gonna get hit next time if they're not more careful."

Better hit by a car than shot by a gun, I feel like informing her.

Instead, I say, "You can drop me off on the side of the building," the entrance being in the rear . . . *No comment!*

Thank God I didn't drive myself. The entire back parking lot is full to capacity once we pull in. Who knew amateur drag night was so popular in Detroit?

"I most certainly will *not* drop you off," Mom adamantly insists.

Wanna know what she says next?

"I'm coming with you."

Jesus!

"That's okay, Mom . . . Really."

"I'm not leaving you here by yourself," she says, protecting me like a mother bird. "How will you get home?"

Good question.

"I'll call a cab."

Mom quips, "Cabs are expensive," not knowing I took them before so I'm well aware of the overpriced fares. "You save your money for school."

Like the messenger from the "Bob and the Kids are Dead" joke, I resist. "But *Mom* . . ."

"Enough!"

This would be her version of *"Sing it!"*

No point in arguing. Like Alexis Carrington-Colby-Dexter, when Laura Victor-Dayton-Victor has made up her mind, there's no trying to change it. After all, she originally hails from Alabama . . . Laura, that is. Not Alexis.

"I think I see a spot," I tell Mom, totally giving in.

She responds, "God's on our side," giving her standard parking-related reply.

Fasten your seat belts, folks . . . We're in for a bumpy ride!

Have you ever seen a Drag Queen? I mean, up close and in person. Believe me, it is *not* a pretty sight! Okay, maybe I'm being a tad bit dramatic. Some of them seem very nice. A few look sooo amazing, you wouldn't believe that's a guy prancing about in a lace corset and push-up bustier singing "It's Raining Men."

Speaking of . . .

"May I borrow your tape?"

Backstage, I'm gathering my *ensemble* together, when a drop-dead gorgeous redhead with a slight Southern accent taps me on the shoulder. I assume she's a fellow drag performer, but her tits sure do look real . . . As does the snake she's got draped around her neck!

Finding it an odd request considering Red doesn't even know what song I'm singing and shouldn't she should have her own music, I say, "Sorry . . . I gave it to the hostess already."

Meaning "The Lady Z."

Picture the joy on Zephyr's face after me and Mom paid the queenie old guy smoking an Eve 120 cigarette working the door our $5 cover and headed downstairs.

"You brought your sister!" Lady Z beamed, making Mom blush.

I almost didn't recognize her all done up as a blonde. Until I remembered she goes platinum when she does the *PTA*. I hoped Mom would get a kick outta that number, one of the only Country ones I imagine we'll hear tonight.

"Pleased to meet you," she said politely after I introduced her to Zephyr. "I'm Bradley's mother, Laura."

Poor Mom . . . She thought Lady Z was really a lady. Or she pretended to. I doubt she would ever point out something as obvious as a man wearing a dress. That would be rude.

"'Blow out your candles, Laura . . .'"

I forgot Zephyr proclaimed herself a Drama Queer from way

back when, so it surprised me at first to hear her quoting Tennessee. You know, as in Williams, from *The Glass Menagerie*, a fellow DQ himself, I'm told.

Then she offered, "Allow me to find you a seat." Lady Z led Mom down to the front row. I couldn't believe how polite she was being. Until I heard her cry, "Move it, Twinkie!" ordering some gay guy not much older than me to give up his chair. "This seat's reserved for a *real* lady."

Mom took her place. "Thank you, Miss Zephyr."

"Call me . . . Lady Z," Lady Z replied zealously. Then to me she said, "This way to the dressing room," curt as ever. *"Move your ass!"*

"You gonna be okay?" I asked Mom, terrified to leave her alone.

She insisted, "I'll be fine . . . Go do what we came here to do."

The way she said those words, I had a feeling Mom knew the exact contents of the paper bag I clutched in my sweaty little hands. Thank God Miss Peter can sew is all I can say. When I told her I needed a costume for my act, she asked me what I wanted and presto! Two days later, I picked it up . . .

"You *made* this?" I asked incredulously, admiring Miss Peter's handiwork.

"Shit! That ain't nothing," she bragged. "Remember Larry?"

How could I forget the hot mechanic from Taylortucky?

"Well, you know how I took his sister to the Prom back in the '70s?"

I nodded, seeming to recall the fact being mentioned in passing. "Uh-huh."

"Who do you think made her gown?"

Back in the Gigi's dressing room . . .

Red looks at me like I never did a lick of drag before. Maybe because I haven't.

"Not your music *cassette*," the Southern Belle clarifies, correcting herself. "I'm talkin' 'bout your duck tape."

"Oh . . . *Duct* tape!"

Why would I have any type of adhesive and what would I do with it if I did?

"Here ya go, sweetie . . ."

A mannish-looking transvestite sporting a Jean Nicole jumpsuit stops tweezing her eyebrows for two seconds. From out of her bag o' tricks, she pulls a roll of extra-sticky silver tape, offering it to the Snake Charmer.

"Thank you kindly."

After Miss Red disappears down the hall towards the restroom, I say to Jean Nicole, "Excuse me . . . What's the duct tape for, if you don't mind my asking?"

"How else you gonna hold down you ho-ho?"

A teeny-tiny Geisha "girl" answers my question. She lifts up her red silk kimono to reveal a strip of silver running from the top of her pubes (if she has any), between her legs—completely concealing her crack. Below her belly button, another smaller piece of tape crosses the first, forming a *T*.

"When you get home tonight, take a nice hot shower," the 6'2" African-American Drag Queen to my left suggests. She reminds me of the chick from the sex-flick, *Emmanuelle on Taboo Island*. "And use *lots* of baby oil."

"I will," I promise, grateful for the inside scoop. Too bad I don't get it. "What for?"

My fellow competitors burst into hysterics.

"You cute," Madame Butterfly coos.

What's that *supposed to mean?*

Removing my costume from the bag, I begin getting ready.

Oh, my God . . . I just realized I haven't said anything about my outfit!

Picture me in a blonde, flippy-banged wig, pulled back into a top-knotted ponytail. Covering my torso, a cornflower blue, one-piece leotard with short-short skirt attached. Flesh-colored tights adorn my silky smooth legs, leading down to a pair of . . .

"I like you ice skates," Madame B compliments. "Make you so tall."

Poor thing . . . She can't be more than 5'5", despite the flip-flop-thingies she's wearing on her feet with three-inch wooden soles.

Emmanuelle Taboo asks, "What do you call yourself?"

Without even thinking, I answer, "My name's Bradley."

Again, my fellow contestants share a snicker at my expense.

"She means your *drag* name," Jean Nicole clarifies.

Proudly, I show off my white Peter Pan collar with the sewn-on letters: L-E-X-I-E.

Yes! That's me.

Alexis Winston, the star of *Ice Castles.*

And now, for my fellow Drag Queens . . .

Jean Nicole formally calls herself "Sally Crockett." Emmanuelle goes by the name "Ebony Sunset," and Butterfly's moniker is none other than "Asia Fantasia." When Red returns (much flatter down yonder), she introduces herself as "Honey from Chattanooga." She's what they dub in the drag biz a *traveling queen,* meaning she (and her snake) goes from town to town performing in various venues cross-country, building up a fan base.

FYI . . . The tits are totally real.

Well, they're implants. And they co$t a pretty penny.

Not that Honey's not a nice girl, but if you ask me, she's taking things a tad too far. I may be sexually attracted to men, but I'm perfectly content being one myself, you know what I mean?

"Good evening, ladies!"

An older man in his mid-30s enters the dressing area unannounced. All decked out in a white tuxedo with silver cummerbund, he ducks his head as he appears thru the door. 'member how I said Gigi's used to be a bowling alley? Well, this explains why the backstage ceiling is so low.

Notice how whenever somebody walks alongside the first or last lanes before disappearing to fetch a lost ball or whatever it is they do behind that tiny door, the further away they go, the *larger* they appear to get? Like in that scene from *Willy Wonka and the Chocolate Factory* when Gene Wilder enters that room with the piano-lock that plays Rachmaninov.

"We're not ladies, sir, we're *girls*."

Miss Crockett gives her Eva Gabor brand wig a gentle once over with her Lady Catherine hairbrush as she informs our visitor of this fact.

Lemme tell ya, the guy thinks he's Robert Goulet. You know, from *The Fantastiks*. Or *Carousel*. Whatever show features "The Impossible Dream." For whatever reason, he's also performing tonight. They call him "Mr. Showbiz."

"My specialty is male-identified show tunes."

What's that *supposed to mean*?

I thought the whole point of a drag show was watching men dressed up as women.

Hence the term *drag*.

Soon as Mr. BS—I mean, *SB*—bids us farewell, one of the Queens insists she saw him the other afternoon working the Drive-Thru at Wendy's in Westland. When they say, *Don't quit your day job*, I guess that's what they mean.

"How do I look?"

I turn to Ebony, after I lace up my skates, asking for her honest opinion.

"You look real pretty, baby," she compliments. "You sure you ain't never done this before?"

"Never," I insist. "It's an amateur contest, isn't it?"

"Shit," Miss Sunset snarls, tossing her long dark hair behind her shoulder. She looks absolutely gorgeous in a glittering Bob

Mackey-esque evening gown. "We all been doing this forever . . . We just none of us ain't never been *paid*."

From beyond the thin paneled wall, the crowd suddenly goes bezerk. Looks like the show's officially begun as Lady Z. Zephyr takes to the stage. Me and the other Queens rush outta the dressing room, taking our places behind the curtained-off area where we wait backstage in the so-called wings. Luckily, the ceiling out front, I'm told, is a good six inches higher if not more. Especially since we're all wearing heels and/or skates.

"I want to tell you all a story 'bout a Harper Valley widowed wife . . ."

Lady Z sounds even better than I anticipated.

"She's good," I whisper. No wonder she's the Hostess with the Mostest. "How does she do that?"

Ebony peeks thru an opening in the curtain, catching a view of the star working the crowd. I think I spot Mom sitting between two (non-drag) queens, both reaching up towards Zephyr, dollar bills in hand. Who knew she got to perform *and* received tips?

"She sounds exactly like Jeannie C. Riley."

This I say in reference to the original "Harper Valley" *chanteuse.*

For the third time, my fellow four bust a gut. Only now, they keep their hysterics hushed. God forbid Zephyr "The Lady Z" has her act interrupted by a bunch of amateurs and their backstage antics.

"Lexie darlin', she is not *that* good." Honey wraps her real-life non-feather boa round her neck. "Haven't you ever seen *Puttin' on the Hits*?"

Of course. I can still picture the Total Babe host, Allen Fawcett, with his blond perm and boyish good looks. Then I *comprendre* the point Miss Honey is trying to make.

"Lady Z's not singing?"

I am stupefied. Isn't this supposed to be a Drag Queen *contest?*

"Nobody sings," Sally Crockett informs me, like it's rule #1 in the *Drag Queen Handbook*, if there even is such a thing.

Why didn't anybody tell me this?

Sure enough, when Sally takes her turn, she performs a one-woman Pointer Sisters "Jump (For My Love)." Sadly, she's not very good. In fact, her only choreography consists of her *jumping* every time Anita, June, and the other one sing the title verb.

Did I mention the time me and Jack went to see the sisters Pointer out at Meadow Brook back in the summer of '85? We got his dad to take us and drop us off, and my mom and his mom came to pick us up. This was back when Jack's mom thought my mom was a (quote-unquote) incompetent buffoon, so I thought for sure they were gonna kill each other on the ride out to Rochester. Surprisingly, they hit it off and had a ball the entire way home.

That same year, we discovered the Vikette advisor, Mrs. Cuccioli, had a picture tacked up on the bulletin board in her office of some Vikettes taken with Anita and What's-Her-Name Pointer out at Metro Airport. You can bet me and Jack spent months coveting that photo. Much like *Operation Revenge of the Band Fags!* back at Webb (long story, I won't go into it), along with Cheri Sheffield, Alyssa, and Luanne, we devised a similar plot to hijack said souvenir in what we dubbed *Operation Grand Theft Photo* . . . We may sound like bad kids, but I promise we're not.

"Cut the music, Chico!"

Once Ebony's song fades ("Dark Lady" by Cher, which explains the get-up), Lady Z calls out to the DJ up in the booth at the back corner of the bar. I'm told he's a totally charismatic, totally hot Arab, but don't you dare call him *Chaldean* because he's not—he's Muslim. Supposedly Chico's got a thing for the young boys, a fact I'm finding more and more common amongst the over-thirty set, even though I don't know why. I mean, what does a man want with a young *boy?*

"Shut the fuck up, bitches!"

Lady Z shouts over the din of the crowd. Like a nervous wreck, I wait in the wings, ready to make my entrance.

"Before I introduce our final performer," she continues, "I need to remind you . . . If you're drinking and driving tonight, drive someone else's car."

How I ended up dead last, I don't know. "*Saving the best for* . . ." I can only hope.

"And now," Zephyr announces, like a gay Shrine Circus ring-master. "I give to you . . . the one and only . . . Miss Alexis Win-ston!"

And the crowd goes wild!

As I step thru the curtain, blinded by the light, my adoring fans immediately recognize my persona, validating my belief in the brilliance that is *Ice Castles.*

With a wink and a smile, Lady Z offers me the oh-so-phallic silver microphone. Graciously, I accept, making sure to leave the switch in the ON position. Maybe all the other Queens here tonight lip-synched, but this girl is out to win the competition with her song-stylings *au naturel.*

As the lilt of the piano plays, a hush falls over the room.

I stare down at the floor, totally in-character.

"'Here's for my mom.'"

Until now, these words were nothing more than a quote from one of my favorite movies. But since she's sitting right here in the front row, about to observe her only son sing the Melissa Manchester love theme from *Ice Castles* before an audience made up of gay men, butch dykes, and flamboyant Drag Queens, the line seems all the more *à propos* to the situation.

I'd be lying if I didn't admit most everybody appears shocked when I open my mouth and actually start *singing* the song. Like I said, I never knew Drag Queens faked it. That's why I asked Mr. Fish to make me a tape using the vocal-eliminating machine he's got. Since his piano playing skills are severely subpar, everything we ever sing in Chorale is accompanied by a click-track.

The next four minutes and thirteen seconds swirl by.

In my mind, I *become* Alexis Winston circling the rink at the Mid-Western Sectionals in St. Louis, Missouri, the little blind skater who could. At number's end, I lean back with a flourish, arms splayed at my side, reminiscent of Lexie's final routine pose.

"The flowers!"

From somewhere, somebody throws me a single red rose. Like Alexis, I receive a standing ovation—initiated by my mother, of course. By the time I finally spot her, just left of house-center, her eyes sparkle with tears of joy.

Too bad I do *not* win the $500 prize.

That goes to Miss Honey and her pet boa constrictor, Bobo.

To help pay for her fake boobs, no doubt!

Is there no *justice in this world?*

Always on My Mind

"Tell me, tell me that your sweet love hasn't died
Give me one more chance to keep you satisfied . . ."

—Pet Shop Boys

On the last episode of *Brad ♥'s Richie . . .*

Richie scan-jul-ously appeared at Brad's back door, wielding a four-pack of Bartles & Jaymes wild berry.

"What's up?" asked Brad, fresh from the shower, wearing nothing but a dirty towel.

Slyly, The Sophomore grinned. "I was just about to ask *you* the exact same question."

Brad let the towel drop.

Richie fell to his knees.

At last, the moment these boys had been waiting for was about to arrive . . .

I wish!

I suppose I should come clean with the *real* story.

"Where ya goin'?"

Richie entered my room, slipped off his coat. From the way he slurred his words, I could tell he already had a few.

"To put some clothes on," I replied, heading for the door.

He cracked open a cooler, kicked off his shoes, making himself comfortable—on my bed. Richie took a swig from his bottle, licked his berry lips. "Don't take too long."

I hate to be blunt, but this damn dick of mine! It would *not* go down.

Maybe it's because I'm seventeen and perpetually horny.

Maybe it's because I didn't get a chance to beat off that day.

Maybe it's because, no matter what I say, I'm still totally in love with The Sophomore.

"Be right back."

I grabbed the first thing I could find: a pair of ratty old sweats and my Blue Lake Fine Arts Camp sweatshirt. Why was I surprised the sleeves came up to my forearms once I finally slipped it on? In my mind's eye, I haven't changed (or grown) a bit since the summer of '83. I can't believe it's been almost *five* years since me and Jack set off on our first Summer Band Camp adventure together . . . Where does the time go?

"I'll be waiting."

Seeing Richie at that moment, sprawled out on my bed, sucking down his wine cooler made me wanna . . . I won't even tell you what it made me wanna do! Luckily, my mom left a copy of *Ladies Home Journal* in the bathroom. There's nothing like an article on toxic shock syndrome to stifle a gay boy's burning desire, you know what I mean?

Fifteen minutes later, I returned to my room . . .

"Sorry about that."

Upon entering, I almost killed myself tripping over the empties Richie left strewn across the tannish-gray carpet. I guess he got tired of waiting, drank his wine coolers, and passed out. But not before taking all of his clothes off.

Like breadcrumbs, he scattered them about the floor . . . First a sock, then another, followed by T-shirt, jeans, and finally, his Fruit of the Looms. Laying facedown on my bed, head upon the pillow, Richie looked like an angel—a naked one.

It killed me to wake him. Not because I'm a perv and I was enjoying the view, even though I was. There's just no way Richie Tyler could stay over my house on a school night. Mom would flip if she woke up in the morning and found a boy in my bed.

"Time to go home." I gave him a gentle shove on the shoulder.

Richie groaned. "I'm sleeping . . ."

You know what they say about two ripe melons? Or a fuzzy peach? Or whatever other ass-related metaphors are out there? At this moment, all applied.

"Wake up, little sleepy-head . . ."

I sounded just like my mother singing in my ear on a Sunday morning.

"Don't wanna," The Sophomore muttered, like a little boy.

Sooo cute!

But I wasn't falling for it. I called out his name, forcefully.

Richie rolled over, curled up in a ball ignoring me, face against the wall.

"You can't stay here," I informed him.

"Why not?"

"Because . . ." I couldn't think of anything else to say. Other than: "You're drunk."

"I know," he whimpered. "My mom's gonna kill me."

I seriously doubted that. I only met her once, after Opening Night of *A Christmas Carol,* but Richie's mom seems like a Total Sweetheart. She's a tad on the heavy side with helmet hair, and works as a secretary up at the Hazel Park Rec Center.

"You should've thought of that before you drank yourself into a stupor," I berated him, sitting down on the bed, trying a more direct approach.

"No stupor."

"You sucked down four coolers in fifteen minutes," I recalled, as if he couldn't count.

He mumbled, "Three . . . Saved one for Opie."

Sure enough, laying on its side next to my bed remained one solitary beverage bottle, fully intact in its colorful cardboard carrier.

"Let's go!"

I tugged at his arm. He wouldn't budge.

If I could just get Richie onto his back, I could lift him up and carry him out to my car. Of course, I'd have to dress him first. Being mid-March in Michigan, I couldn't just wrap him in a blanket and hope he wouldn't freeze.

Big mistake!

'member what I said about Bobby Russell having a big one? Let's just say, The Sophomore may be shorter, but it doesn't mean he's smaller . . . And I thought *I* was prone to things popping up at the most inopportune moments.

Tempted as I was to stare, I had to get that boy outta bed before something happened I was *not* gonna be responsible for.

"Easy does it . . ."

One summer, I worked as a lifeguard at Cedar Point. Originally, they hired me as a performer. Well, not a performer per se, like in one of them cheesy variety shows. I walked around the park wearing one of them costume-character costumes. You know, like at Disney World. Only the CP version was more like a nondescript dog. Or a bear. Or some other animal with fur and short ears. After all of two days, I literally couldn't take the heat. So I asked for a transfer. Lemma tell ya, I much preferred spending my days half-naked in a bathing suit on the beach. So long as nobody drowned . . . Lucky for me, they never did.

Using the skills I acquired, I stood at the foot of my bed, took hold of Richie's upper limbs, and gave him the old heave-ho. By some miracle, he made it to his feet.

"What are you doing here?" He opened his eyes, giggling like a girl.

"I live here," I told him, in no mood for his drunken antics.

"What am *I* doing here?"

"You're drunk," I repeated. "Now get dressed."

Richie looked down at his nakedness. "I've got a woody," he whispered, as if I couldn't feel it poking against my torso. "How'd that happen?"

For the third time I told him, "You're drunk . . . You need to go home."

Richie grabbed my hand. "Touch it."

I yanked my arm away, squealing, "I don't wanna touch it!"

Maybe secretly I did.

He stuck out his lower lip like a pouty 6-year-old. "You don't like me."

Hearing him say that broke my heart. "Richie . . ."

This time I tried the gentle approach.

"I love the way you say my name," he murmured. With his right hand, he reached up to brush my cheek.

"Please don't," I begged. The last thing I needed was to fall under his spell. "It's late . . . We got school in the morning."

He looked up at me with tear-filled eyes. "Why don't you like me, Brad?"

I took a deep breath. "I do like you."

Richie took this as a sign, trying to kiss me.

I pulled away.

"I told you . . ." I swallowed hard. "I'm not a fag."

Hearing myself say these words made me sick to my stomach. Wasn't it just a few months ago when I told Jack I couldn't be his Best Friend anymore if he kept denying who he *really* is? Now here's me, doing the exact same thing.

"Whatever . . ."

I wanted him sooo bad. Not just in a sexual way, it was more than that. I wanted to lie down beside him, tickle his back, run my fingers thru his hair. To hold him in my arms, and make everything better.

But I couldn't.

With only three months left of school, my future would soon begin. For as long as I remembered, I had everything figured out. Falling in love with a boy wasn't part of the plan . . . Not anymore.

Richie got dressed and I drove him home.

Friday night during *Grease*, he refused to speak to me—not even on stage. During the "Hand Jive" sequence, there's a spot where Vince Fontaine (Richie) turns to Doody (me) and ad-libs something about being disqualified from the dance contest for being too vulgar. All thru Act One, I anticipated this moment. How it would feel to have those beautiful blue eyes focus on me, if only for a second.

The Sophomore totally skipped the bit.

After the show, Richie couldn't be found once I changed out of my costume.

"He went to Ponderosa with his parents," Ron Reynolds, aka Johnny Casino/Teen Angel, informed me.

Same thing happened with Closing Night on Saturday.

"He's gotta get up for church in the morning," Michelle Winters, aka Patty Simcox, announced when I asked why The Sophomore wasn't at Ava Reese's post-show party.

Ron and Michelle might both be Richie's classmates, but neither of them knew squat.

Richie hates Ponde*grossa*, and he never goes to church.

His avoiding me was obviously intentional.

"What did you do to piss that boy off?"

Audrey asks me this question, almost six weeks later . . .

It's Tuesday night, we're over her house watching the premiere of some new TV series on channel 7, *China Beach*. I haven't been totally paying attention, but from what I gather, the show is set during '60s Vietnam, and it's all about a group of women from the Red Cross helping the soldiers and such. The only actor I remotely recognize is the woman who played Nancy in *Sid and Nancy,* Chloe Webb.

"I didn't do anything," I insist, even though it's totally not true.

"Are you sure?" Aud asks, giving me her famous furrowed-brow gaze.

What am I supposed to say? *Richie is in love with me, and I'm in love with him. But we can't be together because the world is cold and cruel. So I spurned his affection and now he hates me.*

I don't know why I just don't tell Audrey what's up. She's practically my Best Friend now that Jack is all buddy-buddy with Max again. Believe it or not, I heard he almost got arrested when they were down in Daytona. Something about a girl named Gwendy, a bottle of Baileys, and a Cuban cop.

Instead, I say, "Janelle's working up at Nick's," even though she's eight months prego. "Wanna order a pizza?"

"I'm not hungry," Audrey states flatly. "And don't change the subject."

For this I called in sick to work?

I'm supposed to be at The Gas Station helping Lady Z host the wet-Jockey-shorts contest. She's been super sweet ever since I got my ass kicked in the amateur drag contest, and keeps encouraging me to give it another try. I might. I don't know.

As much fun as I had, as nice as everybody treated me, there's something sorta depressing about the life of a Drag Queen I can't quite put my finger on. It's like nobody gives them the respect they deserve for what they do. It's an art form, really. Just not one I wanna practice on a professional level, you know what I mean?

Aryc is gonna be pissed at me for not showing up tonight, but he'll just smoke a doob or do some coke and get over it, I'm sure. Truth be told, my days are numbered working at the bar. Don't get me wrong, the money is awesome. In the three weeks I been working, I managed to save close to $1,000. But recently, I came to the conclusion: I don't wanna work anywhere other people come for *fun*.

"There's no subject to change."

This I declare, getting up to pee, even though I don't gotta.

Where I should be is at home practicing for tomorrow night's Band concert. I can't believe it's the last time me and all the other Band Fags will play together as Wind Ensemble. I mean, there's still the Memorial Day parade at the end of May, but this is the last concert we'll be giving on the HPHS stage. As much as I may complain about it, I'm gonna miss being a Band Fag come June 16th when we officially graduate.

"Did you fall in?"

When I return from doing my doody, I find Audrey in the exact same spot I left her, riveted to the television. For a show about a *beach*, where are all the hot lifeguards? That's what I wanna know!

"What's your older brother's name, again?"

Sitting on the sofa, I see the framed picture of #63 down on one knee in his HP Vikings football uniform. Every time I take it in, I can't help but think how familiar the guy looks . . . This time, I think I finally figure out why.

"I only got one," answers Audrey. "Mike."

"He doesn't by any chance have a mohawk?"

I try my best to picture the jock from the photo with his

head shaved, save for a six-inch dyed-blue strip running down the center.

"He does now."

I knew I recognized him from somewhere!

All this time, I been hanging out with Aud's totally hot ex-football player brother at the bar, and I didn't even know it. Talk about "it's a small world after all!"

I wonder if she knows her brother's gay. It might just behoove me to ask. Depending on Audrey's response, I can gauge whether or not it's safe to reveal my own Deep Dark Secret.

"What's Mike do?" I ask curiously, even though I already know the answer to the question. "For a living, I mean."

"In case you haven't noticed . . . I'm *trying* to watch TV," Aud whines. "Would you stop your blabbering?"

Attempting to get her attention, I position myself square in front of the set. "'Just answer the question, Claire.'"

Audrey picks up a pillow and pelts me. "He's a bartender . . . Now get the fuck outta my way!"

Dodging the bullet, I ask, "What bar does he work at?"

Frustrated, she exclaims, "One down on Woodward." Then she adds, "What're you asking for? You don't know him . . . Or do you?"

Now she's got me!

"And who's this?"

I opt for the easy way out: changing the subject again.

Next to Mike's football picture, there's a smaller framed snapshot of Audrey's mom looking nine months pregnant, and a man I assume must be her father.

"My parents, who do you think?" she confirms.

I take a closer look at the photo. The man looks exactly like Audrey with the exact same space between his two front teeth. But not so much like her hunk of a brother.

Wanna know her response?

"That guy isn't Mike's dad."

I do a double take. "Isn't Mike's last name Wojczek?"

"It is," she nods.

"Isn't *your* last name Wojczek?"

This time she shakes her head. "Not technically."

Now I'm confused.

At this point, Audrey shares with me her Deep Dark Secret.

"I like to refer to myself as a love child," she begins. "My parents were married . . . But to other people."

For this I better sit down!

"Do you mind if I smoke?"

Aud reaches for an ashtray. "Not if you share."

"I thought you quit."

Since *Grease* ended six weeks ago, I haven't seen Audrey touch a single cigarette. And even in that instance, Principal Messinger forbade Mr. Dell'Olio to allow her to French inhale on stage for real, so she had to fake it. Talk about totally stupid!

"You wanna hear my story or not?"

We make ourselves comfortable on the couch. I shake two Marlboro Lights from the crinkled pack, and light them—both at the same time. You know, the way they do in those old movies from the '30s and '40s. I feel like Humphrey Bogart to Audrey's Kate Hepburn. Or maybe it's the other way around.

"It was the summer of '69," she continues, calling to mind the Bryan Adams song of the same name. "My mom was getting a divorce from my brother's dad—"

"Mr. Wojczek?"

"No . . . Mr. Rogers."

I start to say, "I thought—" Until I realize I should probably just sit here and smoke in silence. Save my questions for the end, you know what I mean?

"Mom moved back to Hazel Park from Minnesota. My father . . ." She pauses a moment to inhale before clarifying. "My *real* father, his name was Frank Hines—"

"Like the ketchup?" I wonder what makes for a worse surname: the one she's ended up with or her original? "I'm sorry, but I can't picture you as Audrey Heinz."

"H-I-N-E-S," she spells, a tad annoyed. Then she growls, "You made me lose my train of thought!" She scrunches up her face, concentrating hard. "My real father, Frank . . . He was a boarder at my nana's. He worked at the racetrack."

I assume she means the one here in Hazel Park, but I don't inquire. In all these years, I find it hard to believe I never been. I know Jack's dad used to take him all the time when he was little, but my dad does not condone gambling—among many other things.

"Frank's wife and kids lived in Nebraska," says Audrey, exhaling smoke thru her nose like a fire-breathing fire-haired dragon. Her mane's even redder now that she spent Spring Break down in the Florida sun.

"How many did he have?" I wonder, interrupting for the final time.

"One wife, three children," she answers curtly. "Two boys and a girl. *Anyhoo!* That 4th of July, he invited my mom up to see the fireworks."

Every year the Hazel Park Raceway puts on this huge display. Last summer, a bunch of us Band Fags piled in Ava's blue Citation, and drove over to the driving range on Dequindre and Woodward Heights behind Kmart's. We spread out some blankets, sat on the grass, taking in the skyrockets in flight. *("Afternoon delight.")*

Thinking about it now, it's hard to recall the way I felt back then. I remember being sooo bic-cited about Senior year starting. All the things me and my Best Friend since 7th grade were gonna do together. And we did for a while. Until I realized I'm a Total Fag and so is Jack, but he's too ashamed to admit it. So for the last six months we've done nothing but avoid each other.

How come nothing ever works out the way we imagine?

"Earth to Brad . . ."

Audrey snaps her fingers in my face, startling the fuck outta me.

"I'm listening."

She says, "No you're not," sounding just like my mom.

"Am too!" I declare, realizing I just wasted an entire cigarette daydreaming.

Audrey grins. "You're thinking about The Sophomore."

"Am not!" I insist, because for once, I wasn't. "Now finish your story."

"If I can remember where I was."

"4th of July . . . Fireworks."

She stubs out her smoke. "My parents started dating—more like *fucking*, I should say." She laughs to herself. "Get this . . . He tells her he's had a vasectomy, so it's all cool—not! Six weeks later, here comes Audrey."

Poor Pat . . . I can just imagine the expression on her face when she goes to the doctor for a checkup, and hears the rabbit's bit the dust.

"So what happened?" I need to know how everything all worked out.

Audrey scowls. "Let's just say, not only did he enjoy the drink, Frank liked to hit things . . . Mom dumped his sorry ass while I was still a bun in the oven."

Now she's cracking herself up. "Can you believe the bastard actually offered to *buy* me for ten grand!"

"You're kidding?" I reply. "What was he gonna do with a baby?"

I could just see this guy trying to explain to the wife and kids back in Nebraska why he's returning home with a little bundle of redheaded joy. In a way, I feel sorry for the man, and I never even knew him. I mean, imagine realizing you have a child, but you can't be a part of its life. Unlike my own father, who *chose* to walk away.

"Mom ended up going back to Mike's dad," Audrey reveals, "I always assumed *he* was my father . . . He did too, till the day he died when I was seven."

"So what happened to Frank?"

Aud forges ahead. "Fast forward to age ten . . . Mom is reading the obituaries one evening and she's crying. I ask her who died. 'A friend from the track,' she tells me. We knew a lot of people from up there so it could be anybody."

Ever the Drama Queer, Audrey picks up a Precious Moments figurine from a shelf above the sofa filled with knickknacks. You know, thimbles, glass bells, spoons from Vegas and other tourist traps like Mount Rushmore.

"She sits me down," Aud says, placing the porcelain doll upon her lap. "'Audrey dear, I need to discuss something with you.' She tells me the story . . . I freak out."

I could just imagine a 5th grade Audrey in her Catholic School girl get-up ripping Mrs. Wojczek a new a-hole. Lemme tell ya, I would *not* wanna be on the receiving end of that.

"I'm like, 'You're a liar!'" Aud continues, "and storming out I go, next door to my nana's. I tell her what mom said, and she confirms the entire story. Then she gives me this old picture of my parents taken on the night of their first date."

This would be the one sitting on the shelf next to #63.

"So what happened with your mom?"

Audrey rolls her eyes. "She took me to McDonald's for a hot fudge sundae." She pinches her thunder thighs. "No wonder food is a comfort to me, huh?" Then she says, "Mom, being spiteful, goes to the wake with bastard 10-year-old in tow . . . I sit with my half brothers and sister who have no clue who I am."

"No wonder you're so fucked up."

And I thought I had it tough. While I might be ashamed to admit it, at least I know who my father is and always have.

"Your turn, Dayton . . . Spill."

How am I gonna get outta this?

"You wanna know my Deep Dark Secret?"

"Don't tell me you don't got one," Audrey warns. "Everybody does."

After the way she just bared her soul to me, how can I not comply?

Here goes nothing!

"I'm gay."

Wanna know what Audrey Wojczek says to that one?

"Now tell me something I don't already know."

Bitch.

Shattered Dreams

"Woke up to reality
And found the future not so bright . . ."

—Johnny Hates Jazz

"No g-news is good g-news."

At least that's what I always used to say.

Not anymore.

'member *The Great Space Coaster*? Me and my sisters used to watch it every morning before school at like 7:30 AM on channel 50. Well, I didn't so much *watch* it as I listened from beneath a blanket, laying on the couch trying to wake up. I particularly enjoyed the animated opening. Baxter the clown picks up Fran, Roy, and the boring blond guy whose name escapes me in the Great Space Coaster *("Get on board!")*, and takes them to his planet. Or wherever they went to put on the show.

It had to be somewhere out of this world because most of the other people were puppets, like the loud-mouthed Goriddle Gorilla, and the turtleneck-wearing newscaster, Gary Gnu. I should probably say, "g-newscaster," since Gary pronounced *gnu* and *news* with a hard *G*.

Hence his catchphrase: "No g-news is good g-news . . . With Gary . . . Gnu."

Now that I think of it, Baxter wasn't so much a puppet, more like a guy in a suit, à la Big Bird. I remember he played this instrument, the *bax*ophone that looked like a piece of black rubber tubing bent in the shape of an *S.*

On another note: *GSC* first introduced me to Mr. Marvin Hamlisch, composer of such Broadway classics as *They're Playing Our Song* and *A Chorus Line,* and the film score to (drum roll, please!) *Ice Castles,* among others.

Anyways!

Three months have passed since my Juilliard audition. Surely the Powers that Be have made up their minds by the end of April as to which twenty actors they're gonna grace with their presence for the fall of '88 incoming class, also known as Group 21. I guess what Juilliard's been doing since the Drama Division's inception in 1960-something is numbering each class in chronological order. For example, Patti LuPone, the original Eva in *Evita,* began training at JSD during the first year, so hers became known as Group 1.

Ergo . . .

Class of '88 = Group 17.

Class of '89 = Group 18.

Class of '90 = Group 19

Class of '91 = Group 20.

This brings me to *my* class . . .

Class of '92 = Group 21.

That's providing everything goes according to plan.

"There's a letter for you, Brad . . ."

When I got home from school this afternoon, I found my 14-year-old sister, Nina, sitting alone at the kitchen table stuffing her face.

"What smells good?" I asked, moving in for a closer sniff.

"'Parts is parts,'" Nina muttered, chomping away on a piece of mystery meat.

I didn't know what the hell she was referring to. No offense, but with Nina's learning disability, I have a hard time deciphering when she's trying to be funny or when she's just plain being slow.

"Chicken McNuggets."

She dipped what looked like a deep-fried golf ball into some ketchup and popped it into her hungry mouth. I knew they couldn't be *real* McNuggets from McDonald's. Not only can't we afford fast food, Mom highly disapproves of us eating it. Sure enough, the box of Banquet frozen nuggets sat out on the table, totally defrosted.

Lemme tell ya, having a sister like Nina can try your patience. Like I said, I love her to death, but sometimes she's a handful. The other day, I discovered her sitting in the family room eating a bowl of ice cream. Meanwhile on the kitchen counter, the carton sat melting all over, the freezer door wide open right next to it, and everything inside—thawed.

"Where's Mom?"

Nina didn't respond, off in La-la Land somewhere.

"Nina!" I snapped before repeating my question softly.

"I don't know . . . She took Brittany somewhere." Then Nina repeated, "There's a letter for you."

Every day for the past month, I been checking the mailbox, like poor Charlie Brown waiting for a Valentine. Amongst a stack of bills, I noticed an envelope addressed to me, postmarked NEW YORK, NY. Sure enough, the return label read *Juilliard School of Drama*. You can bet my heart started beating a mile a minute. That is, after I picked it up from the pit of my stomach and put it back in my chest.

"I'll be in my room," I said, taking my mail with me.

And now, the moment we've all been waiting for . . .

Closing the door behind me, I sat down on the bed, staring at the envelope for five minutes, if not more. It took everything I had in me to muster up the courage to open it. Slowly, I flipped the letter over, preparing to slide my finger beneath the flap. Only it wasn't sealed!

"Ni-i-i-na . . ."

Back in the kitchen, I watched her squeeze a spot of ketchup onto her plate the size of a saucer, even though only two chicken McNuggets—I mean *nuggets*—remained.

"Huh?"

"Did you open my letter?"

"What letter?" my sister asked, crumbs caked in the corners of her mouth.

The sad part was I could tell poor Nina didn't realize what I was referring to.

"The letter I got in the mail today," I explained. "Did you read it?"

Nina looked at me, her expression rivaling that of a lost deer wandering about the side of the road. "I don't think so . . . Maybe."

There was no real harm done. Even if she looked at my letter, I seriously doubted she'd comprehend the contents contained therein. I did my best to remain calm.

"Why did you do that?"

She admitted, "I wanted to know if you're moving away," totally taking me by surprise.

In all the time I been going on and on (and on) about wanting to get the fuck outta Ferndale, I never took into consideration my own family. At that moment, I felt like a Total Shit. Sure, I couldn't stand living here. There's nothing for me to do career-wise, but there *is* my mom and my sisters, and my grandmas and grandpa—even my dad.

Could I just up and leave them all behind, for the sake of some selfish dream?

I decided to cross that bridge when I came to the toll both.

The envelope, please . . .

April 21, 1988

Dear Bradley,

The Juilliard School counts itself among the most prestigious Drama programs in the United States, if not the world. The thousands of hopefuls who audition for us each year are some of the most talented individuals, making our final decision all the more difficult.

Unfortunately, it is with deep regret that we are unable to grant you a place among our actors in Group 21. I want to personally thank you for sharing your talent with us, and wish you the best of luck wherever your dramatic studies may take you.

Sincerely,

Michael Langham

Director, Drama Division

The End of Today Is the Beginning of Tomorrow.

For some, the HPHS Class of '88 motto might hold true.

But not for all.

Case in point . . .

Right now, I feel like the biggest loser on the planet since Judy Tenuta's roommate, Blowzanne. Why am I having the single most shittiest year? I mean, seriously!

Okay, so maybe I made "Top 5" back in the fall, but it's been downhill ever since. First I don't get cast as Scrooge in *A Christmas Carol.* Then I don't get to play Danny in *Grease.* Now this.

How am I gonna face my family and friends?

What am I gonna tell my teachers?

My life is over!

The biggest letdown comes from the fact that it totally looked like a form letter. I mean, sure the signature was authentic. It's not like they stamped it on or anything, the ink's smudged. But does Michael Langham even know who the hell I am? I certainly don't recall ever meeting him. Unless he was either Baldy #1 or Baldy #2 and I was so nervous at the audition that his name didn't register.

You're sooo talented.

You've got what it takes.

You're gonna be famous.

For as far back as I can remember, this is what I heard from everybody.

Maybe it's all just bullshit they been feeding me.

Maybe I suck and they're afraid to tell me the truth.

Maybe this is the reason I didn't get the lead in either play we did this year.

Like poor Charlie Brown, I'm a fucking Failure Face!

For the next hour, I bawl like a baby, biting my pillow so nobody hears my sobs. What the hell am I gonna do with my life? The fact that I didn't apply to any other school (for Acting or otherwise) only makes matters worse. I can just picture myself living at home going to fucking community college at OCC. Or as Stacy Gillespie likes to call it, "Oc," as in *topus.*

I suppose I can always get a full-time job at Cedar Point working as a costume-character dog. Or bear. Or whatever the hell animal suit they decide to stick me in. I mean, that can sorta be considered acting. *Can't it?*

Fortunately, I fall asleep, utterly exhausted.

Last night I didn't get home till after 4:00 AM.

Wanna know what I had the pleasure of doing?

The owner of The Gas Station decided to throw an after-hours party with his harem of hunks, and figured me and Aryc had nothing better to do than babysit them. Sure, I made a shitload of money, but did I *really* need to witness a bunch of guys sitting around the bar in their birthday suits while Grandpa Moses felt them up and plied them with coke—and not the *ca-Cola* variety?

All day in school, I felt like a zombie. In 1st hour Wind Ensemble, I practically fell asleep propped up against my T-bone. It's a wonder I been able to stay awake thru our end-of-the-year concert this evening. . . .

"I wanna thank all of you Seniors," Mr. Klan gushes, once we clear the stage and convene in the Band room, "for making the past three years ones I will never forget."

He wipes a tear from his cheek, and when I look around, most of the other Band Fags are mimicking the gesture. Even the Too Rad crew of Don Olsewski, Curt Chaplin, and Thad Petoskey look a tad weepy.

"Mr. Klan rocks!"

Don shouts this out, launching the rest of the room into raucous applause.

I don't think it's hit me yet that it's *really* over.

No more being a Band Fag.

And with today's big news, my days as Drama Queer are now numbered.

I better get that Thespian of the Year award!

"You sluts need a ride?"

Outside in the front parking lot, me and Zack Rakoff run into Audrey and Carrie Johnson. Like I said, Val is officially retired, so I been relying on the kindness of strangers when it comes to getting my sorry ass around town.

"That's slut *puppies* to you!" Audrey calls back, fanning herself with her program.

"What's a matter?" I ask. "You having hot flashes?"

"Bite me, Dayton!" she bellows. "You know I didn't have to come to your concert tonight."

She's right. None of my other non-Band Fag friends were there. Being a Flaggot, I suppose Aud's got some vested interest in Wind Ensemble and Sophomore Symphony. Why the hell would Jack Paterno wanna support his *former* friends after he up and abandoned them like a sinking ship?

Six more weeks, I keep telling myself.

Six more weeks and I'm outta here.

Then what am I gonna do?

"You want uth to drive you to Big Boyths?" Rakoff lisps, unlocking the door to his shit-brown rust-bucket Dustermobile.

"No thanks," says Carrie, refusing the offer. "We're riding with Ava."

"Don't forget 9 Mile's closed for construction," I remind the girls. "You gotta take Woodward Heights over to the service drive and down."

"I think we can find our way to Elias Brothers," says Audrey, the smart-ass!

Whatever . . .

The inside of Rakoff's car smells like pine-scented puke.

I got news for him: the faux-velvet fir tree hanging from his mirror is doing *nothing* to mask the scent of mothballs and kitty litter. Truth be told, I don't even know if Rakoff's got a cat, but he manages to come to school every day covered in feline follicles.

"What are we listening to?"

The second we're on our way, he turns up the radio.

"Thith would be Ebn-Ozn," Rakoff beams.

Talk about bizarre!

If you can even call it a *song,* I don't know what the hell it's about. Some guy sipping cappuccinos with a Swedish girl named

Lola across from Lincoln Center. Of course, this makes me think of my Juilliard audition and the fact that my life no longer has any meaning.

Forget Big Boy's . . . I need an alcoholic beverage!

"Do me a favor," I say to Rakoff desperately. "Stop at the nearest Party Store."

"There's one right by my houth," he informs me, turning left by St. Mary's off Woodward Heights onto John R.

I can't tell you how many times I drove past Gary's Market, with its green and gold Vernor's sign hanging above the front door, but never set foot inside. In fact, there are tons of tiny businesses all along John R that have been here all my life: Vic's Auto Parts, the B & B Beauty Salon, Koei Kan Karate Club. For whatever reason, I never get around to patronizing them.

The second I push open the door, jingle bells a-jangling, the scent of Party Store hits me smack dab. I don't know what it is exactly, but they all smell the same no matter which one you frequent.

Maybe it's the bags of chips stacked in all the bins.

Maybe it's the rows of candy running beneath the counter.

Maybe it's the guy smoking a cig, watching TV on a five-inch black-and-white.

"May I help you?"

Avoiding eye contact, I place a bottle of Boone's Farm before him. Talk about a cheap buzz! At only two-for-five bucks, you can't beat it.

"Can I also get a pack of Marlboro Lights, please?"

I don't know why it's the case with most of the party store owners in Metro Detroit, but the middle-aged man ringing up my Strawberry Hill is totally Middle Eastern.

"You have ID?" he asks, smoke wafting about his dark head like a halo.

His accent makes me think of hot Jerry from Lakeside Mall. It's been over six months since our last trip to see *Rocky Horror* back on Halloween. How can it be that long ago? Time speeds up the more life winds down.

Six more weeks . . .

Pretty soon, it'll all be over.

Then what am I gonna do?

Opening my wallet, I flash the guy my freshly altered license. "How much?"

When I first started using the fake, I felt a tad freaked out. Like there's no way I could possibly pass for a 21-year-old. I mean, let's face it . . . They don't call me "Opie" for nothing.

Mr. Party Store Owner gives me a look, like he's never seen me before, since he hasn't.

"Remove, please."

"I beg your pardon?"

I can't believe this guy's actually gonna make me take my ID out from the plastic window-thingie and actually present it to him. What's he gonna do, inspect it?

That's exactly what he does!

First he brings it up to his eye, super close. Then he holds it at a distance, in front of the overhead light above the counter, behind the *Newport . . . Alive with Pleasure!* display.

"You know what?" I say. "I don't need the wine."

"No, you do not," Mr. Party Store Owner concurs.

It seems he's used the inch-long, yellow crusted fingernail of his right thumb to scratch at the glued-on double 6's of my DOB, thus revealing the true year of my *naissance.*

"Is there a problem?" I ask, trying to sound as surprised as Mr. PSO.

"1970," he sneers. "You were born 1970."

I can't tell if he's asking or telling me this, so I just nod and smile.

"You can read, young man?"

He points to the orange and black sign taped up behind the counter.

You Must Be Born on or Before This Date
In 1967 to Purchase Alcohol
NO EXCEPTIONS!

I'm thinking, *Oh, shit . . . Now what's he gonna do?*

I mean, attempting to buy alcohol with a fake ID isn't illegal . . . *Is it?*

I reach for my license so I can be on my merry way, and this guy can forget he ever laid eyes on me.

"Just one second," my captor replies, withholding the evidence.

Now I'm thinking, *He's not gonna call the cops* . . . Is he?

Sure enough, he reaches for the phone, and dials. Of course, I can't understand a word he's saying as he converses in some foreign tongue that isn't French, so I don't know what the hell he's talking about.

"I'm sorry," I interrupt. "I gotta go . . . My mom's waiting for me in the car."

Mr. Party Store Owner continues on his tirade, most likely bitching to the person on the other end about how he can't stand these American kids coming into his store, trying to take advantage of him . . . I know that's what *I'd* be saying if I was him.

From far away comes the sound of sirens.

I'm about to be arrested, I know it.

The perfect ending to the perfect day!

My heart rate's a mile a minute, my breathing shallow, my forehead soaked with sweat. I'm having a heart attack. I'm about to drop dead in the middle of some strange party store around the corner from Zack Rakoff's house. Once I depart, he'll probably run home and ask his mom to whip up one of her mayonnaise cakes in my memory.

Next thing I know, I'm climbing over the counter, snatching my ID back, and getting the fuck outta there.

"Unlock the door!"

I been inside the store all of five minutes, it's barely 9:00 PM, and we're in *The Friendly City,* for chris'sakes. Why the hell has Rakoff barricaded himself inside his car?

It's not like we're in downtown Detroit where people get shot and killed on a daily basis.

It's not like anything exciting ever happens in this godforsaken Hillbilly Hick town.

And then I see it . . .

A dark brown blur whizzing past, pursued by two others—these ones white with bright blue and red flashers.

Have you ever witnessed something so frantic, so frenetically frenzied, yet while you're viewing it, every detail sparks with vivid intensity? Each sight, each sound, each smell strikes a chord, cutting thru you to the bone. Like in that moment from *Ice Castles,* just before Lexie Winston takes that fatal jump, everything slows to a standstill.

That's exactly how I feel watching the two cop cars hi-speed-chase the Chevy van up the center of John R, past the party store, towards the corner of Woodward Heights where St. Mary Magdalen protects her personal place of worship.

I stand transfixed, caught in a spell.

This is one of those times you think: *Are they making a movie?*

I mean, I see it happening in front of my eyes. But like I said, nothing such as this ever occurs in Hazeltucky, Michigan.

And then I hear it . . .

Crash!

Metal crunches metal.

Burning rubber fills the air.

Followed by a scream.

Oh, God.

Forever Young

"Let us die young or let us live forever
We don't have the power but we never say never . . ."

—Alphaville

I hate funerals.

In the spring of 1985, I went to one for my friend Paula Cowgill's mother. Part of me thought if I didn't go, if I didn't see the woman's lifeless body laying in a box, she wouldn't really be dead. Somehow I could keep her alive . . .

If only in my memory.

Paula's a year younger than me, but she went to elementary school at Webster, and her mom used to always volunteer because they lived across the street. Not that I'm calling her an ugly duckling, but Paula went from being a shy, glasses *and* braces-wearing 7th grader, to looking like the lead singer from The Bangles the following year. It's amazing what a pair of contacts and a perm can do to improve a girl's self-esteem.

A few days prior to Mrs. Cowgill's death, Mrs. "Friends hold you back" Putnam took the members of Symphonic Band to perform on the steps of the Michigan State Capitol. Back before she blossomed, Paula played clarinet with the Band Fags. Her mother accompanied us as one of our chaperones, along with Zack Rakoff's mayonnaise cake–baking mother, and Ava Reese's mom—who I love!

I remember seeing Mrs. Cowgill sitting amongst the crowd, tapping her feet to the beat of John Philip Sousa. Or whatever the hell march we played that day. This may seem like an ordinary observation, except for the fact that Mrs. Cowgill was totally deaf. Her and her husband both. I don't know how they managed to raise a non–hearing impaired daughter, let alone one as intelligent as Paula, but somehow they did it.

To this day, I'll never forget the time back in 6th grade when she helped Miss Norbert teach a select group of students how to perform several different songs in sign language. Our repertoire included "Coming to America" by Neil Diamond, "I Wouldn't Have Missed It for the World" by Ronnie Milsap, and my personal fave, "Xanadu" by Olivia Newton-John. Surprisingly, there's no single sign for the title of that one, so every time we came across it, we had to spell the whole word out super fast: X-A-N-A-D-U.

Sadly, that afternoon in Lansing was the last I seen Mrs. Cowgill alive.

A few days after our trip, she suffered a heart attack and died.

She was 40 years old.

The news of her untimely death came as a Total Shock. How could somebody so young die so unexpectedly? I mean, my mom's forty-*two* now, and I can't imagine losing her in the near future . . . Why is life so unfair sometimes?

I dreaded the day of the funeral. At the time, I only been to one, for Grandpa Victor when I was seven, and I really didn't get it. I remember the flower-filled parlor, the people I didn't recognize, and seeing my grandfather laying in his coffin at the far end of the narrow room. I knew he wasn't sleeping, that he wouldn't open his eyes, sit up, and say hello. But the concept of never-coming-back didn't quite have an effect, you know what I mean?

By the time of Mrs. Cowgill's passing, I was almost fifteen. I finally understood what it meant to be gone *forever*. Luckily, Ms. Lemieux showed up that day and helped make the proceedings more tolerable.

'member mine and Jack's hot-to-trot 7th grade Enriched English & Social Studies teacher whose first name is Cinnamon? 'member how she up and abandoned us our Freshman year to move down to Florida for a teaching job or a new boyfriend, we're not sure. Well, either the new gig didn't go or the new guy dropped her like a dirty habit, because Cinnamon returned to Hazel Park less than a year later, just in time to pay her last respects to poor Paula Cowgill's dearly departed mother.

Driving from St. Mary Magdalen's out to the cemetery in Ms. Lemieux's car, me and Jack crammed ourselves in the passenger seat, our heads hanging out the window in search of the procession.

"I can't run a red light."

Cinnamon insisted this, stiletto to the pedal, and doing just that as we both egged her on.

Like the blind leading the blind out I-75, we finally caught up to the group at White Chapel, half an hour late for the graveside service. Thinking back, we probably needed one of them funeral flag-thingies affixed to the hood of our car, but what did we know? We were kids. Besides, we got away without getting a ticket, didn't we?

I realize me and Jack probably shouldn't have been laughing our heads off while our friend Paula watched them plant her mother forever in the earth. But we do that sometimes when we hurt . . . Isn't laughter the best medicine?

Well, not today.

"In the name of the Father, the Son, and the Holy Ghost . . . Amen."

I can't say I ever been to Shrine of the Little Flower before. I thought for sure the service would be held at St. Mary's in HP. Considering that's pretty much the place where she lost her life, I imagine her mom didn't wanna have her funeral anywhere near there.

Oh, my God . . . I can't believe I just acknowledged the fact.

Audrey is dead.

As in never-coming-back.

Just to fill you in on the details, from the *Daily Tribune* . . .

> Audrey Melinda Wojczek, 17, of Hazel Park died on Wednesday, April 27, 1988. She was born May 24, 1970 in Duluth, MN. She is survived by her mother, Patricia of Hazel Park, and her brother, Michael of Royal Oak. Her father, Michael Sr., passed away in 1977. She was an honor student at Hazel Park High School where she performed in plays with the Drama Club and marched with the Flag Corps.

According to the police report, some 25-year-old asshole robbed a party store down on 7 Mile in Detroit. All he took was something like a hundred dollars. But then he got into a *stolen* van and tore up John R at 70 MPH, the cops following him the entire way. Meanwhile, Ava, Carrie, and Audrey were heading west on Woodward Heights in Ava's car, en route to meet the Band Fags for a post-concert celebration at Big Boy's.

In the worst case of coincidence, the girls just happened to be passing by St. Mary's as the asshole in the brown van ran the red light, slammed into the side of the blue Citation, pinning it up against the newly built brick wall on the corner. Luckily, both girls wore seat belts in the front. Unfortunately, Audrey in the back did *not.*

The collision with the van literally tore the car in two, the point of impact being precisely where Audrey sat. You can bet the 11 o'clock news had a heyday that evening. Before the ambulance arrived, reporters and cameramen already converged on the scene. And all the busybodies from Battelle to Browning had to come out and gawk, of course!

Standing on the side of the road with Rakoff, across the street in front of Tony's Hardware, we recognized Ava's car right away. And her screams. Fortunately, both she and Carrie only suffered minor injuries, treated at Oakland General. I wish I could say the same for Audrey . . . She died at the scene.

Luckily, the cops were already on hand from chasing the asshole in the stolen van. I recognized one of the officers as Betsy Sheffield's uncle. 'member, from The Gas Station on Valentine's Day? I guess that guy gets around.

The next day in school, everybody walked about in shock, like zombies from that movie *Night of the Comet* with the original Kayla Brady from *Days of our Lives,* Catherine Mary Stewart. During Wind Ensemble, Mr. Klan didn't say much about the accident, the two vacant chairs in the clarinet section serving to remind us why both Ava and Carrie's parents kept them home from school.

The person I felt sorry for was Jack.

I forgot he sits—I mean, *sat*—next to Audrey in Miss Horchik's 1st hour World Lit. From what I been told, the night before, Jack got a call from Betsy Sheffield after she heard the news from her uncle. Neither of them had any details about who the collision involved, other than (quote) three girls from Hazel Park (unquote), as the TV reported later that evening. When he walked into class the next morning, Jack noticed Audrey's empty seat, clueing him in on all he needed to know.

Speaking of . . .

In the pew behind me, over to the left, I see him sitting all by himself.

I can't remember the last time me and Jack ran into each other outside of school. He looks rather dapper in his blue button-down dress shit and khaki pants, his face tanned from his Spring Break adventure with Max, who I do *not* see. I'm surprised since Max used to hang out with me, Jack, and Audrey, back in the day. In fact, I almost forgot he was there the night Audrey singed her bangs lighting a cig on the stove at Luanne's New Year's Eve party.

For a split second, I start cracking up. Like I said, I realize it's inappropriate to laugh when somebody's died, but you should've seen the expression on Aud's face when she smelled the stink of her own hair set aflame. Looking back, I feel guilty for thinking it funny, even though it totally was.

Great!

Now I'm crying.

Ava offers me a Kleenex I use to wipe away my tears.

In Loving Memory of AUDREY M. WOJCZEK.

Looking down at the Virgin Mary prayer card I'm holding in my hands, I can't say I ever expected to view that particular name printed on one of these things . . . At least not for another fifty or so years. Again, I can't believe any of this is *real.* I feel like I'm an actor in a movie or something, waiting for the director to yell, "Cut!" Then we'll do the scene all over again from a different angle.

For the first time, I notice the organ music echoing thru the chapel. A quick glance around, I'm surprised at how many people I see, how many kids from school came to pay their last respects. Of course, we have the Usual Suspects en masse: Tuesday Gunderson, Keith Treva, Will Isaacs, Zack Rakoff, Claire Moody, along with Miranda Resnick, Ashley Lott, Michelle Winters, Ron Reynolds, Charlie Richardson, and Darlene Ellington.

I even saw Joey Palladino and Diane Thompson on the end of the aisle next to Mr. Dell'Olio and Mr. Klan. Miss Horchik is here somewhere, too. So is my favorite most-likely-a-lesbian Gym teacher, Miss Phelan.

Two rows in front of me, Tom Fulton sits with the entire football team, including Allen Bryan. 'member, he played Sonny in *Grease?* I know most of them guys weren't friends with Audrey. Not the way me, Ava, Carrie, and the rest of the Band Fags and Drama Queers are—I mean, *were.* But she was Rob Berger's girlfriend, and they're his friends, so I like to give them credit for being here to support him. Not just because they want a free day off from school.

Poor Rob Berger . . . I haven't had a chance to speak to him yet, but I seen him in the front pew with Mrs. Wojczek and Audrey's brother, Mike, who I almost didn't recognize with a shirt on and his mohawk shaved off. I can't blame him for wanting to look respectable at his (half) sister's funeral. I don't know what I'll say if and when I talk to him, other than "I'm sorry." Maybe he won't even recognize me out of our usual atmosphere.

In the row across the aisle sits the Vikettes: Angela Andrews, Marie Sperling, and Lynn Kelly. Beside them, girls' Varsity basketball co-captains, Natalie Davis and Fay Keating. I forgot Fay and Audrey used to be good friends when they were both at St. Mary's before coming to Webb. Opposite, I see the cheerleaders: Shellee Findlay, Jamie Good, and Betsy Sheffield, along with Liza

Larson, Pam Klimaszewski, and Tonya Tyler from Chorale . . . And who else?

Tonya's cousin, better known as The Sophomore.

Our eyes meet. We hold our gaze. There's so much I wanna say . . .

You were right.

It's my fault.

I do *love you.*

I keep thinking about what Aud said the other night after I professed my feelings for Richie . . .

"What are you gonna do about it?"

"I don't know . . . What *can* I do?"

For that, she just about smacked me upside the noggin.

"You can start by telling him."

Even after I explained what Christopher told me in New York, Audrey still wasn't buying my excuses.

"What if you don't make it as an actor?" she asked me point-blank. "You got a better shot at Aggie Usedly drawing your numbers in the daily lottery."

"Lord knows I could use the money," I replied, knowing Aud was right, but not wanting to admit it.

"Then what'll happen? You'll be sad and all alone, wondering why you never got laid when you were in high school."

The last thing I wanna do is wind up all by myself for the rest of my life. I mean, I know they say high school relationships don't last, but what about Jack's parents? They got married when they were seventeen and fourteen, and they're still together over eighteen years later.

Maybe this thing with Richie (whatever it is) could work out. Just because I'm graduating in six weeks doesn't mean it has to end. Of course, it has to *begin* first.

"Promise me you'll stop acting like a jackass," Audrey implored. "Promise me you'll stop worrying what other people think, and start caring about the most important person in your life . . ." She stabbed me in the chest with her finger. "That would be *you.*"

Massaging my sternum, I swore, "I promise."

Audrey flashed me her gap-toothed grin. "Now go out there and get that boy."

Back in reality . . .

I bow my head in prayer.

Dear God . . . There are lots of other people hurting who need your blessing a lot more than I do. But I'm begging you, Lord, don't let me let Audrey down. Help me find the courage and strength to be proud of who I am . . . And don't let it be too late for me and You-Know-Who. In the name of your son, amen.

The last thing I should be thinking about right now is myself. Audrey is never coming back and it's partially *my* fault.

If only I would've insisted she got a ride to Big Boy's with me and Rakoff.

If only I would've told them to take another route, they would've never crossed that intersection.

If only I would've stepped outta that Party Store sooner, I would've seen the stolen van coming up John R and I could've jumped in front of it and made the asshole stop or something—I don't know.

You can bet I been replaying the scene over and over (and over) in my head since it happened three days ago. Things *could* be different now.

If only Ava took a second longer arguing with Don Olsewski after the Band concert.

If only she waited at the yellow light on Hughes instead of turning thru it onto Woodward Heights.

If only Audrey would've stopped by her house to change her outfit or call Rob at work before continuing on to EB's—I don't know.

If only.

When I open my eyes, I feel like Rockwell . . . *"Somebody's watching me."*

I look over my shoulder and see Jack.

Our eyes meet. We hold our gaze. There's so much I wanna say . . .

I'm sorry.

Please forgive me.

Can we be Best Friends again?

Jack looks away, tears welling, as the service begins.

Speaking of . . .

The funeral itself is long and boring. I don't care what you say about the Baptists, we know how to get in and get out of a church. None of that Catholic up and down, up and down, eat this, drink that, da-dah da-dah. I have to say the best part is when Liza Larson sings . . .

> *"And friends are friends forever*
> *If the Lord's the Lord of them . . ."*

At first, I feel a tad jealous that I wasn't asked to perform. Once Liza gets to the part about *"though it's hard to let you go,"* and I look around and see so many of my friends all together under one roof—for the *worst* possible reason—I realize there's no way I could sing a single note right now. I'm a mess!

Any time we sang that song in Chorale these past two years, I always imagined the lyrics would one day pertain to the fact that we all went our separate ways. Not that we'd be saying farewell forever to one of our classmates before we even graduated.

Goodbye, Audrey, my friend.

Monday evening, the phone rings . . .

From in my room, I hear Mom in the kitchen answering it.

"Br-a-a-dley . . . Telephone!"

I emerge from my cave where I been hibernating all day. To my surprise, Mom allowed me to stay home from school on account of I still didn't have it in me to face anybody. This time we didn't even have to go thru our "Mom, I'm sick"—"No you're not" routine.

I find the phone face down on the counter, and pick it up.

"Hey . . . It's Jack."

"I know." I totally recognize his voice, even though I haven't heard it in forever. "What do *you* want?"

I don't mean to be a dick. This way of greeting Jack stems from the first time he called me back in 7th grade. The love of his life, Lynn Kelly, had just dumped his sorry ass and he started pouring his heart out to me, even though we barely knew each other. Shortly after, we became Best Friends.

In keeping with tradition, Jack starts going on and on (and on) about how sorry he is for being such a jerk this year, for dropping outta Band, and for wasting time being friends with Tom Fulton when we could've spent it together.

"Da-dah da-dah," I tell him, ready to get on with it, no looking back.

"Da-dah da-dah," he repeats, along with, "I'm sorry for being such a jerk."

"That's okay," I reply. "You haven't been that much of a jerk."

I knew Jack would eventually come around. He just had some things he needed to figure out for himself. So long as he did, that's all that counts. Besides, I been a tad busy dealing with my own problems these past few months, you know what I mean?

It's funny, but neither of us says anything about Audrey or the funeral we attended together, yet separately. By the way, Max did eventually show up. I got a chance to talk to him briefly afterwards, but like me and Jack now, we talked about everything but the matter at hand: Spring Break, cap and gown reservations, Prom.

Speaking of . . .

After he asks me about Big Boy's, and I tell Jack I'm no longer working there since I got a job at The Gas Station, he says, "So who are you taking to Prom?"

"To be honest," I answer, "I don't think I'm gonna go."

The last thing I wanna do right now is attend some stupid dance with somebody who means nothing to me. Besides, how can I even think about making merry when one of my Best Friends is no longer living? I know how much Audrey was looking forward to the big night, four days prior to her 18th birthday.

From all the way across town, I hear Jack scoff. "It's our Senior Prom . . . You can't miss it!"

I reply, "I'm not really up for it, you know what I mean?" hoping to leave it at that. Still, I don't wanna be inconsiderate. "What about you? Have you asked anybody?"

"Well," Jack answers hesitantly. "That's part of the reason I called . . ." He pauses a moment before rambling on. "Everybody knows we've been Best Friends since 7th grade, right?"

Chewing the spiral phone chord, I nod. "Uh-huh . . ."

"So it's not like they'd *think* anything if—"

"If what?" I interrupt, getting a sense of where this conversation is going.

"If *we* went to Prom," Jack says cheerfully. "Together, I mean."

At first, I don't know what to say. I mean, yes, I still consider Jack as my Best Friend in the whole wide world. We been thru too much these past six years to throw it all away. But now he's just talking crazy!

"I don't think that'd be such a good idea."

"Why not?" he replies, sounding awfully optimistic for the Jack Paterno I know.

"Think about it . . . This is not a John Hughes film we're living in. I am not Molly Ringwald and you are most definitely not Andrew McCarthy."

"Thanks a lot!" he cries, totally insulted.

"Seriously," I sigh, not meaning to be a Total Bitch. "It's 1988 . . . We live in Hazeltucky and we go to Hillbilly High . . . We'd either be the laughingstock of the school or else we'd get our asses kicked in the parking lot." Just like in *Faded Flowers.*

Did I mention how I went to Homecoming with Luanne Kowalski during Junior year? For whatever reason, she decided to wear one of her dad's old suits instead of a dress like all the other girls. Let's just say, it did *not* go over well with the likes of our classmates! Even if Eden Capwell from *Santa Barbara* did wear a tux to the Emmys that exact same year.

"It's our fucking Senior Prom," Jack spits. He's not about to give up trying to convince me. "We should be able to go with whomever we want."

Now who's being the Drama Queer?

"Whomever?" I repeat, unable to resist mocking him.

"Shut up!"

Looks like I gotta break the news to him: "You know just as well as I do . . . Two guys can't go walking into the Prom together—even if they are Best Friends since 7th grade."

While it sounds like a totally scan-ju-lous idea, I can't see us getting away with it. Besides, if I'm gonna waste $56 on a pair of tickets, plus tux rental, chipping in for a limo and post-Prom hotel room, I wanna make sure I'm with the one I love. Or at least gonna get laid.

"So we're still Best Friends?" Jack asks, as if he's had a doubt.

"Would you shut up, already?"

I realize I could totally call Jack out for treating me like shit for so long. But what's done is done. Time to move on and make a fresh start.

"Listen to me," he sternly demands. "I'm trying to be honest with you . . . Instead of being grateful I had a Best Friend who would accept me for who I am, I tried lying to myself, hoping it would all just go away."

I can't help but think Jack is trying to tell me something serious. Something I been hoping to hear since we had that fight back on Homecoming night.

This is why I gotta ask him: "And did it all just go away?"

Silence fills my ear.

"'member when you told me you wanted a giant Barbie head for Christmas?"

On the other end of the line, I feel Jack ready to make his confession.

"Uh-huh . . ."

"Well, I always kinda wanted one myself."

Not gonna cut it.

"Why's that?" I wonder, wanting him to lay it all on the line.

"Because . . ."

Try again.

"Because why?"

Deeply, Jack inhales, letting out a huff.

"Because . . ." Then in one fell swoop, he spews, "I'm gay, too."

Good boy!

Laying on my bed once I hang up and return to my room, I start thinking about what Jack said. Not about him being gay—I already knew that. (Duh!) Yet it sure made me proud to hear him *finally* say it. I mean, about how he lied to himself, hoping it would all just go away.

I can't believe I thought I could tell myself the exact same thing.

What's more ridiculous is the reason why I felt compelled to do this.

How could I possibly care more about wanting millions of people I don't even know to love me, and not about the one person who matters most in the world?

Me.

Never Gonna Give You Up

"I just wanna tell you how I'm feeling
Gotta make you understand . . ."

—Rick Astley

I feel like Susan Lucci.

You know, *All My Children*'s resident bad girl, Erica Kane.

I don't know how many times the Diva of Daytime has sat in the Emmy Awards audience waiting to hear the words: *"And the winner is . . ."* Followed by *her* name.

Beginning in 1981, she's been nominated for Outstanding Leading Actress every season, and hasn't taken home a single statue.

Last year, she lost to Kim Zimmer (Reva) from *Guiding Light*.

The year before that, to Erika Slezak (Viki/Nikki), *One Life to Live*.

The year before that, Kim Zimmer, *GL*'s Reva—again!

In 1984, Erika Slezak—again!

In '83: Dorothy Lyman (Opal), her *AMC* costar, who later appeared as Naomi Harper on *Mama's Family* with Vicki Lawrence of *Carol Burnett* fame.

In '82: Robin Strasser, *OLTL*'s Dorian Lord, beat her out, and the year before that, *Who's the Boss?*'s Angela (Judith Light) kicked her ass as Karen Woleck, also from *One Life*.

That's a total of *seven* times in a row, plus her first nod in 1978, where she got whipped by some woman from *Another World* who I never even heard of, Laurie Heineman (Sharlene Frame).

Is Lady La Luce ever gonna catch a break?

Maybe 1988 will finally be the big year. Of course, she's up against Marcy Walker (Eden Capwell) from *Santa Barbara*, who wore that tuxedo in 1985, 'member? I got a feeling Ms. Susan won't be taking home Emmy gold anytime soon . . . Poor thing.

Anyways!

Tonight's the big night . . . The Drama Club awards ceremony, where Mr. Dell'Olio will announce Thespian of the Year, and confer upon the winner the coveted "Thespy" award. How many times have I sat in the auditorium, palms wet with perspiration, waiting to hear *my* name called? Okay, maybe only two others ("Top 25 and "Top 5"), but this one's the most nerve-wracking of all.

It seems like a lifetime ago that me and Audrey officially became Thespians, stepping on stage to receive our Certificate of Recognition at the end of Sophomore year. Lemme tell ya, I wish she could be here beside me right now. I mean, what's a President without his Vice?

HAZEL PARK HIGH SCHOOL DRAMA CLUB
AWARDS CEREMONY
MAY 12, 1988
WELCOME AND INTRODUCTION OF OFFICERS
THESPIAN RECOGNITION CEREMONY
MOCK DRAMA AWARDS
1988–1989 OFFICERS ANNOUNCED
THESPIAN OF THE YEAR AWARD

So we've just finished the Recognition Ceremony.

Basically what happened was . . . The current officers: me (President), Claire Moody (Secretary), and Tuesday Gunderson (Treasurer), along with Zack Rakoff (filling in for Audrey) took to the stage, where we each read a speech from the International Thespian Society Handbook.

In mine, I talked about what the ITS is: an international organization with more than a million members, dedicated to excellence in high school Drama, the goal to make good Theatre and honor students who do so.

Claire spoke about how a bare stage can become any place you can think of: the plains of Oklahoma, the South Pacific, or Grover's Corners, NH. How we can travel to any time: ancient Egypt, classical Greece, Elizabethan England. How we can conjur the likes of those who have passed: Henry David Thoreau, Emily Dickinson, Mark Twain, simply by portraying their personas onstage.

Tuesday explained to our audience how people like Hamlet, King Lear, and Eliza Doolittle aren't real people, but mere characters created from the minds of playwrights and brought to life by actors and the Magic of Theatre.

Rakoff lisped his way thru an homage to "Thethpith," detailing the early Greek playwright's history, and explaining how we use the masks of comedy and tragedy etched in blue and gold, bound together with a capital *T*, as the ITS emblem.

"I now ask all *new* members of Troupe #4443 to rise and recite the Thespian pledge . . ."

From his position at the podium, Mr. Dell'Olio made this request.

Dressed in his perennial gray plaid suit, first he announced their names, and invited them to join us on stage. Balding head nervously nodding, next he read aloud the official initiation oath.

Basically this talks about how we promise to *uphold the aims and ideals* of the ITS. How we promise to perform our part and *accept praise and criticism with grace.* How we will work with our fellow Thespians for the *good of the troupe,* sharing our love of Theatre with all.

"Congratulations!" Dell told the newbies. "Welcome to the International Thespian Society."

Now for the mock awards . . .

Like greeting our guests down front of the auditorium after each show, and going to Big Boy's on Opening Night, I don't know how this tradition got started. Earlier this evening, ballots were passed out to Thespians old and new alike, asking us to cast our votes based on performances in both *A Christmas Carol* and *Grease.*

And now for the winners . . .

DRAMA CLUB MOCK AWARDS
1987–1988

	FEMALE	MALE
Best Newcomer	*Jamie Good*	*Joey Palladino*
Loudest Voice	*Audrey Wojczek*	*Will Isaacs*
Softest Voice	*Ava Reese*	*Ron Reynolds*
Biggest Ad-Libber	*Tuesday Gunderson*	*Keith Treva*
Most Likely to Succeed	*Liza Larson*	*Brad Dayton*
Most Likely to Be an Usher	*Claire Moody*	*Zack Rakoff*
Most Likely to Sleep in Costume	*Tuesday Gunderson*	*Keith Treva*
Most Likely to Steal Props	*Audrey Wojczek*	*Allen Bryan*
Best Dancer	*Diane Thompson*	*Joey Palladino*
Best Actor	*Liza Larson*	*Richie Tyler*

How's that for yet another kick in the pants?

There's no way I'm gonna be chosen Best Actor by my peers when I didn't perform a leading part this entire year. I guess I'll settle for Most Likely to Succeed, for whatever it's worth. I just hope they don't take it away once they find out about my rejection letter from Juilliard.

Believe it or not, I'm okay with Richie winning. There's no doubt he's a talented guy, and his turn as Scrooge was spectacular—for a Sophomore. Liza Larson's performance as Sandy in *Grease* knocked everybody's socks off, so I'm happy to see her honored. And how about newcomer Jamie Good getting recognized as Rizzo?

Of course, Audrey got a nod for loudest voice! That girl couldn't keep her trap shut if she had her jaws wired. What I wouldn't give to hear that booming bellow one more time. Yesterday marked two weeks. I keep thinking I'm gonna turn around and see her up on stage where she belongs with the rest of us Thespians.

Is it ever gonna get any easier?

Next up, Mr. Dell'Olio announces the 1988–89 Drama Club officers.

"First we have our new Treasurer, Miranda Resnick."

Miranda takes to the stage over a spatter of applause. I was hoping maybe Alyssa would be here tonight since they're sisters. I can't remember the last time I seen her. Chances are she's still up at Central.

"Our new Secretary, Ashley Lott."

'member our second Sophomore Student Director whose family may or may not be Mormon? She joins Miranda, taking her place next to the podium.

"Our new Vice-President, Keith Treva."

Keith joins the girls as the Peanut Gallery goes wild—led by Will Isaacs, of course . . .

Audrey would have a shit-fit if she knew who was taking over her office!

"And last but not least," says Dell with a smirk, "I present to you the new President of Thespian Troupe #4443 . . ."

Wanna take a wild guess who it's gonna be?

I'll give you a hint . . .

He's the totally hot Sophomore who I'm (once again) totally in love with.

If you said, "Richie Tyler," you win the prize!

As the auditorium echoes with applause, I look over to where Richie waits with his fellow officers, arms folded low across his crotch, chest popping out even more than ever. Did I mention how hot he looks tonight? Pale pink, short-sleeved shirt, showing off his biceps, and what looks like a brand-spanking-new pair of Girbaud jeans, his white slip-on shoes, and no socks.

"Quiet, please . . ."

Dell does his best to calm the maddening crowd.

All it takes is a glimpse of gold.

"Allow me to introduce you to 'Thespy' . . ."

Dramatic pause.

"In all my years of teaching here at Hazel Park, I've never been more proud to present the Thespian of the Year award to the following individual . . ."

Dell takes a deep breath, sustaining the suspense a few seconds longer. He looks down at his cue cards, reading the winner's list of credentials.

"This individual has been a member of Drama Club for the past three years . . ."

Check.

". . . has appeared in productions of *Little Shop of Horrors, The Miracle Worker, Oklahoma!* . . ."

Check.

". . . *A Christmas Carol*, and most recently *Grease* . . ."

Check.

Over his shoulder, Mr. Dell'Olio turns to where I sit beside Gunderson, Moody, and Rakoff, as he continues. "This past February, he traveled to New York City to audition for the prestigious Juilliard School of Drama."

Oh, my God . . .

"And even if he doesn't get accepted," Dell concludes, "Brad Dayton is one of the finest actors I've ever had the pleasure of directing."

Thunderous applause!

Stepping up to the podium to receive my award, I reach out to shake Dell's hand. To my surprise, he pulls me into a big old hug, eyes glistening. From the floor below, Jack gives me the thumbs up. Then he snaps a photo of me and my mentor for the final edition of *The Hazel Parker.*

"Wow."

It's a good thing I actually *wrote* a speech—just in case. Otherwise, I wouldn't know where to begin. Digging into my pants pocket, I pull out the crumpled cocktail napkin, and clear my throat.

"It's been a privilege to be a part of Thespian Troupe #4443 . . ."

So many familiar faces . . .

"And to serve as President."

Mr. Dell'Olio's wife Bonnie.

"I don't have to tell you how important Drama is to me . . ."

Carrie Johnson and Ava Reese.

"I know how important it is to all of you, too . . ."

My mom, my dad, my grandparents, my sisters.

"Or else we wouldn't be here tonight."

All except for Janelle.

Oh, my God . . . I just realized I haven't told you: I'm an uncle!

Janelle and Ted finally had their baby (a week late) on May 10, 1988 at 9:03 PM. His name is Theodore James Baniszewski. He weighed 8 pounds, 3 ounces, and was 21 inches long. You should see him . . . He's got the cutest little head, full of reddish brown peach fuzz, and the widest mouth . . . I swear he looks just like Charlie Brown.

"To quote Mr. Dell'Olio," I conclude, "'This is what our kids *should* be doing!'"

More applause, accompanied by some hooting and hollering from the likes of Will Isaccs and Keith Treva. Dell nods and smiles in agreement, turning a shade of red to rival any I seen on myself.

"I'm not gonna get all emotional here," I promise, "but there's an important member of Troupe #4443 who isn't here with us . . ."

A hush falls over the crowd.

"She was one of my Best Friends . . ."

My throat feels so tight I can barely swallow.

"Her name is Audrey Wojczek . . ."

Many an eye tears up—including mine.

"I loved her . . . I miss her terribly . . ."

The next words out of mouth, I don't know where they come from.

"And I want her to have this."

Holding "Thespy" in my hot little hand the way I always dreamed of, I keep thinking about what Audrey said the night before the accident . . .

"Promise me you'll stop worrying what other people think . . ."

Wining awards isn't what *really* matters.

". . . start caring about the most important person in your life . . ."

Not if you're sad and all alone.

"That would be you."

Thanks to Audrey Wojczek, I know what must be done.

"Now go out there and get that boy."

I will!

Sitting side by side on a bench outside the auditorium, far away from the roar of the crowd, me and The Sophomore (soon to be The Junior) have a civil conversation over post-awards punch and pie . . .

"Congratulations."

"You, too."

Hard to believe this is the exact same spot me and Richie officially met exactly six months ago—November 12, 1987.

"That's a cool thing you did," Richie compliments. The scent of Drakkar Noir drifts in the air between us . . . making me horny as hell. "Audrey would be psyched to be Lesbian of the Year."

I admit, "She's been in more plays than I have," downplaying the gesture. "Besides, it's not like I get to keep the trophy."

Talk about stupid! Giving somebody an award, then stashing it away in some dusty display case for everybody else to admire. Ah, well . . . Someday when I get my Tony. Or Emmy. Or maybe even an Oscar. Heck, I'll settle for a *Soap Opera Digest* award. Just because I'm not going to Juilliard doesn't mean I can't still be on *Days of our Lives!*

"So what's up?"

"Nothing . . . What's up with you?"

This is me and The Sophomore trying to think of something else to say. I can't believe we haven't spoken since that tragic night in my bedroom back in March. Over two months ago. 'member Richie showed up at my door, drunk on wine coolers, after going to EB's on Opening Night of *Grease?*

"Anything new and exciting?"

"Same shit, different day," he reports, flashing me that old familiar shit-eating grin.

Enough of the idle chitchat.

Time to pop *la question* . . .

"You got any plans next Friday?"

Richie takes a blueberry bite, talking with his mouth full. "What's next Friday?"

I'd be lying if I didn't admit I'm distracted by the way his Adam's apple bobs as he swallows. Talk about sexy! "Um . . ."

I down my apple cobbler with what looks like McDonald's orange drink, which I used to love when I was little, but not so much anymore . . . Bogue!

"Isn't that the night of the Prom?" Richie asks, trying to sound nonchalant.

He knows for a fact it totally is.

For the last week, the buzz in the hallowed halls of HPHS has been solely about *An Evening of Elegance*. Claire Moody devoted her final "Fashion Faux Pas" to PROM DOs & DON'Ts. I mean, everybody who's *anybody* is attending. Why would you possibly miss out?

I'll give you three good reasons:

1) You're gay.

2) You can't go with the one you love.

3) All of the above.

This explains why I ask Richie Tyler if he wants to spend the night of May 20, 1988, with me. We may not be able to attend *An Evening of Elegance*, but we can certainly get dressed up and enjoy a fancy dinner at our favorite Backstage restaurant.

"Why would I wanna go and do that?"

This is Richie's response to my query, putting a dent in my otherwise foolproof plan. He finishes his pie, brushing a crumb from his cheek.

"O, that I were a glove upon that hand
That I might touch that cheek!"

"Because . . ."

Now I know how Jack felt when I put him thru the wringer. "Because why?"

Deeply, I inhale, letting out a huff.

"Because . . ." Then in one fell swoop, I spew, "I'm in love with you."

Richie pauses a moment, taking in my confession.

Wanna know what he finally says after what feels like a year?

"I thought you're not a fag."

Reaching out, I take his hand, locking our fingers together tightly. "Would I do this if I wasn't?"

With my fellow Thespians beyond the brick wall behind us, I must be totally out of my mind for doing what I'm about to do. But in the words of Phil Collins: *"I don't care anymore."*

Right then and there, I kiss Richie Tyler—tongue and all.

His lips never felt softer, his breath never tasted sweeter, his skin never smelled sexier.

"Just because you kiss another guy," Richie reminds me once we come up for air, "doesn't make you a fag."

I give his hair a gentle tug, my hand wrapped round his neck. "Then I'll have to prove it some other way."

"What have you got in mind?"

He reaches back, grabs my wrist, getting a little rough for the first time in our relationship. Did I mention I like a man who's assertive?

"Spend next Friday with me and you'll find out."

Gazing deep into my eyes, his face mere inches from mine, Richie Tyler asks the question I been dying to hear all evening: "What time you picking me up?"

7:00 PM the following Friday . . .

For the past three nights my poor sister and her husband haven't gotten a lick of sleep. My nephew, Teddy, came down with a case of colic. So Mom offered to take Nina and Brittany and spend the night over Janelle and Ted's. Originally she suggested they come crash at our house, but Little Brad offered to pay for a room at the Red Roof Inn since he never bought them a wedding present. Plus he wants to have the house all to himself this evening—just in case.

Let's just say, I didn't humiliate myself by walking into Arbor's and buying a box of Trojans just for the hell of it, okay?

"Sorry I'm late . . ."

Richie greets me at his front door, grinning. "Don't let it happen again." Then he says, "Don't you look sharp?"

'member the $1,000 I managed to save working at The Gas Station? Since I won't be needing it for Juilliard, I decided to invest in a new suit. Nothing fancy, just a simple double-breasted beige job I bought up at Oaktree in Oakland Mall. Ninety-nine bucks, what a bargain!

Of course, Richie looks drop-dead gorgeous in a navy number, with maize and blue striped tie . . . *"Let's Go Blue!"*

Right away I notice his hair.

"Nice 'do."

He's got it slicked it back, reminiscent of the style he wore as Vince Fontaine in *Grease.* Considering we exchanged not a single word during the entire production, how did Richie know what the James Dean look does to me?

"My parents won't bite," he promises, inviting me inside.

Like I said, Richie's mom I met at Opening Night of *A Christmas Carol,* and again more recently after the Drama Club awards. But his dad, I never laid eyes on a day in my life. Saying a little prayer, I cross the threshold, where it seems Mr. and Mrs. Tyler have been eagerly awaiting my arrival.

"Nice to see you again, Brad."

Mrs. T throws her massive arms around me, smelling of Chantilly. She truly is the sweetest thing since apple pie. She compliments me on my suit, congratulates me (again) for winning

Thespian of the Year, tells me how much she admires me for giving it up.

Looks like I'm scoring brownie points with Richie's mom . . . How about his dad?

Other than the fact that he works for Chrysler's, I don't know what to expect when we're introduced. But I prepare myself for the worst. For whatever reason, I automatically assume Richie's dad's going to be just like *my* dad: distant, indifferent, and overtly discriminating.

"Pleased to meet you, son."

Sure, he's got a grip like George "The Animal" Steele, but I couldn't have been more wrong about Mr. Tyler. Physically, he appears exactly like what I expected: short, stocky, and Southern. Yet when he looks at me with his son's same blue eyes, I see nothing but acceptance.

"Likewise," I say, even though I never use the expression.

I don't know what Richie's told his parents we're doing this evening. They must be wondering why I'm stopping by to pick their son up all decked out in a suit and tie, with him dressed the exact same way. Doesn't it look the least bit suspect? Or do they really *not* care?

"Have a nice dinner," Mrs. Tyler wishes us.

"You boys be careful," Mr. Tyler warns. "No drinking and driving, y'hear?"

"I'll be extra careful," I promise. "I borrowed my mother's car."

Richie kisses his parents, out the door we fly, and away we go!

But not before taking a few photos . . .

On the front porch. By the bushes. Next to the car.

With all the attention they're giving us, I wonder if maybe Mr. and Mrs. Tyler think I'm actually taking their son to the Prom. Of course, in that case, I would've brought him a corsage—not!

"Sorry about all that," says Richie, once we're at last on the road.

"No need to apologize," I assure him. "Your parents are awesome."

"Not as awesome as you."

Isn't he the sweetest thing?

Dinner's a Total Blur. We get in, we order. We eat, we get out.

"Now where to?"

Like I said, Mom's over Janelle and Ted's with Nina, Brittany, and Teddy, so we got Dayton's Depot all to ourselves for the evening. Once I relay this to Richie, we're back on the corner of Wanda and Webster in less than two shakes.

"Who did all this?" Richie gazes about the family room in utter disbelief.

"Who do you think?"

Call me a nerd, but I took it upon myself to do a little decorating. I figure if we can't physically be at the Vintage House in Fraser, we can at least pretend. After all, we're actors, ain't we?

My date scoffs, "Probably some dork," totally bursting my bubble.

"What makes you say that?"

I hope Richie doesn't *really* think I'm silly for wanting to make tonight Löwenbräu special. All I did was hang some streamers, and make a few *An Evening of Elegance* signs. Did I go too overboard by suspending a disco ball from the ceiling between the chandeliers?

"Lighten up, Opie . . . I love it."

Cue lights.

Stars circling around us, I take him in my arms, holding him close. "You do?"

Cue music.

"So if you love me
Say you love me . . ."

Richie replies, "Not as much as I love you."

Cue curtain.

Hard to believe how truly happy I am at this moment. Back in the arms of the one I love, ready to start a new chapter in my life, full of so much promise.

Isn't that the thrill of the Theatre? With the beginning of each new play, we never know what to expect. Unless maybe we've seen the show before—and believe me, I haven't.

This is one Drama I don't know how it's gonna end!

Graduation Memories

This Book Belongs to Bradley James Dayton

Homecoming King & Queen

Tom Fulton and Jamie Good

Valedictorian & Salutatorian

Jack Paterno and Betsy Sheffield

Lyrics

"Heartland"
FAVORITE ALBUM

Echo & The Bunnymen
FAVORITE ROCK GROUP

Tina Turner
FAVORITE FEMALE VOCALIST

George Michael
FAVORITE MALE VOCALIST

"True Colors"
FAVORITE HIT SINGLE

Tee Vee

"Designing Women"
FAVORITE HALF HOUR SHOW

"Dynasty"
FAVORITE HOUR SHOW

"Matlock"

WORST SHOW

Flicks

"Gone With the Wind"

FAVORITE MOVIE

James Dean

FAVORITE ACTOR

Marilyn Monroe

FAVORITE ACTRESS

Berkley Theatre

FAVORITE THEATER

"Princess Bride"
"Moonstruck"
"Rocky Horror Picture Show"

MEMORABLE MOVIES

Sooner or Later

I predict

Ava Reese marries Don Olsewski
Carrie Johnson marries Peter Reckell
Jack Paterno becomes a Bestselling Author
I win an Academy Award

Autographs

Brad,

When I met you, I thought you were a fag. Now I think your a cool guy.

Don Olsewski, '88

Brad,

We've been friends since Webster, but I'm glad we got to know each other better at HPHS. I'll never forget the good times (and sad times) and all the help you gave me in World Shit—I mean, Lit! ("Don't get my tarp wet you sugar-high druggie")

Love, Ava

Ava loves Don!

'88 dominates

Brad,

What can I say? You're a great guy and a terrific actor. I'll never forget all the fun times—never! The "cookie in the middle," Chorale partners, "Grease," Bloomer State Park. Geez, I could go on forever. Never forget me cuz I sure won't forget you!

Love always,

Jamieleeann Mary Sue Good,
aka Rizzo (Betty)

Brad,

You're a real sweetheart and I'm glad I met you back in 7th grade. You are so talented and you make the lives of those around you so much brighter. I hope to see you on a "soap" someday. May all your dreams come true.

Love, Clarissa Moody (K.I.T. 546-5670)

Brad,

Your the first real friend I ever had. Sorry I been such a dick head this year and we didn't spend much time together (you can blame Jack!) Good luck at Julliard, if you get in. If you don't, there's always O.C.C. (Kidding!)

Max Wilson

Brad,

To my Best Friend since 7th grade. I can't even believe it's been 6 years since we met. (We are sooo old!) I wouldn't be the person I am today without your friendship. Thanks for never giving up on me. I know we'll be friends forever.

Jack

Brad (Opie),

I'm glad you finally got a clue.

Richie "The Junior" Tyler

Drama Queers Rule!

Bradley,

You are a truly talented young man. May you always follow your heart.

V. Horchik

"To thine ownself be true."

A READING GROUP GUIDE

DRAMA QUEERS!

Frank Anthony Polito

ABOUT THIS GUIDE

The suggested questions are included to enhance your group's reading of Frank Anthony Polito's *Drama Queers!*

DISCUSSION QUESTIONS

1. In *Drama Queers!*, Brad meets a lot of interesting characters along his journey. Who did you find to be the most memorable? Who was the most helpful? Who gave him the best advice?

2. Despite being gay, Brad is pretty popular at school. Why do you think this is, compared to Jack, who tries desperately to hide his sexuality and doesn't find this to be the case?

3. Was it surprising that Brad was able to put his past feelings about Richie Tyler ("the faggy little 7th grader who played flute in Prep Band and carried his books like a girl") behind and move forward in pursuing a relationship?

4. Why do you think Brad is so reluctant to open up to Audrey about being gay? How about to his co-workers? Isn't this hypocritical of him in light of what Brad's been telling Jack about being honest about who he *really* is?

5. Brad's mother seems to have known about his sexuality since he was a child, and yet, she's been completely supportive of

him. If you were the parent of a gay son or daughter, how would you handle the situation?

6. Brad's trip to New York City takes place during the height of the AIDS crisis. Being a boy from a small Midwestern town, were you concerned for his well-being at any point while he was traipsing about the Big City?

7. Were there times when you found Brad's character to be unlikable based on his actions in the story? Do you think he is justified in lying to Richie about *not* being gay in order to protect the future of his career as an actor?

8. What outcome were you expecting after Brad's Juilliard audition? Were you pleased or disappointed? Do you find the way things worked out to be a better life-lesson?

9. How did you feel about Brad and Jack's friendship at the conclusion of the story? Was there anything you wished they would have done or said to each other? Based on their past history, do you think the boys will be Best Friends Forever?

10. What do you think will happen next for Brad? Where do you imagine he will end up and with whom?